"It's Midnight."

Once again his body reacted and he had a sense of danger. At last, deep in the core of his torment, he began to freeze and deny the betrayal born of his body, permitted by his head and heart. Only then did his mind become paralyzed and all he felt was a murderous heartbeat punishing his veins. He was dead as stone when she raised herself on tiptoe. Cupped his face in her hands. Laid her fingers against his skin.

"This is from me in honor of your feelings for your wife. Happy New Year." She kissed him full on the mouth, sweetly. Without fever or seduction.

He came to life, profoundly thankful . . .

Books by Jeane Renick

Trust Me
Always . . .
Promises
Loving Mollie
Wish List

Published by HarperPaperbacks

WISH LIST

Jeane Renick

HarperPaperbacks
A Division of HarperCollinsPublishers

If you purchased this book without a cover, you should be aware that this book is stolen property. It was reported as "unsold and destroyed" to the publisher and neither the author nor the publisher has received any payment for this "stripped book."

This is a work of fiction. The characters, incidents, and dialogues are products of the author's imagination and are not to be construed as real. Any resemblance to actual events or persons, living or dead, is entirely coincidental.

HarperPaperbacks *A Division of* HarperCollins*Publishers*
10 East 53rd Street, New York, N.Y. 10022

Copyright © 1996 by Jeane Renick
All rights reserved. No part of this book may be used or reproduced in any manner whatsoever without written permission of the publisher, except in the case of brief quotations embodied in critical articles and reviews. For information address HarperCollins*Publishers,*
10 East 53rd Street, New York, N.Y. 10022.

Cover illustration by Jim Griffin

First printing: August 1996

Printed in the United States of America

HarperPaperbacks, HarperMonogram, and colophon are trademarks of HarperCollins*Publishers*

❖ 10 9 8 7 6 5 4 3 2 1

Romance is a leap of faith, a bridge of wishes:

> *there's more good than bad*
> *believe   in the world,*
> *Loving someone lets you   dare to dream,*
>   *and provides faith . . .*
>   *in yourself.*

Wish List is for:
the men in my life who were Jordan;
my friend, Darren Robinson, whom prayer wheels did not serve;
dedicated Earthwatch friends and volunteers;
and myself—
as reward for finding, and crossing, the bridge.

1

The meter's running on my life . . .

Funny how life's events can sour you on an otherwise innocent place. They'd be passing the church soon. Restless, Charlayne looked out her taxi window at the hully-gully snake fang of a moon. She'd watched it all the way from the airport, committing its slender crescent to memory. "Should be harvest," she murmured absently.

The nervous cabby hit the brakes. "What, here?"

She shook her head at suspicious eyes squinting at her in the rearview mirror. "It's my last Thanksgiving with my family, and I wanted a harvest moon, that's all."

The driver signaled annoyance with a renewed set of his shoulders and resumed his speed. The yellow vehicle meandered in fits and starts along the base of San Francisco's hills, slowing occasionally for pockets of fog; lights reflecting off the bay, slate dull and brooding under an overcast sky, were barely visible in the side mirror as they paralleled the water.

Charlayne tipped her watch to catch the light as they passed under a streetlamp. Six-fifteen was still too early to arrive, so she asked the driver to slow down. Familiar survivors from her youth passed by on either side of the canted street as the taxi wheezed up a succession of steep hills: the greengrocer at the corner of Cattlebury Avenue; her mother's beauty shop; Napoleani's, an Italian restaurant next to the churchyard, had failed and was now an empty store. "I'd like to stop here for a few minutes," she directed.

The driver pulled to the curb and gestured at the gathering fog, as if she hadn't noticed. "I got to leave the meter running, you know."

"The meter's running on my life," Charlayne retorted and opened the door. "I won't be long." She crossed the street to stand opposite the church and watched its slender spire slice through ghostly mares' tails of drifting mist. Ten years ago she'd married tall, handsome Mark Hunter inside those walls. One of those otherwise innocent places.

It had been a perfect wedding, not one glitch to mar the ceremony: California oaks had been green with new leaves, her bridesmaids' gowns in the same soft spring shade; an ivory satin wedding dress with ribbons spilling from the shoulders and seventeen buttons in the back. So much promise; such high hopes on that day. Somber recall arrived as well. Thoughts of Sondra, who'd been maid of "honor."

Charlayne tightened her shoulders and resolved not to weaken in her decision; she only hoped she could maintain sufficient strength to weather the fallout sure to follow in the next few hours. And weeks.

She stood in the gathering mist, waiting for sufficient time to pass, and the harsher side of memory doubled its intrusion. No different from her unpleasant ties to Mark, the feelings refused to go away. Years of them.

She'd met Mark through mutual friends at college. He'd held aberrant views from her own in nearly every area of life, refused to drive, drank only sake, and worked as a bartender and a waiter to support a career as an artist; orphaned at fourteen, he lived in a drafty low-rent loft filled with what were then seductive aromas of canvas, half-emptied tubes of oil paints in bright, primary colors, and sable brushes soaking in solvents. Her mother was appalled—which, Charlayne had reluctantly admitted to herself in hindsight, unquestionably had added to his appeal. He was charming, provocative, and madly attractive and, after achieving moderate success in the fickle world of art, he'd proposed in front of half a dozen of her friends.

She'd accepted. They'd married four months later in the church across the way. A year into their marriage, he'd hit a creative "dry spot," had tried several new directions, none of which were embraced by critics, and not long after, reached an impasse with his agent. The following year they'd managed financially with half a dozen substantial loans from her parents, but when it became apparent that their debt was spiraling out of control, she'd put her aspirations for a career in architecture on hold—much to her father's concern and her mother's disappointment—and left in her senior year of college to go to work. Then, seven years ago yesterday, following a lengthy Sunday service, on the section of sidewalk where she now stood, Mark had called her aside.

"Sondra and I are lovers," he'd announced quietly. "We have been for more than two years."

Her sister had stood in the background, wary eyes confirming the truth of his confession. Two years; more than half their married life at the time.

"I want a divorce so we can get married."

Her sister had been a pale version of herself that day, but beautiful, always beautiful, with dark shadows under her eyes, honey-blond hair adrift around her shoulders. Rocked by the depth of their betrayal and going numb with pain, Sondra's expression had imprinted itself on her memory. No guilt. No remorse even in those blue eyes. Just a focus on getting what she wanted, what she felt she deserved. And what she'd wanted was Mark Hunter.

More than enough time had elapsed, and Charlayne hurried to the waiting cab. Lucille and Henreid Delamere held their holiday dinners promptly at seven. Being late was tantamount to not showing up at all. The taxi crept through thickening fog, and the closer to her parents' home they approached, the more her psyche rebelled. Mark and Sondra. Little Ryan, cute as a cherub, sole and adored grandchild. Dread rose up in her chest.

In the hours and days that had followed her husband's revelation, she'd recognized his careful staging, the prudent choreography—no less effective than his proposal: in front of the church, with its austere presence compelling a minimum of fuss; their mother a few feet away, oblivious. But much worse, she'd been forced to acknowledge the extent of her own blindness where he and Sondra had been concerned; the countless instances of finding them alone together in the kitchens of friends, their bland offers to make each other drinks, holiday snapshots with arms casually entwined, Mark's teasing about marrying the wrong sister, not-so-polite kisses under mistletoe—

incidents of no consequence one at a time, but when added together, forging a picture of the classic unsuspecting wife. More than one sleepless night still had at its core thoughts of her sister and her husband heaving about in their intimacies, laughing at foolish, dim-witted Char, loving wife and sister.

Ex-wife now.

Unfortunately, sibling bloodlines had proved impossible to untie.

It had tumbled out all too soon in a sordid, embarrassing mess. Sondra was pregnant. Very much so. Mark only wanted to do the "right thing."

"It just happened," he'd sworn to her privately. "You were working late. She stopped by one night. From then on it sort of evolved somehow. I swear I never meant to hurt you. I never stopped loving you."

How she'd clung to that myth, fought to make it Sondra's seduction, Sondra's fault, but in the end the explanation wouldn't serve. Having an affair with one's sister for two years wasn't *loving* someone. It was bedding two women at the same time, with one of them living in appalling, humiliating ignorance—until the other one had gotten pregnant. Definitely not *loving* someone.

She still wondered occasionally what would have happened if she'd been the one to get pregnant. Or both of them at the same time? What would have been the "right thing" then, Mark?

Their quickie divorce in Reno had been followed by his and Sondra's marriage the following day in Las Vegas. Charlayne had come home by train, packed her clothing, and moved to Los Angeles to start over; as far as she knew, Sondra and Mark were still living in the loft. Seven months after her nephew was born, she'd hastily married Dr. Roberts Pearce, a specialist in thoracic surgery, also newly divorced. No fantasy trip down the aisle that time, no gown, no maid of honor. Family considerations had called for a small civil ceremony in a judge's chambers.

Once again, hindsight provided an embarrassing, classic picture: marriage between two people on the rebound trying to find in each other a haven of love and security that wouldn't materialize. Shoals in their marriage quickly became visible, insurmountable cliffs.

Thanksgiving at her parents' home two years ago had been particularly gruesome; by then she and Roberts had evolved to being all but strangers. Giving in to her mother's pleas of concern for her father's health, she'd come to San Francisco alone; Roberts had stayed in L.A. to be on call for a precarious postsurgery patient. Wretched and unable to pretend that flying solo around her sister's marriage and four-year-old wasn't upsetting, she'd been desperate not to fail a second time, and had decided to make an all-out effort to salvage things with Roberts.

Braving a last minute trip to the airport, she'd squeaked on board as the final passenger of a commuter flight that had delivered her to Los Angeles—in time to walk in on her husband *en flagrante* with a woman pediatrician that Charlayne had met a few times at various hospital functions. With lawyers involved, divorce proceedings had stretched on, and this time last year she had been declared by the California courts a two-time loser in the marital wars.

Two husbands unfaithful before marriage vows had gotten cold—was it somehow her fault? Mark had desperately wanted a family, and despite their efforts, she'd failed to conceive. Was that her fault as well?

Apparently.

Whatever the problem, Thanksgivings, it seemed, were the kiss of death for her marriages.

2

Don't mess with me . . .

Promptly at 6:35, the taxi came to a stop in front of one of the city's famous Victorian "painted ladies," with a fresh coat of pastel yellow adorned with crisp white gingerbread trim; her parents' pride and joy.

"Thirty-two fifty," the driver said unctuously, "plus the toll." Charlayne counted out a handful of bills and prepared herself for an evening with her family.

Uncle Egan, bless him, emerged from the house and came down the steps to grasp her hands. "Welcome, darlin'." He gave her a kiss and whispered, "They're running late, so you can relax." He'd never forgiven Mark for the circumstances of their divorce, and remained Charlayne's staunchest ally in matters of family.

The weight of dread was replaced with a short but welcome reprieve, and she gave him a fervent embrace. It was going to be all right after all. Her mother and father appeared at the door with Aunt Sophie's face close behind; then it was a gauntlet of hugs and kisses and gentle reprimands for not anticipating the fog and flying earlier in the day.

True to Uncle Egan's forecast, a scant fourteen minutes after her own carefully late arrival, Sondra, Mark, and little Ryan trooped noisily in the front door to shed their wraps in the foyer. Charlayne watched them circle the room in a dance of civility marked with air kisses from Sondra and apologetic rumblings from Mark about expecting a call from a prospective buyer and was there someplace reasonably private where he could phone his answering service?

Six-year-old Ryan, temporarily shy among so many grown-ups, clung to his mother's skirts. Before her sister could reach her side, Charlayne threw a quick wink at her nephew and escaped down a hallway for one final go-round with the bathroom mirror—to stiffen her upper lip, as it were, and remind herself that she was in control, that being here was her choice, and why she was here at all. Her father's health was precarious at best, and . . . and one never knew.

It was going to be a long, emotional evening to get through, so she waited until the very last minute, prepared herself one last time, then inched open the door. At the end of the hallway, Mark was finishing his conversation on a portable phone, his wristwatch held in front of his face so he wouldn't be late for the Delamere toast. ". . . all yours," he was saying, his voice low and insistent. "You know that, whenever you say the word . . . You know how I feel about it, but I have responsibilities to consider. We've talked about this."

When he saw her peek into the hallway, his voice took on an all but imperceptible shift in tone; she realized he was talking to a woman. "Fine. Let me know, otherwise I'll see you there . . . Right. Me, too."

She walked quickly toward the living room to join the others, overhearing his rapid "Goodbye"; he caught up to her in time to slip his hand around her waist. "Well, it looks like I may have a deal for *Toya,*" he announced as they entered the room. "The buyer's going to let me know in a couple of weeks."

"Congratulations, dear. I do hope it works out," trilled her mother. "Is that the green one?"

Everyone had been waiting for their appearance, crystal flutes in readiness for her father's toast. Mark quickly dropped his arm from her waist, crossed the room and seated himself on the piano bench next to Sondra, who thrust a glass of champagne into his hand.

They continued their wait until Ryan had been coaxed onto his grandmother's lap. Lifting her glass as her father rose to his feet, Charlayne fought down her aggravation and successfully avoided her sister's icy glare by watching strands of hollowed-pearl bubbles percolate from the champagne. Her father spoke the words that were now Delamere tradition. "To our loved ones," he intoned, eyes sweeping the room to take them all in and coming to rest on his grandson. "May we live on in peace with charity for others."

Charlayne sipped at the icy wine, still rankled at Mark's behavior. She'd come to her parents' home prepared to hear these words, determined to drink to their meaning and adhere to the well-intentioned message. Unfortunately, again this year, the toast served as little more than salt in wounds so deep there was little chance they'd heal.

The moment passed.

She smiled thinly as her mother stood to deliver her customary follow-up statement. Roberts had irreverently dubbed it the "doomsday warning"—one of the few things in their marriage they'd been able to agree upon, she thought miserably. The message was invariably an affirmation of her father's deteriorating heart condition.

"I know some of you had to make a difficult trip to get here, but we're so *happy* to see everyone again," Lucille Delamere began emotionally. "As you know, I count every day with Henreid as one more blessing, and we have so *much* to be thankful for—our *beautiful* grandson, our children well and happy. Not everyone enjoys the good health of youth...." She paused for emphasis. "For all we know this is the very last time we'll all be together, and I want to make this the *best* Thanksgiving ever." She raised her glass and spoke in a tremorous voice. *"To my wonderful family."*

And, again this year, Mark held up his hand to add to the toast. "Include yourself, Mother Delamere. We all have a lot to be thankful for. I know I do." In the wake of this, his annual tacked-on declaration, he succeeded in making eye contact with Charlayne for a split instant before pulling Sondra close to noisily buss her cheek; Sondra responded by throwing herself into his arms and kissing him with fervor.

"Hear! Hear!" Her mother's voice, delighted at the show of affection, led an awkward chorus of assent and approval around the room; everyone drank except Charlayne, who winked again at Ryan rather than be seen averting her eyes from his parents' amorous display. She grinned when Ryan winked back. He'd stretched up amazingly since she'd seen him last, had feet like little rowboats. All indications were that he'd be taller than Mark, which pleased her greatly. Men hated being shorter than their sons. She tilted the champagne glass toward the little boy in a silent salute and made her own private wish for her mother's good health before taking a sip. She would endure the proximity of her former husband and her sister, and the charming child who was the proof of their adultery, but she would not drink to one word that left Mark Hunter's mouth.

Across the room, her sister emerged from Mark's embrace; her face was stained with dark circles and she refused eye contact. Sondra was as miserable at these events as she was, and every year Charlayne was certain she would beg off, but each year Sondra was here, with Mark and Ryan by her side. Mark's doing. It had to be. Sondra never faced anything. Or anyone.

They adjourned to the dining room, and Charlayne took her usual seat between her father and her uncle, a configuration that prevented direct contact between herself and Mark, and ostensibly camouflaged the fact that there was rarely, if ever, conversation between her and Sondra. She placed her champagne to one side and concentrated on her father, deep in discussion with his grandson. He was thin, she decided, but his color was good and his energy seemed fine. Making no attempt to join in their discourse on the relative merits of Mighty Morphin Ranger power, she tried to assess her feelings at being in this room for another holiday as a single person, her status requiring a discreet removal of the facing empty chair. She studied the ornate moldings that circled the high ceiling, ran her eye down the pale lemon and white stripes of silk wall coverings.

Upon the arrival of roast goose with oyster stuffing perched on her mother's heirloom silver platter, and a barrage of chafing dishes in close attendance, the meal began. Alice, practically a member of the family, whisked the cover from a special plate of turkey and steamed vegetables for her father, who smiled sadly at his fate.

"Want to trade?" he joked, only half serious.

Char watched Alice puff up contentiously. "Should have thought of that twenty years ago." Unquestionably devoted to the Delamere family, Alice had no peer, and no time for self-pity.

Outside the window, fog extinguished the garden and an otherwise beautiful view of the city. Knowing she was captive, and that there was no possible escape to the airport, Charlayne decided to divert her father by sharing her good news with Uncle Egan. "Did Dad tell you I have approval for my trip to Nepal?" Her excited words fell into a lull in table conversation and sounded like an announcement.

Uncle Egan, ever the proud Texan, beamed at her. "Why, honey, that's wonderful. You hear that, Sophie?"

"I wish I were ten years younger." Her father spoke enviously. "I'd be going with you."

"Henreid! The very idea!" It was her mother's reproachful voice. Charlayne edged forward to meet Lucille Delamere's worried frown at the other end of the table. "Now you know I'm not trying to be argumentative, dear, but I simply don't see why it has to be so far away." Her mother eyed her stubbornly. "What if something terrible happened to your father? How would we—"

"Is she going somewhere?" Aunt Sophie asked, looking about myopically.

Charlayne was conscious of everyone's sudden scrutiny. "Nepal, Aunt Sophie." She said it loudly, to make sure her aunt understood.

"What's Napoll?" piped Ryan.

"It's a poor little country halfway around the world, dear." His grandmother's withering tone suggested that it was also populated with half-wits and gorgons.

WISH LIST

"It's a marvelous place I've always wanted to visit," Charlayne defended. "A kingdom, actually."

"For an entire month? It seems to me there are things you could find to write about a whole lot closer to home." Her mother's chin began to quiver dangerously. "And don't be condescending, I know perfectly well it's one of those tourist destinations."

Sondra entered the conversation with a thin smile, her champagne untouched. "I thought malaria was a problem there."

"Malaria?" Both her parents' eyebrows shot upward.

"It's absolutely safe," Char insisted, "but I'm taking precautions, the same as I would anywhere else."

"But, malaria . . . for four weeks!" Lucille's distress was mounting. "That's a ridiculous length of time to be in such a place. You can't possibly mean to go alone."

"I'll be traveling with a photographer." She settled her glance safely on Ryan once again. No point in volunteering that her photographer, Shelley Cox, was a twenty-two-year-old student from UCLA. "We're going into the jungle," she told her nephew, "to write a story about cats about the size of the teddy bear you got last Christmas, only they're called fishing cats."

"How come?" Ryan's little face was solemnly curious.

"Because they catch fish with their paws."

Ryan stared at her, trying to fathom such an animal. Meanwhile, Lucille Delamere was shifting anxiously about in her chair. Charlayne fixed her smile firmly in place before turning to her disapproving parent. Yesterday morning, caught up in the excitement of her editor's confirmation, she'd shared news of her trip with her mother before she'd thought through how to position it where Lucille was concerned. Now she was stuck with the damage of informing her mother so far in advance. No matter really, it was inevitably a no-win situation. If she'd waited until now, she'd have been accused of keeping secrets.

"But, Charlayne, Nepal . . ." Her mother's voice took on an aura of tragedy.

"It's a beautiful country, and if everything goes right I'll come home with a very unique book," she said brightly.

"Henreid, I simply don't understand." Her mother's face was crumpling.

Before her father could respond, Uncle Egan came to Char's rescue. "Now, Lucille, don't go making this high drama." Her mother's older brother was a military colonel; he alone could say such things and be forgiven. Like statements from anyone else would be grounds for high drama indeed. Lucille Delamere sniffed into her handkerchief and changed the subject. Alice came in to clear, and returned with Aunt Sophie's famous pumpkin chiffon pie and a stack of crystal dessert plates.

Despite Charlayne's plea for moderation, a fat wedge of burnt-orange pie loaded with loving spoonfuls of whipped cream was passed down to lurk in front of her.

Sondra took the opportunity to push more of their mother's emotional buttons. "So, this is all very exciting. You must have been working on it for months. When did you know the trip was actually going to happen?"

"I proposed it a few weeks ago," Charlayne admitted carefully. To talk directly with Sondra was to stomp on land mines, and she did her best to prevent an undertone of rancor. "My editor called yesterday to let me know it was on," she continued, and, deciding to get it over with, dropped the final shoe. "I'll be leaving for Kathmandu mid-December."

December twenty-fifth rated right up there in pain level with Thanksgiving, and was also a must-attend holiday in the family—another of their mother's "maybe our last time together" events. Date of departure had not been discussed until now.

At the foot of the table, Lucille's voice trembled dangerously. "You didn't tell me you wouldn't be here for Christmas."

"I know it's awkward, but it turns out to be a good time to travel," Charlayne replied quickly, determined to stick with her decision. "They don't celebrate the holiday the way Americans do, so the flight to New Delhi was easy to arrange." She decided not to mention that flights to Kathmandu were giving her travel agent fits and looked down the length of the table to encourage someone else—anyone—to contribute to their discussion, but since she and Sondra rarely engaged in conversation, this was politely being regarded as "healthy discourse" between sister and sister.

"Are we expected to have Christmas early just because you're leaving town?" Sondra was relentless. "Surely you could put it off until after New Year's if you wanted to." Mark switched Sondra's glass of champagne with his empty one and began to drink, his expression holding faint amusement, but he remained silent at his wife's side.

Charlayne swallowed a bitter response and held to her resolution to maintain peace within the family. "I had no control over the dates, Sondra." It was an outright lie, and she hurdled her conscience; Shelley wouldn't be arriving until after the first of the year. "The research is ongoing, but I need to be there while certain investigators are in the field, otherwise there's no point."

"Mother's right, you are condescending." Sondra dabbed at sudden, copious tears with a delicate damask napkin. "I was merely trying to suggest that she and Daddy might be happier if you were here for Christmas, that's all." Conversation ceased and all eyes turned in Sondra's direction as she ruthlessly smudged streaks of mascara onto the fragile fabric.

"Mummy? What's wrong?" Ryan's eyes filled with sympathetic tears and he began to whimper. Adults leaped to the rescue with elaborate attempts to distract him, but his mother's distress and disconcerted grown-up behavior served to confirm his fears that something serious was amiss; the child's tears escalated to an ear-splitting wail.

Sondra threw an ominous look in Charlayne's direction as she hurried to Ryan's side. "Mummy's all right, darling. Mummy's OK." When it was determined that he was up well past his bedtime and clearly was overtired, fresh sobs gushed into the fray.

Charlayne felt swamped in impatience. When it came to producing tears, Sondra was a pro, turning them off and on at will for as long as she could remember; Ryan was without a doubt her sister's child, and well on his way to beating Sondra at her own game. Risking an outright look at the grandfather clock visible in the hall at the foot of the landing, she saw that it was eight-forty, and picked up her fork. This year's Thanksgiving from hell had a long way to go, and she may as well pave the road with pumpkin chiffon pie.

Eventually, mercifully, the evening ended and she was safe in her room on the second floor and digging into the chest of drawers for her trusty pink flannel nightgown. Flannel: nature's lovely answer to the damp of San Francisco's weather. Snuggling into down pillows and her amethyst patchworked comforter brought back childhood memories: bedtime cups of hot cocoa, and watching the rain form glossy rivulets on the windows, ambered by an old-fashioned streetlight across the way.

Activities ceased and lights were turned off as the household settled for the night. Still keyed up from the stress of the evening, Charlayne watched digital numbers glow red in the dark; the two on the end that signified seconds changed with annoying regularity from 00 to 01 to 02 to 03 to 04 to . . . Turning over and over in the old familiar bed, she tried her best to get comfortable but succeeded only in wrapping the nightgown around her body in an uncomfortable twist.

After an hour, comfy thoughts of steaming hot chocolate began to swim through her fantasies . . . rich with sugar, warm and sweet against her tongue. Mmmhh, hot chocolate! Definitely the answer. Loose in her consciousness, the idea built to obsession. Since she'd been a little girl, Alice had kept a pitcher of chocolate milk in the refrigerator for that very purpose. And it would only take a moment to heat.

Creeping downstairs, feeling ten years old again, her bare feet took her quietly along the familiar hallway to the kitchen. Mark's voice, low and cajoling, was engaged in conversation with someone in the living room. Hopefully Sondra was giving him grief about his predinner conduct. Char smiled with satisfaction. The bastard had it coming.

The refrigerator light assaulted her eyes, and she squinted to locate the pitcher. Alice had failed her. But there was regular milk. A stealthy trip to the pantry for cocoa powder solved that problem. She turned on a burner, lifted a copper saucepan from its hook, splashed milk inside, stirred in sugared cocoa.

Her mission nearly completed, the milk was hissing merrily when a small sound betrayed Mark's silent entrance. Anger bolted up her spine. How dare he sneak up on her! Refusing to acknowledge his presence, she reached into the cupboard for a mug.

"Hello, Charlie," he said quietly, his voice heavy with suggestion.

She clenched her jaw at the hated nickname, aware that he was crossing the kitchen in her direction. Silk pajama bottoms and a bare chest came into view at the corner of her vision as he laid his portable telephone on the counter; he'd been talking on the phone again, she realized. Alone, in the living room. Suspicion caused her to look up at him.

"You still feel good in that thing." His glance slid from her face to her breasts, and he lifted an eyebrow at the braless state of her body under the flannel. "Sometimes I'm not sure I wound up with the right sister after all."

In the half-light from the gas burner, he continued to look her up and down with the attitude of having the right to do it. She was thoroughly embarrassed and edged away. How on earth could she have married this miserable excuse for a man?

Disgust won out over silence.

"You have to be kidding."

"Sorry. Just can't help myself." He positioned himself between her and the kitchen sink, then rested one hand carefully inside his thigh to define his sex worming against the thin, shiny fabric. "Still got a little for me, don't you?"

Refusing to dignify his innuendo with a response, it took all her concentration not to spill the milk as she filled the mug; but anger burned up a hole in her chest. Silence was the best defense. She'd learned a long time ago that one-sided conversations tended to cease a lot sooner if you didn't engage.

Mark refused to give up. "Aw, don't be that way. Your mother's got the right idea. This might be the last time we'll have a chance to be together. You never know."

For an answer she thrust the hot pan past him toward the sink, bumping his bare stomach in the process.

"Damn!" He spun away from the copper pan, rubbing his skin furiously. "What the hell'd you do that for?"

"Just couldn't help myself," she echoed mildly, then ruined the rest of the chocolate by running water into it. She rinsed the pan and turned it onto the wooden drain board in one practiced motion. "Don't mess with me, Mark, and you won't get burnt."

Then, with supreme satisfaction, she made her way out of the kitchen and up the stairs of her childhood, carrying her mug of chocolate, intent on celebrating her freedom.

3

A very short list . . .

Jordan Kosterin looked into the ancient Narmada River valley at the sudden world of modern machinery: monster earthmovers fed massive skip-loaders and dump trucks; overhead cranes swung in lazy arcs; to his left cement-mixing plants shimmered in the oppressive heat. "Twenty-three million cubic feet of concrete," his brother announced proudly. "We're hauling the sand and gravel right out of the riverbed."

Jordan pulled thin linen shirt material away from his sticky chest and groaned at the thought of the cotton T-shirts and blue jeans folded in his luggage. Andrew had been in India for years and was fully acclimated; his thin blond hair had been bleached by the sun, his scalp, face, and forearms burnt gold as a native's, and so far he hadn't broken a sweat. Jordan eyed the pairs of massive stanchions on either side of the valley; half a dozen high-tension cables were suspended between them to ferry giant buckets into position along the dam. "You'll be able to see this thing from the moon," he said wonderingly.

"Wouldn't be surprised. Biggest concrete structure on earth when we're finished." Andy tapped him on the shoulder and pointed out the construction office, then sat back in the Jeep, king of his valley and his beloved dam. "We'll be pouring four more years."

Jordan gazed at the barren rocks of the riverbed. "What'd you do with the water?"

"It's dry season right now, but when monsoons set in, we get huge flood waves rushing down this river. Lots of people killed."

Jordan went silent under the age-old chill; unable to avoid discomfort, he held his gaze on the distant workers.

"Sorry." Andy fussed with the gas pedal for a few seconds and nursed the engine to life. "One of the reasons I came here to work is to make sure they do it right," he mumbled in apology. "God knows it wasn't the money."

Jordan shrugged off the bogies. He'd trade jobs anytime. "Wish to hell I had something that important to do in my life."

Andy gave him a contrite grin. "Hey, you got a right. Natalie was one in a million."

Jordan nodded without comment. Natalie was a painful subject for both of them. His brother threw the Jeep into gear and they began the descent to the valley floor. They'd driven in from Gandhinagar, and until two hours ago the land had been crisscrossed with canals irrigating farms as rich and abundant as anything Arizona had to offer; then had come thousands of acres of rock-strewn, arid desert, its inhabitants clothed in little more than rags. Andy had stopped the Jeep on the top of this hill to show him the view of the dam site.

"Flood cycle's been going on for thousands of years, creating feast or famine. Mostly famine. We'll control fifteen billion gallons a day when we're done with this baby. Irrigate millions of acres of cropland."

Jordan laughed. His younger brother was on a roll. They were together again for the first time in more than six years, and Andy was showing off his dam like a proud father.

"I gotta check in and let them know I'm back." They approached the construction offices. "You want to come in?"

"Next time. I'll wait out here." He'd flown in from Bombay that morning, having made a tight overnight connection through London direct from Los Angeles. Right now his body was going on eighteen hours of being in motion and he was enjoying the sensation of solid ground.

"Half an hour, max," his brother promised, "then we'll get out of here."

Half an hour turned into three. Jordan spent the time taking pictures of the site and sharing shade from a small tree with a Hindu gentleman named Baba. Ageless and spare, Baba sat cross-legged on a small concrete slab with no apparent discomfort; three toes were missing from one of his feet, and his sole article of clothing was a band of khaddar wrapped around his waist. After ascertaining that Jordan had no connection with the dam, Baba allowed his picture to be taken. They discussed the river.

"Mata Narmada." The old man's smile exhibited few teeth as he threaded his way through passable English. "Mata means mother. In India rivers are holy. To free one's self from sin . . . one can bathe seven days in Mata

Yamuna, or a single day in Mata Ganges." Baba waved his hand toward the distant trickle of water. "But merely to *see* Mata Narmada is sufficient. I have walked both sides of this river and she has purged my body of leprosy."

The lawyer in Jordan was curious as to how the pious old man would view the imposition of modern technology on his river. "Do you think the dam will take away her healing power?"

Baba paused a long time, considering. "Perhaps for now it is a good thing to carry her sacred water to those who would not see her." He smiled at the vast concrete structure growing within the valley. "This dam will not last. Mother Narmada will take back her bed in time. Perhaps when our children are no longer hungry," he said slowly. "It is not for me to know. I will sleep with the river long before this answer is given."

Jordan was drowsing in the heat when Andrew returned. They bade the old man farewell, and it was a thirty-minute drive to reach Andrew's home, a kitchenless two-room concrete cubicle amid a cluster of concrete cubicles in a nameless construction town. Inside, noisy air-conditioning blasted away at a wooden table and chairs, a scruffy green couch, an amazing array of stereo equipment, and a refrigerator; the bedroom, a foot larger than its twin-size bed plus a small closet, had an opening punched in one wall that led to a jerry-rigged shower stall.

"Why don't you get a phone? It makes Dad nuts that he can't reach you anywhere except your office."

"They get ten hours a day from my life," Andy exclaimed. "If I had a phone, it'd be twenty. The company pays for my calls anyway, and I'm only a half hour away. If it's an emergency, they can send someone. You ready for a beer?"

Jordan nodded and stripped off his shirt, savoring the

frigid air; Andy raided the fridge's freezer and threw him an icy can. "So, Dad let you have a sabbatical from the firm. Who's handling your clients?"

"I wound up my caseload a couple months ago." Jordan popped the metal tab and drank thirstily; delicious cold numbed his esophagus, and he sprawled onto the couch to concentrate on the beer currently freezing the lining of his stomach. "Haven't accepted anything since July."

"So this is more than your average vacation?"

"Right." Jordan added a sober admission: "I'm not sure I'm going back, and I haven't told him." He took another sip. Drops of condensation from the metal can trickled onto his chest and he absently rubbed the moisture across his skin until it dried. "Haven't made a decision yet, to be honest." Contemplating the dull shine of the can, he found no source of wisdom or knowledge to impart from its label. "I never enjoyed the law, but I always did a good job. Now I have to double check every detail. Can't get myself involved. So far I haven't screwed anything up, but it's no way to represent people. Unfair to them, unfair to the firm, so I decided to take a break. Think things over."

"Sounds pretty serious. What d'you think is wrong?"

"Same thing that's always wrong. She's still gone."

Andy looked away. "Yeah, well, what you two had doesn't come along very often. I guess you hold on to that."

"It isn't enough." Jordan finished the beer and stood, antsy, beyond tired and unable to relax. He placed the empty can on top of the refrigerator and retrieved two more, brought one to his brother. "It started getting to me last summer. From the time we met, I had five years, ten months, and twenty-one days with her."

"I didn't know it had been that long," Andy said uncomfortably. "I remember the first time I saw her."

WISH LIST

Jordan walked to one of the dusty windows and peered out. "This Christmas, it'll be longer that she's gone than all the time we had together. Maybe if I'm not there, it won't be real. Hell, I don't know—I do know I can't spend another Christmas talking to her headstone."

"It won't help. Take it from somebody who's been there." Andy gave him an awkward bump on the shoulder. "You gotta let it go, son. You gotta move on sometime."

"Everybody says that," Jordan growled at him in annoyance. "The fact is, I don't."

"Jord, she was one terrific lady and you know how I felt about her. But I won't let you elevate her to saintdom. She would have hated this."

"What? Keeping her memory alive? Making sure she doesn't disappear?"

"All that's fine, but it's not what she wanted. Natalie didn't have a selfish bone in her body. When she found out about the cancer, she made me promise I'd—"

"I know. Every time we talk, we have this conversation." Jordan tried to keep frustration out of his voice and failed.

"And every time we talk, you're still married to her memory. The only thing she ever asked me to do for her, and I can't make it happen." His brother ran his fingers through his thinning hair, unconsciously massaging his scalp. "Forty's still young. You still got your hair—"

Jordan's temper flared. "I didn't come here to get the same lecture I get from Dad." He paused as a woman of huge girth and shrouded from head to toe in shapeless linen opened the back door and carried in an aluminum kettle. She was followed by a little girl holding a tray of cloth-covered clay bowls. The woman ladled rice and chicken into two of the bowls, and marvelous aromas filled the room.

Jordan held his peace until the woman arranged the meal on the wooden table, then she and the little girl left as silently as they'd arrived. "I'm sorry, I'm tired and I just don't—"

"I'm sorry, too," Andy broke in irritably. "The last thing I want to do is rag on you about Natalie. I loved her, too, you know. Everybody did. C'mon, let's eat while this is hot."

The chicken had been cooked tandoori style to create succulent skinless meat bright red with paprika, and there was nan, India's delicious version of homemade bread. They celebrated the meal with another round of beer. Eventually, thirst and hunger appeased, lethargy began a stealthy trip into Jordan's brain. He knew Andy was right; Natalie had been mulishly determined that he would go on with life. Unfortunately, he hadn't known how.

Their marriage had been seamless; from the moment he'd fallen in love with her there'd been no line of demarcation, no point at which he stopped and she began. They were simply a single entity, finished each other's thoughts, knew each other's choices, fulfilled each other's needs and desires as effortlessly as making personal decisions. When he'd realized she was actually going to die, and that there was nothing medical science could do about it, he'd treated their final days together no differently from the first; he'd courted her. And on Christmas Day, when she closed her eyes forever, it seemed for a very long time that his existence had died with her.

At some point, he'd returned by half. Half of him woke up each day, got up each day, did the things that were required of him, came home, went to sleep, and repeated the process all over again the following morning. Somewhere along the line he began to taste food and engage in conversation, smile at jokes. He couldn't remember the last time he'd laughed out loud.

In the past two years the list of family members, work acquaintances, and friends who'd introduced him to marriage-age women and fixed him up with subtle and not-so-subtle blind dates was as long as his arm. Even his father had taken to assigning him the firm's occasional divorce cases. He'd suffered through endless evenings and paralyzing dinners with any number of probably very nice women, longing for an instant of Natalie's company, her sly wit, her strength of conviction. The smile that broke his heart.

Maybe he'd waited too long. Since her funeral he'd learned to prepare meals for one, become accustomed to the quiet of his Westwood apartment and the silent presence of Frazier, now his responsibility. When he'd decided on the trip, he shipped the cat to San Jose, and he wondered how his grandmother and Frazier were getting on. He'd have to call in a couple of days.

Andy switched off the air conditioner and tossed a couple of blankets onto the couch. "Hotter'n hell in the daytime, but it gets damn cold at night. You'll need these."

Jordan contemplated his brother's tired face. Decent, hardworking . . . unlucky guy, who meant well. Andy had been in love with Natalie, too, had fallen like an ox his first day home from college; but he and Natalie were already in love, engaged, and a few months away from getting married. Six months after the wedding, Andy had moved to Indianapolis to work construction; he'd gotten very drunk at his going-away party, drunk enough to confess that he loved her, that her obvious happiness was the only thing that made his feelings tolerable. Jordan had never said anything to Natalie about that night, nor had Andy, as far as he knew.

The hell of it was, Andy had never gotten over her. "You married her, you watch her die," he'd said brokenly when he learned about the cancer. He'd taken the job in India three months before she passed away, and hadn't come home for the funeral. This was the first time they'd seen each other since.

Jordan grabbed his brother around the shoulders. "Hey, I'm sorry. It's too soon to be an asshole. Hell, I've got weeks to do that. Seriously—"

Andy grinned and cut him off. "Yeah, I know. Look, what's past is past. I got some vacation coming, and a friend of mine has a VW I can use. He owes me a favor, so what do you say we get in it for a couple of days and see what kind of trouble the Kosterin brothers can generate? I'll do the driving and we'll check out anything and everything India has to offer."

Jordan smiled with relief. "You're on."

"Great. My boss gets back in two days and we can take off."

Outside came the wail of the muezzin calling the faithful to evening prayer. Jordan watched in surprise as his brother dropped to his knees; a few minutes later he rose and began preparations to go to bed. Soon his snores filled the room.

Jordan crossed to the window and looked up at the sky, ink-black and strewn with stars. He took out his wallet and looked for the hundredth time at the small slip of paper in Natalie's handwriting. Her "wish list." He'd found it among her things after the funeral. There were several crossed-off items: "Marry Jordan" was one, "piano lessons" another. "Learn to ski" had been lined out as well. His eyes filled with tears as they sometimes did when he consulted the fragile piece of paper. There were other wishes, fanciful, fantasy-laden. Unfulfilled. "Write a book, have ten kids, climb Mount Everest . . ."

Under "Travel" was a sublist. Half a dozen famous

places they'd visited together were crossed off; Easter Island, Great Wall, and Taj Mahal remained. Whenever they'd consulted the list, Natalie's comment had always been, "When we die, this should be very short."

Well, it isn't, he thought angrily. *Not short enough, anyway. And it's too late.*

Suddenly exhausted, he returned the slip to its sheltered slot in the wallet, then moved away from the window to undress. Maybe this attempt to regroup and rebond with his brother hadn't been such a good idea after all. So far, all he'd succeeded in doing was ripping open old wounds. For both of them.

4

A blaze of glory . . .

Charlayne held her mother at bay about Christmas and kept a wary eye on the calendar until December twentieth. Contrary to her inference to her family, she wasn't expected in Chitwan until the first week in January, but traveling ten days early would give her time to adapt to the time zone. Nepal was on the other side of the world, and according to the travel watch her father had given her for the trip, past noon in California was already close to two A.M. tomorrow morning there. It would require an instant day-for-night existence immediately upon arrival. In order to be functional, she'd have to be able to stay awake.

She was also leaving earlier in order to hold to her

decision not to share another holiday with Sondra and Mark. Christmas in particular was too important to have its high emotion and ideals destroyed by her family's pretense in front of Ryan. Since there was no explaining this to her parents without rehashing the past or putting them in the middle where Sondra was concerned, she'd simply take the easy way out until they no longer expected her attendance.

High with anticipation, she arrived at LAX while the local birds were still working on sunrise, unworried that her travel agent hadn't managed a connecting flight to Kathmandu. Despite it being the age of fax machines and credit cards, he'd cited the Nepali Air schedules as erratic and advised her that the airline's policy was to refuse to guarantee seating until the passenger was physically present. Her visa was dated for entry after December 22, and there were always trains, she reasoned; she'd walk if she had to. It was a great deal more important that she stick to her decisions and leave on schedule.

Her luggage, somewhere in the belly of Delta's comfortingly huge L–1011, consisted of lightweight canvas flight bags stuffed with sweatshirts, hiking boots, jackets, and jeans; insect repellent, Pepto-Bismol, and a supply of antimalaria pills rounded out her inventory of smaller survival items. Also, a tent, a sleeping bag, and an air mattress. All this to write a book about fishing cats? Absolutely.

Having successfully lobbied her publisher for the writing assignment, she'd verified with the head of the carnivore study, Professor MacArthur Jamieson, that nothing more rudimentary was likely to be encountered. Of immediate importance, however, was his advice that the nearest health facilities were an hour's drive from the camp and *good* health facilities were available only by flying to New

Delhi, which had encouraged her to invest in a spate of precautionary inoculations—also not mentioned to her family.

It was silly, perhaps, but her fascination with Nepal had begun her first year in college with the exotic promise of Bob Seger's golden oldie, "K-K-K-Kath-man-du!" Cheerful music with lyrics she could comprehend, boiling out of her earphones and stereo speakers while she crammed for exams. Somehow those three syllables had been fascinating, conjuring mighty Himalayas, Sherpas and Ghurkhas clad in felt and furs to blend with *Lost Horizon* legends of suspended time.

Besides, no one she knew had ever been to K-K-K-Kathmandu.

When Judy Baltine had mentioned that her brother, Mitch, had arranged a research trip to Chitwan, Charlayne had jumped at the opportunity to join him. With Mitch on site there was no logical reason not to go, she reasoned, except fear of dying in a twelfth-century country stricken with some unnameable disease, or death and dismemberment by a tiger. Now *that* would be an interesting story for her family to tell little Ryan around future Thanksgiving dinner tables: "How Aunt Char Went Out in a Blaze of Glory."

Guaranteed to give her mother fits.

The hatch doors closed and breakfast coffee arrived microwave-hot in a paper cup. By the time they passed over Las Vegas, her seatmate, Chuck last-name-a-mumble, had assumed an air of having heard it all and that every third out-of-work person he knew was a writer going to Nepal.

"It's to accumulate data on habitat requirements so they won't reduce the size of the game park," she told him.

With no room for his ego to get a foothold, Chuck's

eyes began to glaze. Immediately after breakfast, he opened his briefcase and hooked granny glasses over his nose to bury himself in actuary schedules. Charlayne put three sugars into her fourth cup of coffee and bought headphones for the movie.

By the time she was in and out of JFK and her plane was on approach to Frankfurt, Charlayne had lost track of all logical time. Too keyed up on caffeine and too chilled to sleep even under two woolen blankets, she stumbled stiffly through the jetway, endured Customs in a haze, and sought the warmth of an airport waiting room lounge.

"Don't let me miss my flight," she pleaded. The lounge attendant solemnly swore he'd keep track of her, and did, shaking her from fitful sleep fifteen minutes before she was to board Air India. Through another round of security, down another jetway, and onto another plane, this one with even less space per seat. Oh, joy. She wadded both pillows she'd snagged from the overhead into serviceable lumps and huddled against the window.

Her plan had been to stay awake until Frankfurt, then sleep until she reached Delhi. However, her circadian clock had gone into full rebellion with plans of its own; hours out of its normal time zone, her body was unwilling to allow sleep simply because she had another opportunity. The last time she checked her watch, it was an hour before arrival and her seatmate was rattling on in an Indian dialect. It seemed moments later that she awoke to chaos. Passengers were grabbing and hauling at luggage and packages from overhead bins, jamming themselves and their belongings into the aisles in a gabble of homecoming excitement. Outside the plane window was a night sky and bleary airport lighting.

She deplaned in her turn, only to find New Delhi's airport a scene of deafening turmoil as she struggled with a case of jet lag and caffeine deprivation that surmounted even the excitement of being in India. Plodding on leaden feet with a hastily procured luggage cart in her wake, she made her way through interminable lines that led to customs and immigration officials. Rubber stamps inked permission to enter into her passport; she fielded questions about her visitation purposes.

Unable to face another dose of coffee, tea, or rat-brown liquid of any kind, Charlayne realized she couldn't function much longer without genuine rest; travel logistics to Nepal would have to be tackled in daylight anyway. She identified a money-changing station and signed a receipt for a mass of Indian rupee notes of all sizes and shapes. Not having the faintest idea which was which, she was too exhausted to demand that her brain take care of business. A room with a bed in it was no longer a luxury, it was a matter of survival. Travelers' assistance personnel pointed out a taxi stand and gave her the name of a moderately priced hotel.

She was in the backseat of a dusty, nondescript car before she realized there was a man seated next to the driver. Her concern translated itself into her expression. "Two after dark," they took turns assuring her in brittle English. "It is for your safety. Honestly."

She decided to accept their explanation. *It doesn't matter if one of you kills me and the other dumps my body in an alley, just let me get some sleep first.*

The little car sped onto the highway with unexpected speed, zipping past safety lights burning orange along the center divider. Terror at their breakneck pace and backward driving rules—legacy of British occupation—kept her awake until she reached her hotel.

5

An unexpected opportunity . . .

Morning shone through thin, gaping curtains. The window was barren of blackout drapes that might have shut out the light, and a rude wedge of brightness struck Charlayne full in the face. She twisted her watch around her wrist to bring the time into view. Nine thirty-five.

Outside the window something was moving, awkward and not remotely human. She cautiously lifted her head from the dead-feather brick of a pillow and narrowed her focus to identify the green of leaves. A tree. There was something in the tree, and whatever it was, was black. Centering her awareness, she remembered that she was in New Delhi. Oddments of foreign sounds filtered through the window to confirm it.

Excitement and curiosity propelled her off the hard cotton mattress and she stole barefoot to the window to take her first daylight look at the city. She'd been given a room facing what looked to be an employee parking lot, and had a grand view of a pile of construction sand, a man washing a car, and a barking dog. "It better be a cheap room," she mumbled, disappointed.

Her voice caused a stir and a flop from a nearby limb, and the black things turned out to be monstrous birds. More precisely, vultures. Two big-time ugly carrion feeders were squatting on a tree branch a few feet from her window; long necks covered in crepey, naked skin craned beaky skulls and soulless red eyes at her through the glass. Traditional harbingers of death and destruction, they hopped awkwardly along the branch, balancing themselves with outfolded wings, like massive, oversized bats. What kind of city has vultures instead of pigeons?

Not wanting to think very far along those lines, she quickly tallied the time difference and reached for the telephone. Her father's strained voice caused guilt to tug at her heart. "I'm here, I'm fine," she greeted him. "New Delhi is marvelous and you're not to worry about a thing."

"Well, it's good to know you're all right," he admitted. "So, how were your flights?"

"Wonderful. No trouble. Slept like a baby," she lied.

Her father ran out of questions and her mother took over. "I can't believe you didn't call us. We were so worried, your poor father—"

"Mother, not at these rates. Please."

"Well, you're worrying us to death," her mother insisted.

"I'll call you every day until I get to the game preserve, I promise. You know there's no phone there, so don't start fretting this early," Charlayne admonished urgently. "We've been over all this."

"I know. Don't lecture long distance."

A few more similar exchanges and a declaration of love to them both, and Charlayne was able to hang up, duly absolved. She took a bath and, determined not to set local microbes loose on her unsuspecting stomach just yet, used bottled water to brush her teeth. By the time she found her way downstairs to the coffee shop, she was exhausted.

Menus, thank God, were printed with English explanations. A kindly waiter took her finger-point order for tea and toast. Clearly, more than a couple of days were going to be required to get her body adjusted to being up "all night."

With the strong tea working wonders inside her stomach, she sought the hotel's concierge. "I would like to arrange a flight to Kathmandu."

"You will need a travel agent, miss."

He placed a call to a Mr. Pujji and a meeting was set for that afternoon. Determined to stay awake, Charlayne forced herself to take a walk. The noonday heat was oppressive and the air abnormally heavy; she'd dressed too warmly for the soppy climate and was tiring rapidly.

Halfway down the block, she came upon a sidewalk vendor, barefoot, sitting on the curb next to metal drums of peanuts and pistachios and a vat of cooked rice. Chopped onions in a crockery bowl sat next to a collection of soft drink bottles; the slurry nature of their current contents signaled hot sauces, spicy curries. The teenager in his boredom was studiously examining a couple of dusty toes with his fingers. The New Delhi population could reasonably be expected to survive any or all of the bacteria about to be introduced into the rice seller's food chain, but local germs would no doubt strike her dead; she made a note not to eat anything, however tempting, from street vendors.

Giving up, she returned to the hotel and escaped to the coolness of her room and slumber, with a new understanding of sleep's description as "nectar of the gods." Renewed, refreshed, and thoroughly revived at four o'clock, she took a new look at her world and met the portly Mr. Pujji in the lobby.

"Flights to Kathmandu have been difficult. I must arrange things right away, miss," he advised her. "It may be a two- or three-day wait."

"Why? Is there a problem?"

"Many foreigners travel over your Christmas holiday," he said smoothly. "Not to worry. I, Pujji, will get you there."

She handed over her passport, Nepali visa, and her American Express card. Since it couldn't be helped, she'd have to use the time as an unexpected opportunity. "I guess I'll explore a bit of India," she said uneasily. "Can you help me rent a car?"

Mr. Pujji became alarmed. "Oh, no, miss. It is not a good thing. You must have a guide." He thought deeply. "I have a friend who can take you on a small tour—two days only—that includes the Taj Mahal. You cannot go away from India without seeing this most beautiful place." He quoted a price in rupees. "It includes Jaipur, which you must also see for such a small sum."

It took her a moment to convert the fee to dollars; with hotel rooms and meals included, it was quite reasonable. Plus, she'd have a schedule to keep on local time, and it would keep her occupied through Christmas. "I'd like to leave tomorrow," she said. "Then fly to Kathmandu as soon as I return."

The deal was struck and the rupees paid. Afterward she contacted the hotel in Kathmandu that had been recommended by Professor Jamieson and secured reservations, then celebrated her adventurous change in plans by purchasing a vial of decadent, soul-smoky sandalwood body oil and treating herself to dinner at the Imperial Hotel, a surviving dowager straight out of the British Raj. Unfortunately, a cocktail and two glasses of wine were insufficient to convince her body that it was night, and she was wide-awake until three A.M.

The next morning, however, with the assistance of a nerve-jangling wake-up call and the recurring shaft of sunlight, she got up at seven. She greeted bug-ugly Fric and Frac, who apparently lived in the tree, and called her parents to inform them of her new agenda. Considering it progress, she dressed in a long, airy wrap skirt and matching blouse, caught up her hat and went downstairs to order breakfast; over tea and toast, she made plans to spend the day exploring the city in the company of one of the multitude of pedicab drivers.

6

The second look department . . .

    Jordan reanchored his tripod with several small rocks and made focal adjustments to the camera for the seventh time. He'd been certain he was prepared, but somehow, visiting the world's most famous mausoleum this morning was unnerving. He hadn't had any conscious thought about the place when he planned his trip, no intention of being here at all, but last night he'd crossed *Taj Mahal* off Natalie's wish list and was determined to see it through.

Pacing the entry impatiently, he waited for the sun. He and Andy had arrived late yesterday and, after greasing a few bureaucratic palms with large amounts of rupees, they'd managed permission to set up his equipment in the pretourist, predaylight hours. Andy was currently negotiating an additional permission fee with the morning attendant, fees being the locally accepted version of bribery.

Six hundred feet in front of him, the tips of the monument's slender minarets were beginning to glow faintly in the receding night, to blend with an ice-cream dawn. Behind him in the east, an orange rim of sun was materializing out of the smoke from Agra's smoky cookfires and early morning haze adrift over the city. He needed perfect illumination to photograph the marble dome, and wanted somehow to make the dawning of this day a testament as well, a tribute to Natalie's memory. With luck, the angle of light he was seeking would last approximately one hundred fifty seconds, but he was standing by with half a dozen filters to maximize the color if necessary.

Andy joined him with yet another attendant seeking yet another fee. Walking with them was an attractive woman dressed in a light sweater and jeans, carrying a camera. Even without makeup, she looked decidedly American, and brown eyes smiled their way into his awareness.

"Hey, Jordan, meet Charlayne Pearce . . . oh, and I need another two hundred rupees."

Jordan nodded politely at the woman as he handed over the money, then carefully redirected his gaze to the dome, now warmed to an ashen rose, as his brother concluded bribery arrangements with the attendant.

"He wasn't going to let me in," the woman said at his side, "but your brother was kind enough—"

"Andy," his brother insisted as he moved between them.

"Andy," she echoed dutifully, "was kind enough to include me in his bargaining, so thanks for the use of your coattails."

"No problem," Andy assured her. "Merry Christmas.

For what we've paid these guys, a busload of elves should be able to join us. You don't mind if she takes pictures, too, do you, Jord?"

Andy's voice drew Jordan back to the conversation, and he shook his head. He'd been scanning the graceful lines of the famous monument. In the past few days, the royal forts and palaces he'd photographed had been uniquely, ornately Indian, elegant and charming, but the Taj Mahal was exquisite. The majestic symmetry of the tomb and its minarets had well earned its status as the most beautiful shrine in the country—if not the world.

"Better get ready," he warned her. "We have a very small window of opportunity."

Almost on cue, crystal sunlight broke through the city's dirty mist to a clear space of sky. Softly brilliant, the sunrise caused thousands of gold and carnelian flowers inlaid on the dome to burst into a splendor of fires; Jordan's heart leaped at the sight as he watched the phenomenon of spotless milk-white marble suddenly setting itself ablaze.

Next to him, Charlayne caught her breath, and for brief seconds they shared the luminous vision produced by the pristine light, captured and doubled in the oblong reflecting pools. Spellbound, Jordan forced himself to begin taking pictures. He shot frame after frame, each exposure better than the last. Time spun by in heartbeats, spilled over with magic until the optical miracle faded, disappeared forever, and once again the buildings were merely beautiful.

"Hey, Jord . . . you think you got that?" Andy's voice was hushed with awe.

"Unreal," he heard Charlayne murmur huskily. "I had no idea it was so . . ."

"Incredible," he supplied automatically.

"Mmmm." She nodded agreement. "Created for his wife. I can't imagine loving someone that much."

Jordan's eyes held to the monument. "I can," he said quietly.

"Then I envy you." Her artless declaration drew his full attention. He met guileless eyes, naked in their sincerity, before she turned to walk a short distance away.

Andy held her camera while she opened a new box of film, and Jordan heard her mumble, "If I screwed that up I'll kill myself." Her comment caused a bleak smile as he broke down his tripod and stowed it away, then removed the stones he'd used to anchor it. He knew the feeling.

"What say we look around?" Andy was back in motion. He grabbed Jordan's film bag and hooked his arm through Charlayne's, shepherding the two of them toward the mausoleum as tourists began streaming through the entry gate. "So, do people call you Charlie?" he asked.

"No." After a moment she added, "Friends call me Char. Charlayne's a compromise. My parents were planning a boy."

"Yeah, well, they definitely got a girl."

Jordan saw her glance at his brother and smile the smile of a woman who knows she's being appreciated. Her cheek color heightened and she brought her chin up a notch.

They reached the end of the reflecting pools and paused to remove their shoes at the base of a small marble stairway ascending to the tomb's glistening white platform. As she gave her shoes to the attendant, Jordan took a closer look at Charlayne Pearce. She was pretty, he decided, close to beautiful. Her eyes were an ambered brown with bright glints of rust and copper—almost the exact color of her hair, which she wore in a sensible twist to ward off India's incessant heat.

She had long, lean feet with coral polish on her toes, but her fingernails were buffed and natural. As he watched, she dug in her satchel-sized purse for a slouch hat, which she donned in one smooth motion, then added dark sunglasses against the glare from the snow-white marble. Her eyes disappeared behind tortoiseshell frames. Apple cheeks, a generous mouth— she had a lush body his brother would appreciate—full-breasted with a slender waist, and from his current view as she climbed the steps in front of him, a pert fanny. Definitely Andy's type. Prior to moving to India, his brother had been involved with several women—two blondes, a brunette, and a redhead, in that order—all of whom were as classy and attractive as this woman, but Andy had yet to take a trip down the aisle.

"So, is there a Mr. Pearce?" His brother was wasting no time.

Her voice in response seemed intent on quelling personal questions. "There's a Dr. Pearce."

Jordan's glance wandered to her left hand with its firm grasp around the strap of her purse. Ringless. A fact his brother had no doubt noted as well.

Andy refused to be deflected. "And where is the good *Doctor* Pearce? Can I assume he's not your father?"

"You can. He stayed in California. I'm here on business."

"Oh, really? Jordy lives in Los Angeles—he hates when I call him Jordy—don't you, Jord?" Andy was wholly intrigued. "What business?" he asked.

"I'm an author," she replied. "Here doing research for a new book." More flashing eyes over the top of her glasses, with an amused glance now and then in Jordan's direction; he kept silent, however, observing their ancient, time-honored ritual.

Walking barefoot, they continued their inspection of

the tomb. Andy's interrogation was put on hold while they filed into the massive structure's dim interior to view the small white marble sarcophagus of the queen and the larger matching coffin of the shah on its higher pedestal; the inlaid design of both was identical to the floral inlays covering the interior walls and the dome of the building.

Jordan took a penlight from his pocket. "Watch this," he invited. Switching it on, he placed the beam gently on top of a carnelian petal in the nearby wall; when he took it away, the stone shone warmly for an instant with a soft red-gold glow.

Charlayne removed her sunglasses. "*That*'s why it happened."

She flashed a brilliant smile at him, eyes alight with surprise, and he showed her again. "Holding light is one of carnelian's properties."

"How'd you know that, Jordy?"

He shrugged. In actual fact, he had no idea why the knowledge had occurred to him. Without the light, however, the carnelian petal was the same color as her eyes.

They returned outdoors, then crossed to the edge of the marble deck to look out over a guardrail at the adjacent river.

"The shah died in prison there." The fervent timbre of her voice reflected the extent of her interest as she pointed to a sandstone fortress a few miles downriver. "The shah's son had it constructed on that hill so his father could look at her grave as long as he lived."

"Thoughtful guy," Andy said unceremoniously.

"He'd decided his father was too distracted by her death to run the country. Certainly he was spending incredible sums of money, even for a shah. His son took over the throne before he could build his matching tomb across the river. Its marble would have been black."

Jordan gazed pensively at the barren state of the opposite shore, trying to imagine a glorious ebony twin to the Taj Mahal; half of him listened to his brother's pitch to Charlayne.

"Listen, it's Christmas," Andy was saying, "and since we're all infidel Americans, I think our meeting here is cosmic design and we're meant to have dinner together. Where are you staying?"

She laughed politely and shook her head. "Thank you, but I'm part of a tour and we're on our way to Jaipur."

Andy gave him a surreptitious nudge and plowed recklessly forward. "We're on our way to Jaipur, too, aren't we, Jord? What are you seeing there?"

Jordan watched her favor Andy with a grin that acknowledged his obvious fishing excursion, but her sparkle was infectious and he decided he wouldn't object if she joined them, if that's what his brother wanted. Amused, he awaited the outcome of their social negotiation with growing interest.

Her smile widened and he was unaccountably pleased that she included him in her glance before responding. "According to our guide, we're supposed to ride an elephant up to the Amber Fort."

"Yeah, us, too," Andy lied outrageously. "We'll probably be there when you are."

"No doubt." Her smile disappeared as she caught sight of a flustered, middle-aged man rapidly coming toward them, and she looked guiltily at her watch. "Speaking of my guide, I was supposed to meet him outside five minutes ago. Sorry, I have to go. Thanks again, both of you, for getting me in the door." She dodged Andy's objection with a wave of her hand, hastily descended the stairs to claim her shoes. They watched the guide hurry her past the reflecting pools and toward the exit gate.

Andy breathed a sigh. "Is she gorgeous, or what?"

"Mr. Smooth." Jordan punched his brother in the arm. "'We're going to Jaipur, too.'"

"Well, you sure as hell didn't help." Andy feigned grievous offense as she disappeared from sight. "I think I did pretty well—considering I haven't been around an American woman for almost two years. Man, she is one good-looking female! And my gut says there's no Dr. Pearce waiting for her to come home. If there is, I'll buy dinner. Let's get out of here."

Jordan took a last look across the river at the expanse of ugly scrub where the shah's tomb might have risen had his son not interfered: nothing the old man could have constructed would have brought them together again. He shifted his gaze to the stark fortress where the shah had lived out his life in view of his beloved wife's grave, and a hollow feeling took hold in his chest. Perhaps the son had been the wiser of the two after all. Perhaps enough was enough.

"Are you finished here?" Andy was anxious to hit the road. "You got any more pictures you want to take?"

Jordan gauged the soggy light. Nothing he could photograph now would eclipse the mystical sunrise they'd witnessed. No reason to linger. "Where the hell is Jaipur, anyway?"

Andy grinned and led the way to the stairs. "I haven't the foggiest idea. We should have followed her." He patted his pockets as an Indian ancient, bent and nearly blind, searched for their shoes. "You got any rupees?"

Jordan dug in his pocket for the shoe attendant's fee.

Char climbed into the tour van with her fellow passengers, a Teutonic couple from New Delhi who apparently spoke no English but had glower down to a fine science. She apologized profusely for any delay and went unrewarded in forgiveness.

Their guide was thoroughly rattled by her impulsive behavior this morning and kept checking the rearview mirror as if he expected her to vanish. He'd been horrified this morning when she'd announced that she was abandoning his schedule to take a taxi to the Taj Mahal. She'd done so because, if the past two days were any indication, by the time Mr. and Mrs. Charm had gotten their act together, it would have been well past sunrise. Visiting the monument on Christmas was her present to herself, and no way would she come this far and miss the best time to see it.

She looked out the van window, self-satisfied. Andy Kosterin was cute in a Dennis Quaid sort of way—desert-tanned, all hustle, muscle, and bad boy twinkle; but he brought her ex-husband to mind as well, and under no circumstances was she getting caught in that web again. One snake charmer in her life was sufficient, thank you. Still, a nice, safe little flirtation in the middle of India with an attractive American was supremely satisfying. His tireless attention had gotten her tail up, that was certain; she was feeling frisky for the first time in ages.

Andy, however, wasn't in the same league with his largely silent older brother. Jordan Kosterin was quite probably the saddest, most attractive man she'd seen since . . . She didn't even have a "since." Unshaven, strong features with pain lines at the edges of vague, smoky blue eyes—he'd seen heartache in great quantity, she suspected.

It was probably a good thing he'd been wearing a wedding band, because he was the first man in a long time who had caused her to take a second look. Third-degree burns in the marriage department had tended to keep her second-look quotient pretty low, but he'd definitely been worth adding to the list. And standing at his side when the dome had caught fire in that peculiar sunlight had been magical. An experience she could keep at no cost. And no risk.

The van gained speed on the narrow highway, and Charlayne cautioned herself not to think about the wild-mouse ride coming up between here and Jaipur. If it was anything like the trip from New Delhi, it would be a headlong potpourri of speeding tour buses and commercial trucks and slowpoky camels gallumphing along with their owners unwisely asleep in trailing wooden carts; wandering cattle had a penchant for dodging unexpectedly into their path, as did an assortment of pedicabs, bicycles, stray dogs, unmercifully laden donkeys, not to mention pedestrians, all vying for space on the narrow two-lane roadway.

Her driver alternately sped and braked, flashed his lights to signal his intention to pass, and took her breath away at the minimal space left between deadly oncoming metal and living bodies. Miraculously, they'd hit nothing and no one to date.

Life of every shape and dimension, including birds and butterflies, was sacred to most of the inhabitants of this land, which did not seem to coincide with the plethora of newly wrecked trucks they passed; so far the average was a totaled vehicle about every fifteen miles. When pressed for an explanation, her guide acknowledged the problem with a shake of his head.

"Drivers are inexperienced," he said in clipped English, "and when they brake suddenly, their load sometimes shifts and they wind up crashed."

She no longer questioned Mr. Pujji's insistence that she travel Indian highways with a professional driver.

They arrived post-lunch at the base of the Amber Fort in oppressive midday heat, and the guide led her and Mr. and Mrs. Glum to a platform where they clambered aboard a waiting elephant. Four-to-a-howdah style, they rode majestically through tall, wooden elephant gates to the top of a huge hill.

Surrounded by India's version of a Great Wall, the sprawling, once-royal residence was astonishing in its execution. Cool, smoothly plastered corridors led to bedroom chambers with walls and ceilings executed in delicate mirror mosaics; private gardens for women only—harems, or the Indian equivalent, she suspected—and shuddered at the owned status that those long-ago inhabitants must have endured. She gave silent thanks for being an American born mid-twentieth century with legal, if not precisely actual, equality to men.

She found herself glancing among the tourists as she took pictures of exquisitely fragile carved-marble window screens and burbling indoor fountains, vaguely disappointed that the Kosterin brothers did not appear. Her attention was diverted by an entire quarter of the fort once set aside as stables for elephants, camels, and horses to serve the royal Himself and family, while a man-made, lake-size reservoir provided an inexhaustible supply of showers, baths, and drinking water. "Boy, these guys knew how to live," she said to the guide. "I guess the local people ate cake."

Still no Kosterins; apparently they'd changed their plans.

At the end of the tour, they boarded another elephant. Monkeys perched in nearby trees watched with ancient, uncurious eyes their swaying downhill progress into the valley's heat. Snake charmers were strung along the roadside, plying their trade, tootling wooden flutes to induce small cobras to emerge from their straw basket homes in a dance for the tourists. "It's a Spielberg movie. Where's Harrison Ford?" she wondered aloud. Jordan Kosterin was better-looking, and his scruffy beard would have fit right in.

At the bottom of the hill was a collection of vendors, and while Mr. and Mrs. Don't Speak English were extracting themselves from the howdah, Charlayne broke from the group long enough to purchase a few packets of chocolate cookies; she was on her way to the van when a vagrant cow ambled into her path. She tried to circle the animal, but its walleyes were locked on the cookies and it rapidly nosed its way forward.

"Shoo!" she shouted fiercely. "Get away!"

The cow's response was to pick up speed. From the corner of her eye she saw a group of local boys speculating on the outcome between tourist and heifer. No help there. Outmaneuvering the dim-witted beast was tempting fate at best, so when its stubby horns came too close for comfort, she threw the cookies to the ground. The cow engaged in an immediate scramble with local children. A little boy scampered off with some of the packets, his compatriots in close pursuit; the cow, however, succeeded in grabbing one with its teeth, and plastic wrapping disappeared into its maw along with the sweets.

"Smart move." She jumped at the voice and felt a hand on her elbow. Jordan Kosterin stepped between her and the cow and pulled her behind his body; Andy was picking up a thick wooden stake a short distance away. The three of them cautiously edged around the aggressive bovine, and Charlayne was delivered to her van.

"Thank you. I wasn't sure for a moment what to do," she admitted nervously.

"You did the only intelligent thing." Jordan's voice was firmly approving, and she was grateful for his praise.

Andy agreed. "The kids probably own the cow. They may be sacred but they're half starved."

"Well, I still want my cookies," she joked shakily. "Lunch was a long time ago."

Jordan immediately walked to the vendor, while Andy stayed by her side, hefting the club. "This definitely calls for dinner," he said, a teasing gleam in his eyes. "Damsels are required to share evening meals with their rescuers. It's in the rule book."

"Well, if it's in the rule book . . ." She located her itinerary with shaky fingers. "From here we're going to the Royal Observatory, then the Wind Palace, and—yes, you can buy me dinner." His gorgeous brother returned to stand silently by as she gave Andy the name and phone number of her hotel.

"How's seven o'clock?"

"Seven's fine," she responded, then accepted the packets of cookies from Jordan, who'd taken the precaution of tucking them inside his shirt. He acknowledged her thanks without expression, and she did her best to draw him into conversation. "What did you think of the fort?"

"We've just arrived," he explained, eyes still watching the cow. "Haven't gone up yet."

"Well, don't miss it," she babbled nervously. "Some of the bedrooms are amazing. I had no idea such things were here."

"Really, the bedrooms, eh?" Andy was flirting with her again. "We'll be sure and make special note of them, won't we, Jordy? Always nice to know what a lady appreciates."

Her guide returned with the German couple in tow, rescuing her from the turn in the conversation. "Seven," Andy reminded her, and she nodded confirmation before taking her seat, aware that she was already looking forward to an evening with the two Americans. No harm in having dinner.

She broke into the package of cookies as they left the parking area and, happy when they were declined by her fellow passengers, ate them with relish as she reflected on the Kosterins. Jordan seemed to be warming up a bit, and indulging in flirtation with his harmless brother would be fun; certainly it was preferable to sharing another meal with her humorless companions, who had yet to smile at her, or each other, for that matter.

She looked out at the exotic city of Jaipur speeding past her window in a blur of wooden sidewalks and open-air markets next to blacksmith shops, with cows in the streets amid pedestrians, camels, and bicycles, and laughed. She and the others were scheduled to visit a carpet merchant this evening; her guide was going to have a coronary when he found out she was having dinner with strangers instead.

7

Three is safer than two . . .

Jordan looked up from shaving to find Andy in the doorway eyeing him with amusement; he was unaccountably irked and tried to cover. "What?"

"I thought you said you didn't think she was cute."

Andy's machismo had been building since the arrival of Ms. Pearce and the brother-versus-brother act was beginning to wear out its welcome. If anyone had reason to know that he had no interest in her, it had to be Andy. Loving Natalie aside, they'd never in their lives competed for the same woman, and as far as Jordan was concerned, never would. "She's attractive, I told you that. You want me to show up with half a beard to make you look good?"

Andy's image studied him from the mirror. "Scruffy wouldn't hurt."

"Get off my case, or take her to dinner and leave me in peace," he threatened.

"No way. First date, women think three is safer than two. That's why they always bring girlfriends. We've already moved into her hotel, and I don't want to start out on the wrong foot by having you disappear. She'll think I'm coming on too strong, it'll all go sour and I'll hate you."

Jordan frowned against the drag of the razor, unsure why he was shaving a three-day growth of beard in the first place. It was merely being courteous; nothing more than the polite thing to do for a female, even if he didn't know her. A round of drinks, hopefully a couple of steaks in lieu of India's incessant vegetarian fare, and he planned to be history. Andy could figure it out from there.

He rinsed his face and dried his razor, contemplating his reflection; hard steel-blue eyes, effective with opposing counsel, stared back at him. He'd turned forty in September, was pushing middle age, and the gray at his temples was gaining on him. Fine lines that he didn't remember creased the corner edges of his eyes. He dropped his gaze to a firm but no longer washboard abdomen; he'd drifted out of shape in recent years. Not good. He ran his hand through the satisfying thickness of his hair and relaxed his face, wondering if a woman who hadn't been "introduced" would find him attractive.

"Any time, old man." Andy's voice was impatient. "We're picking her up in twenty minutes and I still have to shave. Ladies prefer smooth cheeks. Top and bottom." He parodied a rough approximation of a samba in the narrow hall in response to Jordan's scowl. "The night is young, dear brother, and has great possibilities."

Jordan wiped his face and decided to skip aftershave; his participation was, after all, nothing approximating a date. His job was being the he's-a-nice-guy brother, and he was damned if he was going dancing. He surrendered the bathroom to Andy and pulled on chinos and a green polo shirt that had survived the road trip relatively unscathed; he smoothed out a few wrinkles here and there, but what the hell, it matched his face.

The door buzzer sounded, and she was standing outside with a bright smile, holding a hotel message slip. "I see I have the right room, seven o'clock, right?"

His watch read 7:05. "Seven-thirty," he said stupidly. He was certain Andy had said something about changing the time while he was in the shower. Maybe he'd misunderstood. Whatever, she was here.

Her gaze flickered approvingly over his clean-shaven face. "I guess that makes me 'fashionably early.' Sorry."

Not exactly transformed from the woman they'd rescued that afternoon, she was a great deal prettier than he remembered. Same richly brown eyes, but her hair was now free and framed her face; it floated to her shoulders in shiny layers. Coral lipstick had been freshly applied, he noticed, and it followed the curves of her lips precisely. Finely worked gold hoop earrings threw off glints of light; a sleeveless blue linen blouse was loosely belted with strands of amber beads over matching pants, strap sandals.

She was suddenly hesitant. "Was I supposed to meet you downstairs? The message says—"

He woke up. "Uh, no—come in. That is, if you don't mind him getting dressed."

Shirtless, his face half lathered, Andy leaned out the bathroom door to wave to her. "Ten minutes," he called with a grin, then whistled appreciatively. "Five, for you. Jordy, entertain this lady for me. I promised her a drink."

A faint breath of sandalwood passed him by and Jordan watched her circle the room, not completely comfortable. Not completely comfortable himself, he concentrated on amenities. "We have an assortment of—uh, things I've never heard of, actually." The miniature bottles clinked around in the minibar as he searched for something familiar.

"I'll pass, thanks," she said. "I'm not much for alcohol."

"Not without ice, anyway," he agreed. He looked up to find her perched tightly on one end of the couch, feet neatly together in the manner of a schoolgirl, with the huge satchel purse clutched in her lap. Apricot polish peeped out from her sandals. Natalie had never worn polish on her toes, considered it "tarty." It didn't look tarty on Charlayne, he reflected, merely nice. He began the search for conversation. "So you enjoyed the elephant ride."

"Loved it. I was a head of state making a royal entrance." Her voice was jovial and enthusiastic. "How about you?"

"Used-camel dealer." His response seemed odd to him; humor had been absent from his repertoire with women for quite some time.

She laughed and shifted her feet, lowering the bag to her side. "You're enjoying India," she declared shrewdly.

"An unexpected surprise," he admitted. "I usually visit countries after a great deal of homework. My wife always—" He floundered awkwardly, then recovered. "But not this time."

Andrew sauntered into the room to pull a fresh shirt from the closet; he moved between them, slowly buttoning the buttons. "Ms. Pearce, you look fabulous. Did my brother mention how good you look or has he been boring you?"

She denied being bored, but fastened her attention on Andrew. Jordan encountered annoyance. Just because the kid was five years younger didn't heave him entirely out to pasture. Baloney. From a woman's perspective, Andy had ten times more energy, knew how to make them feel special, and was interested in the same things they were interested in. Jordan dismissed his irritation as a nuisance and watched his brother escort Charlayne out the door.

On the recommendation of the hotel clerk, they drove to a nearby restaurant that appealed to American palates. The waiter located a surprisingly decent bottle of wine and they toasted her trip to Nepal.

"They don't permit vehicles in the park," she told them. "We'll travel by elephant."

"Rough terrain?" Andy guessed.

"It seems elephants create the least disturbance—"

"Among the wildlife." Jordan absently completed her thought; and nodded in agreement; it made sense. "They've been used for centuries as safe methods of transportation. They're like bulldozers. Very little—"

"Stops them," Charlayne finished for him.

Andrew glanced at them oddly, then began to add more wine to her glass.

She waved the bottle away. "All I care is they're big enough to push rhinos around and they're not afraid of tigers."

Jordan was intrigued with her adventurous nature. "You expect to see any?"

"Tigers? I sure hope so. They're so rare now—poaching and lack of sufficient habitat. Professor Jamieson says it's not out of the question. But . . ." She raised her glass. "Here's to getting lucky."

"I'll drink to that." Andy clinked her glass with a cheeky grin.

WISH LIST

She saluted Andy in return, then soberly touched Jordan's glass as well before drinking the toast.

Andy looked at his watch. "I should check in with my office. Someone's usually there until eight." He left the table to find a telephone.

There was silence in his absence. Determined to stay out of his brother's territory, Jordan searched for neutral questions. "You said you're an author?"

"Children's books, actually. Six- to eight-year-old market. Naturalist and ecology-based for the most part," she explained earnestly. "They're studying several animals in the park—sloth bears, palm civets, fishing cats—things kids don't normally find in zoos. Plus the tigers, of course. And the rhinos."

Interested, he questioned her at length about the aims of the research teams, and they were concluding their discussion when Andy returned. Jordan felt very much the third wheel as his brother immediately began to wheedle personal information. "OK, you can admit it," Andy bantered. "There's no faithful Dr. Pearce back home with a candle in the window."

Jordan felt rather than saw her minuscule hesitation.

"You obviously know Dr. Pearce," she retorted wryly. After a moment, laughter warmed her eyes once again. "That poor little candle blew out years ago."

"I knew it," crowed Andy confidently. "I told him the minute I saw you that you were not a married lady. Didn't I, Jord?"

Jordan nodded and smiled an accommodating-older-brother smile. Her eyes were always serious when she glanced in his direction; all during their conversation, there'd been no merry twinkle designed to draw him in. Not at all the way she was flirting with his brother. His idle musing was interrupted when she switched her attention to him.

"If I may, I'd like to ask a favor."

"Jordy'll do anything you want. If he doesn't, I will."

"I'd really like to have one of your photographs of the Taj Mahal."

Jordan went silent at this unforeseen request. Intent on her petition, she brought the heel of her hand to rest lightly on his wrist; when he met her eyes, she became self-aware and removed it. "Of course," he responded, and watched her search in her purse for a business card. "I hope there's something to send. I'm never sure till they're developed." His caution was automatic, lawyer-ingrained; he had no intention of exercising the caveat. The fact that she wanted something from him gave him a good feeling, curiously welcome in this place and time in his life.

He retrieved his wallet and slipped her card inside. When he looked up, Andy was staring a hole through him with deliberation on his face, before abruptly turning to Charlayne. "I'd like one, too." She gave his brother a card, and Andy changed the direction of their conversation. "So tell me about the park."

Her attention returned to his brother, but the small place on Jordan's wrist where she'd touched him burned brighter somehow than the rest of him; a bizarre feeling, actually, and odd that he would notice such an obscure sensation.

"It's a hard six-hour drive from Kathmandu, according to Professor Jamieson," he heard her answer, and mentally shook himself alert. She was a physical person, someone who touched easily; some people were like that. He personally was not, but Natalie had been. It was one of the qualities he'd loved most about her.

". . . an airstrip there?"

"I don't think so. According to camp literature, they use

a nearby park for emergency evacuations in the event of injury. There are all kinds of warnings about rhinos."

He noticed that she sat as calmly as if she were discussing weather, but talked about going into a situation where an injury would risk her life. An unexpected facet in this woman that Andy was doing his best to charm.

"Well, if they have an airstrip, I can fly in to see you. I'm in and out of Mandla all the time. Shouldn't be more than a couple of hours from there," Andy pursued.

"There's no way of knowing when I'll be available. Civets and fishing cats are nocturnal so we'll be tracking at night most of the time."

His brother wasn't ready to throw in the towel. "Here's my number."

Andy produced a business card from his shirt pocket, and Jordan realized that he'd been angling for a reason to give it to her.

"I know they have phones in Kathmandu. You'll come back through New Delhi and I'll fly up and take you to dinner. Deal?"

She laughed, but took his brother's card. "I don't make deals."

"Sure you do," he teased.

She studied him before making a careful reply. "If I get a chance to call, and depending on how much time I have, maybe I'll take you up on it."

"That's a deal where I come from." Andy kissed her fingers then pulled her to her feet; immediately he cocked his head and cupped a hand to his ear. "You hear that?"

She stopped, listening intently as he closed his eyes and brought her fingers to the center of his forehead in mock concentration. "It's very close by, I can almost see it . . . it's rock and roll! My rich lawyer brother is going to pay for dinner, and you and I are going dancing." He shepherded her, laughing, toward the door of the restaurant.

Resigned, Jordan dug in his wallet for rupees; unless he called a taxi, there was no way to get out of going with them. Besides, at the moment he wasn't too sure he wanted to be in a hotel room with himself for company. When he noticed that he'd tucked her card into the same slot with Natalie's wish list, he started to remove it, then changed his mind.

The restaurant bar was dingy and breathless from the damp heat of too many bodies, and Jordan had hated it on sight. Thick layers of cigarette smoke were floating as green murk in the garish lighting, and strident music jarred the room from a jukebox with half the plastic kicked out of its front. He'd been nursing a glass of thin beer for half an hour now, watching Andy dance with her. The current song was an ANYME standard, and he absently tapped his ring against his glass in time with the rhythm.

Charlayne danced sedately, nothing suggestive or in any way provocative, but now and then Andy led her through a series of steps that caused the amber beads at her waist to slide with lazy promise across her hips and midriff. Jordan knew the effect was totally inadvertent, but the swaying beads were vastly seductive, and every man in the room had his eyes on her. Two in particular had been feeding coins into the music machine with regularity.

In the past few minutes, however, foreign patrons had been leaving and some subtle shift in tension made him take a closer look around. Two granite-eyed women remained; both wore brash colors and westernized makeup. Most of the young men in the room wore traditional shapeless djellabas.

The bar was being taken over; vibes were changing quickly and dramatically. Jordan's nerves went on red alert. He didn't need a road map to tell him things were headed south in a hurry. When the music came to an end, Andy escorted Charlayne back toward the table. Unfortunately, he was walking directly behind her and Jordan was prevented from making eye contact. When he tried to grab Andy's arm, Andy veered away before he could stop him.

"Don't dance with her while I'm taking a break," his brother called back, dodging his way to the men's room.

Over Charlayne's shoulder Jordan surveyed the growing number of agitated men watching her every move. Flat black eyes held age-old male challenge as the next song began. Unable to leave without his brother, the safest place seemed to be on the dance floor. "My turn."

She looked up at him, skeptical. "Andy said you wouldn't dance."

"Yeah, well, I don't mind slow tunes like this one." He led her onto the tiny floor. With his cheek next to her ear, he settled his face into a primitive glower. Unable to relax or get into the flow of the music, he saw two young men form couples with the women and join them on the floor; within moments both men had deliberately brushed an arm against Charlayne's back.

The second time, he felt her stiffen and murmur, "Excuse me." Hostile eyes challenged him to do something about it, and he knew he'd have to get her out of there in the next few seconds or go down swinging.

Respectable women here didn't dress in pants, didn't dance in public, and certainly didn't go to bars, that much he knew. They didn't have long, loose hair on display, a free attitude about their body. As neutral and inoffensive as her clothing might be in America, in this country it was just possible that she was dressed in a suggestive or morally inciting manner.

Andy came out of the men's room, and Jordan instantly steered Charlayne toward the edge of the dance floor to meet him. "It's time we left," he said abruptly. "Things are getting tight in here."

Andy looked around. "Hooo-boy!"

With Andy leading and him bringing up the rear, they made their way out the exit and walked quickly to their car. Three men followed as far as the door, glaring in angry silence. Andy jumped in the driver's seat and started the engine. Jordan slid into the passenger side and quickly drew Charlayne onto his lap; he pulled her legs inside the car as more men crowded the bar's exit, their outrage apparent. Jordan slammed the car door. "Get us the hell out of here," he said tersely.

Andy gunned the motor and the VW flew out of the parking lot; halfway down the street he reported cautiously that the road was empty in their wake.

Jordan released his breath but tension still ran a high, constricted tide in his chest. Charlayne's body was strained against him, the cheeks of her buttocks hard and round against the tops of his thighs. To clear the roof of the small car, she'd had to tilt her head at an awkward angle, which placed her lips bare inches from his own. Her eyes were closed, and her breathing strained and shallow in his hearing; he was vividly aware that he was inhaling her breath, a warm, moist fragrance that passed along his jaw and into his mouth. The air surrounding him held the sweetened scent of her lipstick.

The coarse road bounced the car, causing her head to brush the roof and roughly jostled them even closer; her open mouth skimmed his lips in a brief electric contact. Without thinking, he spread his legs and shifted his shoulders. She lowered her body into the hollow he'd created between his knees and the soft feminine flesh of her slid along his shoulder and down his chest to press full against his ribs.

Air from the open window caused her blouse to creep forward at the neckline; he saw the swell of her breasts and the deep crease between as they spilled in tight curves over the satin cups of her bra. One side gaped for an instant at the clasp to expose a puckered smoke-rose aureole and a rigid rust-brown nipple. Thoroughly disquieted, he compressed his mouth and looked away; the intimate taste of coral lipstick bled onto his tongue.

The motor blared in the quiet night as they sped through the darkened city. Strands of her hair trailing lightly along his cheek, occasionally brushed his lips; it curled and drifted into the opening of his shirt, sleek and languid as silk against his throat. Awareness flumed and soared through his chest. The cream and rust and smoky rose of her would not leave him alone. Heated sandalwood fragrance lifted into his nostrils, pooled slick on his skin, and he wondered if she was as conscious of his body as he was of hers.

Hoped?

He was no longer sure of anything.

"Well, that was invigorating." Andy's voice sang out over the whine of the laboring engine. "Nothing like a little one-on-one with your local militants. Extremists. Growing movement all over the country. They're convinced the sole function of foreigners is to use our money to destroy their culture."

His brother's noisy humor jolted his senses, sharply reminding him that the woman pressed against him was his brother's date, and she was in their company solely at Andy's invitation. Andy punched him in the arm. "Thanks to your quick thinking, older brother, we are fleeing safely into the night."

"He saved our beans, younger brother," Charlayne quipped edgily.

Her tension continued its flow into Jordan's chest, adding to the primal pleasure engendered by the touch and warmth of a woman's breast—her breast—cream soft and supremely pliant, subtly conforming its shape yet firm against his body. The mate to the rose-rust nipple he'd glimpsed was separated from his skin by thin layers of fabric: a green shirt, the blue curve of her linen blouse, and a wisp of satin.

He tried to fight the emotion swimming thickly in his head, but the short drive back to the hotel was charged with the dense, compact beating of his heart. The lightness of her body against him, quick and alive, added to the awareness of the intimate spread of his legs; the confined fullness of his sex gained heat against her thigh. It took every ounce of control he could muster not to embarrass himself, or her, with an erection.

At the hotel entrance an attendant helped them out of the car. A light evening breeze caused his clothing to glow damply cold where she'd been next to him. Confused at this sudden, overwhelming attraction to her, needing time to pull himself together, Jordan bade the two of them a swift good-night. Unsure of his place in this picture, unsure he wanted a place in it, he headed toward the lobby elevator before he could be shanghaied into having a nightcap.

This morning all he'd been able to think about was Natalie. This morning was suddenly a hundred years ago, and the stunning truth of it was, he hadn't thought about his wife for several hours. Nearly the entire evening. Not since Charlayne Pearce had danced with his brother. Not since dinner. Not since the Taj Mahal.

Her scent and feel clung to him like an aura, surrounded his senses, swamped his emotions in chaos. For the first time since his marriage, he'd allowed himself to enjoy the touch of another woman. His brother's *date*, for God's sake, and the effect was staggeringly uncomfortable! He was mired in a hideous sense of disloyalty.

Charlayne caught up to him in the lobby. "You have my lipstick . . ." She reached up with her thumb and wiped it from the corner of his mouth, an innocent gesture, while he tried to find somewhere to look beyond her eyes. "Thanks for getting us out of there," she said gravely. "I knew things were getting pretty weird, but I hadn't realized it was dangerous."

Before he could respond, Andy arrived and the three of them stepped into the tiny elevator. His brother's manner was teasing and cheerful; as if nothing whatever had happened, he began fishing for another date. "So, where will you be tomorrow night? You want to go dancing again?"

Jordan forced a smile, too aware of her presence next to him, of the heat from her; the bare arm with baby-soft skin that had slid around his neck in the car was jammed tightly against his own in the small space, tingling and electrifying their contact, making him want her. Despite his control, desire pressed its way to his loins, set his flesh on fire. He wanted to smooth his fingers along her skin, longed to taste the cream and the rust and the smoke-rose of her, to run his tongue down that crease. . . .

"I'll go dancing with you two the next time I have a death wish," she retorted, and her laughter filled his ears.

Her words were still an echo in his brain when they arrived at her floor. Andy got off to accompany her to her room, and she called a good-night before the elevator doors closed them out of his view, but Jordan made no response. Desire melted dully into a sea of pain. The anniversary of his wife's death, and he was looking at another woman. More than looking. Wanting to bed her.

A woman attracted to his brother—who was going all-out to seduce her.

He knew rationally that his feelings were false. Some kind of anomaly. Had to be, for there was no doubt in his mind that he still loved his wife totally and irrevocably. And being false, they would pass, but his pain was indescribable. It was some kind of bizarre reaction to the three of them behaving like teenagers this evening, some cross-purpose acting-out of what he should be doing versus what he wanted to do. What he *wanted* to do was go back to being numb.

He let himself into the room. When Andy didn't return right away, he emptied a couple of bottles from the minibar. Half an hour passed. He called the lobby. Thirty American dollars quickly produced delivery of a questionable bottle of Chinese vodka, and as soon as it arrived, he proceeded to get rapidly, thoroughly drunk. Drunk enough to shut off his mind and go to sleep.

He woke the next morning to find his brother in the opposite bed, with a faint smudge of coral lipstick along his cheek. A few minutes later, he was heaving the contents of his stomach into the toilet, praying his brain wouldn't explode in the process; Andy announced that he had invited Charlayne to join them for breakfast. Jordan knew an intense mixture of loss and relief when Andy called and there was no answer in her room; he gleaned from his brother's end of a conversation with the front desk that she'd left a note thanking them for dinner and had already checked out.

Curiously, Andy made no mention of his obvious hangover; nor was anything volunteered about the reason he'd had been delayed in Charlayne's room. Jordan was all too aware that his brother could be incredibly charming, not to mention persuasive, when the occasion arose. If she'd been receptive . . . he convinced himself that he didn't want to know about it.

Her tour van was no longer in the parking lot when they left the hotel. End of situation. Life could return to normal.

It was a long, miserable ride back to the valley. Shards of sunlight pierced his eyelids to ricochet through his brain; guilt at his betrayal of Natalie fed on his soul. It was unmercifully hot in the little car and his shirt stuck to his skin, irritating and uncomfortable; a faint sandalwood fragrance lingered in the fabric.

He wore it all the way to Narmada as penance.

8

Sorely tempted . . .

Charlayne compared her watch with the airport clock. They should have boarded an hour ago. She walked nervously to and fro in front of the Nepali Air counter. Anxious to get to Kathmandu, she'd been delayed a full day after returning to New Delhi because this was the first, and only, available flight until after New Year's. She'd requested and received the same room at the little hotel, become friends with Frick and Frack. Yesterday, she'd taken a tour of the older portion of New Delhi, and each time she'd seen wandering cows among the shops and pedestrians, she was reminded of her rescue and the Kosterins. She found that she was still looking for their faces among the crowd of men in djellabas and veiled and gowned women in the waiting room.

Outside the airport window heat waves were beginning to shimmy over the tarmac, but ground activity was zero in the immediate vicinity of the plane. All the fuss this morning to be here early was for naught. She yawned. Getting up to catch a taxi at five A.M. was exhausting no matter what time zone you were in.

It hadn't helped that she'd been adrift in exotic fantasies about the Kosterin brothers for the past two nights. Closer to erotic, if she was honest. Like no dreams she'd ever experienced—or remembered if she had. In black velvet rooms with the ambience of the harem quarters of the fortress, it wasn't clear which of them—she or the brothers—had been prisoner, and all of them more or less unclothed. Unable to escape for unclear reasons, the men had openly competed for her, challenging each other in escalating bouts of seduction.

She'd been embraced by first one and then the other in some kind of dizzying ritual, and the dream-she had enjoyed it immensely. Sometimes both brothers had merged into one homogenous, very male presence with Andy's teasing eyes and Jordan's mouth, Andy's smile and Jordan's arms; and always, always, she was tight against Jordan's chest, as close as they'd been in the car. Both nights had been a continuous, sensual state of somnambulance, kissing and caressing her dream-Jordan until he became Andy, at which point she'd pull away until he became Jordan again, unwilling to wake up and unable to sink into deeper sleep. All very potent and very confusing.

Not an unpleasant experience, she conceded honestly, but what was the message from her subconscious? That both Kosterins were attractive? Nothing to deny there. Andy had been cute from their first encounter in the parking lot, but meeting Jordan a few minutes later had been positively devastating, unkempt growth of beard and all. When she'd seen him clean-shaven, she almost lost her cool. Fortunately, he'd been totally upfront that he was married, backed up by the large gold ring he wore; when he'd spoken about his wife, something in his voice had made it clear that his marital situation held great importance for him. From that point, she'd deliberately countered her interest in him with increased attention toward his brother.

The wild ride in the little car crossed her mind again, drifted in without conscious thought, accompanied by a physical surge of feeling. Her mouth against Jordan's, inadvertent or not, was technically kissing a married man; he hadn't kissed her back, but her reaction and the intimate closeness of their bodies, the hypercharged sense of danger—real or imagined—had combined to make it a very potent memory.

For a while, hard against him during that ride, sliding her body into the intimate space between his legs, she'd forgotten that he was married; somehow she'd come under his care and he was cradling her, protecting her, and would look out for her. Heady, powerful emotions had poured into her body, and she'd given in to them, reveling in his strength until they'd reached the hotel. He separated himself immediately, almost as if he'd sensed her attraction. Clearly he was uncomfortable with her presence, had held her awkwardly when they'd danced. Maybe her dreams were an admission of what she'd been denying: that she *hadn't* fought her interest in Jordan Kosterin, which brought her perilously close to duplicating her sister's behavior.

She shrugged in resignation. It was a good thing she was getting on a plane this morning—assuming it ever got off the ground. Flirting with Andy and playing at being carefree had nearly gotten out of hand. He'd spent more than an hour in her room under the guise of quizzing her about her private life, and she'd been sorely tempted to drown her interest in one brother with the body of the other. But kissing Andy good night had only verified that he wasn't the one.

A flurry of activity caught her attention. The departure gate had opened at last. She hurried to join the crush of passengers in the boarding line.

Descending into the Kathmandu Valley, she looked out the window, eager for her first glimpse of the magnificent Himalayas—that line of snowy, crystalline peaks revered by the Nepali people and known around the world. This day, however, gray rain clouds obscured her view from the air, and after they'd landed as well. Nevertheless, standing at the top of the plane's metal exit ramp she felt an enchantment the instant she took a breath; clear, chilly mountain air assaulted her lungs and caused her eyes to water. K-K-K-Kathmandu. Nothing could dampen the sense of mystery that emanated from this valley.

A veteran of airport procedure by now, she negotiated the customs and immigration bureaucracy with the confidence of a pro and excitedly procured a taxi; it was a forty-minute ride into the city proper, and she arrived at Jamieson's recommended Kathmandu Guest House slightly after noon. Despite not having a phone in the room, her fourth-floor single was practical in its dormlike simplicity and provided a smashing view of a nearby temple tucked into a low round of foothills.

From her tiny balcony the view of hodgepodge city rooftops gave the impression of urban combat between unruly gangs of square, three- and four-story buildings. Constructed mostly of brick, some were stuccoed, and all were bleached to muddied pastels by relentless sun and snow. Wooden, rain-blackened window frames and doors lent an air of being down-at-the-heels, and edges of this otherwise ragged profile were smudged with charcoal outlines of skeletoned, winter-bare trees.

Unpacking took a quick five minutes as she debated whether or not to wake her parents. It was well after midnight at home, but best to notify them she'd arrived.

Impatient to explore, Charlayne speared her toothbrush into a glass in the bathroom, then ran downstairs. She sought the hotel's central operator and gave her the San Francisco number. Her stomach dropped when the woman looked at her cautiously. "Miss Pearce? I think there was a call for you about ten minutes ago. Someone in California."

Before she could check, the connection went through and she was speaking on a scratchy line to her parents. "No, I haven't called, but we were just about to," her mother scolded sleepily. "It's bad enough you weren't here for Christmas." Maternal grievances were replayed once again.

Charlayne assured her mother for the sixth time in six days that she was absolutely in the best of health, and reminded her father when he picked up the extension that it was going to take a massive hunk of her royalties to pay the phone bills. "I'll call before I leave for Chitwan," she promised. "That's two days from now. Have you received any of my postcards?" They hadn't.

She filtered out her father's amiable good wishes from her mother's fretful warnings about everything from water to weather. "The trip's been smooth as silk," she shouted over the faulty line. "We'll be taking tons of pictures, so buy stock in Kodak." She sent loud, smacking kisses down the long distance from Kathmandu to Baywatch Street and hung up, then retrieved her message from the front desk.

Discovered I'm pregnant. Can't travel to Nepal. Max and I are thrilled but feel terrible at letting you down. Shelley.

Charlayne's first reaction was astonishment; she'd known Shelley and Max were engaged, but a pregnancy hadn't been in the picture when she'd left Los Angeles. A child-to-be would certainly cause a major change in their plans, not to mention her own. Damn! She couldn't provide the promised book without proper photographs, and locating an alternate someone was all but impossible on such short notice. Inoculations alone would take three weeks.

Her dilemma was compounded by the knowledge that her personal skill as a photographer was point-and-shoot at best. Plus, she didn't want to divide her focus between making creative observations and peering into a camera lens. Pictures were to be the basis for a sketch artist's illustrations, and it was essential that they be captured with a naturalist photographer's eye. The loss of Shelley was major.

She hurriedly scanned the Kathmandu phone directory, to discover no listing whatever for *Photographer*—not even *Portraits*. Surely there was someone in Nepal who was proficient with a camera! At least until she located a replacement. Maybe someone from the local paper. She placed a call to *The Rising Nepal*, whose editor politely agreed to post a notice in their office and took her number.

Thwarted for the moment, she found a local restaurant and ordered lunch. Jordan Kosterin kept pushing his way to the top of her mind, and that magical morning at the Taj Mahal. Was this already the third day since that had happened? *You don't suppose . . .* She ran down what she knew about him as she ate her sandwich. He was a lawyer, in India on vacation, apparently without his wife. She remembered very clearly the look on his face when he'd mentioned her—uncomfortable. But what if she'd read his demeanor incorrectly? What if there was a reason he was traveling alone? What if they were separated? In the middle of a divorce, maybe . . .

Too much to wish for. Back to the problem. But the idea wouldn't go away. He'd taken photographs that morning with some very sophisticated camera equipment, had a carrying case full of filters and different-size lenses. If he was an amateur, he must be pretty good to lug so much specialized gear.

And he'd been very interested in Professor Jamieson's research, had asked her all kinds of questions at dinner the other night. Maybe she could invite him to the game park for a week, in exchange for taking her pictures and free room and board; at least she'd have some of the photos she'd need, which would be better than nothing. If he said no, she hadn't lost anything.

She dug Andrew's number out of her purse and returned to the hotel. This time the phone connection was crystal clear and Andy's voice was filled with surprise. "You don't know how glad I am that you called," he greeted her happily. "Where are you?"

"I'm in Kathmandu." She decided to get straight to the point. "I know you didn't expect to hear from me so soon—"

"No, it's great," he insisted eagerly. "What's going on?"

"I've encountered a stumbling block over here and— uh . . ." Suddenly it was a stupid idea. Worse than stupid, not thought through. She didn't know Jordan Kosterin from Adam. *Or* Andy, for that matter. She suddenly felt ridiculous, aware that she'd panicked. The man was a lawyer, for heaven's sake, and probably happily married. Even if he wasn't, a *GQ* type like that wasn't likely to be interested in midnight mud and pungent elephants. Besides, everybody knew lawyers had no sense of humor and were right up there next to dead fish in the ability to lose their appeal.

"So, what's up? What do you need?" Andy's voice was a mixture of concern and helpful intent.

"A photographer," she muttered, and cringed that she hadn't come up with an alternate story.

"A what? I can't hear you. The phone system's rotten."

She spoke louder. "My photographer can't make it after all, and, well, there doesn't seem to be any local talent. I know it's pretty left field but I thought maybe"—at the very last instant she found an exit door and bailed—"you might know someone. It's a free trip to Nepal," she finished resolutely, and treaded water through his pause.

"Uh—sure. Maybe. Let me work on it. Where can I reach you?"

She gave him the number of the Kathmandu Guest House.

"I just may know someone," he said thoughtfully. "How soon would you need him?"

"Day after New Year's. Anytime that week, actually."

"I'll see what I can do. Just a second."

She heard a frizz of excited voices in the background until he came back on.

"Sorry about that. Anything else?"

She thought madly for something more to say. "Uh—no. That's my only crisis at the moment."

"OK. I'll call you if I have something. Otherwise, shall I have him show up at the park?"

She paused. Would an unknown quantity be better than nothing? Probably. "That would be fine. Thanks, Andy," she tried to convey her appreciation. "You're really terrific to try and help me out. I'll let you know right away if I'm able to locate someone." She paused, then added politely, "Tell your brother I said hello and I hope he's having a good trip."

"I will. Listen, I'd love to talk, but they just told me some moron's pouring cement into the wrong hole, so I gotta go. See-ya." The line went dead.

She got off the phone thanking her stars that she hadn't offered Andy's brother the job. What a blunder that would have been. In her limited experience, lawyers weren't the roughing-it type. He was probably on his way home anyway.

Faced with the end of her immediate possible solutions, she computed the time difference with New York. Later this evening would be early morning there; she'd have to notify her publisher and see if they had something or someone to suggest. The rest of the day was devoted to touring the city in a taxi, taking amateur photographs that would have to do, and making notes. Her last stop, a temple with an unpronounceable name, Swayambhunath, was otherwise known as the Monkey Temple—aptly, for there were scores of the scrawny-rumped, long-limbed creatures scrambling about, nimbly plying tourists for handouts.

Making an offering of rupees as she passed through the gate, Charlayne mounted the steps to stand on the holy mound of earth and stone. Known as a stupa, it was essentially a grave for a portion of the Buddha's ashes; atop its white dome was a squared gold face. Each side featured a pair of enormous stylized blue eyes that were visible for miles. Above the eyes, and reaching to the sky, was a tall, pagoda "hat"; streamer ropes holding colorful ribbons and prayer flags fluttered from its peak in the manner of a maypole.

In a ritual aged in centuries, caretakers slowly circled the temple's shoulders, emptying buckets of whitewash down its sides to erase rusty stains; in their wake the stupa glistened a wet, brilliant, beautiful white. Charlayne had the eerie sensation that from any direction, the Monkey Temple had its eye on her and could see through to her soul.

At its base she paused to examine the surrounding bank of wooden prayer wheels and wondered whether a nonbeliever's petition might be heard. Concentrating her thoughts on her father, she spun one of the elaborately carved cylinders around and around, praying fervently that he enjoy good health. On an adjacent wheel she made a similar request on behalf of her mother and amended it to include her family in general; on a third she made a brief, selfish plea for an answer to her dilemma concerning a photographer, spinning it three times—just in case someone was listening. And in the mood to grant her wish.

Jordan followed his brother into the concrete house. Since they'd returned from Jaipur he'd done little more than sit with Baba in relentless, weltering heat and watch Andy's construction crew pour cement into the wrong hole.

Andy had worn the subject of Charlayne very thin during their return trip. "Didn't you think she was terrific? I mean she really handled herself in that bar situation. Most women would have gotten hysterical but she hung right in there. She's got guts, I'll give her that. Not to mention the fact that she's got some kind of body on her. Can't really blame those guys for getting nuts."

By the time they'd arrived, it was clear to Jordan that his own feelings where she was concerned had been properly assessed. They were false and had disappeared under the weight of Andy's obvious infatuation. An anomaly, nothing more. He resolved to get a stronger handle on things. "I'm getting bored," he admitted over dinner. "I don't have any better idea about my life now than I did when I got here."

"They didn't build Rome in eight days, either."

"No kidding, Sherlock," he retorted with ill humor.

"What are your options?" Andy was staring at him as if he expected some sort of breakthrough insight. "What're you gonna do?"

"I don't know, probably go back to L.A." It was the last thing he wanted, but cabin fever was setting in. For all practical purposes, he and Andy had exhausted small talk, and as yet he had no answers to the bigger questions in his life.

"And do what?"

"Christ, if I knew, I'd do it." He walked around the jail-cell room, trying to pull his frustration under control. "I don't know. Get my act together. Admit I'm no different than the rest of the working schlubs and go do a job I hate. Hope it gets better."

Andy opened a couple of beers. "Can I ask you a personal question?"

"If you leave out any mention of Natalie."

"Had anyone in your life since Natalie?"

Jordan paused to fight down annoyance. "You mean am I getting laid?" he responded bitterly. A vision of Andy and Charlayne disappearing down the hotel hallway in Jaipur flashed into his memory. He pushed it away. "No, I'm not."

"Choice, or can't get it up?"

"It's not a matter of getting it up, it's a matter of wanting to. Not that it's any of your business," he said rudely. He had wanted to with Charlayne Pearce, and if Andy hadn't been there . . .

Truth? The minute he'd started thinking, his interest in her would have disappeared. *That* was truth. And if Andy hadn't pursued her, asked her out, would any of it have happened? The question was no longer on the floor. The minute his brother had gone to her room, none of it mattered anyway.

"I don't want to fight." Andy was staring again. "The only way I know how to get through a bad situation is to tear it apart. Get in with both feet and do a job on it." His brother moved to the green couch and slumped heavily onto its cushions, a baleful eye in Jordan's direction. "Your choices, as I see it, are to continue to be miserable or—painful as it is—do something about it. You're bleeding to death. A blind man could see it. Nothing could hurt more than this—"

Jordan interrupted. "Problem is, I don't know how," he heard himself confess. "Every time a woman causes a reaction in me—even friendship—one thought of Natalie and I completely shut down. It's hard to explain to someone who's never been married, but when you take a vow based on everything you believe in . . . when you swear to forsake all others . . . "

"Till death do you part."

"Even acknowledging that," he retorted with anger, "even knowing intellectually that she's gone and will never know . . . emotionally it's like cheating on her, and I never did that, not once. Wasn't even tempted."

He sat next to his brother on the couch. "It's still getting worse, not better. I still have dreams about her. . . ."

He held up his left hand, and the gold ring glinted in the harsh light. "You can tell me this isn't healthy—and you're right—I'm smart enough to know that. Give me some credit. But settling for just sex . . ." He tried again. "Settling for that much *less* with another woman would be slow death. You of all people ought to understand that." Having said it at last, he drank the beer.

"You're right, I do. But you gotta do something and—" His brother took a deep drink and deliberately changed the subject. "—it's too soon for you to go home." Andy pushed himself back into the couch and propped his feet up on a stack of bricks that served as a coffee table. "I have to go to Mandla in a couple of days. They need a revised set of construction plans. We can take 'em up in the company plane and hop on over to Tiger Tops. Chase a few cats over New Year's. What do you say?"

Jordan was grateful for the shift in topic. "I tried getting us in there when I knew I was coming. They're booked solid."

"The rooms are booked, but I made a few calls today and we can get in a couple of game runs. There are a bunch of tourist traps nearby with pretty rustic accommodations, but what the hell, you're not doing anything anyway."

Jordan felt a surge of enthusiasm awaken in his chest for the first time in years, the call to adventure. He hesitated. "Tiger Tops is in Nepal."

"So?"

"What about visas and all that jazz?"

Andy punched him in the arm. "Hey, you forget who you're talking to. I got friends of friends who got friends. . . ."

9

Into another world . . .

Jordan looked out his window at the thin brown line of grass his brother was calling the Meghauli airstrip and wondered which was worse: staying aloft in the rollicking updrafts or landing on a pinstripe in the Terai foothills between an otherwise solid mass of trees. Already today they'd flown over more landscape than he'd thought possible, arid desert giving way to scrub, then lush tropical jungle in the Himalayan lowlands; the famous mountains, to his frustration, had remained hidden behind thick layers of clouds.

The plane plunged into a sudden, rapid descent with Andy yakking into a radio transmitter all the way down, and Jordan's pulse rate hiked another couple of notches.

Eventually, they whumped and rattled their way along a shadowy clearing marginally wider than their wingspan. He caught himself pushing his feet against the floorboards—the same as twenty years ago when he'd taught his brother to drive. It hadn't worked then either.

Andy revved the small plane smartly into an adjacent field of potholes and killed the engine. "Welcome to Tiger Tops, older brother. Help me tie her down."

Jordan helped him secure the light plane to a steel pin buried in the ground.

"Wouldn't want some jocko joyriding in it. You think you have cabin fever, wait'll you check out some of the locals."

Two hundred yards away the famous lodge was obscured by a stand of trees, but once inside, it had the modern appearance of an American resort: showy glass windows, thick cross beams and high ceilings of natural wood, with a profusion of potted plants hanging above the booths in the bar area. Andy bought their beers and used the change in the public phone; he returned a few minutes later. "Afternoon run's already gone out, but we're set for tomorrow morning."

They settled into a booth and Jordan felt a renewed surge of excitement at the prospect of actually photographing a tiger in the wild. "What about tonight?"

"We'll drive to Saura. My friend's sending one of his kids with the keys to his Land Rover. He's set us up with his brother-in-law who has a campground. We'll stay in one of the tents."

Minutes later a small boy arrived, not more than six years old and all eyes; he handed over a circle of twine holding car keys. Andy gave him a hundred-rupee note and the little boy flew out the door.

"How far's Saura?" When Andy shrugged, Jordan asked the bartender.

"'Bout an hour."

One of the bar patrons turned around. "Where y'all goin'?" His eyes behind a thick pair of wire-framed glasses were the weak, watery blue of the nearsighted, and his most striking feature was a neatly trimmed, carrot-red beard. When he bent to pay his tab, a lengthy ponytail slid over his shoulder onto the bar. "On up to Chitwan?"

The name caught their attention and Andy grinned at him. "'Y'all'? Where you from, son?"

"Mis'sippi."

"Well, Mississippi, are you talking about the national park?"

Jordan watched the man nod confirmation. Something about the situation was making him uncomfortable. He wasn't sure exactly what. Just that it did.

"I'm on my way up there in a coupla days." He gave them full directions before sliding off his bar stool and heading lazily toward the exit. "Right nice place."

Andy smiled into his beer, then peered at Jordan, obviously intrigued. "Isn't that where Charlayne Pearce was going?"

"I think so." He'd made the connection the instant the name of the park had been mentioned, and knew suddenly what it was that made him uneasy: the fact that he wanted mightily to know if she'd arrived.

"You suppose she's there?" His brother echoed his thoughts as he led the way to his friend's Land Rover. "If she is, it sure solves what I'm doing tonight," he said with a confident grin. "I don't know about you."

Jordan shrugged in response, trying to separate Charlayne Pearce from whatever else it was about the turn of events that was giving him the willies.

○   ○   ○

Stiff with fatigue, Charlayne stepped off the public bus, relieved to find a waiting station wagon with a Royal Chitwan National Park emblem on its side; she crossed the road, supremely grateful that she'd made the tenuous connection with no trouble. Making plans via short-wave radio was a new experience, and she was still getting used to the casual way things were accomplished in this country.

Her driver's name was Joseph and he spoke English very well; after nine hours of mimed communication with her fellow passengers, her own language was balm to her ears. Joseph tossed her bags into the back of the vehicle and they were off. Immediately outside the village he turned the car onto little more than parallel dirt tracks between unfenced fields, and identified their route as "the back way"; loose children and attendant farm animals were present in the vicinity of occasional thatch-roofed dwellings, and cattle yoked to primitive wooden-wheeled carts were courteously led aside to allow them to pass.

They drove across a series of creeks bridged with wood planking, and once, they forded a stream deep enough to allow water to seep through the floorboards. Eventually Joseph turned the car onto a small graveled road that led to the gate of the park headquarters.

There she stepped from the vehicle into another world.

Halfway down the camp's wide grassy compound, a tame elephant walked toward her with lumbering majesty; a bundle of half a dozen lush green banana trees was tied to its saddle. The trees were easily ten feet in length from base to crown, their broad leaves sweeping to the ground on either side of the huge animal's girth. A smiling driver stood upright on its back to wave a salute. In the golden light of late afternoon, man and beast were outlined in living amber. Charlayne was too entranced to move.

All the dust and sweat and misery of the past several hours disappeared in that single moment, the discomfort of the bus's punishing wooden seat, feelings of being hopelessly out of step with this timeless country, and, after the first hour or so of scenic excitement at the steeply terraced hillsides, the boredom of bumping along an endless ribbon of dusty road, enduring tedious hairpin turns that sent her back an equal distance toward the direction she'd just come—all gone. All worth it. She returned the driver's wave and the elephant raised its trunk. This was going to be her home for the next three and a half weeks, and Charlayne was thrilled.

Professor Jamieson, a spindly, graying man in his early sixties, opened the door to the compound's office and motioned her inside. "I see we didn't lose you," he offered by way of greeting. "I appreciate your traveling a few days early. I don't think you'll regret it."

"Almost lost me on the bus ride," she admitted breathlessly, "but just now, seeing that elephant . . . Where is it taking the trees?"

"They'll be cut up for fodder. We're allotted five elephants for our use, and since they can't graze and work at the same time, they have to be fed every evening."

Reminded of the reason she'd traveled all this way in the first place, she reverted to being as professional as possible. "Well, it's a pleasure to meet you at last, and I'm very excited to have this opportunity. I'll do my best to stay out of your way," she assured him.

"We can go over the camp schedule tomorrow morning, I think. Do you know how soon your photographer's going to arrive?"

She was tempted to throw her dilemma into the bargain, but decided she'd best wait until she knew him a little better; perhaps a solution would present itself among his staff. "I'm hoping he'll join me in the next couple of days," she improvised.

"We'll reserve the room next to yours. If you'd like to settle in, freshen up a bit, I'll have Sunita show you your accommodations."

"Right now, a bath would a very welcome idea, thank you."

He looked at her blankly. "It's a bit of a rationing situation. River water has to be hauled in, you see. We'll make an exception, of course, for this evening, but in future bear in mind—"

She felt like an idiot. It had all been in the instructions. "A bucket of hot water is just fine," she insisted quickly.

"Fine, we'll manage to heat it for you as well. Ah, here's Sunita. She'll show you to the bunkhouse." He rose to his feet to introduce her to the Nepali girl who'd arrived at the door; she appeared to be somewhere between eight and ten years old. "You have a flashlight, I trust? Otherwise we can provide one."

"In my pack," Charlayne said confidently. She'd brought every item that had been recommended.

"Best locate it. Electricity is also limited. We're on solar power, you see. Sunita will explain." Charlayne shook his hand and followed the young girl to the bunkhouse, an unpainted wood-plank structure built some three feet off the ground, with a small porch entry to three rooms. A quick glance inside confirmed no indoor plumbing.

"Make sure you look carefully." Sunita moved the pale beam along the sparse growth of bushes under the line of trees that marked the camp's perimeter. They'd progressed only a short distance on a stone walk that skirted the bunkhouse, and the little girl was flashing the light up and down in a specific pattern. "Do it from here," she instructed, indicating their position on the walk. The lavatory, a small whitewashed-brick building, stood about thirty feet distant. It was still very much daylight and she could see that there were no signs or other markings posted among the shrubs.

"What am I looking for?"

"Rhino," Sunita replied casually. "At night their eyes will shine in the light. If you see red eyes, it's a rhino and you must go back very quietly. Turn off the light because they can see it moving and might charge."

The outlandish instructions—and their reason—caused the reverberation of a drunken drumbeat in Charlayne's chest, slightly off its rhythm and jarring. "Don't worry," she said nervously. "It'd be too late to use the place after that, anyway." They had to be kidding. "How often do rhinos come 'visiting'?"

"Not often, but it's best to be careful."

"You got it, Tonto."

The girl looked at her, not understanding. "It's really safe, but don't take chances. Just check for red eyes." She demonstrated again.

"Any other potential killers out here I should know about? What if I see green eyes?"

The girl smiled broadly. "Green is tigers . . . "

"Not really!"

"No." Sunita was joking this time. "They don't like people."

"As friends, or for lunch?"

The young girl laughed out loud and waved as she ran back toward the camp office. "Dinner is six," she called over her shoulder.

Charlayne tried not to think about what she'd gotten herself into. Theory was just dandy, but wild animals were suddenly ruling the roost as a very real and dangerous presence. She took a firmer grip on the flashlight and hurried around the bunkhouse to her room, glancing back twice to make sure she wasn't being followed by a rampant rhino.

Her bed was little more than a raw wood frame with a thin cotton mattress, and surrounded by a length of mosquito netting attached to a nail in the ceiling. Open shelving had been provided for her clothing. Sunita had warned her to keep any food sealed in plastic, preferably suspended on twine from the ceiling, to discourage unruly field mice. No hangers, two thin blankets, no electric lights. Solar power was rationed as well, apparently.

She unpacked her sleeping pillow and a few other essentials; ten minutes passed before a slight knock on the wooden door alerted her to Sunita's arrival with the promised water. The small metal bucket was warmer than its content. She undressed to take a quick marine bath and readjusted her thinking as to what constituted proper hygiene.

"When all else fails, keep to basics," she muttered for her own benefit. The human race had managed to evolve rather efficiently from the ice age without warm, daily soap-and-water ablutions, and she would simply adapt to a similar situation. Still, the tepid water was heaven against her skin; sighing with pleasure, she cleansed road grime from her face and throat, trickling water over her shoulders and breasts to enjoy the cool sensation of evaporation. The sexy Kosterin brothers should see her grubby little self now, she thought, and giggled at the idea.

A second tap on the door interrupted her thoughts.

"Who is it?"

"Charlayne?"

She was shocked and mystified. It sounded like Andy

Kosterin, but couldn't be. Unless he'd found a photographer. Flown him up here? Entirely too much to wish for. It had to be someone else. Before she could answer, there was another rap, this one cautious.

"Charlayne? Do we have the right room? I thought the little girl said—"

We? "Just a minute." Flummoxed, she threw a shirt over her damp skin and stepped barefoot into a pair of shorts before pushing the door open wide enough to see who was speaking. It *was* Andy Kosterin, and Jordan was standing in the grass a few paces away, looking up at her, a camera slung over his shoulder. She could feel amazement freezing her face into an open-mouthed gape, while Andy broke into a grin.

"We were in the neighborhood," he said with a jovial air.

She was too astonished to respond. Jordan approached the bunkhouse and nodded up at her, his dark gaze quietly appraising. She was suddenly aware of her limp clothing and suspected he could tell she had nothing on underneath.

"We flew into Tiger Tops this afternoon," Jordan explained, his fixed look held carefully at eye level. His expression suggested a longstanding tolerance toward his brother's humor.

"Not true. We flew up here to take you to dinner," Andy contradicted, laughing at her confounded demeanor. "The man has no romance in his soul whatever," he stage-whispered, "but it didn't seem right to leave him behind."

As Andy spoke, she saw Jordan drift away to evaluate the compound. A few yards from the porch, he stood with his back to them, shielding his eyes from the lowered sun to follow the flight of a pair of birds. Charlayne self-consciously crossed her arms in front of her chest and addressed herself to Andrew. "I've been here exactly half an hour," she marveled. "I mean, my fanny doesn't even know it's not on a bus." She blushed at her choice of exaggerations. "How . . . what are you two. . . ?" For a wild moment she allowed the possibility that he was indeed delivering Jordan as her photographer.

"Really. We came to take you to dinner," Andy repeated cheerfully, then dashed her hopes. "I called your hotel this morning but you'd already left. I didn't have any luck with a photographer. Sorry."

"Hey," she dissembled through a blur of disappointment. "Thanks for trying. I couldn't find anyone either. Someone from the newspaper was interested, but at the last minute they wouldn't let him leave his job for more than two days. Travel eats that up." Her glance strayed briefly to Jordan's outline in the afternoon sunlight, then, deciding it was pointless to give him any more thought, she wrapped her arms around the nearest post and concentrated on Andy. He'd been sweet as Christmas to come all this way to tell her, so she trotted out all the enthusiasm she could manage. "My publisher says to keep looking, but I think I'll just muddle through and hope for the best."

Jordan sauntered up during the last of her statement. "Is something wrong?"

"Her photographer didn't show."

Smoky blue eyes hit her full in the face. "What about your book?"

Jordan's response confused her. Surely he and Andy had discussed her call for help at some point, but his demeanor was guileless and his concern seemed genuine. A sliver of hope resurrected itself. Now that he'd seen the place, maybe this was his way of signaling Andy that he was willing to reconsider.

"My editor's attempting to locate someone," she said

quickly, "but it doesn't look promising." There was a lull and she knew there was no chance. The man was on vacation; if he'd been willing or available to help her out, Andy would have said so. Giving it up as a lost cause, she sought a new subject. "I hear Tiger Tops is wonderful. Have you been on a game run?"

Jordan's gaze had shifted again to hover in the middle distance between them. "We have one tomorrow morning."

"Seriously, we want to know if you're free for dinner." Andy took her by the arm. "There must be somewhere to eat in this hamlet. It's only an hour to Tiger Tops. We'll even buy you a beer."

"No liquids, thank you." Her flip response brought curious looks from both men. "I'm trying to avoid run-ins after dark," she explained, and launched into a blithe interpretation of Sunita's instructions about flashlights, red eyes, and rhinos. "I'm to sprint in the dark, hope I don't kill myself when I hit the bunkhouse—or die of fright—whichever comes first. Given the conditions that would force me outside in the first place, I don't think running is going to be an option," she finished delicately.

For the first time since they'd met, Jordan Kosterin smiled all the way to his blue-steel eyes. For a brief moment his good looks were transformed from passive to devastating, before he grew serious again. "You have very pale skin...." His glance dropped to her throat for an instant before he continued. "Make sure you wear dark clothing, and cover most of the beam with your hand. Use just enough to see the ground."

She nodded, fascinated with his voice and his thought process, and the change she'd just glimpsed. His eyes held hers intensely, and she felt the power of his concentration. A problem solver. Caretaker. Her conviction about him protecting her in Jaipur hadn't been wrong. Probably came with being a lawyer.

"Wouldn't hurt to carry something that'll make noise if it hits the ground. A tin can ought to do."

Of course, and how smart of him. The simplicity of his solution made her grin with appreciation. "The cow and the cookies."

She was rewarded with a tilt of his head and an appreciative smile that lingered, even white teeth dazzling against a faint four o'clock shadow. "Precisely. Throw like hell and run like hell," he emphasized, blue eyes reading her face; the tug of his full attention was disturbing, nearly physical. "Whatever you do, make sure you kill the light. Throw it, too, if you have to."

Andy, who'd been vigilantly following their conversation, was incorrigible. "Well, now that that's settled, we can go get something to eat."

His voice brought her back to the moment, and she flashed them a smile filled with genuine regret. "My host is expecting me for dinner, I think. I haven't even been around the compound yet." An alternative occurred to her. "How about a tour instead, if I can get one?"

She saw keen interest cross Jordan's face before he looked away in silence. When Andy, who'd been watching his brother closely, openly expressed his enthusiasm, she quickly excused herself. Inside her room, she was careful to get properly dressed, changed into a fresh shirt, and dug madly in her purse for a lipstick. Just in case.

10

Too difficult to manage . . .

A few minutes later Charlayne introduced the Kosterins to the professor. "We met in India," she explained. "They're staying at Anup's Campgrounds."

"Best in the village next to us," Jamieson acknowledged expansively. "Let me show you around, and then I do hope you'll join us for dinner."

Andy's acceptance was immediate, and Charlayne stole a quick glance at Jordan. The somber, detached look, she noticed, had not returned and he seemed more open. He was attentive to every aspect as their host described the park facilities.

"Do you mind if I take photographs?" he asked courteously. "Or is there a policy?"

"Not at all. Blaze away," invited the professor.

"Portrait of a rhino, maybe?" Andy's devilish grin was irresistible, and he winked at her. "Get many in camp?"

"Not too often. They avoid the elephants." The professor led them across the compound toward a second bunkhouse and an equipment shed. "Our staff is housed here. Each animal has its own drivers, a saddler and feeder, all of which report to Joh. He decides when the elephants work and oversees their training for us."

The three elephants in camp were leg-chained to monstrous stumps, and each was systematically stepping on and crushing cord lengths of banana trees. Probing trunks, facile as hands, selected the soft centers and placed them delicately into their mouths; utterly content, the animals chewed with relish. "They have to be tethered?" she asked curiously.

"They act as lookouts. Otherwise they'd go foraging. We feed them instead." In the dying light, a fourth elephant came up a small rise and entered the compound with Joseph standing on its back. "That's Mala, our newest addition. She's been out for a bath and is ready for dinner. We only use females. Males are too difficult to manage."

"I know the feeling," Charlayne cracked, and laughed as Andrew, with an air of great innocence, looked around for a culprit.

Beside her, Jordan's camera whirred and clicked, catching photos of Mala as the animal crumpled to her knees, lowered her hindquarters to the ground, then settled her belly onto the dirt. Joseph sat on her back, slid to a foreleg, then hopped to the ground.

"That's your method of disembarking," the professor advised. "Getting on is the other way 'round. You'll get the hang of it soon enough."

When Joseph signaled Mala with a hand against her

body, the young elephant lurched ponderously to her feet. She raised her trunk and snorted, eyes alert behind long, elegant lashes as Joseph led her away.

In the near distance came a shrill "Kee-*yahh!* Kee-*yaahh!*" Charlayne stopped to listen. The screeching sounded again. "If I didn't know better, I'd swear that was—"

"Peacock," identified Jordan, his blue eyes seeking hers for confirmation, and she knew he was right. How would a lawyer know about peacocks? "My grandmother keeps a pair in San Jose." He smiled another devastating smile at her.

"They're wild here," the professor acknowledged. He consulted his watch and then led them toward the meeting room. Sandwiched between the professor and Andy Kosterin, with Jordan on the outside, Charlayne wondered why fate would dally with her at this point in her life by introducing two splendid men, then ruin matters by not allowing her to have the one she wanted. Remembering belatedly that she was embarked on a colorful adventure for the first time in her life and—thanks in part to the attractive brothers at her side—had survived her first Christmas in several years outside the bosom of her family, she dismissed her thoughts as ungrateful, fingered the comforting presence of her flashlight and fervently hoped they weren't having soup for dinner.

There was no question in Jordan's mind that his brother was smitten. Throughout the meal Andy was highly attentive, almost overboard in a determined attempt to hold Charlayne's interest. Quietly assessing conflicted feelings of his own where she was concerned, he sat at the table lit with flickering candles, ostensibly listening to American idiom as it blended with softer Nepali accents; in reality, he watched Charlayne.

Seated to his right and next to his brother, she was deftly deflecting Andy's flirtatious comments one moment and engaging in knowledgeable ecological discussion with the professor the next. Never ruffled, confident in her opinions, she resorted to gentle wit on those occasions when Andy's demeanor made her blush. He knew why his brother was attracted to her. Who wouldn't be? When she'd stepped onto the bunkhouse porch with long legs dripping from a pair of shorts, wearing that damp shirt, he'd had all he could do to ignore the sight of her nipples budding through the fabric. Cream and rust and smoke-rose.

He'd had to turn away to keep from staring. Hell, he'd have been dead from the neck up if he hadn't noticed; from his neck down, however, there'd been no repeat of anything remotely similar to his reaction that night in the car. Just an ordinary appreciation of her physical attributes, no different than any man. As he watched her face in the candlelight, he searched his emotions very carefully to be sure. He found a vague annoyance at Andy's behavior—she was, after all, in Chitwan to work, not to field suitors—but there was no hint of the madness that had occurred in Jaipur.

His feelings confirmed, he observed her more carefully.

Her thick hair had been smoothed into a topknot, but strands had feathered loose about her ears and at the nape of her neck. Firelight from the room's central hearth surrounded her features, brightening her profile with a warm carnelian halo, almost but not quite the magic color of the sunlit Taj. He drifted with the conversation, aware of his growing preoccupation with her.

"Marthae says I refuse to grow up," the professor was

saying, "and she's right. I've been known to fish with a bow and arrow."

To Jordan's surprise, for the first time that evening Andy showed enthusiasm about something other than Charlayne Pearce. "Mind if I have a look at what you're using? I've wanted to try that for years."

"I've a dandy bow, carved right here in Saura," Jamieson bragged. "Anyone else?" he invited.

Both women's faces wrinkled with distaste for the subject. His disinterest in fishing born of aversion to water in general, Jordan declined as well. Mrs. Jamieson and the remaining staff unexpectedly excused themselves, and, too late to join his brother without being openly rude, he found himself alone with Charlayne.

Her hair continued to burn in the fire's glow with richly auburn highlights. A single button of her shirt was undone at the throat; the chaste opening above the rise of her breasts was enough to remind him of his secret glimpse of her and the vivid memory of the soft flesh giving shape to the fabric. Smooth ivory cleft. Rust and rose. The rolled sleeve of her shirt came to just above her elbow, exposing more pale skin; a blue vein was visible at the bend.

She was remote as she moved to a chair near the fire, half the room away. "Andrew seems very intense. Is he always this . . . "

"Persistent?" She regarded him carefully until he continued. "Only when he finds someone as attractive as you are." It was more than being attractive. She was interesting and intriguing and adventurous. Everything Andy would find irresistible.

She blinked rapidly, but let the comment pass. "I'm surprised your brother isn't married." When he didn't volunteer a response, she changed the subject. "When is he going back to the States?"

Aware that she might not consider a man stationed in India an ideal romantic candidate, he did his best to be loyal and honest at the same time. "He says another four years. I think it'll be sooner." He moved to a chair a few feet away from her.

"What about you?" She wasn't looking at him, and he couldn't tell from her tone whether she was genuinely curious or merely being polite.

"I haven't decided, actually." He kept further explanation at bay by letting the conversation die. Light continued to play across her face as she absently bit her bottom lip. The taste of her mouth passed through his memory: moist with the feminine flavor exclusive to women. It seemed like forever since he'd had an appetite for that particular taste. The ripe coral lipstick she favored had worn away from the fullness of her lips, but a perfect outline remained. She was chewing it away as he watched.

Long fingers, strong, with sensibly blunt nails, held the half-full glass of tea she hadn't finished at dinner, and she was watching the hearth fire through the amber liquid. The brown of her eyes had taken on golden centers, and her face became more solemn.

"Tomorrow night's New Year's. I feel a long way from home."

The sudden melancholy in her voice triggered his emotion. He didn't want a reminder of New Year's. Needing activity to counter his growing fixation, he got up and walked to a window. The first woman he'd noticed since . . . forever, and his brother had already staked a claim, had already kissed her, maybe taken her to bed. "It's pretty dark," he said abruptly.

He heard her rise, cross the room to blow out the table candles before joining him to look at the night. "You're right. I should be turning in."

He expected relief at her statement. Received none. The moment stretched on; a burnt-wax smell of candlewicks hung dry and acrid in the room, then disappeared. Uncomfortable, he reached for humor. "Bring your flashlight?"

A small smile crept onto her lips, crinkling her eyes at the corners. "Yes, but I forgot my tin can. Got any advice for mosquitoes?"

"Outrun 'em," he sallied in return. She was still perfumed with sandalwood, and he followed the elusive scent out the door and into black velvet.

It took a moment to adjust to the night. Swift-moving clouds hid a slender moon; still, a quarter-million stars were visible in the sky window above the camp. A vague rustle of fabric told him she was unrolling her shirtsleeves to cover her arms. He smiled into the darkness, having no idea why he felt better.

Andy and the professor rounded the building to join them.

"Well, I have a few remaining things to attend to this evening, gentlemen, Charlayne, so I'll say good night." Jamieson shook hands all around and disappeared into the black, his flashlight illuminating his feet as he walked toward his office.

Jordan was surprised when Andy's best efforts weren't sufficient to persuade Charlayne to join them for a nightcap, and she kissed his brother on the cheek as she bade him good night. A different kiss, Jordan wondered, than he might have received had they been alone? The flirtatious behavior she'd engaged in with his brother in India was gone, but this was her work environment, and her professional demeanor made sense. She was firm in her refusal to join them, citing a long travel day and a need to get settled in.

He was self-conscious when she lightly pressed her mouth against the stubble of his jaw as well, and his awareness of her hung like a millstone around his shoulders. The weight of his interest did not lessen as he and his brother drove through the park gates and toward their campgrounds. Nor did Andy's uncharacteristic silence.

At Anup's, they unrolled rented sleeping bags inside their tent and turned in for the evening. It was highly unlikely he'd see her again, he told himself, and in view of Andy's situation with her, getting out was definitely the answer. They'd spend tomorrow at Tiger Tops, and he'd head for the States as soon as he got to Narmada. But she wouldn't leave his mind. He tried for a while to shut out her sadness, did his best to concentrate on the wilderness noises that heralded a Nepali night, but her pensive voice stayed with him, provoking his own self-awareness.

New Year's. The annual date for personal accounting. He was also a long way from home and introspective. Why had he forgotten that the year's end was always harder to survive than the actual anniversary of Natalie's death? The specter of life without her stretched before him as never before. And once again he discovered that until this moment his wife had been out of his thoughts for several hours.

Because of this woman? Or was he, too, simply far from home? Or had her interest in Andy given him rein to indulge in a nice, safe, foreign affair of the mind?

His brother's too-casual voice came from the other side of the tent to shatter his contemplation. "So, did she say anything about me while I was gone?"

Jordan shifted in his sleeping bag, trying to locate an accommodating spot on the hard ground. "She wanted to know why you weren't married."

"What'd you say?"

"I told her you had six wives and seventeen kids."

"You're a pal. She say anything else?"

"About you? No."

There was a significant pause. "What else *not* about me?"

"She said she was lonely." A confidence betrayed. He was uncomfortable talking about her, and it annoyed him. Andy's flashlight snapped on, and Jordan raised himself on one elbow to blink past the harsh light; his brother was staring at him again. It seemed to be all he'd been doing lately. That and chasing Charlayne Pearce. It occurred to him suddenly that the three of them being at Chitwan tonight might not be coincidence after all. That his brother could very well have used their visit to Tiger Tops as an excuse to see her again. "Now what?" he said bluntly, in no mood for conversation.

Andy's distorted face spoke at him above the light. "I want you to help her out."

Had he missed something while he'd been daydreaming at dinner? "Does she need a lawyer?"

"She needs a photographer, pee-squat. You want some time to think, I want to know more about her. Gee . . . what does that suggest?"

"No way." He emphatically shook his head. "Uh-uh. Not a chance."

Andy barreled past his resistance. "Shut up and listen, gonad. You're bored out of your skull and you don't want to go home, so why don't you help her out? You're here, you got all your stuff in the Land Rover—"

"Out of the question. First of all, it's not what I do."

Andy lurched to a sitting position. "You been taking pictures since you got here. Suddenly you don't know how?"

As he warmed to his theme, Jordan quickly saw where his brother was headed.

"If you won't do it for you, do it for me," he urged. "Find out about her. Check her out. She's beautiful, she's too good to be true . . . find the flaws. Help me out here," he warned with a macabre grin. "If she's too lonely, I could wind up getting engaged again."

Jordan didn't see the humor. "Find your own flaws!" He rolled over, refusing to listen. "Besides, I'm an amateur. She needs a professional." The excuse was lame and he knew it. He was a damned good amateur.

"Right now she needs anyone she can get. Besides, it's not like you haven't been published."

"One photo. One magazine. In the real world, I'm a decent beginner, that's all."

"Versus what? Hanging around with me? Taking another thousand pictures of 'Construction of the Narmada Dam'?" Andy was on his usual roll. "It's a couple of weeks out of your life, for crying out loud. You stay here and I'm guaranteed another crack at her."

"It's ridiculous. No way." The whole idea was a few bricks short of a load, but Andy was relentless.

"I've never asked you for a favor in my life, and I wouldn't now except I can't take any more time off. I'm begging you to do this for me. I am pleading, Jord. I'm serious."

Jordan blew out his breath. He had to admit it wasn't likely that he'd get this close to the Himalayas again in the next couple of decades. It *would* be fascinating to see a game park from an insider's point of view; wild animals had always been high on his interest list.

Was Charlayne Pearce on his interest list, too? As a serious matter and not some sort of aberration?

His *and* Andy's?

He refused to give the possibility merit. Yes, now that he'd spent some time around her, there was something nice about Charlayne Pearce, something unusual, but if Andy hadn't been attracted to her, hadn't reined her in at the Taj Mahal, she'd have been just another tourist as far as he was concerned. They'd never have met. Plus, she'd showed no notice of him whatever. A one-sided interest in some woman thousands of miles from home didn't give him license to meddle in his brother's personal life. "No," he repeated.

"You don't have to fall in love with her," Andy pushed at him. "I'm working on that part, just help me out a little. If you hate it after a week, rent a guide and go trekking. Get the scoop on the meaning of life direct from the source, I don't care." Andy was practically on his knees. "Hey! I've never asked a damned thing from you," he repeated strongly. "And you know it. But I really want this."

"Jesus, Andrew!" Jordan heard himself cave in. "OK, I'll think about it."

"Yes!" Andy grabbed his victory, switched off the flashlight, and began jerking his sleeping bag into place. "We'll skip the game run tomorrow. We can go when I come back."

Jordan knew he should call a halt to the whole situation. All it would take was a firm, final refusal; Andy might moan and groan for a while, but he'd accept it when he had no other choice.

"Helping a lady in distress *and* helping out a brother." Andy's voice crowed excitedly in the darkness. "Whatta guy! I'm gonna owe you for this one. OK, now, the main thing I want to know is what happened with the infamous *Doctor* Pearce, why she's single, and anything else you can find out about her. If she's as genuine as I think she is, talk me up. Take care of me."

Jordan stared into ink. "When's the last time you needed an advance man?"

"Since I'm thirty-five," Andy responded happily, "and if I don't find someone soon, I'm going to be a crabby asshole like you and too old to raise kids."

The mention of children chilled any extension of their fractured camaraderie; Natalie's pregnancy had led to the doctor's discovery of cancer. Andy was still pumped up with excitement over the girl, and Jordan scrambled to amend his commitment. "OK. But only till the end of the week—and no promises on the spying."

The flashlight came back on and Andy began to struggle out of his sleeping bag. "Hell with tomorrow. You'll flake out on me."

"What are you doing?"

"Getting dressed. I'm taking care of this right now."

"You sleep here tonight or all deals are off."

Jordan grabbed the flashlight and shoved it under his sleeping bag. He settled into the darkness trying to counter his nerves with the knowledge that the principal player in this scenario hadn't agreed to it as yet, and whether she agreed or not, he could always change his mind.

11

Any lawyer worth his salt . . .

He'd given his word, but he knew it was wrong, all wrong; from Anup's camp to the park, he knew it. He'd known it the whole damned sleepless night. He'd known it while he was drinking witches' brew coffee this morning, boiled over a wood fire and gritty with local sugar, while Andy whistled and grinned like a kid with a stash of cookies; and he knew it standing on the bunkhouse porch outside her room. Whether or not she and his brother were destined to be a pair, for the life of him he couldn't find a viable reason not to take pictures for Charlayne Pearce over the next few days.

Andrew's infatuation was all too evident; he'd been eager to see her again this morning and cheerful as hell during the short drive to the park. Instinctively, Jordan was certain that even a hint that he'd noticed her as well would go down hard, and wasn't worth the possibility of a rift with his brother; not at this stage of their lives when he was promoting a renewed relationship between them, not sibling competition. The only solution was to have her turn him down. Any lawyer worth his salt could manage that, surely. He rapped again on her door.

"Hi! Are you looking for me?"

He wheeled to find her striding toward them in walking shorts and a long-sleeve sweatshirt; canvas shoes and thick white socks had replaced her sandals. He felt a lift at the sight of her, even as his brother's elbow battered his ribs. "Actually, yes. Andy suggested that you could use—"

His brother's voice overrode his words. "He's volunteering to be your photographer this week if you're interested."

Annoyed at himself for not anticipating Andy's glib interference, Jordan realized that it was too late to sidestep offering to help; he shifted his thinking to how best to extract himself from the situation. They met her at the foot of the bunkhouse steps.

"Interested?" she echoed vaguely.

She was clearly cautious, and Jordan saw her eyes question Andrew. His sixth sense told him that something was going on between them, which confirmed his decision to set up an exit. "Well, maybe it's not such a good idea, I'm not that experien—"

"He's been published." Andy's voice was sheepishly insistent, and he grinned at her. "My own brother, and I never even thought of him."

"Well, I'd certainly be grateful," she said, and it was obvious to Jordan that she was still being careful in spite of her words to the contrary. "But I feel I should warn you that field conditions will be pretty grubby. Sleeping in tents on occasion. Mud galore," she concluded.

Already irritated with his brother, he was doubly offended at the obvious parachute. What did she think, that he was too prissy to get his hands dirty? "I think I can stand it for a few days," he said stiffly, neatly catching himself in a trap of his own making. Some lawyer.

"I just meant that you seem to have pretty expensive equipment," she went on carefully. "Are you sure?"

Irked at not only muffing a potential escape, but misreading her hesitation as well, he softened his stance, paid more attention. She'd said something about working nights. "I didn't bring a very good strobe. Probably couldn't get anything after dark without additional lighting," he warned quickly. "Nothing underwater, either. I think I could pretty much handle the standard day-to-day kind of thing." That ought to be vague enough.

She pursed her lips, considering his words. "Can I afford you?"

A fee hadn't occurred to him. He was still out to lunch and about to get nailed. If he'd been in court, any decent judge would have tossed him out the door as being unprepared.

Andy jumped in, interfering again. "How about whatever you were going to pay the other guy?"

Still annoyed, Jordan shot him down with a look. Feeling the net of commitment closing in around him, he thought rapidly. Charging a fee would make her his boss, a situation he definitely didn't want to live with. "I'll do the shoot for nothing and keep ownership of the negatives. Name credit on anything you use, OK?"

"Done."

She grasped his hand in a firm shake and her face broke into a radiant expression; brown eyes sparkled at him happily, and he became aware that the lady writer was a pretty canny negotiator in her own right. Oddly enough, he was no longer upset at being outmaneuvered.

"Welcome aboard. And thank you," she said enthusiastically. "You're pulling me out of a very deep hole."

His brother unlocked their handshake by possessively pulling her hands into his own. "Promise not to forget who delivered your photographer."

"I won't, I promise." She kissed Andy's cheek exuberantly then pumped Jordan's hand one more time. "I'll let everyone know you're staying on. This is super!"

Andy thumped him roughly on the shoulder. "Well, I'll leave her in your capable hands, big brother. If I'm going to refuel and fly to Narmada today, I'm going to have to toddle. You two get your pictures taken and I'll be back this weekend. Where do you want his gear?"

She pointed past him to the room next to hers, and Jordan's pulse picked up a beat. Five minutes hadn't passed, and now he'd be sleeping ten feet away from her at night. Another matter that hadn't dawned on him. Christ, what else wasn't he thinking of? It was his last chance to cut and run. But one look at both grinning faces and he couldn't do it.

While she notified the professor, he and Andy made a quick trip to Anup's to rent camping equipment. Andy thanked him all the way.

"When she was gone the next morning, I didn't think we'd see her again, but I probably got too pushy at the hotel," he admitted warily, "so don't start out asking her about that night." Excited, he pounded his palm against the dashboard. "I won't forget this, Jordy, and you can count on it. Now listen to your blue collar brother. You only got a few days, so skip all the lawyer crap and don't waste a bunch of time being polite."

"Yeah, yeah, I got it," Jordan answered touchily, absorbed in Andy's reference to their night together at the hotel. He'd forgotten about that. And the lipstick on Andy's face the next morning. Maybe there'd been an incident that had caused her to be resistant at first. Maybe she hadn't counted on running into Andy again. He knew in his bones that there was something between them, the same way he knew when clients were lying and juries would come in with "Guilty." He hadn't sensed discomfort from her regarding his brother, but she hadn't seemed overly encouraging either.

Unfortunately, Andy was playing it unusually close to the vest about his relationship with her. Among men, lack of discussion and detail where a woman was concerned was an understood indication of respect. Only a major asshole talked openly about his conquests or mentioned private moments with someone he had feelings for, all of which signaled that his brother had a genuine, serious interest in Charlayne Pearce. Whatever the situation, he'd given his word that he'd stay the rest of the week, and he was now committed to keeping it.

It took a few minutes to transfer luggage, camping gear, and camera equipment into the bunkhouse, then they said a hurried goodbye at the entrance gate; Andy was anxious to get in the air. "Remember, everything you can find out about her," he called over his shoulder, then barreled the borrowed car toward Tiger Tops.

Jordan shrugged, resigned to compliance. He watched his brother disappear down the gravel road, a powdery trail of dust billowing in his wake, then returned to the bunkhouse to survey the small room that was his temporary home. His pledge was fresh in his mind as he sat on the bunk, surprised at himself and his situation. New Year's Eve, and here he was in a wooden room, in Nepal, working for a woman he'd seen three times in his life, and committed to photographing animals he hadn't known existed until a few days ago. All because his brother was fascinated with the lady who'd be sleeping next door.

And, to be honest, because he was drawn to her as well, to her energy and commitment and willingness to gamble on a stranger. And nothing else, right? Wrong. He was too smart a lawyer to sell himself that one. The fact was, Charlayne Pearce was the first woman he'd been able to see since Natalie died. And another fact occurred to him. Neither she nor his brother had outmaneuvered him. Consciously, or subconsciously, he'd managed that all by himself.

He stood, aware of an alien sound. The second time it was louder and bounced eerily from the wooden walls. Astonishingly enough, for the first time in years he'd laughed out loud.

Charlayne practically skipped toward Jamieson's office in her glee—relieved, excited, and plain old-fashioned happy at having her problem solved. As soon as she got her feet down she'd find out why gorgeous Jordan Kosterin had decided to come to her rescue, but for the moment she didn't care. The book was saved. She had a photographer, and he was here and ready to start working this morning.

He was also married and leaving this weekend, but that was unquestionably a good thing since he was entirely too good-looking and she had the potential of getting much too turned on. Getting involved with a married man would lower her to the same level as Sondra, and that thought was not only ugly but chilling. She resolved to put any attraction for him absolutely out of her head. From now on and until he left, she'd concentrate solely on getting as much coverage for her book as possible. To try, anyway.

Twenty minutes later she collected him from the bunkhouse, and they spent the balance of the morning going over the camp's schedule with the professor. Fishing cats had been captured several weeks ago and fitted with radio collars; they were being monitored each night to map the extent of their hunting range. She and Jordan would have their first go at tracking one later this evening.

"We check on the sloth bears in the afternoons," Jamieson stated. "We've collared a mother and cub. A slightly different area from the cats, so you'll have a daylight look at the park before you do night duty. Be ready at three o'clock, if you will." He looked at Charlayne. "Brush is quite high this time of year. No trails past the river, so longer pants might be advisable."

At the appointed time, duly changed into jeans and hiking boots, Charlayne emerged from her room to find Jordan waiting on the porch with the straps of two cameras slung over his shoulder. Cartons of film in the loops of his safari vest gave him the appearance of a proper photographer, and in spite of her pledge, his extraordinary looks sent a shudder through her stomach.

"Do you want a cover shot?" He stepped back to frame her with one of the cameras, and his wedding ring reflected glints of sunlight, reminding her once more that he was entirely out of bounds.

"A glamour shot, you mean?" Full of high spirits and unable to contain her energy, she chose to abandon professional behavior and struck a ridiculous pose; his being married didn't mean she wasn't allowed to enjoy herself in his presence. So long as she was careful not to be interpreted as flirting. The shutter clicked and captured her face.

"Now a real one," he directed seriously. "As official photographer, I want at least one picture of you I can put my name to."

She complied and gave him a genuine smile. He took three in a row before he was satisfied.

At the elephant shed, they found their driver talking with Professor Jamieson, who introduced the young man as Jimi. Mala was waiting with a stirrupless saddle fitted across the ridge of her backbone. The wooden frame, approximately three feet square, rested on a thick burlap-covered body pad stuffed with coarse grass, and a similar pad on top provided cushioning for her passengers.

"We don't use the tourist howdahs," the professor explained. "Facing one direction is useless for our purposes. Makes for wider seating, to be sure, but much more sensible."

At the driver's signal, Mala settled ponderously to the ground, and Jimi, who might have weighed eighty pounds if he were soaking wet, scrambled up her trunk and across her forehead to seat himself behind her skull on a folded length of burlap. He wedged his bare feet under the lead rope around the elephant's neck. "You first," he indicated.

Charlayne thanked her stars she wasn't expected to walk up its face as well, but felt clumsy following what seemed to be simple directions. She stepped onto Mala's foreleg and grabbed onto the saddle to haul herself up. Climbing onto a living elephant, she discovered, was akin to scaling a lumpy, hairy, lavishly padded rock, the top inches of which shifted unpredictably under her feet. With the help of an embarrassingly firm fanny-push from Jordan, she managed to reach the elephant's back.

Working her way forward on the thin cushion punished

her knees, but she triumphantly slipped her feet onto either side of Mala's shoulders and settled securely onto the front half of the saddle. Looking down at Jordan, it seemed at least twenty feet to the ground.

"Him next." Jimi's eyes were amused. "The equipment will be tied onto the back."

Jordan, being taller and stronger, was able to pull himself up with ease. Charlayne realized that once the tracking device was on board, they'd be out of room on the saddle, and that, of necessity, Jordan would be riding very close behind her. Mala began to heave herself from the ground: a giant seesaw motion of front first which brought them firmly back-to-belly, then thigh-to-thigh, as the elephant lunged forward to make room for hind legs and an abrupt leveling out. It was now thirty feet to the ground.

Undeniably thrilled, Charlayne allowed herself to twist around and whisper, "We get to do this every day." Jordan's amused chuckle sounded through his chest wall as he leaned forward to wrestle with the tracking equipment that the professor was handing up, then secured it onto the saddle behind him.

"It's set at the frequency to locate the bears," Jamieson explained. "See you at dinner."

They were off.

With the swing and sway, dip and glide, of a small rowboat in a large lake, Mala picked her way down an inclined path into the surrounding forest. Crowns of tall trees blocked out the sun, and a thousand hues of shaded green became their frame of reference. Birds in brilliant feathers fluttered above and ahead of them among leaves and underbrush, scolding their progress with warning calls and generally alerting the neighborhood to the alien presence of humans.

Bold *kee-yahhhhs* of peacocks fell silent at their

approach, and strutting, jewel-eye feather displays collapsed; hens flew into trees and males scuttled off the path. Charlayne watched impossible lengths of tail feathers disappear into thickets that wouldn't accommodate a cat. Jimi's feet under Mala's ears sent guidance signals as he pushed aside low branches with a short wooden staff, and the young elephant carried them deeper into the park.

They emerged suddenly from the tangle of trees into a belt of low scrub that bordered a broad, murky stream. Charlayne felt Jordan's thighs stiffen against her.

"I take it that's the river." A thin edge had come into his voice. "How deep is it?"

"Two feet, maybe, where we cross," Jimi replied.

Jordan said nothing further, and Mala proceeded along the bank to an area of shallow riffles. They splashed across, ignored by colorful wads of wild duck families, then frantically grabbed hold of the saddle as Mala lurched up the opposite bank. The trail soon dried to dust, then disappeared. Jimi pointed his stick at the sea of scrub mixed with tufts of gray-green elephant grass stretching before them; the faded grass reached well above Mala's chest.

"Rhino," he said quietly.

Mala advanced unconcernedly as Charlayne and Jordan both scanned the sweep of grass. After a moment a bulky shape the color of old tar shifted in the brush and an adult rhinoceros became visible; its ponderous head swung nearsightedly in their direction, coned ears pitched alertly forward. Behind her, Charlayne heard Jordan's sotto oath as he muttered in her ear. "There's another one! Two o'clock!"

From the elephant's swaying back she had trouble at first spotting the second animal, but she aligned herself with Jordan's body, identified straight ahead as noon, and moved her focus slightly on an imaginary clock to two. He was right. "Are they close enough for pictures?"

"We will be nearer than this," Jimi advised. "Wait."

Again, Jordan's voice, tight with excitement. "All *right*."

Safely aboard an elephant and wedged firmly against her handsome photographer's vest, all *right*, indeed.

He'd relaxed the moment he'd boosted her on board the elephant. There'd been no reaction to touching her, no unusual response to the feel of her hips under his palms. He'd swung up behind her on the saddle and moved forward until she was snug between his legs, and still no improper repercussions; nothing more than a sense of surprise that he was at ease with her body. Her shoulders rubbing against his chest in time with the animal's motion had induced nothing more than his enjoyment of the scent of sandalwood that he'd come to associate with her proximity. He was relieved, and a little hollow at the same time, that his feelings about her had been false.

Crossing the river, unfortunately, had awakened deeper, more ancient fears, chilling all other sensations, and he'd been busy fighting them down until they'd sighted the rhinos. More thrilled at that moment than he could remember, emotional restraints had disappeared and he'd felt himself fully engage in the excitement of riding a working elephant in Nepal!

Zoos would never be the same, he realized; it was not in civilization's power to house such animals without destroying the image of raw competent might staring at him from the matted growth. Riding the elephant was a bizarre experience as well, but had lulled him into the belief that it was merely another means of transportation. In actuality, the animal beneath them was every bit as capable as those in the bush of pulverizing the three of them. What wonderful knowledge to have, what a rich perspective to regain. He felt the tingle of a long dormant process. Discovery.

Her back taut against his belly, he felt Charlayne's hips in gentle motion between his thighs as she sat high to peer this way and that around Jimi's body, trying to see everything at once, and her enthusiasm jacked up his enjoyment. The rhinos' slate hides had the peculiar appearance of medieval armor-plating. As Mala brought them closer, he was able to take wonderful close-ups until the pugnacious beasts lost patience with the crowding presence of the elephant and thrust their way into the dense growth, to disappear.

"Designer rhinos," Charlayne quipped, making rapid notes on her pad, and Jordan laughed out loud at her unscholarly but entirely apt description.

Shaking his head at indecipherable American humor, Jimi set Mala on a new course and they struck off across the boggy flatland with their oversize mount maneuvering around tangled brush and pulling high grass aside with her trunk. As they worked their way deeper into the vegetation, Jordan helped Charlayne keep her balance, both of them using their feet to push aside thorny shrubs that found no purchase on Mala's hide but were capable of puncturing denim, and human legs.

They continued to encounter rhinoceros in singles and threes and pairs, all intolerant at being observed, and Jordan began to give serious appreciation to being seven feet above the ground. Deer scattered and vanished well ahead of them, but at the edge of a pond, he was able to photograph a wild pig family whose members burst into high-tailed retreat. At the water's edge, a group of basking crocodiles dashed into brackish depths, exhibiting an unexpected and eye-opening speed; woe be it to slow prey, human or otherwise. Strong signals on the headphones shifted their attention to locating the sloth bears, and Jordan quickly prepared his cameras as they headed toward a group of trees.

"Any possibility of photographing from the ground?" His blood was up, and the idea of being at eye level with a bear suddenly seemed intensely exciting. As long as the elephant was there to protect him, of course. Otherwise, for a lawyer, it fell into the realm of the severely stupid.

Charlayne gave him an incredulous look over her shoulder, but before she could speak, Jimi shot him down emphatically. "These bears weigh sometimes three hundred pounds, and sows are especially belligerent. When we trapped this cub, four elephants could not get the mother to abandon it. We finally had to sedate her. We must keep our distance, be very still, very quiet."

The vicious scrub gave out to smaller growth, but the ground became an uneven mire of black mud trampled into the consistency of a badly plowed field; it was tough going, even for Mala. The radio receiver was capturing full-volume signals from the collared bear, and at the site of a dead sal tree scrape-marked at its base, Jimi pointed to a fresh scattering of wood and bark. "Recent feeding," he whispered. "We are very close."

Suddenly, he stopped Mala and pointed out a shaggy black sow and cub shuffling along a narrow clearing toward the dead tree. Jordan swung his camera around Charlayne's body and into position, took a quick focus, and was able to capture several photos before the mother, unnerved by the foreign sound of the shutter, shepherded her cub to the safety of high grass.

They moved into a downwind position and settled in to wait. Charlayne twisted around to look at him with an unspoken question. *Did you get them?* He nodded, and her eyes brightened with pleasure at his success. Amply rewarded for being prepared, he handed her the first camera, then resumed his vigil with a longer lens in case the sow returned.

Jimi permitted Mala to graze. Silent patience granted them a second opportunity. The bear, with its distinctive necklace of white fur and a blazed face, emerged from the grass; the cub was clinging tenaciously, if precariously, to her hindquarters as she scraped away at the rotted trunk with three-inch ivory claws, and the pictures were priceless. Bark and dead wood flew and the noisy snuffling of the mother feeding on termites was clearly audible. Jordan shot the full roll, and Charlayne smoothly passed back the first camera with fresh film in it. Not having to reload gave him precious time and he was able to get another half a roll before the bear became agitated and left again. This time she did not return.

Jordan rewound the exposed film from both cameras and secured the cartridges in his vest pocket. After nearly an hour of total quiet, Jimi signaled that it was time to pack it in, and the patient Mala was turned toward home.

Charlayne jiggled in front of him, openly delighted. "The *cub!* Could you believe how adorable it was? This makes another book possible. Thank you, Jimi." She locked her arms around the driver's shoulders and squeezed until he laughed out loud, his ears red with embarrassment. Jordan laughed as well; in all probability, the young man had never encountered an exuberant American woman. He was still chuckling when Charlayne reached backward to grab a firm hold of his belt loops. She jammed her hat under his chin as she rested her weight against his chest to give him a reverse hug. "You, too," she crowed, basking in her joy. "I'd *never* have gotten those photos. You're wonderful. Both of you."

Before he could react to her embrace, she released him

and reached down to pat Mala's hardworking shoulders. "You, too, Mala. I love you all." Her enthusiasm buoyed him all the way to the river, where her bright chatter and camaraderie made recrossing the shallows tolerable. Moments before they emerged into the compound, they encountered a final treat that left even Jimi speechless: a pair of hornbills in flight. Huge banana-yellow beaks and black-and-white wing feathers flashed among the trees for an instant and then they were gone. Too quick to photograph, the rare birds would exist again only in memory, he realized, and was pleased to have shared the brief sighting with Charlayne.

For the balance of the journey to the compound, Jordan became strongly introspective. Being here, taking pictures for her, had not been a mistake. He'd had more adventure, more new, rich experiences in the space of eight hours, than he'd had in the past six years. The minute he slid off Mala's width, however, he knew he'd be adding another: a bronc buster's walk. The physical cost of the afternoon, aches and pains and cramps in muscles he didn't know could hurt, became apparent. Charlayne clambered off on rubber legs as well, only to collapse in giggles; he held her upright until she was able to stand on her own. "Yippie-ki-yay," she whooped.

They walked together toward the bunkhouse and he manfully forced his legs to carry him without a limp, but she eyed his gait with a grin. "See-ya, pardner." She lightly bopped her fist on his arm muscle before disappearing behind her door. He heard the distinct sound of stifled laughter and was forced to laugh at himself as well. So much for being macho.

It wasn't until he'd settled onto his bunk that he began to assess. For the first time in forever, he'd enjoyed spending time with a woman. He wasn't dead in his chest or busy constructing defenses against his guilt, and he hadn't shut off his mind. He still found her attractive, hell, yes, but even riding intimately close behind her for hours hadn't produced the sexual reaction he'd been worried about. Wishing for?

Probably, if he was honest.

As long as he was being honest, he also had to admit that she was quirky and funny and intelligent, and enjoyed life on a moment-to-moment basis, something he'd forgotten how to do. And, if he was *completely* honest, sometime during the afternoon he'd allowed her to cross an invisible line to become his friend. He'd lowered his guard, he realized, and he genuinely liked her. And surprisingly, there was no guilt attached to that admission. In fact, the feeling was fine.

He heard lissome rustlings next door and wondered what she was doing. Probably changing for dinner. Technically, he was eavesdropping, but he listened in spite of himself. A man and a woman could do exactly the same thing, and her sounds would be subtle, mysterious, and intriguing; a man's, noisy and obvious, drawers banging and shoes hitting the floor. Women had a gift for positioning things, placing them in a quiet manner. Men shoved stuff around with little patience for particulars; two weeks with Andrew had convinced him that his brother couldn't cross a concrete room without rattling the windows.

Andrew and Charlayne. His brother would be a lucky man indeed if things worked out between them. But the thought was nowhere near as comfortable as it should have been.

12

If wishes came true . . .

At dinner, Professor Jamieson congratulated them with cheerful amazement on their success in photographing sloth bears and was downright askance at the unusual sighting of the hornbills. "You've had a proper welcome to the park indeed," he assured them. "Now then," he continued benevolently, "there's been a rather exciting change in plans. I hadn't confirmation when I suggested you arrive early, Miss Pearce, but we received word this afternoon. King Birendra's granted permission and his elephant troops are being made available to help us catch a juvenile rhino. We'll use our animals as well."

Jordan looked at the man, unable to believe he'd

heard correctly. A rhinoceros hunt with elephants in the twentieth century? "For what purpose, sir?"

"We're selling a pair of calves to the Bangkok zoo for breeding purposes. Funds will be used to support the park. We've completed a holding pen, and with luck, we'll capture the first one the day after tomorrow."

"And we're taking an active part?" Charlayne verified cautiously, and her eyes brightened with jubilation at his brisk nod.

"Certainly, as my guests, and I should hope you'll have an even more exciting opportunity for photographs, Mr. Kosterin."

A rhino hunt! Jordan's heart beat heavily in his chest and he made a silent vow that the next time he saw Andrew Kosterin, he was going to kiss his brother's balding little head!

Details of the hunt were fleshed out as they finished their meal, and Charlayne left the two men deep in discussion of the relative merits of zoos and animal gene pools. She walked toward the bunkhouse with a wary eye on the perimeter; it was going to be a long night, and common sense said to get as much rest as possible in preparation. She crawled into her bunk still wearing her socks, secured the mosquito netting in place, and closed her eyes to listen to the calling peacocks. If things kept up at this pace, she'd have enough material for a dozen books before the week was out.

Images of the day's events kept coming to rest on Jordan Kosterin. Worn denims had seemed to hang just right on his hips, and a faded navy sweatshirt under the safari vest had removed all vestiges of *GQ* lawyerism; his body was firmly masculine—close contact on Mala's back this afternoon had confirmed that as a stone fact. And she'd been pleasantly surprised at the ease with which his photographer had melded with her writer, creating a smooth, effective partnership when they'd taken pictures of the bears. They'd soon be out for the evening's run together, and the anticipation of spending more time with him took center stage in her thinking. She frowned at the quickening in her body. "You're too attracted to this man," she warned herself unhappily. "Keep your head."

In all the time they'd spent together, he hadn't once mentioned anything relative to his private life. In fairness, they'd been fully occupied all afternoon, and both their personal lives had taken a backseat. Other than the singular comment a week ago in Jaipur, the subject of his marriage hadn't surfaced, even obliquely. Andy had been forthright about being single, but for the life of her, she couldn't remember either of them making any reference to Jordan's marital situation. It was almost as if it were a closed subject.

Why he'd made an overnight decision to abandon vacation plans with his brother and volunteer to take pictures for her, was puzzling, too; unless there was a phone in Saura she didn't know about, he'd done so without consulting his wife. Then logic kicked in. Any man who wore a wedding ring ten thousand miles from home was happily married. He'd probably driven to Tiger Tops and phoned home from there. No great mystery to solve and so much for wishful thinking. "That's the end of it," she announced.

The sound of her voice was followed by suspicious scuttlings in the corner of the room; a well-aimed flashlight revealed a lizard skritching its diminutive body down the wall on noisy toenails.

She giggled with relief. "Hiya, sailor. New in town?"

The animal resembled an actor posing in a spotlight as it cocked an arrogant eye in her direction; eventually it nodded its head up and down at her with more than a little attitude, clearly unafraid. She nodded in return and it froze in place. Lizards dined on mosquitoes if she wasn't mistaken; definitely an asset from her point of view and someone to hang out with.

Sailor leaped to the floor and Charlayne watched him tour her belongings for a few moments before reaching for her notepad to begin roughing out storylines featuring errant sloth bear cubs with lizard sidekicks and belligerent moms. Jordan's footsteps sounded lightly along the porch; the scrape of the door to his room preceded the bump of his shoes hitting the floor and a wooden squeak when his bunk took the weight of his body. After a moment all was silent.

When she looked for the visiting reptile, it was no longer in sight. "If wishes came true . . . photographers would be single," she quietly advised her vanquished green visitor, then switched off the flashlight and slept.

Light peeking through a crack in the wood of their common wall brought her awake. It was too dark to read her watch, but she had the sense that it was late from the barrage of night sounds: a large animal of some kind was bellowing a lewd mating call, and legions of basso frogs were issuing social invitations. The air was uninvitingly cool, and she hunkered under the blanket to absorb one last moment of warmth. The thought of her first night ride and a possible glimpse of a fishing cat shook off her lethargy; she'd traveled halfway around the world to see one of these little guys, and now was the time to make its acquaintance. Her bunk protested with a squeak of its own as she lurched stiffly to her feet and immediately became entangled in mosquito netting; the gauzy material clung to her face like spiderweb, frightening her at first, then merely irritating.

The pencil of light from Jordan's room was accompanied by creaking floorboards as he moved about. Chilled from sleep, Charlayne reached for her boots. The lizard shocked her by making a frantic, last-minute exit across her hand, avoiding her oncoming toes with the barest of margins. "You better work on your timing," she muttered jerkily, and shook her other boot to make sure no one else was home. She plaited her hair into a loose braid, donned a canvas jacket against the nippy air, then grabbed her hat.

They greeted each other on the porch, flashlight to flashlight; a dense blanket of fog soaked up the night. No wonder it was cold and dank in her room.

"I've brought my strobe." His words drifted toward her on a cloud of vapor. "But not much of anything's going to work in this."

"Maybe it'll lift." She shivered involuntarily and led the way down the steps on stiffened legs. "At this rate, I'll be happy just to find the elephant."

He walked on the outside, she noticed, between her and the compound's perimeter, and she shivered again. "You suppose rhinos can see in this soup?"

His sideways glance into the glistening mist revealed his apprehension. "Let's hope not."

They made a double row of tracks in the grass until they found the path to the elephant shed. There, the distinguished belly of Khalli, oldest and largest of the elephants, loomed next to an incandescent dot glowing red in the mist. An old man was smoking a cigarette and a puff of smoke steamed upward; standing next to him was Jimi, and ageless faces, young and old, crinkled into broad smiles of greeting.

"I am Joh." The old man tugged a knitted cap close around his ears. "It is cold tonight."

Charlayne introduced herself and Jordan. "Are we still going out?"

"Oh, yes." Joh's eyes disappeared into the folds of his face as he smiled again. "It will clear in a little while, I think," he said. "Good for fishing cat. Bad for pictures."

Khalli lowered her bulk to the ground and tilted her huge body to make it easier to climb up her side. Having learned from her earlier experience with Mala, Charlayne had the satisfaction of being more graceful about getting into the saddle and made it without Jordan's help. When he settled his body in behind her, she welcomed his warmth against her back. Joh climbed on as well and stood on Khalli's rump as the elephant launched herself to her feet.

As soon as Jordan had secured his camera case to the rear of the saddle, Jimi handed up their tracking equipment; moments later he was swallowed up in the fog as they began their float across the compound to enter the jungle. The trees Charlayne knew to be overhead were impossible to make out, and under them everything below the level of Khalli's knees was equally invisible; with no up, no down, and no guidelines, she had the sense of bobbing about like a cork in a fluorescent ocean. Pallid branches laden with wet, colorless leaves emerged and disappeared from time to time, their only reminder of being on land after all.

They crossed the river and entered the scrub, the elephant competently picking her way through ghostly brush and tall wet grass, visible in intermittent degrees of gray mist. Sudden rustlings and crackling noises indicated rapid departures, large and small, and Joh's quiet voice provided identification of unseen creatures.

"Barking deer," he would say. "Wild boar. Rhino." She was lucky to see her hand in front of her face, and he could tell the difference between a pig and a deer in this stuff? Unbelievable.

Occasionally, the sounds of fleeing animals were attributed to local cattle. When questioned, Joh explained that villagers sometimes defied park regulations by bringing their stock in to graze under the cover of darkness. "A risk with the tiger," he added. "He will hunt by smell this night. They don't see him."

They soon pinpointed the direction of the radio beep issuing from the fishing cat's collar, and after a few minutes they arrived at the site of a monstrous wash. Here the fog hovered ten feet above the water, and Charlayne almost wished it wasn't clear: coal-black on the surface, pooled at the bottom of a steep embankment, the wash was easily fifty feet across. Jordan's body went rigid against her and she felt his intake of breath.

"Tie the radio equipment in front of you, Mr. Kosterin, if you will. It's the last place that might get wet. We will dry, it will not. Also, you will need to hold on with both hands."

Jordan's warmth disappeared and the cold of the square metal box penetrated the back of her jacket as he repositioned the tracking device and retied it between them by means of thick leather thongs.

"Ready?" Joh's voice was a light whisper that did not carry in the night.

Jittery, Charlayne wrapped her fists in the lead rope encircling Khalli's neck. "Did we miss the bridge?" she wisecracked. "No jokes about Chappaquiddick."

Jordan's voice was sternly void of humor. "Let's do this if we're going to."

Khalli's descent down the steep incline seemed all but

perpendicular; Charlayne let go of the lead rope to brace both hands against the elephant's skull and threw her weight backward to keep from taking a header between the animal's ears. The metal box dug keenly into her back and she let out a gasp. Jordan held fast to her shoulder until they reached the bottom.

When they came to a halt at the edge of the water, the elephant was up to her knees in mud; Charlayne practically hugged the surefooted creature. No matter how ungainly her appearance, Khalli's agility was outstanding.

Jordan's tense voice spoke in her ear, his breath curling warmly along her cheek. "Let me have your hat." She complied and felt him stuff it between her back and the cruel metal box.

"Thanks," she said gratefully. "That thing's a killer."

Joh's powerful flashlight played along the rim of the opposite bank; its beam mirrored across dead-still water in a perfect straight line. "Be prepared to lift up your feet as we cross," he said.

That meant it was deep. Her nerves began to get the better of her. "We're going across?" Fifty feet of black loomed in front of her. "I'd rather go back and come down the bank again," she joked nervously. "We'd pay money for that in California. Call it a theme park."

Her sarcasm was rewarded with Jordan's pithy, "Yeah, right," and the old man's laughter, making her feel better. She was still apprehensive, but common sense told her that Joh wouldn't do anything dangerous. Deciding she'd rather drag her feet in the water than fall off, she firmly gripped the elephant's neck with her thighs, hoping she wasn't sending some kind of command to take a bath or, God forbid, roll over. Behind her, Jordan practiced lifting his knees jockey-style and took a firm grip on the saddle. "We're ready," he said tightly.

Joh's flashlight continued its search for rhinos on the far bank as Khalli pulled her feet from the sucking mud and moved forward into the wash; they sank rapidly into black water, and a series of shining ripples pushed ahead of them. At eight feet, Khalli was the tallest of the camp's elephants, but the oily water rolled up her belly to a level just below the saddle. About the time they'd reached the center of the wash, a fish of some kind suddenly flipped itself through the air and splashed them in its wake. Jordan flinched and Charlayne jerked her feet higher. "Hey, Joh, cat food," she gasped shakily as circles danced through circles on the water, creating choppy patterns of light.

A silent Jordan braced her again as they negotiated the equally steep far bank with the same awkward ease of elephant power; she heard a rigid sigh as he released his breath and reached for the headphones to check the fishing cat's position. It had moved on in the few minutes it had taken to cross, and they started forward in the new direction.

She knew the question was futile, but asked anyway. "Will we see it, do you think?"

Joh laughed. "In the daylight maybe, not at night. He's too quick, too small."

A short time later they paused on the bank of a small creek. The cat continued to forage in blanket-thick fog, while an unseen herd of barking deer coughed at them in warning; their namesake barks had the eerie sound of suspicious dogs. Fording the shallow water, they disturbed a sleepy mother rhino midstream; she grunted her irritation in an unmistakable pig-voiced protest before collecting her calf and graying into the night. At the next crossing Charlayne noticed an uneasy, blah feeling in her stomach, but refused to give in to it. It didn't go away. By the time they'd upsy-daisied the banks of a third stream and were searching the perimeter of a marsh for a suitable place to wait, she was positively queasy. Her body was breaking into a sweat.

"I'm going to lose dinner," she said quickly to Joh. "Either I get off or you're going to have to give Khalli a bath."

She felt Jordan's hand on her forehead, deliciously warm against her skin; if he wasn't careful, he'd need a bath, too.

"She's pretty clammy, Joh."

The old man brought Khalli to a halt. "It's cold on the sand," he said worriedly. "Best to stay warm on the elephant."

"I'll lose lunch *and* dinner if I don't get on the ground," she warned; her vision began to spin into tight loops and bursts of light. "Breakfast, too . . . and that's if I'm lucky," she said thickly.

"Joh, we better get her down."

"Oh, God, hurry," she moaned.

The world went whirling as the elephant dropped to her knees. She felt Jordan jump stiffly to the ground in time to help her off; her legs buckled, but he held her steady and her head stopped spinning almost instantly. "Uhhn, thank you," she babbled incoherently. "I'm nnngh . . ."

"Breath deep. You need oxygen."

She did as directed, until her stomach dropped anchor and things stopped drifting sideways. Eventually she was able to stand upright again, but spasms were rippling and shivering through her body, setting her teeth on edge. "Joh's right," she admitted. "It's freezing down here."

"Try to relax." Jordan handed over her hat then gathered her close inside his jacket. Folded into his arms, his

WISH LIST 133

body tall and strong and solid as oak, and warm, please God, warm, she nodded gratefully, unable to speak. Joh was gathering armfuls of dry grass into a pile on a sandy area near the swamp. Jordan's voice rumbled above her head as he chafed her hands. "Hang in there, he's building a fire."

"What about the fishing cat?" she said uneasily. She'd caused enough trouble without interfering with the collection of data. "Won't a fire chase him away?"

Joh laughed and pointed into the marsh. "Nah, he's busy in there, I think. He likes this place." He struck a match to the grass.

Jordan walked her forward to the fire, then left to collect dead bark and driftwood to add to the flames. As Joh had promised, a light breeze began to disperse the fog. She stood as close as she dared to the warmth while the men returned to the elephant. Joh grabbed Khalli's ear and raised his foot; he was effortlessly lifted on her trunk high enough to scramble across her head and onto her back, where he untied the receiver and passed it down to Jordan. Then he moved the elephant to a patch of grass a small distance away. "I will keep watch from here," he called to them, and lit another cigarette.

Fire warmth was beginning to penetrate her jacket and she saw Jordan studying her in the firelight. "Do you ever get seasick?" he asked casually.

"Every time I look at a boat. Why?" She frowned at him. "Crossing that little bit of water shouldn't do it. Do you think?"

"When it comes to water, it doesn't take much."

Kneeling to operate the tracking device, he handed the headphones up to her, and she took a moment to listen to the steady beep. "He's still there," she confirmed. As they waited and warmed themselves by the fire, Jordan's assessment began to make sense. "No horizon," she deliberated. "Not enough—"

"Visibility to keep your equilibrium."

"Oh, great," she said, and grinned apprehensively. "And it's at least two hours back to camp."

"We'll know well before then."

His voice somber as he stared into the blackness of the marsh, she watched him work his shoulders in an obvious attempt to relieve his tension. A mask of resignation veiled his eyes, and she had sudden insight into his feelings. "You hate water."

It struck Jordan instantly that she'd used an absolutely correct word. Hate. In truth, he hated water with a passion beyond measure. And feared it. Water equaled death. It was phobic, as permanent as life could make it, and ate at his soul like a cancer.

"I nearly drowned once." He blew out his breath and admitted, "If I'd known crossing rivers was part of the deal, I wouldn't be here." He'd expected to recross the shallow stream that bordered the compound, and had handled it OK, but at the bank of the wash, fear had wiped out all but the most basic ability to function; from that point forward terror had canceled any enjoyment of the mystical night or the pleasure he'd derived from riding close behind her again. Crossing that black expanse of water had nearly torn it; he'd come within inches of balking, until he'd reasoned that savvy old Joh would not risk taking them into water more than five or six feet deep. Still, crossing depth of any kind was excruciating, and after that it had been harrowing each time they'd forded a stream.

He'd gradually become aware of Charlayne's descent from gallows' humor to silence and had sensed her discomfort as they'd continued to track the cat. When she'd admitted to being nauseous, he guessed the reason and had gotten her onto solid ground as quickly as possible. If she'd gone into full equilibrium imbalance and vomiting, it might have taken days for her to recover.

Folding her into his jacket had been instinctive; getting her warm was the next best thing he could think of. He had to give her credit for hanging tough, though. She hadn't buckled until it was absolutely necessary, but she'd gotten thoroughly chilled and he wondered if he should offer to hold her again.

Joh and Khalli were moving. The massive animal approached a driftwood snag and used her foot to shove it loose from the sand; with no visible commands from the old man, she wrapped her trunk around the awkward limb, dragged it close to the fire, then backed away. With a great deal more effort on a human scale, Jordan and Charlayne bullied it into the flames.

Sparks scintillated upward and the rotted wood caught fire within seconds, increasing the ambient heat. Charlayne seemed to be getting warm at last. "OK if we stay down here until the cat moves?" he called to Joh.

The old man lit another cigarette, studied the night, and finally nodded reluctant permission. "You keep track of him and let me know." Khalli returned to her patch of grass and Joh stretched out on the wood of her saddle.

Jordan grabbed a handful of sand and dry-scrubbed mud off his hands. Charlayne did the same. "I warned you it would be grubby," she reminded him. "Your brother's a witness."

"Grubby, I don't mind," he replied. "Could use a little more heat, however. Are you warm enough?"

She nodded and smiled up at him, her eyes clear and honest in the firelight, reflecting camaraderie and friendship in this most unlikely place. The hiss of burning wood blended with a night alive with noises and rustlings of unseen creatures, all damped to a murmur in the hovering mist. Her reference to his brother reminded him that he hadn't as yet honored his word to Andrew. His mind turned to what he knew about her. She was susceptible to motion sickness. Other than that, he had to admit he had little more information now than when he'd said goodbye to his brother.

She was adventurous and gutsy, but what had he actually learned about her? Her home was Los Angeles, same as his. She was divorced, but hadn't mentioned children. Or made reference to a current man in her life. Surely a woman as attractive as Charlayne had someone waiting in California. She was lonely, far from home, and had chosen to travel by herself during what were usually very important holidays. He hiked his shoulders again to relieve their stiffness from the damp, and saw that Khalli was alert, but the old man was no longer smoking and probably asleep.

He checked the monitor and assured himself that the fishing cat's signal had not changed. Since they were going to be stuck here awhile, he might as well use the opportunity to make good on his pledge. He owed his brother that much, at least.

13

Tiger tidbits . . .

Charlayne relished warmth from the fire and studied Jordan Kosterin as he checked the cat's location. If he was right and she'd been seasick from Khalli's motion, getting back to camp was going to be hell. For both of them. A near drowning was a life-altering thing, and he had to be dreading the return trip as much as she was. It wasn't a huge amount of information about him, she conceded, but it was more than she'd known an hour ago.

"Still steady," he reported, and joined her by the fire. Flames consuming the dried wood grew higher and they were obliged to rotate exposure to their fronts and backs with greater frequency as they waited out the fishing cat's business. "How'd you find out about the research projects here?"

"My college roommate's brother, Mitch, had this great professor—"

"Jamieson."

"Right, and when Judy told me Mitch was here doing research—he studies bat species and everyone—"

"Calls him Batman."

Aware of his expectant gaze and amused at how quickly he could finish her thoughts, Charlayne grinned. "Anyway, Professor Jamieson agreed that I could come as well. Mitch is collecting samples near Tiger Tops at the moment, but he'll be back in time to help capture the rhino calf."

"I don't suppose he's from Mississippi?"

Her jaw dropped in surprise. "You know Mitch?"

His eyes warmed when he smiled. "Lawyers are good at guessing."

Mystified, she searched his face for clues, stalling the conversation until finally he laughed and owned up. "I think he was in the hotel bar when Andy and I arrived. Close to my height, reddish hair?"

"We've never met, actually, but Judy's a redhead from Biloxi." Emboldened by his humor, she readied herself to satisfy her curiosity by broaching the subject of his altered trip.

"Why did you—"

"When did you—"

"You first," she insisted.

"I was wondering how long you've been divorced."

He glanced away and it was clear that he felt awkward raising the subject. She was surprised. Less than a week ago she'd been very open with Andy about her marital history. Was he double-checking her story or clarifying details, or whatever older brothers did for younger brothers? She felt her way cautiously into the conversation.

"A little over a year . . . this time." When he didn't ask the next obvious lawyer question, she answered it anyway. "I've been married twice. Four years the first time. The last one didn't make it to an anniversary." His attention told her that for some reason Andy had not shared this information. Very odd.

"My turn," she said. "I was surprised when you changed your vacation plans. If I were your wife, I'd be upset that I couldn't reach you by . . . pho—" She stopped short. Something was terribly wrong. "It's none of my business," she backpedaled hastily. "I really didn't mean to—"

"My wife is dead."

His leaden delivery of the statement rocked her as much as the content. Why on earth hadn't Andy warned her? "Oh, God, I'm sorry." Totally thrown, she fumbled for an escape. "You're wearing a ring . . . I just assum—" She forced herself to shut her mouth.

"It's not a . . ." He cleared his throat. "Well, actually it was. I had our wedding rings melted down and this one made." He twisted the worked-gold band around his finger, staring past her into the fire. "Six years ago Christmas. Her name was Natalie. I couldn't stand not wearing a ring on top of everything else." He kicked smoking embers at the edge of the fire toward its center.

"Oh." There seemed very little to say as the timing assumed its importance. Christmas had been the sunlit morning at the Taj Mahal, dinner in Jaipur, the near-incident in the bar; his ill-at-ease behavior most of that evening began to make sense, as well as his tension during their wild ride in the car. Six years ago this week would have been his wife's funeral. "Oh," she said again, feeling terrible for him. "This must be an awful time of year for you."

His voice remained flat. "It is that."

"Should we talk about something else?"

He glanced at her. "No, it's all right. Everyone I know is tired of hearing about it. It's just that I loved her a great deal. Totally, as a matter of fact." He moved to the tracking equipment, held an audio phone to his ear to take a reading, then replaced it. "Sometimes I think, too much. Everyone says I can't let go."

She stared at him, puzzled. "Why should you have to? She was your wife."

The simplicity of her response released a barb of emotion and Jordan turned away. Why, indeed? It hit him, basic as pain, that Charlayne was the first woman he'd met who seemed to get it, who had some comprehension that his love for Natalie was forever, and wouldn't change just because life kept on happening. He looked at her strongly, his need rising. "Most people don't understand that."

"Then that's their problem," she said forcefully, then laughed with unmistakable irony. "Two husbands combined didn't care that much about me." Her irony faded and once again she gave solace with her words. "I think it's all that counts, really, how much you love someone."

He joined her by the fire, hungry for more.

"How did she die?"

He heard himself recount Natalie's bitter history, bore the hurt of it, as always. "Bone cancer. We found it too late. She refused chemotherapy." Past an expression of sympathy, he'd learned that people rarely wanted the circumstances of Natalie's death. Most were uncomfortable when he tried to discuss his grief, inevitably attempting to change the subject or urge him with well-meant platitudes to move on with his life. When Charlayne listened in silence, empathy obvious in her expression, he continued.

"She suffered . . . I lost her in a matter of months. I don't even remember the next two years."

"I can't tell you I know what that's like," she said softly. "I've never lost anyone."

"It's hell on earth," he assured her.

"I can see that." She was quiet for a long time before she added, "She knew how much you loved her." It was a statement that assumed the fact. "You'll always have that." She was obviously pleased with him. "It's all any woman really wants."

His throat closed over for a moment before he succeeded in forcing out his question. "You have children?"

"I have a nephew." The irony returned, cutting this time, which surprised him, but her voice changed immediately and became caring. "Ryan. He's a terrific kid and I love him a lot. I also fear for him." She became aware of his gaze and looked at her watch, suddenly restless. "Hey, it's five minutes to midnight. Tell me what you and Natalie did for New Year's."

Warmed, his back to the fire, he was pleased to share his feelings with this woman who understood. "It was our private night together. Never went out, didn't allow anyone in." He slid into memory. "We'd have a bottle of champagne. She'd buy it every January and we'd look forward to it all year. . . . The last one's still in my apartment." He stopped.

"A bottle of pain," she said, precisely identifying it.

He nodded, tears released by her understanding. The champagne was something he'd never spoken of to another person; and the fact that he hadn't been able to dispose of it or drink it, had been a yearly reminder of his loss. He rode out an upwelling of sorrow, then was able to find the warm comfort of the way it had been with his wife before their life together had been destroyed.

"I used to buy her a trashy negligee every Christmas. I'd have to look all over town for it. She was always so thin—I should have known . . ." This time he was able to rise above the really bad part to find intimate memories he'd carefully hidden away. "Some of them were pretty tacky, I can tell you, but she had a model's body and looked incredible in everything from lace to feathers." As he refined the memory, his pulse increased and his skin reacted to his thoughts. "There were only two rules. It had to be satin and it had to be a different color every year. She'd put it on and be sexy and adorable. . . ." Pressure began its course, working low in his abdomen, heating his blood to a subtle swell of arousal. "We'd drink the champagne and then we'd make love. We'd start early in the evening and keep each other wai—"

He stopped, abruptly aware of the pulsing in his groin, the near-erection. Christ! He was well on his way to getting hard in front of a woman he barely knew. Shocked and astonished at his behavior, he looked away. She said nothing, seemed oblivious as he fought down a hot tide of sensation flushing his skin. "Then we'd check her wish list and it'd be midnight," he finished lamely.

"That sounds wonderful." Her voice was wistful. She'd turned her face away from the fire.

"It was." He tried not to look at her, and failed.

"Mark always insisted on a family party." She laughed softly, no pleasure in the sound. "Now he has his own family. My second husband was a surgeon, spent New Year's—"

"At the hospital."

She nodded, then considered him briefly. "What's a wish list? Christmas presents?"

"No." He took a breath, still bewildered by the impossibility of his body's exhibition, and tried to focus. "It was, uh, a special list of goals. Things we wanted to share in life . . . places. . . ."

Her eyes filled with compassion. "And there are too many left."

He looked away, unsurprised and immensely grateful that she would know that as well, but gratitude raced headlong into another jolt of arousal and he experienced an intense desire to kiss this woman listening so carefully to him—seal her in his arms and really kiss her. To take his time doing it and sample the taste of her past the lipstick.

Confusion sped blindly through his thinking. They were talking about *Natalie*! How could he be missing his wife and wanting to kiss another woman at the same time?

This was haywire! Things like this didn't happen to him. Thoroughly bewildered, he fought for control. His mind and body were at such extremes it was frightening. What the *hell* was going on? He would have walked away, given himself an opportunity to pull himself together, but she held out her watch to show him the time.

"It's midnight."

Once again his body reacted and he had a sense of danger. At last, deep in the core of his torment, he began to freeze and deny the betrayal born of his body, permitted by his head and heart. Only then did his mind become paralyzed, and all he felt was a murderous heartbeat punishing his veins. He was dead as stone when she raised herself on tiptoe. Cupped his face in her hands. Laid her fingers against his skin.

"This is from me in honor of your feelings for your wife. Happy New Year." She kissed him full on the mouth, sweetly. Without fever or seduction.

And it was Natalie's kiss.

He came to life, profoundly thankful; suddenly he was

able to open his mouth to her, taste her sweetness, for it was exactly right. Moments passed and he felt a pumping rage begin in his chest, a hunger to have her, but by some power buried in his psyche, an older discipline won out; he held their kiss instead, missing her, wanting her, enjoying the peace of Natalie. When it ended, it was Charlayne who smiled and rested her head lightly against his shoulder before walking quickly away to check the monitoring equipment.

A black hole opened under his feet and he dropped into it, stunned into silence, unable to believe what had just happened. Her voice came quietly toward him from the real world.

"I think our friend has moved."

Still too shaken from the bizarre experience to make sense of it, he tried to assimilate her words, saw her frown of concern. *God, if she had any idea . . .*

"The signal seems much fainter. What do you think?"

She held out the headphones, and he seized the opportunity to smother his guilt by managing to regain a hazy command of his behavior. Manning the tracking equipment, he swung the detector in circular arcs until he found the signal. She was right. The cat had moved on. She called to Joh, and the old man was instantly awake. When he confirmed their opinion, Jordan spent as much time as he dared, kicking sand and stomping embers until the fire was thoroughly extinguished as well.

Damn this insanity!

Rattled by her actions, Charlayne wasn't certain if she was glad or sorry that the fishing cat was taking his invisible self elsewhere. When she'd noticed it was midnight, Jordan's obvious pain had triggered an irresistible urge to go to his side. To kiss him as his wife might have done. A joining of mutually lonely spirits so far from home and family, nothing more. The instant she'd kissed him, however, things had changed. Emotional doors long closed and nailed shut had opened in a heartbeat. Now she was slowly going through the motions of preparing to move on while her thoughts tripped headlong into a whirlwind.

Neither of her husbands had enjoyed kissing simply for the joy of it; both had considered two or three kisses a female requisite for having sex and had gone about it in a hard-lipped, hurried fashion, anxious to get to basics. But Jordan Kosterin was a revelation. His mouth had opened to her naturally, perfectly, and he'd kissed her without demand, turning her head around in the process.

She'd been dismissing his silent looks and sideways glances since they'd met as nominal male observation on behalf of his brother. Had she been wrong or was wishful thinking carting her merrily down a garden path? Her confusion was total and there was no time to deal with it. Joh was waiting for her by the elephant.

Fear of becoming ill interrupted her thoughts as she approached the giant animal. The last thing she wanted to do was revel in that kind of moment with Jordan Kosterin then lose her dinner in front of him five minutes later. She appealed to Joh. "Can I walk behind until we have to cross water?"

"Too dangerous. Rhinos are here," he objected. "Tigers, also."

"I know, but they're not going to argue with Khalli, surely, and I'll stay right on her heels, I promise."

Jordan looked at her once in silence, his handsome face wary and restrained under her glance before he gazed off into the marsh. Joh's brow had furrowed in concern. "It is not good."

Jordan seemed not to hear as she pled her case. "I'll hang onto her tail if you want, but please don't make me ride until I feel better. I know I can keep up, and if you see anything dangerous, I promise I'll get on."

"It will be too late." Joh was brusque. "Can you climb a tree?"

"Like a monkey," she bragged audaciously. "Want me to show you?"

To her relief, Jordan spoke at last, but still did not look at her. "I'll stay on the ground with her."

Joh reluctantly gave permission, and Khalli lumbered toward the fading radio signal with the two of them walking a few paces behind. As they followed an animal trail along the edge of the marsh, Jordan made no eye contact with her, rarely said anything except to point out hazardous rocks or holes in her path. Once, he steadied her over the trunk of a fallen tree. Something definitive was altered between them.

Attempting to decipher his thick silence, she reassessed, trying to relive those fragile moments. He had seemed to like kissing her, but he hadn't put his arms around her. Hadn't initiated a kiss of his own, and his mood had changed from that instant. In her excitement, lost in her enjoyment of him, could she have been totally wrong? What if he considered her attempt to honor his wife ill-timed, or insensitive, or inappropriate altogether? Would he think she'd used his wife as an excuse to kiss him? Had she? Was she being manipulative after all?

She quickly searched her conscience and found no intent. Subconsciously? She shook off the possibility. Her actions had been spontaneous and unthinking, a response to his pain, she was sure of it. But if he thought otherwise, she needed to clear things up as soon as possible.

Before she could attempt discussion, they entered wild

grass three and four feet above Khalli's head, and in order to match her progress, it was a full-time job fending off the stiff, wet fronds being swept aside by the elephant's bulk only to swing back and occasionally smack them in the face. Conversation of any depth was impossible.

Despite the diminished fog, cloud layers blurred the moon to the color of ashes. After half an hour of Jordan's protracted silence—and from following an inelegant rump featuring a hair-fobbed tail centered as steady as a plumb line—Charlayne's anxiety transferred itself to her sense of the absurd. Which promptly slipped its mooring.

As the elephant lifted and planted her back feet with care, loose gray skin sagged and drooped at her knees and ankles, and her ample hips rose and fell with the economy of the very old: nothing taken for granted or left to chance. Little by little Khalli's haunches began to resemble the wrinkled pulchritude of a giant human behind, and the more Charlayne tried to deny the vision, the more it was so. She clamped a hand over her mouth, determined to suppress her ribald laughter, but her shoulders began to heave.

Jordan caught her elbow and looked her in the face with concern. "Do you need to stop? Are you all right?"

"I'm fine." Relieved that he'd spoken to her at last, she made a frantic effort to rein herself in. "When I'm this tired, I get silly," she explained giddily. "My imagination gets away from me ... sometimes it goes around the bend, that's all." But it was no use; the moment she glimpsed Khalli's gray keister in motion, she was gone.

He glanced over his shoulder to see what was so funny and got a look at the elephant's rear end; her laughter became contagious, and his handsome features softened into an irrepressible grin as he recognized the likeness, monstrous ghostly buttocks churning in the moonlight.

"Put that in your book."

His dry comment ruined her resolve to shape up and hurled both of them into fits of laughter.

"Please, God, she doesn't get offended, or we're rhino bait."

"Tiger tidbits."

Tears streamed down their faces while they struggled to keep Khalli's wondrous behind in view. Staggering through grass and sticks and mud, over rocks and under fallen limbs, they helped each other conquer one obstacle after another, and Charlayne had trouble believing her luck. Next to a delicious midnight kiss—which she'd remember until she had more wrinkles than poor old Khalli—and finding out that Andy's gorgeous brother wasn't a married man after all, chasing a fishing cat through Nepal's tropical lowlands, all agiggle with Jordan Kosterin, was the most delightful New Year's she could ask for.

14

Happy New Year . . .

    Their frivolous humor vanished into the effort of keeping pace with Khalli's baggy buns, and forty-five minutes later the radio signal came to a halt deep in the marsh. After they both made humble apologies to the elephant for laughter at her expense, Joh permitted them to climb on board, and the three of them waited, dozing on her warm, motionless back. At four A.M. Joh concluded that since the fishing cat should normally have returned to its den by now, it had either slipped its collar or might have come to harm; sobered, they headed toward camp and much needed rest in the pale predawn light.

The cat's location allowed them to circumvent the wash. Worn-out from walking miles of rough terrain, too tired to take more than halfhearted interest in passing wildlife, Charlayne sagged against Jordan's chest as the old matriarch swayed toward home. When they came at last up the small rise to the camp, she welcomed Khalli's rumbled greeting to the other elephants and slid numbly to the ground. She bid Joh good-night, then accompanied Jordan on leaden feet toward the bunkhouse. "Nothing tomorrow until the sloth bears at three," she confirmed, one zombie to another.

"Right." They climbed the steps to the porch, and she was once more reminded that there'd been no reference to her having kissed him. Nor did his proper, gentlemanly good-night before disappearing into the blackness of his room give her a clue as to what he thought of her behavior.

It was just as well. She was too tired for discussion or clarification, or anything else for that matter, besides which she'd gone over it in her head for so long that she was no longer certain it had happened at all. Standing inside her doorway, swaying with fatigue, she tried to remember what to do first. The squeak of his bunk sounded through the wooden wall, followed by light boot thumps against the floor. At this rate he'd be asleep before she could find her bed.

Moonlight illuminated 5:35 on her watch and the dull sky promised dawn soon. Seven hours until New Year's at home, she thought light-headedly, vaguely aware of an odd pungent-must odor in the room. Probably her own clothing from prolonged contact with Khalli's hide; maybe the layer of bog mud clinging to her boots. Maybe space aliens. Legions of lizards; lots of 'em. Hmmm . . . Ought to write that down.

She took care to coax her door quietly closed, and her mind meandered erratically to whether or not Sailor Green had used her absence to take up residence in her bed. Whether her parents would stay up until midnight this year. How long it would take to cross the room.

She succeeded in finding her bunk in the dark, remembered the mosquito netting in time to ease it aside, and slumped onto the mattress. Unbidden, her body went limp with fatigue and a huge yawn nearly allowed her to give in to sleep.

Boots. Boots were first. Untying laces in the dark and extracting her feet from heavy, muddy boots and disgusting socks. Unable to remember being so exhausted, she gave up wet, gummy shoelaces as far too complicated and decided to let her feet hang over the side of her bed. Encouraged by this utterly brilliant solution, she felt her way to the opposite bunk, groped under the netting, and yanked off the blanket.

Belligerent snorts roared through the room followed by ominous poundings on the wooden floor; something a whole lot bigger than she was began flailing wildly in the small space between the bunks. Then the source of the sour smell whacked her solidly in the stomach and she lost all her air.

Jordan sank onto his bunk and kicked off his boots, unaccustomed to the ache of physical exhaustion melting through his muscles. A replay of the evening's events dominated his thinking. Within the space of an hour she'd kissed him senseless and damned near reduced him to tears before making him laugh until his stomach hurt. No one had put him on that kind of roller-coaster since . . . Christ, it wasn't possible.

He peeled away his shirt and tried in vain to put things in order so he could sleep. He still had trouble believing that kiss. No two women kissed the same, and the instant it was over, his brain had shut out the world and gone into overdrive, expending every available second to seek an explanation. The end result: he'd been unable to deny it. For that brief space in time, and for whatever reason, he'd made her his wife. It was that simple and that troubling.

What he couldn't account for was the fact that she bore no resemblance to Natalie, not physically, facially, nor in any way he could assemble. She'd *been* Natalie. Outside of logic, and beyond sense.

None of which even began to deal with breaking the pledge he'd made to his brother. Loss of control over his sexual urge had been embarrassing, but explainable, and he'd come up with a reasonable answer: abstinence for an unnatural length of time combined with an awakening of his feelings in general. It could all be accounted for. The unexpected fording of deep water had ripped open his stock of fear, for certain, complicated by emotional highs from the unusual adventures they'd been sharing.

It occurred to him, jarringly, that his response to her that night in Jaipur had followed a harrowing evening— also high in emotion: he'd had apprehension, if not outright fear, toward an unruly pack of men . . . definitely anger at not being able to protect her on the dance floor. Maybe he'd thought of her subconsciously as Natalie then, as well. Not a particularly welcome idea, but worthy of being considered. What was it about her . . . ?

Christ, *Andy*. Why the hell couldn't he remember that part of the problem? Andy, who'd gotten him into the goddamn situation in the first place! Andy, who was gaga over the lady next door—whose innocent kiss had created havoc with his common sense!

He stripped off the rest of his clothing, tossed everything that smelled of elephant onto the opposite bunk, and stretched out on the mattress. He pushed sexual matters and Andy's stake in the situation into a side compartment for the moment, determined to sort it out. If he took Charlayne's kiss—and his reaction to it—out of the picture, the time he'd spent with her these past twenty-four hours had been as close to normal as he'd felt since Natalie's death. He'd genuinely enjoyed himself. Following Joh's elephant through high grass . . . he hadn't laughed so much in years.

For that reason alone, exposure to this woman was important and, selfish as it might be, he wanted his response to her to linger. At least until he was certain what was happening. Not too much to ask, surely, and if his feelings disappeared as fast as they had from the incident in Jaipur, his conclusion would be verified . . .

Loyalty to his brother pushed its way into his argument. And . . . *if* they disappeared , there wouldn't be a problem with Andy. If, on the other hand, his emotions had some valid basis that he couldn't currently define, then what? Depending on the depth of his brother's interest in her, the situation had all the earmarks of triggering a serious problem. Andy had never questioned the fact that he'd met Natalie too late, and he had acted with absolute honor; other than the one drunken instance of confessing that he loved her, his brother had never exhibited his feelings in front of either of them. But now, if they were both attracted to the same woman, the script would be vastly different. This time Andy had first claim and could not reasonably be expected to step aside.

To admit his own attraction to Charlayne was asking for hell on a silver platter, especially under these unexplainable circumstances. The whole scenario would require a great deal of additional thought. When he wasn't so exhausted.

Besides, how could she *be* Natalie . . . ?

He was going in circles. Time to put aside deliberation.

In the meantime, there was tomorrow—today, he realized foggily, and the taste of her came back to him. It had been a hauntingly wonderful kiss. Common sense and evaluations aside, he'd spent a lot of time reliving that kiss the past few hours, with the weight of her body slumped warm and welcome against his chest.

No lipstick this time . . . just the taste of her mouth . . . Wet . . .

Lethargy had crept a couple of inches into his body and he was entering a vivid dream when he heard the commotion next door. Shocked and bleary, he grabbed his flashlight as the handiest weapon and charged through her door, readying himself for just about anything. He found her a few feet from some jerk who was wrapped in mosquito netting and reeling between the bunks.

He snapped on the flashlight and advanced into the room, prepared to do mayhem. "What are you doing in here?" he demanded angrily.

The man was belligerent and clawing at the netting. "I work here!" The stale smell of beer flumed into Jordan's face. "Who the hell are you?"

Illuminated in the light was the redheaded patron from the bar—in all likelihood "Batman" Baltine, who stopped fighting the netting and squinted myopically into the brightness, bare-assed as the day he was born.

"Shet that damned thing off, fool. Cain't you see I'm nekkid!"

A look of amazement was creeping onto Charlayne's face as she blinked in the sudden glare; Jordan saw her do a wide-eyed take on the man's unabashed nudity, then move toward the open doorway. And him. Unfortunately, being vastly underdressed for the occasion, his own hitherto private state of affairs had also gone on parade; he was strongly aware that his briefs weren't necessarily his most subtle asset at the moment.

Baltine succeeded in freeing himself from the net but fell across one of the bunks in the process, barked a shin, and swore bloody murder; between his drunken oaths and making no move to cover himself, Jordan's self-control reached its limit. "This room's occupied, *fool!*"

"Yeah, well I can see that now." Baltine struggled to his feet, airing complaint. "Wadn't nobody here when I came in. What time is it anyway?"

"Late. Get your things," Jordan ordered sharply and threw the beam of light to the ceiling. "You'll bunk next door with me."

The man began to gather his clothing. "I'd take that right kindly, thank you." He carefully tossed his shirt and trousers over one shoulder before grabbing his shoes, and was apparently unconcerned that his naked body was whitely on display. Frustrated, Jordan doused the flash and edged toward the door, fighting an urge to cover himself as Baltine's pale buttocks ambled past him out the door.

For her part, Charlayne was losing it. Viewing Jordan's considerable assets was interfering significantly with her effort to pull herself together. "*Happy* New Year," she sang out, barely able to concentrate. "I won't make any more noise, I swear it. Please come to bed."

Come to bed?! She *was* losing it.

"We'll straighten this out tomorrow." Jordan's brows were grimly pulled together.

I'd love to straighten it out.

Inch by inch, moment by moment, she was sliding tidily over the edge. He looked so protective and adorable in her doorway, with enormous bony feet planted for combat, and long, hairy legs hanging out of his underwear—the fit of which could best be described as magnificently undignified—that she had to remember how to nod.

"If you need anything else—"

"I'll whistle." She bit her lip and held her breath to keep from babbling. Her mouth was out of control. Everything—mind, body, libido—was flying solo, no brain attached.

His gorgeous frown relaxed into puzzlement at her ditsy behavior; then he blinked in recognition of her reverse on the famous repartee, but made no further comment. She shook her head, biting down on her lip as hard as she dared. She'd be drawing blood soon. He backed outside, depriving her of profile, as well as much anticipated rear view, and closed her door. The instant he was gone, she stuffed the tail of her sweatshirt into her mouth and willed herself not to make a sound; burying her head deep in her pillow, she gave in to silent laughter until tears wet her cheeks.

Jordan's well-filled jockeys had left nothing whatever to her writer's imagination, and she'd been as fascinated as a three-year-old with those husky bulges. She laughed some more. Dark body hair, aimed thickly south from a masculine V on his chest, had disappeared into thin white cotton, cradle to those most interesting protuberances, and emerged in a light coating over lean, muscular thighs. The overall picture struck a deep chord in a very inviting manner. Very deep. She didn't even want to think about how deep. Deep enough to keep her awake nights.

The redheaded stranger could only be Judy's brother, and he had indeed been totally "nekkid." Well-endowed in his own right, with skin chalk-white as a miner's, he'd been sprinkled with curly fur from his beard all the way to the russet patch surrounding the southernmost tip of his anatomy that had come under her scrutiny, loose and perky as the cheeks that had sauntered out her door. Not exactly a propitious moment to introduce oneself.

Abruptly her laughter ceased; the frantic energy waned and her exhausted body took on the weight of concrete. With the hard-won blankets draped around her shoulders, she sank onto her mattress to dream dreams of fascinating white-marble knights and blue-eyed kings with flags at full staff, moving across her private chessboard.

15

No compromise . . .

  Charlayne woke a little after eleven and startled the cook when she made a barefoot raid on the kitchen for leftover coffee and a pail of water. Jordan's room was blessedly silent. Under the baleful eye of Sailor Green, she washed her hair, did hand laundry in the shampoo water, then soaked her feet while she finished her field notes.

Hair still damp, and behind her darkest glasses, she ventured to the meeting room for lunch and made the formal acquaintance of Mitch Baltine, seated opposite Jordan at the table. Both men got to their feet.

"Judy sends her regards," Mitch said affably, eyes twinkling at her bold as brass. "She mentioned you was cute. I guess she's sure right about that."

"Thank you." Distracted by his colorful speech, she took a breath and decided to get it over with. "I'm really sorry about last night."

"Now, I'm right sorry, myself, Miss Charlayne."

He dipped his head and a braided ponytail slid into view. It reached well below his shoulders and was a paler shade of red than his beard. And the rest of his body hair. She flushed at the memory.

"I got in purty late, New Year's and all, and since I always stay in that end room . . . Wal, I seed your gear, but I sware I didn' see nothin' female, so I just took th'other bunk." He winked broadly at her. "I wadn't exactly sober, but I's doin' fine till somebody yanked my kivers. Put my bootie in full view. Guess I better locate some perjamas."

By this time Charlayne was crimson, and remained so until after Jordan had provided a more complete explanation to the professor and his staff. After which, he caught her eye. "I couldn't sleep so I went out with Jimi this morning to see what happened to the cat."

Her embarrassment dissolved into disappointment at being left behind.

"It seems our friend gave up fish for meat. He was feeding on a tiger kill last night."

Her eyes widened as she recalled Joh's warnings, and their having been on foot most of the night at her insistence. Dismayed that she'd missed the run, and his company, not to mention sight of the cat, she nodded blankly, still jolted at the thought that she may have risked their lives.

Professor Jamieson took the floor. "We won't monitor the bears this afternoon," he announced. "Joh's suspending any further use of the elephants. They'll need to be fully rested tomorrow, for the rhino hunt. Also, Joseph's driving over to Tiger Tops this evening to visit his family.

The hotel has telephone service, which I'm sure will be welcome. If you go with him, however, please be prepared to have dinner as well, since he generally spends most of the evening with his family."

Jordan indicated his interest in going, and Charlayne pounced on the opportunity as well. "I'd love to call my parents."

"Wal, if it's safe to move the rest of my things out of your room, I got mist nets to repair." Mitch was grinning at her.

Charlayne looked at the redhead warily; she hadn't noticed anything of his in her room, but she hadn't made a search.

"Didn' know you'as gonna sleep till noon, or I'da took my seein' eyeglasses," he pestered cheerfully.

Jordan was staring a hole through Mitch's forehead.

"As you know, I tend to make myself t'home," he went on, "so my undies is probly in there, too. You didn' happen t'see'm?"

"Your red frilly ones are hanging on the porch rail right next to mine," she retorted sweetly, "but the black lace pair really ought to soak awhile." She tapped the eyeglass case peeping out of his shirt pocket. "Now you be sure and wear these when you come by to pick them up. Wouldn't want you to take my little old drab things by mistake."

The staff broke into laughter; Mitch had met his match and everyone at the table knew it. The country twang disappeared and he gave her a good-natured grin. "I see I'll have to get up earlier in the morning where you're concerned."

"I'd stay awake, if I were you." The professor's dry comment brought another round of grins.

Lunch proceeded and Charlayne perceived a subtle

distance in Jordan's manner as he gave her a description of the sighting. "The cat was sleeping next to the kill and ran when the elephant got too close," he said, eyes midrange. "Beautiful jaguar-type markings down the middle of its back. Sorry I couldn't get a photograph."

"Maybe we'll get another chance." He'd been fine when they'd said good night, she was sure of it. The change had to be due to her demented behavior with him last night. She'd have to work in some kind of apology during the drive to Tiger Tops, at least an explanation. Definitely make sure things were cleared up between them before he left. It hit her then that he'd actually be gone in two days. She'd be here without him. The realization created a hollow place under her ribs, and she finished her lunch in silence.

Jordan checked his watch, then slipped into his green polo shirt. He found an aluminum juice can to use as a mirror to brush his hair. They were supposed to leave at five for the drive to the hotel, and it was close to that now. Following lunch, Charlayne and Sunita had gone with Joseph into a nearby town to do some shopping and still hadn't returned.

The can distorted his image back at him, reflecting his dilemma. After they'd driven away, he'd managed a couple of hours of restless sleep and woke up with a hard-on from an erotic dream about a woman—Charlayne's face, but he'd been making love to Natalie. The ramifications had gnawed at his principles despite his best efforts to explain away what had happened.

His wife was dead. An unalterable fact. Something he should have accepted by now, and he'd been shaken by the uncomfortable knowledge that even in his sleep he'd been using one woman to keep an emotional hold on another. That he was capable of imagining someone in Natalie's place—replacing her physically as well, if he included last night's kiss—was not only jarring, but unconscionable.

Added to that admission was a growing, insidious temptation to find out if she'd remain Natalie to him sexually. Instinctively he knew that if he permitted himself to listen, to tolerate even the possibility, it might well become the mindless quest of an addict. To have what? A few hours of fantasy at Charlayne's expense? Respite from the living hell that was his life without his wife?

Would she be harmed if he allowed himself to push his moral self aside in the process? Would his brother? A long, hard examination of his soul left him with no resolution. Surely Andy would understand. And forgive. Even if he didn't, was it so great a cost to ask? Was it so wrong to want to hold on to the woman he loved? Even for a little while? What kind of asshole would that make him?

Selfish? . . . absolutely.

Deceptive? Unfair? . . . unquestionably.

A liar. Yes, and despicable. He got angry. It was *his* soul, *his* need, and his chance to have someone to live for again. A reason to get up every morning and face reality. And to care. Most of all, to give a damn!

Outside, the station wagon pulled to a stop and his rage dissolved as car doors slammed and Sunita's sunny chatter filtered into his hearing, followed by the crackle of packages. They were back. And the familiar lift in his stomach at the sound of Charlayne's voice told him his response to her had not changed.

His quandary unresolved, he took one last swipe at his hair and reached for his shoes. So far it was just him and Charlayne at dinner, no Mitch, whose local-yokel sexual harassment routine had been an embarrassing reminder of his own condition in front of her last night. He'd been self-conscious as hell at lunch. Not so much so that he hadn't enjoyed her nailing Baltine's rubber ego to the wall. He snorted with grim satisfaction. The guy was as irritating as a rash, but unless the Batman was a total idiot, he'd keep his distance for a few days —the naked son of a bitch.

He came to an abrupt decision. The minute they reached the hotel this evening, he'd call Andy and tell him not to fly halfway across India to pick him up this weekend. And why. And take the repercussions. If it was being greedy and self-indulgent and half a dozen other unpleasant things, so be it. It was what he intended to do. That, and to stop fighting his conscience for as long as his attraction to her lasted. Andy would just have to understand.

Her footsteps crossed the porch and he heard the soft scrape of her sandals on the floorboards as she moved about in her room. His mind enveloped the feminine rustlings, the subtle rhythms of a brush sliding through rich, slick hair, the mysterious pauses. Suddenly, he knew he wouldn't do it. Even if she hadn't shown herself to be a gracious and caring person, to subject her to lies and deceptions for his own benefit, sexual or otherwise, was indecent.

And he couldn't do it to his brother, who'd entrusted him with honest emotion about this woman. It was up to him, at the very least, to act honorably in the situation. He'd been thinking like a certifiable jerk!

Disconcerted at this unexpected reversal, he left the bunkhouse and took a quick walk to the elephant area, more to prepare himself than anything else. Three possibilities were open: he could conduct himself with care for the next two days and enjoy every instant with her, but allow absolutely no compromise —and keep his sexual fantasies in check at all times; he could tell her, and Andy, what had been happening to him and see where it went from there; or, the simplest solution of all . . . get the hell out of both their lives as soon as possible. Which was a waste of time to consider because he knew he wouldn't do it.

He closed Charlayne's passenger door, then rounded the back of the station wagon to slide in behind Joseph. Once again he was aware of her fragrance. Her arm slid bare of her shawl for a moment as she settled herself for the ride, and he studied her profile. There was no question in his mind. Nothing in her features, her demeanor, her movements—nothing—reminded him of Natalie.

She was wearing the blue blouse from the night in Jaipur tucked into a long, loose denim skirt and belted with the same strands of amber beads. He rigidly held his thoughts well away from the cream and rust and rose of her and concentrated on the slight sunburn on her face and forearms from her outing this afternoon. Darkened lashes, he noted. Carefully applied lipstick. A hint of blush on her cheeks, as well. It was more makeup than she'd worn in the past and enhanced her looks, but not remotely suggestive of the woman he'd married.

Their conversation during the drive was light, mostly his comments on Joseph's excellent command of English and her questions about his pregnant wife and extended family living near the famous resort; a graduate student in the field of landscape ecology, Joseph had hopes of being able to salvage the park's land from the encroaching demands of his countrymen.

Ahead of them a troop of twenty or so monkeys was

crossing the road with slender tails curled high in question marks.

Charlayne reached for her notepad. "Langurs, aren't they?"

Joseph nodded and slowed the car to a crawl as Jordan readied his camera, but the approach of the station wagon sent the animals skittering into the nearby forest. Gray-white, spider-limbed, they sped through the waiting trees; saucy juveniles, grizzled ancients, and mothers entwined with newborns disappeared from one limb to appear on another with the elegant grace of their species, providing mere humans with a lofty quicksilver ballet.

Charlayne got out to stand next to him beside the car, transfixed at the sheer beauty of the sight. "Truly free," she said to him earnestly. "I can't imagine what that's like."

"Neither can I," he responded, aware more than ever of the constraints his brother's interest in this woman had placed upon him.

Under the luminous sky, her brown eyes exposed innocence and emotion for the world to see, and he watched her search the trees for one last glimpse of the amazing creatures. Then she looked at him and smiled. At that moment he snapped probably the best picture he'd ever take of her. He knew he'd been right, that he could never compromise her for his own needs, but he had another forty-eight hours to enjoy her presence, and he intended to make every instant count.

Joseph started the car as they got in. "There's an observation tower nearby," he said. "It should be an unusually good sunset tonight. Do you wish to see it?"

She glanced at Jordan for agreement, and he would have granted her anything. "We'd love to."

A few minutes later the station wagon glided onto a faint path that led into riverine forest; Joseph turned off the motor and allowed the car to coast to a halt near a tall woodframe structure at the edge of a large natural meadow. Cautioning them to silence, he began the climb to the top.

Jordan waited for Charlayne to transform her full skirt into makeshift pantaloons before she followed Joseph up the ladder; when he joined them on the platform, he was spellbound at the view until she gently tugged at his sleeve and pointed to a small herd of spotted deer cautiously entering the near corner of the open grassland. As they watched, the does began to graze while the bucks remained nervously on the alert.

High-stepping out of the trees to join them was a magnificent pair of borang, resembling American elk. The borang quickly trotted into the distance to become little more than putty-brown smudges, blending with the grass and the chalky gray-green dusk of the jungle; the distant tree line dissolved into layers of blue-gray foothills under a mass of slate mountains, their tops glistening with pristine snow. But crowning it all was the sweep of the mighty Himalayas forming a majestic border with Tibet; snow-laden crags were tinted in blue-purples, mauves, and mystical lavenders, but their peaks were topped with a golden-rose wash from the setting sun.

He tried to capture the magnificent scape with his camera, but gave it up after a moment, satisfied merely to watch and enjoy the hush, celebrate the shift and ebb of living, vibrant colors. When the sun's rim disappeared, regal hues of the snowy pinnacles began to fade into afterglow and the temperature dropped like a stone. Without her shawl, Charlayne's linen blouse was little protection from the chill. Jordan quickly pulled off his jacket to drape it around her body, carefully smoothing the fabric across her shoulders. She accepted his gesture with an absorbed nod, unable to pull her gaze from the dying fire on the mountains.

When Joseph moved to the ladder to begin his descent, they were discovered and the air was filled with the haphazard pounding of hooves as the deer darted for cover. The borang melted away as well, silent as ghosts. Joseph continued his way down and Charlayne was alone with Jordan on the platform.

He'd been rivetingly silent during the drive, speaking mostly to Joseph, and she'd been going quietly crazy, worried that she would have no chance for privacy at the hotel, none on the return trip; tomorrow was the rhino hunt, and who knew if she'd have another chance before he left? It might well be now or never to have her say.

She paused at the head of the ladder, deliberately blocking his way as she caught up her skirt, and launched into apology before she lost her courage. "I've been wanting to talk to you about what happened." Embarrassed, she spoke as low as possible so Joseph wouldn't overhear, and kept her eyes on the hem of her skirt, getting it tucked just right into her waistband. "To try to clear things up, if I can. About midnight, I mean. I hope you didn't misunderstand when I kiss—uh, I wasn't trying to . . ."

When she looked up, he had a strange expression on his face and everything she'd planned to say about kissing him went racing out of her head. Unnerved, she began to ramble. "I don't want you to think I was . . . because really it was nothing more than, uh . . ." His silent gaze became more and more disconcerting. Time was speeding by and she could see in his face that she wasn't making herself clear, so she abruptly changed course to tackle the more embarrassing event with Mitch. "And as far as the other, in my room last night, I mean, I don't want you to leave with an idea that I normally act like that when I see—"

Unwilling to embarrass either of them by being specific, she found herself mired in euphemisms. "I think my reaction to his—your—everything was due to being very tired, actually, because it's been a very strenuous couple of days and I've never done anything so out of character in my life. It didn't mean anything, except . . . I was . . . "

"I understand," he said quietly. "It's not a problem." His expression was kind as he swung onto the ladder. "It wasn't my normal behavior either."

At the base of the tower, Joseph was looking up at them, waiting. She watched Jordan start down the ladder and realized she hadn't begun to make her apology understood. If anything, she'd botched matters further. Somehow she would have to fix it. She made one last try. "This *has* been a wonderful trip."

He paused to look up at her, his manner solemn, and she spoke hurriedly, before she thought. "You know what's best? Being able to share it with someone I like." She gestured toward the range of mountains behind him, cold and austere, stately in the growing twilight. "I'll always know how they looked, but whenever I think of this night . . . I'll know you were here, and it'll help me remember how it felt to be in this place. It's the same with the Taj Mahal. It was shared. I wasn't alone."

He was watching her face, his blue eyes deepened to a rich violet-black in the dimming light, and he grinned at her at last, breaking the impasse between them. "That's exactly what's best about it."

Jordan climbed carefully to the ground and stood by to help her down the last few steps; if he'd understood her intentions just now, she was telling him that she genuinely considered them to be friends, but not to assume anything more just because she'd kissed him. Still, there was light in his body from her admissions, and he knew he'd chosen his first option. He'd spend the next two days sharing everything he could with her, enjoy the pleasure of her company and learn to feel again, but he'd stay true to his word to his brother and he wouldn't compromise her in any way.

But as he looked up to monitor her progress toward him on the ladder, watched the smooth roll and sway of her hips, assessed the curve in the small of her back, his vow not to fantasize vanished under the heated pressure of blood. Need rose from his chest, blathered his head, and sirened his ears as a roaring heartbeat; he wanted to kiss her again. She would be perfect wrapped in his arms, and he wanted to put himself through her body to the other side. Own every inch of her. Find someplace and . . .

He forced himself to bring the rise of emotion to a halt and reined in his feelings. No compromise. He'd sworn it.

A small cough brought him back. Joseph, who had moved a discreet distance away, was studiously examining the sky. "There will be a storm soon. Clouds will cover the mountains tomorrow," he said quietly. "This time of year we don't see the peaks for days at a time." He looked around at the lowering night and smiled in innocent collusion. "It must be something in the air."

No compromise.

Somewhere, Jordan heard Joseph's voice; somewhere on some ordinary little side street in his thinking that didn't relate to the present. Charlayne returned his jacket, and he seated her on the passenger side of the station wagon, helped her pull the light shawl around her shoulders, vaguely aware of little else. He slipped on his jacket, absorbing her heat and her scent; he got himself into the backseat by some means or other that had no bearing in reality. The two feet of space between them, from where he ended and she began, was all he could think about.

16

Two women in his life . . .

They arrived at the lodge and made arrangements to meet Joseph promptly at nine o'clock for the return trip. Charlayne watched the station wagon swerve around the hotel driveway and disappear into full darkness. When she and Jordan entered the lodge's dining room, the tables were crowded with tourists; she stood by while he made reservations for dinner. Unlikely she'd be able to resurrect any kind of conversation about last evening in this room.

It would be a few minutes' wait for seating, so they went to the bar. Heartened that it was relatively empty, she chose a booth while he placed their drink order with one eye on his watch.

"I'm going to try to catch Andy," he said. "See where he wants to meet on Saturday. Will you be OK for a few minutes?"

She managed a nod. "Tell him I said hello."

He disappeared and Charlayne's hopes began to deflate. He was still leaving. For a while she'd had the sense that something had changed. Since they'd left the tower, his behavior had seemed much warmer. Maybe bumbling through that absurd apology had helped after all, but she longed for a glimpse of the man who'd shared his soul in the firelight.

Their beers arrived and she studied the thin amber liquid. She'd allowed herself to hope that he'd decide to stay on. That their friendship might grow into something more. But forty-eight hours from now he planned to be on a plane out of her life.

Jordan pushed a multitude of coins into the phone until an operator came on to place the call to India. Six long rings finally produced Andy's frustrated voice. "Yeah, what is it?"

His decision made, Jordan steeled himself to go forward. "Happy New Year to you, too, younger brother."

"Jordy! Damn it, man, I was halfway out the door! How come you're calling? Is anything wrong?"

"Things are fine. Great, actually. I'm at Tiger Tops. Uh . . . Charlayne and I are about to have dinner."

There was a pause. "You're doing what? I couldn't hear you."

Jordan heard a banging in his ear. "Andy? Can you—"

His brother came back on. "That's better. So, all *right!* It's been thirty-six hours. What do you have to report? Is she terrific or what?"

Taken off stride at Andy's unexpected opening, Jordan tried to regroup. "She's terrific, all right."

"I told *you* she was terrific." Andrew seemed impatient, almost curt. "Tell me something I *don't* know. And make it fast, I gotta get out of here. Are you spending a lot of time with her?"

"Actually, yes. You were right, she's very special and . . ." *I've already kissed her.* There was no way around it, he had to be honest with his brother. He took a deep breath. "Listen, Andy, something very odd has happened between us and—"

Andy wasn't listening. "She's not still hung up with that doctor, is she? I don't want to hear she's carrying a torch."

Jordan hesitated. Andy was entirely too intense; he'd passed infatuation and was well into being possessive. "Not that I can see," he answered carefully. Thoughts of leveling with his brother began to recede. What could Andy say? *It doesn't matter that I care about her? Go ahead, cut me out and forget I saw her first?* Not with their history.

"She's got a great sense of humor and I like her a lot, kid. If I were you, I'd get my ass up here and make my pitch," he said doggedly.

"That's it?" Andy's voice thundered at him. "What the hell have you been doing? I'd know her passport number by now."

"We've been busy, Andy." Stalling for time to think, Jordan filled him in on their tracking activities. "You haven't lived until you've spent a couple hours following an elephant's ass through tall grass." He liberally borrowed from Charlayne's more irreverent observations. "We laughed so hard we were crying." His brother's corresponding laughter rang through the phone as he finished. "We're going on an honest-to-God rhino hunt tomorrow." Jordan found himself bragging like an excited adolescent.

"That lets me off the hook for sandbagging you into this. By the way, how are you handling the water?"

"It's been a little tough," he admitted, "but I'm getting through it. Better than I expected, actually. I talked to the elephant keeper this morning and he's promised his guys will keep me out of the deep end of things."

"So, where is she now? You didn't lose her somewhere, did you?"

Of course Andy would want to speak to her. Jordan winced as he realized that he hadn't given a thought to having Charlayne share the call. "We're about to have dinner, actually. Hell, she's right down the hall, let me get her. . . ."

More banging. "Damn these phones anyhow. Can you hear me?"

"Yes!" he shouted.

"Dinner, huh? Now *that's* more like it! So, is she wearing that great pink lipstick?"

"Coral."

"OK, coral. She looks gorgeous?"

"Yes, she does." Jordan dutifully answered his brother's rapid-fire questions with as much truth as he could muster, doing his best to find a segue into getting her to the phone. Each time, Andy interrupted with a demand for further information. Finally, he tackled the subject of this weekend and found a way to include her in the plan. "Ask her to join us for the game run. I'll bring her to the phone and—"

"Obviously you didn't get my message."

"What message?"

"I thought that's why you were calling. I left word two hours ago to have someone drive up to Chitwan. I can't make it this weekend. Gotta fly a couple of guys to Delhi. Right now, I'm keeping my boss and his boss waiting, and I have *got* to go. I take it you can handle another week?"

Tell him no, Jordan pressured himself. *Another week around her is going to land you in serious trouble.* His mouth made him a liar. "Yeah, sure." If he could do two days, he rationalized selfishly, he could do ten—as long as the ground rules remained the same. Ten was better than two. Eight times better.

"OK, fine. Now don't let me down. I'll expect a full report when I get there. I haven't stopped thinking about you two for an instant."

This was crazy. What if he couldn't make ten days? "Andy, we should talk about this."

"Talk about what?"

"Damn it, man, I don't know how to say this, except . . ." He took a deep breath, then followed his brother's advice and plunged in with both feet. "I have to tell you that I'm attracted to Charlayne, too. In fact, it's very possible that I'm falling in love with her . . . in some very bizarre way that I can't explain right now."

There was a lengthy pause and then Andy's voice was swearing at him. "Goddammit! Is this happening again? Jordy, if you're there . . . Hello? *Damn* it anyway!"

The phone clattered harshly in his ear and Jordan shouted into the mouthpiece, trying to talk through banging and nonstop profanity. "Look, I didn't want this to happen. I don't even know if it's real."

There was silence at last, and then his brother's angry voice. "Jordy, if you're still there, I'll wait five minutes. Five minutes, you got it? Call me back! Otherwise, I'll be up as soon as I can!" Jordan heard faint mutterings. "Tell 'em I'll be out in five minutes. *Hello!* Christ, I don't believe it!" The phone went dead.

Jordan pushed more coins into the slot and managed to reach a helpful operator. They were reconnected within Andy's five minute deadline, but the phone rang seventeen times before Jordan asked her to ring again to make sure they hadn't reached a wrong number. No answer. Upset, he gave it up and returned to the bar. Charlayne had sipped her beer halfway down.

"Andy sends his regards." He slipped into his side of the booth and tried to cover his anxiety. His brother could be leaping to all sorts of conclusions about now, none of them good. "He's looking forward to seeing you. Says he hasn't stopped thinking about you."

She laughed. "Let me guess. 'Remind her she owes me a photographer'?"

"No, he missed that one." Jordan watched her carefully as he delivered the change in plan. "He has to fly to New Delhi over the weekend. Won't be able to pick me up till he gets back."

"If that means you're staying on," she said brightly, "I can manage to keep you busy."

"Only if you want me. I can arrange transportation to Kathmandu. Get home from there."

"Oh, I want you." She looked at him, blushing. "Of course I want you to stay on, are you serious? It's just that this is unexpected. However, I certainly plan to take advantage of it."

His guilt and his temperature each shot up ten degrees. "Looks like I'm all yours." His vow not to compromise was already getting hard to remember.

Until he could talk to Andy, there was no possibility of straightening things out, so he salved his conscience over dinner by keeping his word to his brother and getting to know her. He'd have a "full report" if it killed him.

Conversation began to flow between them, light as smoke; by unspoken mutual decision, they avoided discussion of their former spouses, and spoke instead about everything and nothing. Her decision to be a writer, the joy of being published, things they loved about California. He carefully kept Andy's name in the conversation as much as possible while they compared their experiences of growing up the eldest child, dumb foods to eat with peanut butter—Andy won with kiwi and pine nuts—learning to drive, worst hangover. Foods she loved; things she hated.

All the while, her eyes occasionally met his in open estimation, and he tried to evaluate himself from her point of view, found a new course of energy pulsing through his chest in acknowledgment that her opinion mattered very much indeed.

Two hours flew by. Charlayne saw the waiter approach with their check and glanced at her watch in surprise. "Oh, boy. I almost forgot my family."

"I'll take care of this while you make your call, and meet you in the bar." He escorted her to the phone booth and she felt his shoulder brush lightly against her own as he helped her count out the necessary number of coins; as soon as the overseas operator came on the line, he withdrew. She placed the call collect and reflected on their dinner together as she waited for the connection.

His penchant for staring into her eyes had paved the way to unlocked secrets, an unorthodox quickening of her inner responses, an exchange of confidences, personal and revealing. It seemed easy to tell him silly things she'd never shared with another living soul.

All the signs of falling in love. If the interest he'd shown was genuine and she allowed herself to get involved, then what? She'd been so sure that nothing of a personal nature could possibly come of this trip that she hadn't even considered birth control. Not that it had ever been necessary. She'd tried for two years to become pregnant to please Mark, without success—in either department apparently.

Maybe Sondra was pleasing him; she'd certainly provided the child Mark had been so determined to have.

The call was accepted and a male voice yanked her attention through the line to San Francisco. "Hello, Charlie. How're things in the jungle?"

It was the last voice she expected to hear. "Mark?"

"Your loving ex. Thought about you over Christmas." His voice dropped an insinuating degree. "You miss me?"

She ignored him. "It's seven A.M. there. Why are you answering the phone?"

"Your sister and I spent New Year's with your folks."

There'd been an abrupt change to brother-in-law mode. Someone must have come into the room. Charlayne was suspicious; New Year's was always a heavy drinking night for Mark. "And you're up at this hour?"

"Oh, we had what you'd call a double celebration. Sondra couldn't drink this year, so we're all up early to go to breakfast. Hold on, here's Mother Delamere."

"Charlayne?" Her mother's voice held its usual accusatory edge. "Why are you calling? You said you couldn't phone from the park."

Her father's voice came onto an extension. "How are you, sweetheart? Happy New Year."

"Happy New Year, too," she responded blankly, still assimilating Mark's comments. "I'm at Tiger Tops. It's near the park and I had a chance to call, so—"

"Well, it's good you did," her mother broke in. "We have wonderful news. Your sister's pregnant and it's going to be another boy!"

Charlayne switched to automatic pilot, buying time to deal with the dull weight lodging itself inside her stomach. "That's great. Tell her that I said congratulations."

"She's having a bit of morning sickness, ah, but didn't we all?" prattled her mother.

Charlayne couldn't help it, it just came out. "No, Mother, we haven't all been pregnant."

"Well, it's no picnic, I can assure you. I was sick with both of you for weeks. Wasn't I, dear?"

"Yes, you were." Her father was his usual tolerant self. Suddenly she missed them terribly.

"I'm just calling to let you know everything's ten times better than I'd hoped," Charlayne inserted quickly, "and if there's an emergency, call this hotel and they can send someone with a message." She gave them the number on the phone. "I'm only an hour's drive away."

"Mark and Sondra are giving up their apartment," her mother announced happily. "They're going to be here until the baby comes."

"They're moving in with you?"

"Well, she's certainly not strong enough to handle another miscarriage, and her doctor says—"

Shock seeped through Charlayne's chest. "Sondra had a miscarriage? I didn't know that."

"She says she's had two in the past eight months, which is entirely too many. I'm going to insist that she see Dr. Leonard. I don't trust these clinics. It's not something she wanted anyone to know, apparently. Anyway, she's giving up her job and they'll be living with us."

Startled at this avalanche of information, Charlayne had to scramble for something to say to avoid making a pointed comment. Where was Mark "I Swear I'll Repay Every Dime" Hunter in all this? Another child was an expensive proposition. It didn't look like the Thanksgiving sale of his painting had gone through after all. "Another boy. Well, you two have been wanting more grandchildren."

"We're delighted, naturally. All she has to do is make it through the next two days and she'll start her second trimester."

"How's your trip?" her father broke in.

Charlayne gave them a brief description of tracking the sloth bears and the night run. "We're going on a rhino hunt tomorrow," she said vaguely.

"Good lord, I'm hanging up." Her mother's insistent voice brought Charlayne's attention back to the conversation. "With your sister being pregnant, I don't suppose you'll be willing to come home sooner?"

It was hopeless to remind her mother that writing was a job and that she was working. "I'll be home in three weeks."

Her mother left the line and her father's voice perked up with interest. "It sounds like you're having quite an adventure, sweetheart. Did you manage to find a photographer?"

"I've found someone who's working on a week-to-week basis." She fought an urge to build any hope in the Jordan Kosterin department by admitting her feelings to her father. "When's Sondra moving in?"

"Gave up their apartment over Christmas." Her father's enthusiasm waned. "Have most of their things stored in the garage. They've taken over your old room, and Ryan's in the guest room. Your mother's got all kinds of plans for turning Sondra's room into a nursery."

"I'll bet she does. It must be great having your grandchild full-time."

His joy in Ryan was evident, and she allowed him a full two minutes of bragging before ending the conversation. "I love you. I'll see you soon."

She hung up the phone, troubled. Sondra's having been pregnant, twice, without her knowledge grated on her conscience, and her sister's strained face at Thanksgiving took on a totally new significance. But why had Sondra waited until she was out of the country to make her pregnancy public? Their parents were rabid for another grandchild, and terrified that her father would die before Ryan was grown. Why hadn't Sondra paraded it down Main Street? She'd hate having a huge belly and swollen ankles, but it had to be more than that. If Sondra had been having miscarriages, maybe she wanted to be sure before flaunting it.

Jordan was waiting in the bar, and she was aware of his questioning glance.

"My sister's pregnant." She hadn't intended to say anything, but suddenly it hit her, hard, that if Sondra was nearly three months along, she'd have been pregnant at Thanksgiving. And Mark would have known. She knew from personal experience that Mark kept a mental menstrual chart, and if Sondra was two days late, Mark would *definitely* have known about it. The bastard. She got angry.

"What's wrong?"

For the first time that evening, the conversation moved into a personal arena, fraught with emotion. She told him about Sondra and Mark moving in with her parents, the revelation of her sister's miscarriages; then everything surfaced about her own marriage to Mark and his affair with Sondra, and of her humiliation at the manner in which things had been forced into the open. "If she hadn't gotten pregnant, they'd still be lying to me, I suppose. I don't know. And now she's pregnant again and it feels like it's all—"

"Repeating itself."

"That, and the fact that six weeks ago my ex-husband made a pass at me knowing that my sister was expecting his child! Now he's sleeping in my room—oh, God, in my bed!" Her eyes filled with tears and she turned away, upset.

"I've tried to accept what happened, I really have, and I'm glad Ryan has a father, even if it has to be him. It's the lies I can't stand. I'm tired of being forced to pretend there's nothing wrong in front of a sweet little boy. It makes me a liar by default, and I have to be dishonest to people I love. I hate deceit! I hate it!" Her shoulders shook with the depth of her anger, and tears slid down her cheeks. "It's so unfair, and he just did it again!"

"Did what?"

"Came on to me over the phone." She swiped at her tears, furious. "He does it all the time. Every time her back is turned, and I despise him for it. He uses me to keep up this private little fantasy that he still has two women in his life. It's not fair. . . ."

Jordan started. *Two women in his life.* The words scalded their way inward to lay open his own guilt and deception. Charlayne's rage and loathing sealed his decision. Resolutions not to compromise ought to be a hell of a lot easier now. But at the moment, with her weeping and him ready to tear the sleazy, two-timing bastard's head off, he wasn't so sure.

"You're right. It's unfair and no one should have to deal with that," he said with difficulty, determined to rid himself of his own dual preoccupation.

"And you know what's really crazy?" She laughed through her tears at him, and began to blot her face with a tissue. "I miss my sister. As mixed-up and angry as she is, I wish we could just forget everything and be family again. I love Ryan and all I want to do is spoil him and hug him and be his dotty old aunt. I'll probably never have children—" Her voice halted and she stared at him, eyes brightened with the intensity of her feelings. "You know what I wish? I wish we'd both had a family. You'd have something of Natalie and—"

His blood drained and he couldn't prevent it from showing in his face; his sudden emotion stopped her.

"Oh, God, no chemotherapy." She gripped his fingers and closed her eyes. "You lost them both. Oh, Jordan, I'm so sorry."

They sat in mutual, silent misery.

Finally she released his hand and looked up at him, tears very near the surface. "Does it ever turn out the way you want?"

"It did for a while. Then she died." It occurred to him from a far place that, removed from this woman's touch, his fingers were suddenly quite naked. He glanced at his watch. "Joseph should be here any minute."

They shared a long, quiet ride back to Chitwan.

17

Adventure of the first order . . .

It was barely daylight, but adventure of the first order was due today and Charlayne got briskly out of her bunk; a sleepy Sailor Green bobbed his head in consternation as she tiptoed quietly about her room. Last night seemed a hundred years ago. Knowing the basis for the pain etched in Jordan's face seemed to lighten her own troubled history. To lose a child . . . and its mother. Hideous.

Next door, he and Mitch began to stir before she'd finished getting dressed, and they joined her as she was heading for the kitchen. The three of them gulped down boiled coffee and added their excitement to the cook's generally disorganized breakfast.

Everyone was abuzz with anticipation over the hunt, then it was suddenly time, and they piled into the camp station wagon with Professor Jamieson driving; his wife and Charlayne and Sunita were stuffed into the front seat, Jordan, Mitch, a man introduced as a veterinarian, plus two other staff members were scrunched together in the back. Next to Jordan, the veterinarian gripped a small rifle, its butt between his feet and the barrel carefully aimed at the car's ceiling; a box of tranquilizer darts to immobilize the rhinoceros calf for capture was entrusted to Mitch.

They left the gravel road to drive cross-country through a farming community for a mile or so, then veered toward the jungle once again; after sifting their way through droves of local villagers and children who'd come to be a part of the event, Professor Jamieson halted the station wagon in a field at the edge of the park. Charlayne got out of the car a few yards from a loose congregation of the king's elephants, manned by soldiers in khaki uniforms.

Jamieson indicated the head elephant, a tusker with chalked pink-and-green symbols high on its haunches. Carrying ivory nearly four feet in length, it was clearly in charge. "Our people should be here," fussed the professor.

Jordan pointed out Joh and Khalli, and moved away to get a shot of their group emerging from the forest to join the elephant troops. Charlayne saw Jimi up on Mala, plus Joseph and two drivers she didn't know riding the other three.

In a flurry of kneeling and rising elephants, she was seated behind a driver introduced to her as Madhav on a young elephant she'd never ridden; Mitch boarded as the second rider. Jordan had been paired with Jimi on Mala, and the veterinarian with his dart gun stood on Khalli's rump behind Joh and Professor Jamieson. Twenty-five orderly trunk-to-tail elephants formed a double row in the field and filed into the scrub. A quarter mile into the jungle they split off into a right and left pincer configuration ranging across an area the size of a soccer field. Charlayne's elephant was directed right, Jordan's left.

"How are we going to find it?" she asked Madhav dubiously. Surely they weren't going to walk the elephants through the bush until they scared up a calf the right age. The driver shook his head, indicating he did not speak English.

Mitch pointed to soldiers standing on a pair of stationary elephants barely visible amid the trees and brush ahead of them. "They've been watching the mother and calf all night and are monitoring their position."

Charlayne watched the lead elephants of each line meet near the guardian soldiers, and one by one drivers wheeled their animals into side-by-side positions. Madhav did the same, and she was amazed at their precision in the midst of what appeared at first to be little better than chaos. Behind them the last half-dozen elephants on both sides quickly moved to close the gap, and formed a living enclosure of gray hides.

The large circle began an inexorable drift toward the perimeter of the park, forcing a rhino mother and calf along inside. Deer skittered by, and wild pigs, scooting erratically through the underbrush; peacocks and birds of every size and color fluttered out of the path of oncoming elephants. As they approached the edge of the park, smaller elephants began to drop out on either side, contracting the circle; only the oldest and largest animals were on the front line as the frantic rhino and her bleating calf, outgunned and aware of the unusual and dangerous situation, made threatening charges this way and that, seeking escape.

Simultaneous with the sharp crack of the rifle, Charlayne saw the tusker and three others charge the mother in a wall of squalling, trumpeting force, to drive her from the circle. A dozen smaller elephants from both sides moved in to follow the path of the darted calf, while others reinforced the group holding the furious parent at bay in a slow push back toward the park's interior.

She saw Jordan's shirt and shoulders as Mala joined the circle escorting the juvenile toward the edge of the park, and was frustrated at being relegated to rear guard. "Can't we get closer?"

"It'll be going down any second," Mitch said excitedly. "Once it's sedated, they have to work very fast. I'll have him try to get you a better view." He spoke to Madhav in Nepali and they began to work their way toward the calf.

For Jordan, the coordinated efforts of man and beast had been the closest thing to an old-fashioned cattle roundup he could imagine—except that everything was oversize, pursuer and prey, and ten times more hazardous in the dense brush. He took his attention away from photographing the ground activity long enough to search for Charlayne. He'd been pleased that her elephant had been placed well back from the dangerous front line, but had gotten so absorbed in capturing the event on film that he'd momentarily lost track of her position.

Jimi had managed to keep Mala well into the circle of action for him until the juvenile had gone down; the calf was being converged upon by Jamieson and the veterinarian, and Jordan quickly took the opportunity to reload his cameras and look for Charlayne. Jimi spotted her coming toward them, and it was a great opportunity to provide her with a wide shot.

She looked vibrantly alive, ready to take on the world single-handed; her ex-husband should only see her now.

The mere thought of the asshole tightened his jaw. As he focused, the aggressive rhinoceros entered frame; snorting her way through the scrub, she violently rammed bushes and tree stumps in her fury. In a split instant the crafty animal veered away from her pursuers and lunged in Charlayne's direction; there were several villagers on foot, and Jordan yelled a warning amid shouts from other drivers. The men, whose curiosity had pulled them into the park, immediately scrambled for the safety of nearby trees; three and four in the branches, their excited cries and laughter added to the confusion.

Jordan yelled again, trying to warn Charlayne. Jimi urged Mala in her direction. Half a dozen elephants wheeled to cut off the rhino's charge, trumpeting and snorting in their pursuit, but too late. Calls to Charlayne's driver were lost in the din of crackling brush and mahouts shouting fierce commands; Jordan's heart leaped in terror at their collision course with the maddened animal.

Charlayne saw the rhino coming, chugging away like a freight train. "Mitch," she said nervously, "it's coming at us."

"Don't worry, we're fine." He spoke to the driver, and Madhav urged their young elephant forward; she fanned her ears and lowered her head in a threatening gesture, trumpeting at the charging rhino. The ferocity of the encounter was primal, and at the very last second the elephant gave ground, crunched her ribs against a sal tree as she sidestepped the rhino's charge, leaving just enough room to allow the enraged attacker to glance off her shoulder.

Charlayne nearly lost her seat from the shuddering impact as the rhinoceros scraped its way down the elephant's hide. More from luck, she managed to jerk her foot aside to keep it from being crushed between the two animals.

Madhav had nearly been unseated as well; Mitch had paled, and Charlayne felt her heart boiling out of control in her chest at their close encounter with disaster. She could have been knocked to the ground and trampled. Her leg could have been mangled against the tree. Had it gone one second wrong, she knew she might be writhing in agony at this very moment, on her way to a hospital, half a day from here. She tried not to shiver, but her body wouldn't come under control.

Still a few yards away, Jordan swore at her driver's actions; when the young elephant advanced toward the charging rhino, he'd been forced to watch in horror as the two beasts collided with a resounding whump, nearly pitching Charlayne from her saddle. As the rhinoceros was driven away from the area, they were able to approach the shaken elephant; Jimi shouted to the driver and there was a brief exchange.

"What happened?" Jordan demanded furiously.

Jimi shrugged. "Was foolish," he said tersely. "The driver was asked to challenge the mother rhino."

"*What!*" Jordan's fear went to outrage. Challenge a crazed animal? She could have been killed! It had to be Mitch. A local man wouldn't risk answering to a woman in front of his superiors, even if she'd been stupid enough to request such a thing. And Charlayne was anything but stupid. He saw she was pallid, and he fought the urge to call Mitch out and thrash the idiot on the spot; he'd cheerfully kick the driver's ass as well.

"Were you hurt?" he yelled.

She nodded unsteadily, then shook her head, confused and shocky. "I don't think so. . . ." He noticed blood on her fingers at the same time she saw it. "Scraped my hand. Scared to death." She was hyperventilating and her arms were visibly trembling.

He stared Mitch down, his vision blackened with rage. But this wasn't the time—or place. Rationally, he knew that causing a scene in the middle of the hunt could serve no purpose. Of immediate importance was making sure Charlayne was all right.

Mitch looked away first, then spoke to the driver. Before he and Jimi could come alongside, her elephant limped past them toward the immobilized calf. Jimi swiveled Mala in pursuit, and Jordan was still fuming when they caught up to the animal. Charlayne's driver was deep in conversation with Joh, whose face was fixed in a scowl as he examined the injured elephant.

"She should not carry weight," Joh pronounced, and motioned to Jimi, who moved Mala in closer.

With Jordan's help, a still-wobbly Charlayne managed to crawl onto Mala's back behind him; her arms immediately snaked around his waist for security and she trembled against his body as she held herself close. He examined her hand: a broken nail had been torn to the quick on her little finger and was bleeding; her third finger had shallow lacerations and was bleeding also.

"I'm not about to leave, so don't tell me anything bad," she said, her voice quivering only slightly. "Delameres are a sturdy lot. And I have a first aid kit in my room."

"Delamere?"

"That's my maiden name."

He wrapped her fingers in a piece of linen from his camera case. "It's going to hurt like hell, but I don't think there's anything broken." Relief began to seep into his chest.

"Thank you, Doctor. What are they doing? Are we missing anything?"

He laughed at her gumption. "I take it you want pictures instead of first aid."

"All you can get. I don't plan to be a part of something like this again, so if you don't mind . . ."

Jimi moved Mala forward, and Jordan returned his energy toward recording the men's straining efforts to secure the calf; its ears had been stuffed with cotton and its body was covered with a wet blanket to protect it from the sun, now high in the morning sky. Mitch had joined a dozen villagers who were rolling the animal, inert as stone and nearly as heavy, onto a canvas tarpaulin. It took all their efforts to heave the calf onto the bed of a small flatbed trailer attached to a modern tractor.

Jordan felt a return of irritation at the sight of the man, but Charlayne was slowly relaxing her hold around his middle and taking a firm grip on his waist with her good hand; his happiness that she felt safe momentarily overrode his rancor. When the tractor began its slow pull out of the area, he got some great shots of the exuberant elephant troops urging their excited mounts into an impromptu race, literally hightailing the massive animals toward the border of the park while behind him, Charlayne joined the villagers in cheering them on.

By the time they'd dismounted and had walked to the waiting station wagon, she seemed fully recovered and was gabbling with excitement about everything that had happened, making notes with a pen held carefully between the thumb and forefinger of her injured hand. He left it wrapped until they'd escorted the tractor to park headquarters. Then, in the camp's kitchen, she took some aspirin while Jordan doused her bandages in alcohol.

She was determined not to miss the juvenile's recovery and insisted on deferring further treatment until after the calf was revived; he asked the cook to put water on to boil. By the time they arrived at the pit, the trailer had been backed into position and Jordan was able to get coverage of the groggy calf, still on the canvas, being slid down wide wooden planks that served as a makeshift ramp.

The veterinarian cautiously climbed into the pit to inject an antidote. Holding his thumb against a blood vessel in the calf's ear, he administered the shot, then speedily scrambled out again. With good reason. Twenty-five seconds later the juvenile rhino was on its feet and ready to roll; shaky and disoriented, frightened by the surrounding humans to be sure, but fully prepared to do damage.

Convinced the animal hadn't been physically harmed, Charlayne relaxed, but her face was drawn, and Jordan realized she was probably in a good deal of pain. "The water should have boiled by now. We'll wash your hand properly and make sure there's no infection."

They returned to the kitchen and he removed the bandage from her swollen fingers; he could tell from the cautious manner in which she extended her hand that in spite of the aspirin, it had begun to ache pretty good. Removing the soaked linen caused her lacerations to start bleeding again, and he could see now that there were small splinters from the wooden saddle driven into her flesh. Impatient for the water to cool sufficiently, he trimmed her broken nail and poured on more alcohol, hurting for her as she winced.

"I'm sorry." He examined the splinters. "This isn't good. Is there a needle in your first aid kit?"

She nodded. "In my duffel."

Sunita ran for the kit, and the cook produced a small pair of tweezers. Jordan worked the larger slivers of wood out of the pads of her fingers as gently as he could, alternating with liberal doses of the stinging alcohol, and when the little girl returned with the kit, he probed with a needle to coax the last of the broken wood from her flesh. "I'm sorry, I know this hurts."

She nodded tearfully, her jaws clenched in acceptance. When he finished, she was pale with pain, and quivering. He carefully soaped her hand then plunged it with his own into the near-scalding water; when he'd had all the heat he thought she could stand, he applied antibacterial ointments and wrapped her fingers in fresh bandages.

He gave her more aspirin for pain before walking her to the bunkhouse, eased her into her bunk, and began to unlace her boots.

"You don't have to do that," she said woozily. "I'm getting good at sleeping with my boots on."

"You'll rest better."

She looked up at him tiredly, the aspirin adding to her drowsiness. "I know this will be a terrific story someday," she confessed, "but that rhino scared the hell out of me."

"It should have," he said tersely.

"Will you see if the elephant's OK?"

He sat on the opposite bunk. "I'll check on her as soon as you go to sleep."

She nodded and closed her eyes. After a short time, she rolled onto her side and he reached under the mosquito netting to pull up her blanket. He waited until he was sure she was genuinely sleeping, then left her room and went looking for Mitch Baltine.

18

"Sorry doesn't cut it . . . "

Jordan stalked the compound from the bunkhouse to the elephant sheds. Joh assured him that Charlayne's elephant hadn't sustained serious harm but would not work until it was fully recovered. From there he went to the capture pit, asking for Mitch. Eventually he spotted him leaving Jamieson's office and followed him to the meeting room. When he stepped inside, Mitch was defiant. "I suppose you think it's your turn. Have a few comments you want to add, do you?"

It was the wrong approach and his jaws tightened in an effort to keep it civil. "I'd like to know what happened out there."

"I've had enough of this." Mitch tried to shoulder his way out the door, and Jordan moved to block his exit.

— 193 —

"I want an answer."

"I don't answer to you."

Jordan ran out of restraint. "You do today!"

Mitch shrugged sulkily, unwilling to push it further. "We made a mistake, that's all. The elephant balked and things got out of hand."

Jordan wasn't satisfied. "That's not the way I heard it."

"Just what the hell does that mean?"

Not the day to mess with me, pal. "It means you were careless, and people got hurt."

"It was an accident," Mitch insisted. "She wanted—"

"Correction. You caused it to happen and it was stupid."

"Says who?"

Jordan held his temper by the thinnest of margins. "Says your driver if I decide to ask him."

Mitch paused warily. "OK, lawyer, I'm sorry. Is that what you want to hear?"

"Sorry doesn't cut it. You damned near killed her."

"Who the hell are you to give me grief about this? It's nobody's fault and no one got hurt except an elephant!"

"And Charlayne."

"Yeah, well, I've already apologized about that, and a cut on the finger is a long way from being killed—"

Jordan didn't realize he was going to hit him. Mitch was looking up at him from the floor with astonished outrage in his face when he became aware of his stinging knuckles; pain worked its way up his wrist as he grabbed Mitch by the shirt and yanked him to his feet. "No thanks to you, she wasn't killed! Do you know what happens when people die, Mitch? *Do* you? They don't come back—*ever!*" He shook the man like a giant doll. "You don't see them, or hear them, or have them in your life!" he screamed, nearly out of control. "And you *know* you're responsible every day you breathe!"

Mitch fought to free himself and Jordan pushed him away, unnerved at the depth of his own rage. "You don't take stupid chances."

Mitch gingerly rubbed his cheek. "Hey, nothing happened! Nobody got really hurt. So the elephant's banged up a little. I've already apologized to Jamieson and I'm sorry about Charlayne. So what else do you want?"

"I want you to be careful." It was a warning. "No more macho routines."

Mitch jerked his shirt into place. "So I'll be more careful. Whatever." He retreated to the other side of the room, his temper rising. "What is it with you? How'd I step on your tail?" Agitated, he began to pace back and forth. "She wasn't the only one, you know. I was out there, too. But it seems you're all puffed up about Charlayne." He stopped pacing to sneer. "You and the lady writer have a thing going? Is that what this is about? You musta really been pissed when she seen me naked."

He fought the urge to punch the redhead again. "It's not like that."

"Oh, yeah, right! You didn't hit me because of what happened out there today. You had an attitude since the night I got here. Her being with me today didn't sit too well, I take it. Well, I'm not making moves in your territory, if that's your problem."

"She's anything but my territory. I've told you the problem and I'm not going to repeat it."

"Glad to hear that," Mitch said acidly. "You sure you won't mind if I take a shot at her?"

Jordan saw black. "You've made one mistake, don't make another one."

"Don't threaten me, lawyer. The only reason she's here at all is because I got her in the door, and I can make that go away in five minutes." Mitch moved toward the door.

That the miserable coward would try to intimidate him by compromising Charlayne sent rage boiling up again and Jordan knew he had to hold on to his fury or take it the full ten rounds. "You heard me."

Mitch slammed his way out of the room.

Jordan waited an hour then pushed Charlayne's door open a crack to make sure she was still sleeping. Her poor bandaged hand was curled under her chin, which set off his anger once again. He stomped to the meeting room for lunch. Mitch and his bruised face kept his distance, and his mouth closed, when the professor brought up the necessity of rearranging the camp's schedule.

"One less elephant requires us to set up a temporary base in the park. We'll locate near known fishing cat lairs, which will save hours of commuting from here. Monitoring operations will resume tomorrow night. Joh says we can use the remaining elephants to set up camp and take specimens for Mr. Baltine this evening, but they have to rest tomorrow." He looked across the room at Jordan. "We'll need to replenish our food supplies. Mr. Kosterin, in the absence of Miss Pearce, would you mind going with Jimi into the market this afternoon?"

Jordan nodded, grimly pleased to be doing something besides waiting for Charlayne to wake up—and glaring at Mitch.

By the time he'd traveled to and from the local town, and helped purchase sacks of potatoes, onions, a couple of live chickens, and dal—a bland local grain and staple of Nepali diets, eaten with rice—Jordan's mood had improved greatly, but it was still a good thing they were going to be camping out for the next few days. There was no way he could share a room with Baltine at the moment. He and Jimi delivered the supplies to the cook, then

Jordan made his way to the bunkhouse. Easing onto the porch in case she was still sleeping, he paused at her door and heard the sound of her voice, low with concern.

". . . your poor face, I didn't realize you were hurt, too."

"I think I hit a tree or something when the rhino charged us. I'm not sure."

Anger spit through Jordan's body. The lying son of a bitch!

"Your cheek looks terrible. Too bad there's no ice to put on it."

"I'm sure it's fine, but I wish you'd talk to your photographer. Jamieson thinks I'm responsible for getting you hurt this morning. I've tried to tell both of them it was the driver's idea but—"

He rapped on Charlayne's door with his bruised knuckles—glad for the painful reminder of how they'd gotten sore, and more than ready to bruise them again.

Mitch opened the door. "Hey, as I live and breathe. It's the lawyer."

"Photographer," he corrected tersely, and looked past the smug redhead to Charlayne, who was padding around the room in bare feet. "If you don't mind, we have a few things to talk over."

"I'as just helping her pack."

"That's all right, I'll take over from here." He dropped his eyes significantly to the welt on Mitch's cheek and hoped it hurt. A lot. He'd like nothing better than to work on the other side—make his two faces match—and gave Mitch a look he kept in reserve for skeazeballs and screw-the-client-for-a-buck attorneys.

"Sure thing," Mitch said carelessly. "See you tonight, Miss Char." He sauntered next door and Jordan took a moment to let the sight of her calm him down.

"How are your fingers?"

"Pretty good, actually." She stopped stuffing clothing into her duffel to demonstrate and bent her hand into a slow, careful fist. "I'm almost finished packing. I'll need help setting up the tent when we get there, but otherwise . . ."

"Think we ought to change your bandage?"

"Sunita helped me do it a little while ago, thanks. You must have done a very good job. Everything's already starting to heal."

He circled the room restlessly, aware of Mitch next door, eavesdropping, no doubt, and was sorely tempted to haul the whole incident out in the open. Make the bastard eat his lying allegations. But that might cost her Jamieson's support, and was not his decision to make. He held his tongue with difficulty.

"So, are you ready to camp out?" She had resumed packing. "Mitch said you and Jimi went into town to get supplies."

"Yeah. Stay tuned for more porridge, rice, and dal. Fried potatoes." Failing to find an excuse that would keep him in her room, allow him to touch her, or keep Mitch at bay, he gave it up. "I'll carry these out for you."

"Actually, Mitch said he'd do it."

Yeah, I'll just bet he did. Ignoring her statement, he stuck around to help her finish packing, then swiftly stacked her gear next to the porch railing, mentally defying Mitch to so much as lay a hand on it.

Charlayne tried to ignore the obvious tension between the two men, openly apparent to everyone. Both were civil, bitingly polite, and clearly ready to take each other apart. Her own loyalties were divided. Mitch was interfering with the short time she had left with Jordan before his brother arrived to spirit him away; on the other hand,

Mitch had a legitimate complaint if Jordan had unnecessarily disrupted his relationship with Professor Jamieson. Unsure how to mediate the situation without bringing the two men face-to-face, an extremely ill-advised move at the moment, she stalled for time. When the elephants returned from delivering supplies and foodstuffs to the campsite, and it was their turn to be ferried into the jungle, Professor Jamieson carefully assigned Mitch and Jordan to separate animals.

They arrived at the site in the late afternoon with no break in the standoff. Tents and equipment had been piled next to a rough lean-to constructed at the edge of a small clearing, shaded and sheltered under the umbrellas of old growth trees. The cook and his helper had a cheerful fire going, and the savory odor of cooking chicken permeated the immediate vicinity. Charlayne claimed her things, and Mitch and Jordan began setting up her tent; neither gave ground in helping her, and for a while she was concerned that the canvas might not survive their efforts.

Relieved when they finally pronounced it finished, she did her best to keep herself neutral in their war. "Thanks, guys."

If it hadn't been so annoying, it might have been funny when she realized that Mitch was determinedly pitching his tent on one side of her, and a stone-faced Jordan had begun on the other. Deciding to absent herself in the hope that they'd work it out, she walked the short length of the clearing to where Khalli and another elephant had been stationed. At the opposite end of the camp a third elephant had been leg-chained to a tree as well.

When Joseph and the professor arrived on Mala a bit later, she noticed that she, too, was positioned at the perimeter of the camp. Literally, the elephants were being placed every fifty to a hundred feet between humans and wild animals. Charlayne wasn't certain if her discovery made her feel better or worse. Still uneasy at the situation between Jordan and Mitch, she joined the professor while he outlined the evening's events.

"We'll have an early dinner, then use Mala to help stake the nets which will stay up overnight. Morning runs will begin just before daybreak. Those who work evenings won't be required to get up early. Sort out your duties to suit yourselves."

Jordan didn't leave her side during dinner and sat quietly by as she formulated a rough schedule with Mitch. "I'm not sure what I can do with just one hand."

"Jimi and I will set up the stakes," Mitch decreed. "If you could help tie nets onto them, it would go faster. When we run the nets, I'll deal with any bats. They take special handling. Don't want anyone getting bit 'ceptin' me. You can help remove birds or leaves or whatever else gets caught."

She glanced at Jordan, who seemed to approve. "You have gloves?" was his sole comment.

She nodded.

"Nets will be set up within walking distance," Mitch continued, "and I'll make rounds every hour. Nights are easiest. Only two runs. Three in the morning when the bats're on their way to their roosts."

Jordan spoke up at last. "I'll do mornings."

She saw Mitch's jaws tighten; he didn't challenge Jordan's decision, but rose to his feet and walked away.

"You want pictures this evening?" Jordan asked her quietly.

She studied his face. "What's going on with you and Mitch? He says you told the professor he was responsible for—"

"I haven't talked with Jamieson," he interrupted sternly.

"What, then?"

"Me and Batman have a failure to communicate."

"What does that mean?"

"It means he's reckless, and I don't like reckless people."

"Well, the two of you are making things very difficult for me."

"You're right, I'm sorry. I should have realized." He threw up his hands and looked her full in the face, eyes contrite. "It's gone, it's over. It never happened."

She contemplated his opened expression. "I could have gotten hurt anyway, you know. Accidents happen."

"I know. It's over, I swear it."

She saw truth in his eyes. "Thanks. I appreciate it. And to answer your question, yes, if you don't mind I'd like a few pictures of me stringing mist nets. Bats aren't my forte, and I hate what's going to happen to them, but they need to be studied, and if the only way to get accurate information on how to protect them is to—"

"That'll look great on their little headstones."

His unusual sarcasm took her off guard.

"Sorry. Bad joke." His apology was strained. "I don't like things dying either. I'll get my cameras."

True to his word, Jordan's attitude toward Mitch softened; a truce of sorts seemed to go into place between them, and she was able to relax. With the four of them working, and Mala ferrying bamboo poles across the water, it took about forty minutes to string the three nets along the wash, by which time it was dusk.

On their return trip they scanned the nets with flashlights. The wash was indeed a flyway. Mitch was able to claim four specimens while Jordan freed a small white bird that looked as if it had been spattered with black paint, and she busied herself disentangling a brilliantly feathered kingfisher. Jordan took pictures of her freeing the turquoise water bird, and they returned to camp with the mystery bird.

Charlayne carefully extracted the terrified creature from her jacket pocket, and the professor identified it as a harlequined dove; it was examined and photographed and freed as well, then it was deep dusk and she left with Mitch to check the nets again. They walked along the edge of the wash, with Jimi following on Mala. An owlet and a couple of bats were entangled in the nets; she freed the tired little night bird while Mitch and Jimi retrieved the two bats at the middle of the wash. When they'd quickly met their destiny with fatal doses of chloroform, she couldn't watch.

Most of the camp had settled in for the night by the time they returned, but Jordan was waiting outside his tent.

"Safe and sound, counselor," Mitch said bitingly.

To her relief, Jordan merely smiled. "Guess I'll get some sleep, then. I hear it's an early morning." He disappeared into his tent.

Too charged up from the evening to turn in just yet, Charlayne sat on a camp stool to enjoy the fire. Holding wild birds in her hands was exhilarating, and there was an incredible joy in examining them up close, then setting them free. Mitch sat across from her, looking at his watch from time to time. "What do you think?" he said quietly. "One more run?"

It was after nine o'clock. Tempted, she glanced at Jordan's tent. The flap was closed and he was silent. Night birds would be on the prowl. Fruit-eaters and insect hunters. Bats were creepy, gargoyle-faced, contorting creatures whose terrified squeaks twisted her innards, but who knew what other kinds of treasures might become entangled? The possibility of holding another beautiful bird was too enticing. Besides, it would be hours before he and Jordan would check in the morning, and something might get hurt in the meantime, she rationalized.

"OK, one more."

She was drowning. He strained to reach her and saw relief flicker in her eyes for an instant before he was torn away; then, as always, acquiescence—the gentle giving up of herself to the inevitable, and her lowering eyelids as she sank into dull chocolate turbulence. Out of his sight forever.

The dream since Natalie's death, which wouldn't go away.

Jordan shuddered awake, his heartbeat rapid and futile. Something was wrong. He could feel it. He became aware of the shadow of someone standing quietly in front of his tent. The shadow moved to the left; disoriented from the nightmare, he couldn't discern if it had moved to Charlayne's tent or Mitch's. Charlayne's, he decided. He listened intently to stealthy unzipping sounds. Had she been up while he'd been sleeping? Slick liquid noises he couldn't identify were followed by subtle slaps and rustlings of cloth. Light footsteps. Low murmuring voices.

Charlayne, and Mitch.

"I'll be fine." Her whispered voice held an odd inflection.

He ripped open the flap and saw the two of them next to the campfire. Bare-legged, she was bent over with one leg halfway into a pair of jeans; soaked from head to toe, he thought at first she was naked. Then he saw she was wearing a waterlogged T-shirt that barely reached her hips; thin wet panties failed to sufficiently cover her pale butt cheeks gleaming in the firelight. Facing away from her, Mitch was crouched by the fire, nervously poking wood into the embers; shirtless, beard and braid dripping water onto his chest, his pants and boots were muddied as well.

Startled by his sudden appearance, they turned in unison to look at him. He crawled out of the tent and got to his feet, blood surging in his temples; tact went out the window. "What happened?" It came out thick with suspicion, and he did not care.

Mitch took a stance and held firmly to his stick of firewood. "She fell in the water." His voice echoed in the clearing.

"Shhhh!" she hissed. Bedraggled as a drenched cat, embarrassed, she finished hobbling into the jeans before looking up at him. "I slipped on a rock and went under," she stage-whispered guiltily. "Mitch hauled me out, and it's a good thing it was shallow, 'cause I can't swim."

It was the worst thing she could have said; he lost it and went at Mitch. The son of a bitch was going to need a whole lot more than a stick to defend himself on this one. She stopped his charge by stepping between them.

"It wasn't his fault. I swear it."

Mitch hurriedly crossed to the opposite side of the fire, and Jordan followed him with a glare, then brought his eyes back to her; her long hair was plastered wetly to the crown of her head and had separated into wide strands across her brow and along her cheeks; water seeped steadily into her collar, and her T-shirt was a muddy second skin, its weight clinging to slick curves and clefts. Her nipples, puckered to rigid nubs at the centers of her breasts, were highly visible to him through the fabric. He sustained a rush that bent his will. Cream and rust . . .

He saw Mitch openly staring at her breasts and moved to shield her from the ill-mannered bastard's view. "What happened?" This time he wanted an answer.

He saw her become defensive and self-conscious; glancing down at herself, she immediately crossed her arms to hide her breasts. "I wasn't sleepy. We decided to check the nets one last time. I waded in trying to free an owl and tripped. Nearly drowned the poor thing." She followed his gaze to her bare feet. "It wasn't deep, just muddy. I washed off as much as I could in the water." She stopped, embarrassed, and made an awkward gesture toward her tent. Dripping blue jeans had been draped over the peak of the canvas; boots were upside down on two of the tent pins. Her duffel lay open at the entrance to her small tent.

Mollified for the moment, Jordan looked around the camp and saw only the three of them. Cognizance and fear burned their way to the tips of his ears. All four elephants were tethered. "You went out alone." It was an accusation.

Her attitude wavered, then she nodded, shamefaced. "Just to the first net."

Mitch chimed in. "We could see Khalli from there."

He turned a quiet burst of rage in Mitch's direction for the space of an instant. "Khalli is chained to a tree."

She went silent in the face of his anger before admitting, "You're right. I didn't think about that."

He deliberately picked up her wrist to examine her injured fingers; the bandages were sodden with mud and her watch had stopped at 9:27. His own watch read ten-fifteen. They'd been at least forty-five minutes without safe escort; he blew out his breath. If he said anything else, he'd regret it. "Better change this. Who knows what kind of bacteria's in the water. I have to get some sleep. I'm supposed to go out at dawn."

She nodded again, didn't look back as she made her way to her tent, and slipped inside without a word. He took one last look at Mitch. "You're one lucky fool," he said tersely, then retreated to his tent and crawled into his sleeping bag. Next door, Charlayne was stirring about, hopefully redressing her hand. He'd been too furious to offer to help. If anything had happened to her, hell wouldn't have stopped him from making Mitch pay in blood.

As his temper cooled, his mind distracted him from sleep by replaying the sleek perfection of her thighs and buttocks, long suspected and, as of this evening, committed to absolute fact. It was a long time before he was able to doze off, but the dream did not return.

Charlayne sat on her blanket in order to avoid wetting her sleeping bag. Awkwardly stripping off her shirt and bra, she threw the soggy clothing to the foot of the tent; her fury built. Who did Jordan Kosterin think he was? Who bloody died and proclaimed him king of the mountain? He'd interrogated her as if she were a truant six-year-old, embarrassing her in front of Mitch and any number of people they'd awakened in surrounding tents—people she would have to face in the morning—including her host. The skin on her face burned with mortification.

She found her first aid kit and proceeded to soak her fingers in alcohol and change the bandages. So she'd forgotten that Khalli had been chained. So she'd fallen in the water. Why was he so bent out of shape? It wasn't as if he'd gotten wet and muddy dragging her out of the wash. And he'd held Mitch responsible for no reason, nearly attacked him when he tried to explain. She'd started out defending her actions like a naughty teenager, and wound up explaining herself like a disobedient employee. The person she thought she'd gotten to know reasonably well in the past few days had turned into a raging, possessive tyrant, somewhere between her bossy mother and her controlling ex-husband.

Fuming, she yanked a brush through her wet hair, then pummeled her sleeping pillow with her good hand. First chance tomorrow, she had a thing or three to straighten out with Jordan Kosterin! If he was going to behave like this, he could bloody well leave tomorrow, and good riddance!

19

. . . something's come up . . .

Jordan was up before daylight waiting for Mitch to crawl out of his tent. They ran the nets on foot, with Joseph keeping watch on one of the elephants; he worked the near side of the wash, freeing entangled kingfishers and another harlequined dove while Mitch and Joseph worked the other. One additional species of bat bit the dust as Mitch's newest specimen; a dozen exhausted fortunates were released squeaking into the dawn.

There was a minimum of conversation between all parties concerned, and nothing beyond necessary questions or responses. Mitch was light on making a jerk of himself, and Jordan made no overtures as his mind combed through the obvious problem. It wasn't going to work. He couldn't handle another week of getting nuts every time Baltine bent the rules. Plus, like it or not, Mitch hadn't coerced her last night, Charlayne had made a decision to go with him; the bottom line was, if he didn't get his act together, and quickly, she'd have to find someone else to take her pictures.

Or, he'd have to make a clean slate of his feelings . . . which brought him to the bridge of straightening things out with Andy, and he was right back in the trap of his own making. Caught in a lousy circle, getting tighter, he was in a slow drift toward disaster.

It was full daylight by the time they'd finished the final run, furled Mitch's nets, and pulled the stakes. Breakfast was waiting when they arrived back at camp. Skipping the usual porridge for coffee and scorched toast, he decided not to aggravate himself with a cold-water shave, in order to concentrate on his next move. When nothing came to mind, he took it as further proof that things were getting out of hand. Charlayne was not in sight, and apparently sleeping in. Freed from the distraction of her presence, he sank onto a stool in front of the cookfire to watch her tent for signs of activity. Absently rubbing the stubble of his beard, he stared at her boots; he'd moved them close to the fire this morning and they should be dry soon. The boots and the water-logged jeans still draped over her tent were mute testimony to last night's turmoil. Like it or not, he had to make a choice where she was concerned before something came along to take it out of his hands.

Joseph joined him, squatting on his heels next to him. "I have heard of your brother's troubles." He proceeded to enjoy his porridge. "It is too bad. Anup says he loves to fly."

The young man's stilted English took a moment to assimilate, and Jordan looked around at him, confused. "I'm sorry, you said what?"

"The accident. It's a bad thing to happen."

The back of his neck began to chill. "What accident? My brother?"

Joseph's brows lifted in surprise. "Yes, Andy. Is he not your brother?"

Jordan nodded, concerned. Why hadn't Joseph mentioned it before now? "You have a message from Andy?"

Joseph shook his head. "Anup told me. Yesterday." He reacted to Jordan's confusion. "Do you not know this? I'm sorry. I thought you call your brother from Tiger Tops."

"I did. What do you mean he can't fly?" Jordan asked uneasily. "Are you sure?"

"Anup said." Joseph abandoned his porridge to frown in deliberation. "They're good friends, he should know. He said it happen a week ago."

Jordan relaxed a beat. Not possible. Obviously someone had mixed up a few facts, because he'd talked to Andy since then. "What kind of accident?"

"A car, I think. I don't know," Joseph repeated. "I'm sure he's OK by now. Anup said he talk to him yesterday and he's fine."

Here was a major glitch in the chain of information—and perhaps the problem. As far as he knew, Andy had never met Anup prior to this trip. Jordan began fishing for details. "Did you say Anup's known my brother for a long time?"

"I think a long time. He came here just three months ago."

"My brother was here?"

"Not here, Tiger Tops. He stays every year with Anup."

Every year? Something was very wrong about this conversation, and very right. Jordan's mind began sorting through bits and fragments of thoughts that he hadn't realized were in limbo: Andy's invisible friend with the convenient Land Rover. The little boy who showed up with keys within minutes of their arrival, who hadn't been standoffish in a land of perpetually shy children, and who'd quickly been given a huge amount of money by his brother—who never seemed to have rupees. And probably the biggest piece of all: instant visas and the ease with which everything about this trip had fallen into place.

Plus, the day they'd arrived at Tiger Tops, Andy hadn't asked where the phone was located, he'd gone to it straight as an arrow. Had managed to get them on a game run within minutes. Or had he? No game run had materialized. Yet . . .

He ran out of string and started again.

Andy couldn't possibly have been seriously injured a week ago, he'd been at his office the day before yesterday. There'd been plenty of opportunity during their conversation to say something about not being able to fly. Actually, he'd been very specific about flying to New Delhi. However, they had been cut off. He shifted uneasily on the stool.

It might make sense if he had an accident yesterday and called Anup to ask him to notify me. But why let a stranger know he was OK, and not me? If Anup was a close enough friend to receive such a call, why pretend not to know him? Why not admit he'd been here before?

Joseph was staring at him with concern. "Is something wrong do you think?"

"I don't know, maybe." Jordan saw Charlayne emerge from her tent, and was distracted. She was tucking strands of hair under her hat and didn't look like she'd slept well either. He watched her stop for a brief conversation with Professor Jamieson then head toward the cook, and he knew she was looking for coffee. "Excuse me, Joseph."

He intercepted her at the cook's elbow and held out his cup for a refill. "Good morning." She didn't answer, and he could tell by the set of her jaw and her short manner that she was ticked; an apology of the first order was due. "Something's come up and I need to talk to you," he ventured.

"I'd wait if I were you," she said sharply. "I'll be in a lot better mood after I've had some caffeine."

He ignored the warning, and the knowing smile of the cook. "I'm aware that I owe you an apology." The whole camp probably knew about last night's incident by now. They'd hassled in the midst of the staff lean-to and half a dozen tents; people had had hours to pass it along a grapevine. "You want it public or private?"

Her shoulders were set, stiff as cardboard. "Public isn't necessary." She stirred sugar into her coffee, caught up a few slices of toast, then led him to a relatively secluded area of the camp before exploding all over him. "The next time you lecture me like a little girl with a hand in the cookie jar will be the last. If I want to get wet or risk my neck, or change my clothes in public, or walk around . . . naked if I want!" Confused, she came to a halt and blushed in spite of her ire.

The idea of her being naked leaped through his head: how many others had witnessed her unclad cheeks last night? Those long gorgeous legs . . . Under the weight of her irritation, the thought disappeared as quickly as it had come. Her eyes sparked with righteous anger and her color ran high as she wrestled her train of thought back on track. "It's my career and my neck and my . . . business, and I won't have you jumping my associates over it."

"You're right. I was wrong." *Man, are you gorgeous when you're angry.*

"It so happens that I was very careful last night. We were only going to check the one net. I wanted to make sure nothing was caught and choking to death!"

"I was wrong and I embarrassed you."

"You were wrong and you embarrassed me," she scolded, then realized he'd already admitted it. Placated somewhat, she ate her toast, glancing up at him with leftover pique. "Mark used to do that, and I won't have it from you or anyone else," she justified in a last attempt at defending her rights.

Ex-husband territory. He should have known.

He nodded, understanding her completely, and waited until he felt she'd be receptive to an explanation. "It was the water," he conceded. "Seeing you soaking wet, I knew you'd fallen in the wash, and I lost it. As far as Mitch is concerned, I don't like him and I won't pretend to, but I was angry with him about something else entirely and shouldn't have—"

She pounced like a cat. "About what?"

He walked a careful line, wanting very much to rat the guy out. Unfortunately, exposing Mitch's threat to get rid of her would do little more than open a my-word-against-yours can of worms, and solve nothing. He decided not to take the chance. "How I feel about him is unimportant. He's your contact with the professor, and what matters is properly researching your books. The two of you will be here long after I'm gone, and that relationship takes priority."

"If you know something I should know . . ."

He proceeded cautiously. "In my opinion, he acts before he thinks, and he's too quick to take easy outs. Just be careful around him. That's all."

"That's all?"

He nodded, and she looked at him with suspicion, toward him or Mitch wasn't clear.

"Apology accepted."

Relieved that she was no longer angry, he gave her a

silly grin; it was Andy behavior and it felt foolish on him. What he should be doing was getting into the rumor situation instead of appreciating her stormy face in early morning sunlight.

"On one condition," she tacked on severely.

"Name it. Anything you want for the next seven days." *Jesus, was it really only seven more days?*

"If you have any future problems with Mitch . . ." She tipped her head to study him beneath her lashes, and he saw her change her mind. "No. On the condition that from now on, whenever I ask you a question, you will tell me the absolute truth."

"From now on?" He hid behind a sip of lukewarm coffee, grimaced at the taste, and tried to see into the coming week. He and Mitch would hassle only if he bought into the Batman's bullshit, which he did not plan to do. "I swear on my honor that I will never lie to you." He grinned again and the lawyer in him added the inevitable caveat. "Not knowingly."

She broke into a small smile. "This is the first time I'm sure you and Andy are brothers. For a moment you looked just like him." She tilted her head sideways, a new, less cautious glint in her eye. "Speaking of Andy, there's something I've been wondering about."

Her manner set him on guard. "He's a Pisces," he dodged, trying to keep it light. "No scars, tattoos, or other distinguishing marks. Clever. Hardworking. Serious . . ." *About you.* Maybe injured. His humor flattened. "A few minutes ago, I found out—"

"Did he tell you I called his office from Kathmandu?"

". . . No," he said slowly, stalled in place.

"I asked him to help me find a photographer." She examined his face, openly evaluating. "You didn't have a conversation about it?"

Trying to divine her intent, he found himself haplessly out of sync. "No."

Her skepticism was evident. "Would you tell me if you had?"

Genuinely mystified, he lapsed into legalese. "I'm not his lawyer at the moment so, yes, unless I'd agreed not to . . . which I haven't." More instances of Andy not being forthcoming, he realized. Shades of the curious revelations from Joseph came flooding at him and he held them at bay with difficulty in order to concentrate. "Is there some reason you're asking?"

Her face closed over the least bit and he thought for a moment she wasn't going to answer. "When you two arrived, the first thing he said was that he hadn't found anyone, but the next morning, you agreed to help me out. I mean, you saved my life—liter-arily speaking." She stumbled over the word, then pursued her point. "But it's just seemed odd to me that you changed your plans, that's all. You appear to be very close as brothers, and you're sure he didn't mention it?"

"I'm positive." In his zeal to convince her, he wandered into quicksand. "The first time he said anything about taking pictures for you was that night. He didn't say you'd called, he said . . ."

She cocked her head, and truth became stickier. "He pointed out . . . that you needed someone, and since I wasn't ready to go home . . ." He was mired to his knees with no plan of escape. "It seemed like a good thing to do."

She processed the information instantly. "So this was his idea."

The sand began to suck him down. "It didn't occur to me, at first, that it was something I could . . . should do . . . wanted to," he amended as fast as he could, "but, really, it's been the best time in my life, since Natalie . . .

and . . ." She began to seal him out. He could see in her face that she was battening hatches. Preparing to abandon ship.

Suddenly she changed up, switching subjects like a good legal opponent. "What about after dinner, at the hotel in Jaipur? What did he say about that?"

What the hell was she searching for? He reached for the unknown rather than go under. "He's never said anything."

"Nothing? All those questions about who I'd married, and for how long, and why I'm divorced, and where I live, and he hasn't said anything about that conversation either?"

He stared at her blankly, unsure whether or not to believe her. Conversation wasn't what had concerned him that night, but the smear of lipstick on his brother's face. "The only thing I know about your life is what you've told me."

"Why *are* you here?"

The truth, the whole truth, and nothing but. He'd lived by the pledge his entire professional life. The essence of his promise to her a little more than ninety seconds ago was staring him in the face. He gave her the only honest answer he could assemble. "Partly . . . because my brother's interested in you."

Surprise flashed through her eyes, and something else. "Your brother?"

Nowhere in conversations with Andy had he been requested to keep the situation privileged, and in a way, it would be a huge relief to stop carrying it around. He bit the bullet. "He wanted me to get to know you and see if there was room in your life for him, but—"

"So it *was* his idea." Her face recomposed; her expression became carefully neutral. "And the other part?"

No compromise, he'd sworn it. Still trapped, he opted for the truth. "I didn't want to be anywhere else."

"I see." She looked away from him and carefully emptied her coffee onto the ground. "Well, that answers all my questions. I need a refill, will you excuse me?"

He stopped her from walking away. "There's more to it—"

"I'm sure." Her smile and her voice were extremely polite, but she did not meet his eyes. "There's Joseph, I need to speak with him."

He saw Joseph also, and the anxiety about Andy that had been held aside took over. Somewhere in the translation, part of this morning's information was clearly bollixed. His gut said that if his brother had indeed been in an accident, information on the extent of his injuries might be screwed up as well. He restrained her again. "Char, something's come up." He told her about his talk with Joseph. "There are a lot of details that don't make sense, so I need to make sure Andy hasn't been trying to reach me."

Her reserve disappeared, and he was thankful that her capacity to care exceeded her distrust of the Kosterin brothers.

"You think it's serious," she said, cutting to the core.

"Probably." He scraped his fingers through his beard, and was reminded of his rough appearance. "Hell, I don't know what to think. Unfortunately, it'll take most of the day to get to a telephone and find out for sure. If he does need me and I have to fly out . . . I'll get word to you. Otherwise, I should be back sometime tomorrow."

She was nodding, eyes wide with understanding.

They quickly located Professor Jamieson and explained the situation. "Best take your things," he counseled. "Won't be able to pick you up this evening, but Joseph makes a trip every day to check on his wife. Park business as well. Arrange things with him." He got to his feet. "I'll send him early so you can leave right away. Anup should be able to get you on to Tiger Tops."

Jordan thanked the professor with genuine appreciation.

"Not at all. I just hope things aren't too difficult. Not good to be injured in this part of the world. Make sure he's gotten proper care."

Charlayne and Jimi helped Jordan pull down his tent while Joseph transferred his gear onto an elephant's saddle. With so many people surrounding them, there was no opportunity to continue their discussion, and Jordan bade her goodbye with foreboding in his stomach. As he left the camp, he watched behind him until she was swallowed up in the green.

20

You screwed it up, that's what's going on . . .

Charlayne waved goodbye and followed Jordan with her eyes until he was out of sight. Her concern for Andy ran the gamut: if he'd been able to send word, chances were the accident hadn't been life-threatening, but if it was even moderately serious, she might not see either of them for a long time. If ever. Numbed by that possibility, she dismissed further speculation until she had more information. Forcing herself to make reference notes on the sights and sounds of the camp, she found it increasingly difficult to concentrate. Everywhere she turned was either evidence of Jordan or an indication of his absence, and she felt surrounded; the space next to hers where his tent had been, the very boots on her feet, warm and dry, were constant reminders of her inability to talk with him, share her thoughts, simply study his face.

After lunch she wandered to the end of camp to visit Khalli, another giant, gray reminder of Jordan—of the night in the fog when she'd kissed him—and the force of that moment came thundering into her chest. Now she knew why he hadn't pursued the kiss. Andy was the one who was interested, not Jordan.

Joh appeared with Madhav, who began to remove Khalli's chains.

"I thought she didn't have to work today."

"Madhav is taking her for a bath," Joh replied.

"Is it OK if I go along?"

She waited while he spoke severely to Madhav, who'd been demoted from driver to saddler and caretaker. "Don't leave his sight. Not for a moment," Joh admonished her.

She agreed and followed the two a short distance to a small stream. She found a perch on a convenient tree limb to watch the elephant lower her body into the center of the water and allow Madhav to vigorously wash her back with the aid of a burlap mop; from time to time Khalli spouted water over her head to aid in the process.

Jordan would have had a grand time taking pictures of this, she thought, and realized that she was terribly lonely for his company. Other than his ride to check on the fishing cat, Khalli's bath was the first thing they hadn't shared since he'd come to the park. Replays of their exchange over coffee—memories she'd been using all her energy to shut out since he'd left—leaked into her thoughts.

She'd asked the right questions; gotten the wrong answers. Since their dinner at the lodge, she'd dared hope that he had stayed on because he was becoming interested in her. This morning her original suspicions had come true with a vengeance; he was here because of Andy. References to his brother during past discussions began to surface and she realized that Jordan had introduced Andy's name into nearly every conversation they'd ever had. He'd been a twentieth century John Alden—speaking for his brother—and her disappointment was supreme.

She'd made the mistake of creating her own private wish list, with Jordan Kosterin at the top of the page. Determined to make the most of their last week together, she'd "set her cap for him," as her grandmother used to say. Indulged in baseless fantasies that if he got to know her, there might be a future in here somewhere for the two of them. She cringed at the memory of her fishwife attack that had led to his owning up. *Got more than you bargained for, didn't you, my dear? Next time, if you don't want to know, don't ask.*

He'd taken all his belongings in case he'd had to travel to India. Since it was Andy's idea that he was here at all, she realized that he might well decide not to return— whether or not his brother was hurt. What would be the point?

Madhav and Khalli lumbered out of the river. She hopped to the ground to follow the two of them back to camp, her discouragement building on disappointment. Without Jordan, her sense of humor had evaporated as well; ahead on the path, Khalli's derriere held no more charm than the north end of an elephant traveling south.

She was on the verge of tears when Mitch collared her at the edge of camp. "I've been looking for you." He fell into step at her side. "Joh's changed his mind again, says we can't use some of the elephants for two more days. Camp schedule's blown to hell, so I've decided to drive into the Churias to try a small river up there. If I hurry, I can arrive while it's still daylight, and be back tomorrow. Since nothing's going on here, I thought you might want to go."

The Churias were the nearby foothills that she and Jordan had witnessed from the observation tower. The memory was split between their beauty that night and the pain of reality. She caught herself up. It was going to be a long evening in camp, and anything was better than letting her anxiety build up an all night head of steam. Jordan's warning to be careful around Mitch slid through her thoughts. *He acts before he thinks. Too quick to take easy outs.*

Catching sight of Joseph's elephant trudging into camp, she put Mitch off. "Let me think it over and I'll let you know."

"Well, hurry. We'll have to leave by two."

She nodded vacantly. Mitch veered toward his tent and she waited for Joseph to dismount then asked about Jordan. "I left him with Anup," he informed her. "Anup said Andy is injured for sure, and they went to Tiger Tops. That's all I know."

Her hopes foundered. Then she remembered to inquire about Joseph's wife. It was his first child and he was greatly nervous.

"Maybe tomorrow." He grinned. "He takes his time."

"Oh, so you know it's a boy," she teased.

"Of course." He laughed, then spied Joh and bobbed his head at her before sprinting toward his boss.

The hollow spot under her ribs enlarged. If they weren't going to track bears or fishing cats for two more days, keeping herself busy was the best remedy for potential wall-climbing. She debated Mitch's offer: she could mope around and wait and worry about Andy, and wonder about Jordan Kosterin, or she could visit another locale in the park and add to her research. She went to find Mitch.

"Jamieson says we can use Mala," he told her. "She's being saddled, and when we get back to base camp, we take the Jeep. An old logging road goes halfway up. I've been there before."

"What about food?"

"Scrambled eggs and fried potatoes?"

Reprieve from rice and dal was the clincher. "OK, I'm in. As long as it's just overnight. I want to be back tomorrow in case things change."

"Piece of cake. Let's get your gear."

She interrupted the professor and Joseph mid-conversation to briefly advise him that she had decided to accompany Mitch back to the compound. The professor nodded in agreement and she excused herself to begin packing.

Anup swerved the car to avoid a monstrous hole hidden from view in afternoon shadow. "I am sure he said it happen last week," he said. "I don't think I am mistaken."

Jordan watched the road, pleased the man was a careful driver. The last thing he wanted was to end up like Andy, with cracked ribs and a broken leg, according to Anup. Anup's daughter was married to Joseph, and Jordan liked him, understood why he and Andy would be friends.

"He stays with me when he's coming to Tiger Tops. Three years now since his job in Narmada." Anup laughed. "He enjoys seeing the tigers."

Jordan thought back to Andy's conversation with Charlayne the night they'd gone to dinner. If Anup was telling the truth, and he had no reason to suspect otherwise, clearly Andy's ignorance of Nepal's parks and tigers had all been bogus. But why? For what purpose?

They arrived at the lodge and Anup waited while Jordan arranged a room. "I will be here tomorrow morning to check on my grandchild." The man grinned broadly. "If you are ready to come back to Saura, I will take you." The grandfather-to-be took his leave.

Jordan dropped his bags in his room and placed a call to Andy's office with a certain amount of trepidation. Things regarding Charlayne had been left pretty high and dry during their last conversation, and he hoped there was no connection to Andy's accident. In any event, his high-octane brother was bound to be upset at being incapacitated; not being able to fly would seriously curtail his work schedule as well.

The phone rang at length and his apprehension grew. Finally someone answered and immediately disconnected him. Frustrated, Jordan re-placed the call.

The voice answered a second time.

"Andrew Kosterin, please," he demanded.

"No here." Followed by thick silence.

"I understand he's been injured. Is he at home?"

"No. No home. Here soon." More silence.

Jordan pushed his end of the conversation. "Do you speak English?"

"Ah-hanh, English. I am speaking."

"This is his brother, Jordan. You said he'd be there today?"

"Ah-hanh, today."

He tried an end run. "Is anyone else there?"

"I am here."

Dead end. "Have him call me? Tell him it's an emergency. You understand 'emergency'?"

"Ah-hanh, emergency."

Three more ah-hanhs later he gave it up and left the phone number. He'd have to call back every half hour until he found a voice with a larger "English" vocabulary. In the meantime he'd look into flight possibilities to Gandhinagar. Just in case.

He located his passport and found the concierge, who directed him to the travel deputy, who provided the next in a series of brick walls. Without Andy and his private plane, a visa was required to establish visitor status and date-of-entry data for all passengers leaving Nepal; he remembered, entirely too late, that he'd never seen the thing. Andy hadn't given it to him. After explaining to the travel officer that the visa was lost and that his brother had been badly injured in an automobile accident, the man advised him most apologetically that he would have to go to Kathmandu to arrange a flight to India. A reissuance of his visa could only be accomplished there, and, since air service from the lodge was only to Kathmandu, it would be most convenient. If he wished, he could have the number of the embassy to begin things in advance.

Defeated for the moment, Jordan returned to his room to regroup. Too upset to sleep, not hungry, he was in limbo about travel until he could talk to his brother. He decided to shave since he had a mirror, and took advantage of a hot shower. Then he alternately paced and worked the phone.

The third time he spoke to "Ah-hanh," it occurred to him to ask for Baba. After what seemed an interminable wait, the old man came to the phone. "Yes."

"Baba, this is Andy's brother, Jordan."

"Yes, I remember you. How are you?"

Struck by the old man's formality, he responded in kind. "I'm fine. And you?"

"It pleases God that I am well, thank you. How can I help you?"

"I am worried about my brother. I received word that he was in an accident. Do you know if it's true? Can you tell me where to reach him?"

"He is here."

"I've been calling there for two hours!"

"He has just arrived. I will get him. Thank you for talking to me. It is my only phone call."

Jordan sighed with relief. "You are most welcome," he said fervently. If Andy was at his office, his injuries couldn't be too bad. Maybe he wouldn't have to fly to India after all. A breath of calm overtook his frustration.

His brother came on the phone with a surly attitude. "Now what? I talked to you two days ago."

"Word in this end of town is that you rolled the Jeep," he said bluntly. "Any truth in it?"

"Word from who?"

Suspicion descended and Jordan scowled, irritated at his brother's manner. It didn't take a legal mind to recognize that Andy's surprised response was neither denial nor admission. "So you're not hurt?" he pursued. "You didn't send a message?"

"I didn't send a message, but I'd sure like to know where you got such screwball information."

More nondenial. "Obviously you didn't fly to New Delhi. But that's not because you've been grounded?"

There was a surrendering sigh. "OK, so I blew a tire. Cracked a couple of ribs. No big deal, and I didn't see any reason to bother you with it. Where are you calling from, Tiger Tops?"

"Came all the way in from a field camp to do it."

"How's Charlayne? Is she there with you?"

Jordan paused. He planned to lay his interest in Charlayne on the line this time, and since candid conversation had all the potential of getting volatile, he didn't want to talk about her just yet. "She stayed in the field. I also heard you broke your leg—plus there are one or two other details that have come to my attention, things you haven't bothered to mention. You want to talk about any of this?"

"How much do you know?"

He ran it down. "You're friends with Anup, you know your way around Saura, and you've been on crutches for a week." He tried to reach out on a brother-to-brother level. "What's all this about, Andy? Are you in some kind of trouble?"

"Nothing you can fix." His brother was abrupt and determined to stay on another track. "Tell me what's going on there. Any progress with the gorgeous lady? How are you two getting along?"

Jordan sidestepped, unwilling to bring his escalating feelings for Charlayne into the mix until he had a clearer picture. "How bad were you hurt?"

"When you answer my questions, gonad, I'll answer yours."

Andy's obstinence was the topper to a perfectly rotten day. Tired and lonely and wanting to be somewhere else, Jordan lost his temper. "How are we getting along? Well, how's this? Last night we had a fight and this morning she told me I reminded her of her ex-husband." Determined not to be sidetracked further, he instituted a counterattack. "I'll be happy to discuss her later. Right now, we're talking about you! What kind of trouble are you in?"

"Damn! I knew you'd screw it up!" Andy shouted back at him. "She's beautiful. Intelligent. Available! Everything a man with blood in his veins could want and I gave her to you, you lawyer *moron*! You screwed it up, that's what's going on!"

Flummoxed, Jordan searched for solid ground. "What the hell are you talking about?"

"Your ears went up like a bloodhound at the Taj Mahal! You were interested in that woman!" Andy was practically frothing at him. "What *happened?* I know it was you that messed up, 'cause she was looking at you, too!"

Jordan was struck all but speechless. The man had lost his mind. "What do you mean, gave her to me?"

Andy ignored him to continue his tirade. "I should fly up there and break my other leg kicking your ass! When you didn't make a move on her in Jaipur, I went to a hell of a lot of trouble—not to mention expense—to get you two together! Do you have any idea what using that plane *cost* me?"

"Wait a minute!" Jordan scrambled for logic. "How'd you know I was interested in her?"

"My brother, Joe Solid Citizen, drinks half a bottle of Chinese vodka, for starters, pukes out his guts the next morning, but never says a word about why he's boozing. I get you to Chitwan, you don't take your eyeballs off her for twenty seconds, so I know I'm right. I make her the safest girl in town by hitting on her in front of you, made myself a major jerk in the process, then got the hell out of the way. Did it work? *Nooooo!*"

His brother was on a roll and Jordan began to laugh.

"So I figured out a way to leave you there. Practically tied you to her doorknob! Did everything but put a ribbon on *her* neck. I'm matchmaking my ass off, what do you think I was doing, getting you work? I got spies all over camp, I'm getting daily reports. I even thought there was hope when she kissed you. What was that, a week ago?"

Joh, the spy? Jordan laughed harder. "Four days, asshole." He slid off the bed and landed on the floor, laughing so hard he could no longer speak.

"Call me a liar for seventy-two hours, you jerk! You dimwit! All I want to know is, was there any progress before you blew it? And don't tell me no or I'll hang up on you again."

"What?"

Loud banging erupted from the receiver. Jordan recognized the "phone interference" and shouted with helpless glee, nearly drowning out his brother's voice.

"So what about the progress, numbnuts?"

Jordan wiped his eyes and confessed. "I want her so bad I can't tell you."

"Yaaaahooooo!!"

Andy's whoop on the phone shattered his eardrum, but he was equally joyous. "I owe you for this one, little brother."

"You're damned right you do, and it'll cost you like you are not gonna believe!"

"Anything you want. Name it."

"Marry her. Be happy, asshole."

He came down a bit. "Well, that's going a bit fast."

"Oh, get over it, lawyer. You're nuts about her. I know all the signs."

"Yeah, well, she's got a say in this, too."

"You wanna know what my gut says?"

"Well, let's hope your gut is right." He struggled back onto the bed. "I can't believe you set me up."

"I can't believe it actually worked."

"So did you really have an accident or was that—"

His brother chuckled wryly. "Unfortunately, that's real. I walk a little funny but everything that counts still operates, except they won't let me fly a plane. You'll have to figure another way out of there when the time comes."

At the moment all Jordan wanted in life was to wrap his arms around his brother and keep him safe from the world. "I can get there in a couple of days if you need anything."

"Hey, I'm the guy who knows the guy...."

"Yeah, oh, by the way, can you have the 'guy' send me my visa? They want one before they'll let me leave the country."

Andy was suddenly silent. "Uh, actually, there were no visas. I sort of faked it. They'll probably make you get one. Sorry. Didn't have time to plan that part."

Jordan didn't care. "I think I can handle it. I'll tell them my elephant ate it."

"Right. See, lawyers know all that stuff. Look on the bright side. You'll have to stay with her until it gets straightened out. Awww, gee." Andy laughed uproariously. "Just don't come back here."

"Are you sure?"

"Trust me, you get on my nerves and you frighten the natives."

Jordan fought sudden tears. "I love you, man."

"I love you, too, older brother. Now go get her."

21

Rhinos and tigers and bears . . .

Jubilant, Jordan hung up the phone. No encumbrances. No more fence-sitting. An end to pretense and deception! He could cease avoiding his feelings and explore the possibilities of Charlayne Pearce! The cream and rose and rust of her, too, if she'd have him. He checked the time. It was not too late to hie himself to Saura and maybe bribe one of the king's elephant soldiers to ferry him to the field camp so he could feast his eyes on her and make a full confession this very night.

Excited by the challenge of getting back to her, he called the number his brother had given him for a local driver. When there was no answer, he made a quick sortie into the bar and, just in case, struck a discreetly masculine

– 231 –

bargain for a few personal items with one of the bartenders, a wild-eyed man named Roget. Simultaneous in their negotiation, he was able to arrange an immediate ride to Chitwan. Roget was a one man, one-size-fits-all hustler, precisely the man he needed at the moment.

He waited while Roget arranged coverage with the night-shift bartender. When the man showed up twenty minutes later, Jordan notified the front desk of his imminent departure, put the bill on his credit card, grabbed his luggage, and headed for the exit.

"See you later." Charlayne waved to Jimi and settled herself into the Jeep next to Mitch. The mournful bleating of the rhino calf as it called for its mother was giving her maternal instincts a beating and the sound followed them out of camp. The calf had been heartily suckling a mixture of powdered milk and vitamins from a bottle a few minutes ago, and the veterinarian had assured her it was doing fine, but a full stomach did not a parent make. Distressed at the reminder of its plight, she busied herself with checking to see that her duffel was well-packed into the backseat and held onto her camera, determined to keep her mind off Jordan and survive her own weaning process.

They drove half an hour along the gravel road, then onto a dirt track for several miles, higher and higher into the foothills. The weather was perfect and she spent much of her time enjoying the late afternoon sunshine and open air of the ride. Without the usual breeze crisply tainted with mountain snow, it felt like a humid April day in California.

Wildlife other than a few langurs and half a dozen deer fled well ahead of the noisy Jeep. Even the birds were quiet. To keep the subject of Jordan Kosterin from coming up, she entertained Mitch with tales of her college days with his sister, and he threw in a few escapades of his own. The loss of Jordan's company receded a bit, and she began to look forward to their adventure.

When they entered rougher terrain, the trail disappeared and she helped pick their way cross-country through stands of trees and low brush by standing on her seat, spotting rocks and other obstructions in their path. Mitch handled the Jeep with confidence born of experience, and eventually they arrived at the top of a bluff, one side of a sharp bend in the river. He brought the vehicle to a halt close to the edge. From her seat she could see into the riverbed, nearly empty and possibly thirty feet across.

"This is it. We'll camp over there." Mitch pointed down at a sandbar on the opposite bank; centered in the river's curve, there was plenty of room on it to set up both their tents.

Jimi and Mala were nowhere in sight as she helped him unload their gear. "How are they going to find us?"

"Who?"

Mitch's offhand attitude struck a nerve, and she whipped around to face him. "Jimi and Mala, that's who."

He looked at her with disdain. "I told you, I've been here before. They know where we are."

She backed down a notch, only slightly reassured. "Isn't it dangerous until they arrive?"

"Not if we build a fire right away," he said casually. "Wait here."

It took him two trips down the steep bank to transfer the food and tents, while she stood lookout for Mala and Jimi. At the foot of the bluff, the dry river bottom resembled a winding, roughly cobbled road striated with black where small streaks of water trickled along its course. Pretty, actually. In the late afternoon light, the pale ribbon of sky visible above dense stands of trees on either side was the same oyster color as the river's paving stones and boulders. She wished Jordan were here to take a picture for her.

She shouldered her duffel and helped carry down the last of the netting equipment, highly aware of how small she felt in the midst of the wilderness. They quickly set up their tents, pounding the pins deep into the sand with handy rocks.

"We'll have to hurry and string the nets." They were both panting from exertion in the unusually warm evening. "Why don't you round up some wood for a campfire. It's not a good idea to go where I can't see you, so don't go up in the trees. There should be enough by the water."

"Sure, OK." Increasingly nervous, she collected an armful of driftwood along the riverbed while he separated the nets and stakes. She dumped the kindling next to him on the sand, convinced more than ever that they were courting disaster. "We're not going out until they get here," she confirmed.

"Can't wait. Bats go out at twilight, come back at dawn." He looked up and down the river. "We'll set these up at either end of this stretch of water. When it gets dark we can see the fire."

She balked. Something was wrong here. Other than an occasional deer, they hadn't seen animals of any kind for the last several miles of the drive, but that was no guarantee a rhinoceros or worse wouldn't show up any second. Without an elephant, it plain and simple wasn't safe, fire or no fire. She caught Mitch's arm. "Mala and Jimi *are* coming?"

"Look, I've stayed up in these hills lots of times. There's no reason to have an elephant with us every minute. It's not that dangerous."

It wasn't an answer and she knew it. Jordan's warning about being careful around Mitch clarioned in her mind. "What about tigers?"

"There's no problem with tigers unless they've turned man-eater, and everything else will stay away from the fire."

"This is crazy. You said Jimi and Mala were coming."

"No, what I said was, we could use them to get back to the base camp and we'd take the Jeep."

She dug in her heels. "If they're not coming, I want us to leave. I won't do this. It's stupid."

"OK, I have an answer to every problem." Mitch reached into his pack and brought out a large revolver; its stiff leather holster was attached to a belt. "This is all the protection we'll need in the event anything goes wrong. I camp out all the time and I've never had to use it." He proceeded to buckle the gun belt around his waist.

Charlayne was appalled. "I didn't agree to this and I'm not doing it, period." She began to yank at her tent pins. "This is nuts."

Mitch stopped her. "We're here. It'll take thirty minutes to string up a couple of nets. Stay with me until the bats go out, then we can go home. Just let me get a couple of specimens. Jesus! We can drive back tomorrow morning."

"Not good enough. You lied to me."

"No, you heard what you wanted to hear. This is wasting time. I'm stringing the nets, and you can do what you want until I'm ready to leave. If you're smart, you'll help me because it'll go faster with two of us. If anything dangerous is in the area, I'm the one with the gun."

Enraged, she weighed her options. There was nothing

particularly safe about waiting him out in the Jeep. It might be protection from snakes, but that was about all since it had no top. Besides, who knew when he'd decide to leave if she didn't stay on his case? Her tent wouldn't keep out anything with teeth. Or claws. Helping this mutant jackass went hard against the grain, but he was right. If she had to be here, she'd best stay with him—at least until she could build a fire big enough to keep a tiger at a distance.

"You win, I'll start the fire."

"When the nets are up," he blackmailed. "Otherwise we'll lose the light. Putting them up after dark takes twice as long and would only be an exercise. Wouldn't get anything until dawn that way."

Angry to the point of being fearless, she nodded tightly. Being lectured on top of being bullied, on top of being lied to, was her limit. God help him when they got back to civilization. If he lived that long. She picked up a bundle of stakes and waited, blood in her eyes. "Let's go."

Instead of two nets, Mitch insisted on five, and they walked to the bend in the river to begin setting the stakes. Then he decided that rather than placing up nets in view of the tents, he wanted them upstream, enraging her further. She tried to keep track of the river's configuration as she went, in case they got separated. Anything was possible at this point, and if he pushed her much further, she just might make a decision to push back.

Working in dogged silence, she made sure each time they rounded a curve that she didn't become disoriented and could find her way back to the tents. Occasionally she noticed that the river split into a V that created a small island when it rejoined itself; other splits were all but dry tributaries coming down out of the hills, but there were deep pools of water at their base where the riverbed had been undermined and washed away. At last the fifth net was up and they began the return trip.

Mitch gave her a good-ol'-boy grin. "See, I tol' ya we'd be perfectly safe."

"We're not out of here yet," she gritted back at him.

Her only salvation from fury was in being able to work the nets, but even freeing a small flock of finches, half her mind was distracted with how to solve her predicament. There was no question that he'd refuse to leave as promised, and unless she could figure a way to get her hands on the keys to the Jeep, she'd be stuck here overnight with him and that ridiculous gun.

When they came to the bend with a clump of brush growing on the left side of the stream, she crossed her fingers that she'd kept track accurately and the tents would be about fifty feet away. If so, at least she'd know where she was on the river; stepping into the clear, the tents were on the sandbar where they should have been, but she couldn't believe her eyes. Mala was a gray ghost in the trees and a sober Jimi was sliding to the ground at her side.

Mitch gave a brittle, satisfied laugh. "I figured he'd send someone. See, they knew where to find us."

Charlayne saw through choler. The whole thing had been more of Mitch's callow, one-sided humor. Too happy to see Jimi and that bulwark of safety, Mala, to indulge in a proper fit of temper, she left Mitch's side to climb onto the bank and run along its animal trail, nearly bowling Jimi over in her eagerness to make sure he was real. She hadn't known she was so frightened. Jimi's face went taut with concern.

"Snakes lie along the path," he cautioned. "Do not go there unless I walk first." He demonstrated by swatting weeds and vines that matted the sides of the trail with his wooden staff.

Dear God, she thought, what else? How did people live here? Answer: people didn't. Snakes did. Rhinos and tigers and bears, and who knew how many other potentially lethal biters and eaters did, but people sure as hell didn't.

"I'm going home with you," she informed him. "I don't care what this"— she bit back a decidedly unladylike epithet—"miserable person decides to do, but I'm leaving when you leave."

Jimi smiled for the first time. "Joh said to travel at first light. Too dangerous tonight."

"First light is good with me." She reacted to the rest of his comment; they were here with an elephant. "What's too dangerous?"

"A big storm is due. Joh didn't want to send us."

"That's baloney!" Mitch had joined them in time to overhear. "The sky's been clear all day, no thunder. I told Jamieson, there's not going to be any storm."

Charlayne stiffened. "You were warned?" She ground her jaws in frustration and looked to the pale ribbon of sky easing into early twilight. It was actually warm and there were no clouds, not even a breeze; as much as it galled her, she had to agree with Mitch that a storm didn't appear likely.

"It may pass." Jimi said nothing further.

"Well, as long as you're here, we can put out the rest of the nets," Mitch directed. "I have six left and we can work the ones that are already up as we go."

Charlayne shot Mitch a look, in no mood to watch Jimi be pushed around. "I intend to build a fire first," she insisted stubbornly, and drew a mental line in the dirt. She wasn't going anywhere without a fire to return to. "You want to give me the matches or do you want to light it?"

Mitch gave her an affable grin. "Hey, a fire'll take five minutes, then we got work to do, right, Jimi?"

He bent to start the fire, and she reassessed the situation. Since Mala was here to protect them, it was probably best to try to take advantage of the experience. If she made a mutiny of it, Jimi would be forced to take sides and possibly get in trouble. So, when the fire was well started, she raised no objection and they set out with the additional nets. The elephant picked her way upstream in the rocky creek bed, and they worked the existing nets. There were several birds ensnared, but no bats.

Charlayne carefully removed the largest bird caught so far; its wing feathers were an incredible blue-purple hue. From beak to tail it was easily thirty inches long, and instantly became her newest potential character for a children's book. "Magpie?" she guessed.

"Black-headed magpie," Jimi confirmed with a nod.

Black feathers indeed crowned its head, blending to a strikingly purple body and magnificent tail feathers that were triple its body length; its overall color was the same as the mountain range that flanked the Himalayas. She held it gently by its legs, its white belly feathers resting against her fist; sharp talons curled around the bandage on her little finger while she stroked its feathers. Unalarmed at being her prisoner, the magpie cocked its head and calmly inspected her with bead-black eyes; she realized that it had probably never encountered a human being. Never having met a purple magpie, they were even. She opened her hand and the bird perched a few instants on her fingers, then flew away.

Mitch had already rounded the next curve in the river. She and Jimi and Mala followed at the elephant's leisurely pace. In subsequent nets there were several multicolored barbets, which reminded Charlayne of South American tri- and multicolored parrots in miniature, with the straight beaks and body size of canaries; there was also a juvenile kingfisher, its heartbeat racing under her gentle fingers; but no bats. Mitch chafed at the loss of time required in freeing the birds and was irritable until they began setting up the rest of his nets.

Charlayne was breathing heavily from the effort of navigating the tricky river rocks and climbing onto slippery banks to tie the net strings, particularly following Mitch's rapid pace, and she was soon perspiring in the unusually close air. This time of day should be dropping into chill and a brisk breeze, but was not. They were piling stones against the last stake when suddenly it grew visibly darker and the impact of stillness became apparent.

Charlayne wiped moisture from her forehead with the back of her hand and stood upright, uncertain what had caught her attention. Something about the charged intensity of the quiet. Nothing was moving, not high in the trees nor low to the ground; not leaf nor twig nor bird nor insect. There was literal silence in the stilled air, and it seemed as if the immediate world was holding its collective breath.

Suddenly she recognized it. Twister weather in Kansas. She'd been there once as a child and experienced this kind of calm before a massive thunderstorm. People had been killed. "Is it the storm?" she whispered to Jimi, her neck hairs standing on end.

"Yes, I think. It comes too quickly. We should go back to camp."

Mitch looked about uneasily, checked the lowering sky. "Yeah, he's right." He savagely kicked a small rock aside, venting his frustration. "Bats won't go out to feed until the rain passes through. May as well yank 'em out as we go. We've wasted our time."

It would be a long trek down the riverbed under shadowy daylight, and for the first time in her adult life, Charlayne was frightened of weather. The last net they'd set up was thankfully empty, and they were taking it down when they heard it in the distance in the form of a low roar. Jimi motioned her to Mala's side.

"Stay next to me," he instructed and pulled a knit cap down over his ears. "You have a flashlight?"

She shook her head. "It's in my pack."

He handed her his wooden staff. "Take this. Try not to fall."

The storm came at them within seconds, beginning with a monstrous whoosh of wind that whipped the tops of trees on the far side of the river nearly sideways; tree trunks and limbs gave unearthly groans as living wood was strained to the breaking point under the force of the gale. Dead limbs snapped and arched to the ground in the wave of creaking, whining flux through what had been motionless green. Dust and twigs and dried leaves were swept up from the ground and tumbled out of trees to pelt them from all sides as bedlam swirled across the river and began on the other side.

The sounds of thrashing trees became a howling roar as the storm increased in strength. It became impossible to hear; mindless cacophony added to her expanding sense of chaos. Charlayne bent into the wind, trying not to stumble over uneven stones in the riverbed as the air coiled around them, flinging grit in her eyes, choking her, and bringing the taste of mud to her mouth. Loose rocks covered in algae and slime slipped and slid under her feet. She used Jimi's staff to keep her balance as twilight disappeared and the sky turned black.

Lightning, sudden and dangerous, was followed by instant clashes of thunder in deafening impacts; slamming, near-physical body blows of sound that reverberated through her chest. The storm was in full fury above and around them.

It was mad and howling and bat-out-of-hell glorious! And hideously frightening.

Beside her, Mala was ponderous in the maelstrom, visible in incessant flashes of lightning as she slowly worked her way down the river, choosing her footing with care. Charlayne found that the elephant provided a lee against stinging fragments in the driving gusts of wind, and marveled at Mala's peaceful demeanor; wondrously calm, she didn't shy or wave her trunk or exhibit fear in any manner. Jimi sat hunched on her shoulders, shining his flashlight in Charlayne's path, helping to light her way.

A gray wave of rain came out of the trees and punished them with huge, splashy drops, hard-hitting and cold as ice; water ran into her eyes and it was all but impossible to see. She opened her mouth for a drink and laughed into the rain with a sudden thought. Maybe she'd be a headline yet. If this kept up, maybe Aunt Char would go out in a blaze of glory after all.

The minute Jordan stepped out of the hotel, the menacing rotten-egg color of the sky threw an edge of concern over his anticipation. There was a pretty good squall coming, maybe worse. Driving in whatever it was, was bound to be dangerous. Roget pulled up in a wheezing, bedraggled mixture of what had once been several vehicles—the base most likely a convertible, since it was lacking any semblance of a top, canvas or otherwise; its motor spit and hacked in uneven rhythms. "We got a helluva storm coming and we better haul," the ersatz bartender called above the rattling engine.

Jordan refused to hesitate, closed his eyes to common sense and climbed into the car.

"We get these late storms once in a while," Roget informed him as they picked up surprising road speed. "Bastards they are, some of them."

Jordan fought his fear, convinced himself that Jamieson wouldn't risk staff and crew in the field under this kind of threat. Joseph had mentioned something about a storm a couple of nights ago. People here didn't have radios, let alone a TV weatherman to rely on; they were alert to their surroundings, made their own observations, and . . . and sometimes terrible things happened. Freak rainstorms happened. People weren't always careful. Even careful people sometimes died. His anxiety grew.

In spite of the car's shortcomings, they arrived in Saura inches ahead of the storm, now rumbling and flashing at their heels. He jumped to the ground in front of the park entrance and grabbed his things. Roget honked a quick farewell and the car disappeared into a thick blanket of dust being kicked up along the gravel road.

Jordan ran for the bunkhouse, dust and detritus passing him by, riding on the gale; he was pushed by the blustering wind until he ducked onto the porch. He looked back at the entrance to see a wall of oncoming dust, his worry for Charlayne growing stronger. Canvas tents would be no match for a windstorm of this size. He paused at the railing to search the compound in the disappearing light. Khalli and the other elephants were tethered, as far as he could tell in their usual stations, and he heaved a sigh of relief. Obviously Jamieson had brought his people in.

The bunkhouse strained and creaked under the weight of the storm as he shoved his gear into his room, then knocked on Charlayne's door; when there was no answer, an ominous feeling took root in his stomach as he pushed it open. It looked the same as when they'd departed for the field camp; most of her things were still gone. Surely she hadn't stayed in the field. Most likely she was with the professor and his family, he reasoned. There'd be no point in remaining alone in her room.

Light vanished from the sky and the evening became an unlit nightmare; a carpet of black rolled over the bleak pus-yellow clouds and shrieking claps of thunder assaulted his hearing. A firestorm of lightning plagued the area as far as he could see, eerily illuminating stray laundry and thatch from local roofs that had become airborne.

Fascinated in a horrific sort of way, he saw a crippled tree on the perimeter sway drunkenly in the wind and sag to earth, splintering smaller saplings in its path in a whirlwind of destruction. A stray cow ran bawling through the compound, a metal bell clanging drunkenly under the frenzied animal's throat as it disappeared into the forest. This booming, clangorous cacophony must be the origin of the sounds of hell, Jordan thought recklessly. Nature's energy; not to be trifled with.

Please God, she was secure somewhere here in the park's headquarters. Waves of rain descended out of the black in a massive downpour, hissing and pounding relentless fists against the bunkhouse and blocking out his view of the remaining world; he sought the relative safety of his room against the gusting winds, and after a moment realized that Mitch's gear was missing also.

22

. . . a very dangerous place . . .

Jordan made himself wait until the brunt of the storm had passed. When the thunder had rumbled into the near distance, he ran through the driving rain to the professor's quarters; Jamieson's wife let him in, and he found him inside talking to Joh. The old man was upset. "All the elephants will be needed here," he was saying. "There is much damage and there will be injuries. Jimi and Mala are with them. We must see to the village."

Jordan's hopes sank, and he knew without asking that Charlayne and Mitch were out there somewhere, with Jimi and Mala. He tried to keep panic out of his voice. "How long have they been gone?"

"Since this afternoon." Jamieson turned to look at him,

his face grim in the thin candlelight. "I personally told Mr. Baltine that we were breaking camp due to the storm and that elephants would not be available to him. Joh was forced to send Jimi out with Mala to protect them, and now we're short-handed. It's not the first time the young man's seen fit to ignore my decisions."

Jordan joined them at the table, rigid with concern, as the professor continued his tirade. "I had no idea what they were up to. However, there's nothing to be done at the moment. As Joh says, we must check on the people in our village. When things are put right here, then we'll consider the matter of locating Miss Pearce and Mr. Baltine."

"Do you know where they are?" Jordan insisted, unable to restrain his anxiety.

Joh picked up his jungle knife and rose from the table, his face grave. "At a small river in the foothills, I think. If it was possible to keep them safe, Jimi has seen to it." He motioned to Madhav and the two went out into the rain.

Fighting a spiraling mixture of rage and fear, Jordan watched Jamieson struggle into a raincoat. The foothills? With Baltine? After he'd warned her against him? In a monstrous rainstorm like this one, being anywhere near a river was courting peril. What on earth had possessed her?

The professor handed him a slicker. "We'll need everyone at the moment, Mr. Kosterin."

He nodded grimly. "Yes, of course."

For the next two hours he worked with the professor, Joh, and Joh's drivers as they coordinated their efforts with soldiers and villagers in a search for missing and injured residents of Saura. Roofs had been torn off, store windows smashed; felled trees and broken limbs blocked the roads. The elephants were being used to clear debris and help pull apart the collapsed walls of mud huts.

Jordan worked in the pouring rain with a mindless dread aching through his shoulders; fright for Charlayne thick in his throat. How soon would this be finished? How soon could he reasonably expect to begin the search for her? *Damn*, why had she gone with Mitch?

Tragedy focused him on the situation at hand. At the far end of the village, Sunita's home had collapsed and her parents had been crushed; Joh and Khalli were working to lift portions of a mud wall, and Jordan was unnerved at the sight of the bloodied bodies. Their six-year-old son stood by in shock, rain washing mud and tears from his face while his sister clawed at the ruin in Khalli's wake. Jordan leaped to her side and found a wooden cradle filled with dirt and sodden bedding. Inside was another child, a baby, limp as cloth. He snatched it from the cradle, placed it on the ground, and as gently as possible cleared mud from its mouth with his fingers, then began mouth-to-mouth resuscitation. After endless moments the baby began to struggle, vomited dirty water, and set up a wail. The sweetest, most beautiful sound in the world. The sturdy cradle had withstood the weight of the wall, but had filled with mud and water. A few minutes more and the baby would have drowned for certain. He closed his mind to the thought in order to function.

"Is there anyone else in there?" he demanded, terrified the little girl would say yes, but Sunita tearfully shook her head, and he sagged in relief as he examined her wriggling sister; rain washed mud from her body and she flailed arms and legs in squalling distress. When he was reasonably certain nothing was broken, he handed her to Sunita and looked to the boy, who'd sustained a fractured arm.

He bandaged his cuts from broken glass, and the little boy watched stoically as Jordan secured the broken limb between two lengths of wooden stake from what had been their garden. After tying the makeshift cast with strips of cloth, Jordan lifted the naked child to his hip and walked the children toward park headquarters. A few minutes later, when Mrs. Jamieson had them wrapped in blankets and settled in a bedroom, Sunita and her brother with cups of hot cocoa, he stepped outside to return to the rescue effort. Joh and Khalli were coming through the park gate. The old man looked at him, rain running in rivulets down his slicker. "We can go now," he said quietly.

Jordan bowed his head in gratitude, fighting profound emotion that the old man had not forgotten. "How far is it, do you think?" he asked when he'd recovered himself.

"Maybe one hour," Joh replied. "Longer perhaps, depending on what we encounter." He gestured toward the bunkhouse, and Jordan ran for the porch to use the rail to clamber onto Khalli's back. The stormy sky shed no light and rain continued in a steady downpour as the elephant made her way into darkness dense enough to eat. They crossed the shallows and seemed to set off in the general direction of the tree where he'd photographed the sloth bears. From there he became hopelessly disoriented in the black and rain. Actuality began and ended with the elephant beneath him and Joh in front of him, and the terror in his heart.

Storms meant flash floods, and she was camped along a river. Water equaled death. Sudden and permanent. He knew death intimately; had seen it again this evening. Please God, they would find her well and safe.

Lightning crashed in split-second intervals, creating a strobing, surreal sense of fractured daylight, and thunder crashed around her unabated. The wind had lessened only slightly, and rain slashed down without mercy. Water in the stream had deepened, and even with Jimi's staff, it was a struggle to keep her footing next to Mala. Mitch's occasional oath reached her ears as he plodded along ten feet in front of the elephant.

Over the din of the storm, she heard a series of rending cracks and watched with terror and fascination the slow-motion lean of a massive tree as it took a hit from lightning. Blue-white sparks flared up and down its length and it split in two to become a twisting, unstoppable, pile-driving force that smashed into another tree fifty feet ahead of them. The stench of scorched wood assaulted her nostrils as a domino effect went into motion; the second tree broke away from the earth under the weight of the first and the two spiraled into the river in a spray of water and a maelstrom of flying leaves and branches. Within seconds, the water became appreciably deeper, and she realized that the stream had been blocked. Jimi quickly worked Mala onto the bank and around the trees, searching the area with his flashlight.

Roots were still attached on one side of the second tree's base, and the rest, pulled free from the earth, were sprangled in the air, split and fractured. Limbs from both had been driven into the soft ground from the force of their impact, and water was piling up dangerously behind the sudden dam. As they watched, it began to spill over the trunks in an impromptu waterfall even as the river sought passage around the obstruction and began to wear away the bank beneath their feet.

"It will wash out from the bottom and the water will come, whoosh!" Jimi shouted. "We must leave the stream and go into the woods."

"It'll just go around," Mitch argued. "It'll take a monsoon to move those trees. Besides, anyone trying to find us isn't gonna look in the forest."

Charlayne gauged the rising water and knew Jimi was right. "I say the forest," she concurred. "Mitch, no one's going to search for us tonight."

"I'd rather risk high water than dodge falling trees. Stay with me," he insisted stubbornly. "When we get to the Jeep, we can drive out and be home in a couple of hours."

Charlayne looked at him. "What about Jimi and Mala?"

"Jimi can make his own decisions. I'm sticking with what I know. Are you coming with me?"

"No!"

Mitch turned and they watched him begin to splash his way down the stream. Added to the rolling thunder and sizzling cracks of lightning was another sound, a slick, whispery, sucking noise. Under Jimi's light water began to burble from under the trees; within instants a whirlpool began a slow swirl in the dammed water behind.

"Mitch, don't be crazy," she called after him. "The water's coming under!"

Mitch did not pause and his light bobbed in the darkness ahead of them.

"We must cross quickly to higher ground," Jimi yelled to her. "Climb on one of the limbs." On the bank, her feet were already under several inches of water. She scrambled onto a nearby branch and walked up as far as she could manage; he brought Mala close alongside, then made room for her to crawl across the elephant's skull and seat herself around Mala's neck. She scooted backward and they managed an awkward trading of places. "Hang on," he shouted, and urged Mala forward into the rising water.

It was after midnight when he and Joh came upon the empty Jeep parked on the bluff; its reflectors glistened a wet bloodred in the beam of their lights, and Jordan's stomach twisted with rage. Rage that it had taken so long to find a sign of them, rage at Mitch for causing the situation, rage at being so helpless. She was somewhere nearby, but where? Khalli's screeching trumpet rang out over the storm and he prayed for an answering response from Mala. But above the rain and the grumbling river at the foot of the bluff, all was silence.

The ground was saturated with water and the bluff too steep for Khalli to safely negotiate an immediate descent to the river, and Jordan seethed at more delay. Eventually the animal found safe passage and they reached the water; here the current was shallow but mud-chocolate under his light and moving swiftly. His stomach tightened. This was the river of his nightmares. Apprehension had long since numbed his mind, and Jordan stared at the brown, hating it with all his being.

Khalli splashed through the riffling water to the sandbar. He and Joh played their lights across the area. Newly charred logs were lolling in two inches of water and both tents had been ransacked by the wind; hooked to their tent pins, their flattened canvas trailed ominously in the dirty stream.

Joh cupped his hands and called up and down the river, "Hello!" Jordan timed his voice with Joh's and they alternately called and waited. At Joh's signal, Khalli trumpeted again. If there was a response, it was impossible to hear.

They started upstream and found the first mist net blanketed with leaves and debris and floating in the stream; one side was still attached to its stake in the bank. Where it had been tied to the pole, the bottom of the net was a foot under water. Jordan caught his breath. Mitch normally set the nets at least a foot above the water level. The river had risen two feet since they were placed. Two feet of rushing water was life-threatening if you lost your footing. His fear multiplied.

Khalli continued to work her way up the river in the driving wind and rain. At a second site they found one stake with its net torn away entirely. Midstream, water overran what had been a low island. They and Khalli called out into the blackness at intervals until they reached a small fork in the river. On their left, mud and stones and rushing water from a good-size tributary plunged down a steep gully into the main stream, washing earth from around the roots of nearby trees; Joh sent Khalli on, and Jordan leaned forward to be heard. "Shouldn't we go up and check?"

Joh shook his head. "Not a flyway," he insisted. "Ahead is more possible. We'll follow the nets, then check the side streams if we have to."

Several yards farther on they found another net, windblown and canted sideways but still intact. It was the last net they were to find.

They followed a snake bend in the river, and a few yards beyond the second curve, where two streams converged, Joh brought Khalli to a stop. Jordan swore softly under his breath. Under the play of flashlights, he recognized a true division of the river. Damage was apparent everywhere. Young trees had gone over, ten and fifteen in a tangle. A dead deer tumbled past them in the water, its spotted back rolling over and over in the current.

"The storm hit very hard here," Joh said solemnly. "Both streams should be searched."

Jordan nodded. "I'll take the right." Joh moved Khalli onto the bank and Jordan lowered himself onto the muddy ground. "Any advice?"

For an answer, Joh held out his staff in one hand, the steel knife in the other. Jordan chose the staff.

"I will search upstream one hour, then cross and come back down to meet you," the old man said. "Do not look for me, I will find you. Shout every five minutes so we can stay in touch."

Jordan blinked, blinded by the rain leaking into his eyes. "Just find her," he said tightly.

Joh nudged Khalli with his foot and the animal disappeared into a curtain of rain, silent as air itself.

Elephants don't make noise, Jordan thought absurdly. They're like ghosts, they walk and they don't make sounds. He shook his head to clear his brain and started along the bank of his stream. After a few yards he heard Joh's "Hallo!" and Khalli's echoing screech; he yelled an answering call, and relaxed enough to concentrate. If there were no mist nets in the next hundred or so yards, chances were she and Mitch had taken Joh's fork in the river.

Thirty yards and there were none. He decided to continue another twenty minutes upstream just to be sure before switching back to wait for Joh. He hallooed every five minutes, straining into the wind, but Joh's answering call was no longer audible. Once, he faintly heard Khalli trumpet and knew they were a large distance apart. When he came upon a stretch of bank where the stream had narrowed, he was forced to enter the water to see beyond. He'd been soaked for hours, but its coldness shocked him, and he knew he was reaching exhaustion. He'd been working half the night on less than six hours' sleep, without food or a break for rest, too uptight to think about it until now. The powerful beam from his flashlight illuminated the water and he could see the tops of large rocks and boulders as the current tore at his knees.

He examined the area with the light; directly ahead was an impassable collection of dead limbs and forest debris that had washed down the ravine to become lodged between the stream banks. They had combined to form a tiered spillway which was rapidly eroding away at the bottom. He grasped the danger of the situation instantly. It could give way any minute. "This is far enough." The sound of his own voice was startling.

Rattled at the perilous position he was in, he quickly turned to retrace his route, felt the shift as he stepped backward, the pressure against his boot as the rock settled against his ankle; he was forced to pitch the light and use both hands to jam Joh's staff into the stream bed to keep from going over. He teetered dangerously, but was able to retain his balance and prevent his ankle from being snapped. He went to one knee and knew instantly that it was bad. Dazed with fear, he watched a patch of light appear and disappear as his flashlight washed past him downstream until it, too, became caught against a rock; two feet away the powerful light shone dully in the water, barely visible, out of reach.

Even before he tried to move, he knew his foot had become wedged between stones too large to push away, too heavy to lift, too big to pry aside with the wood in his hands; a freak of circumstance that the weight of his body and the flood of water spilling down the steam had been enough to shift the base of the rock. It started as a litany in his head: *Oh, no! Please!* He fought panic, rushing in waves through his body, crushing his mind and beating through his brain. *Oh, no! Oh, Christ, not like this!*

23

. . . not going to forgive me for this one . . .

In the black hole that was his trap, Jordan jerked at his bootlaces, frantically trying to release his foot, but he was neatly caught with no room to maneuver. Using Joh's staff as support, he tore off his slicker and tied it around the wooden stake; then he forced his face underwater in order to reach toward the flashlight. After nearly a dozen attempts he succeeded in touching the hard rubber handle, and it seemed hours until his fingers were able to grasp it firmly enough to bring it to his side. Regaining light gave him a sense of control over his nightmare and allowed him to hold on to his sanity.

Gasping for air, he gathered his breath to shout Joh's name again. When there was no response, he heaved in three quick gulps of air and bent himself double to plunge the flashlight toward the river bottom, trying to see the position of the rocks that held him prisoner. It was impossible, and his ankle protested his actions until he came up for air.

He paused to regain strength and shouted, *"Jimiiii!"* Jamming the flashlight under his belt, then three more quick breaths for oxygen, he pushed under the water again, feeling the contours of his trap with his hands; his ankle had swelled, drawing the bootlaces into a stranglehold. He was anchored to the bottom worse than ever.

Up for air again, he was desperately cold, beginning to shudder with waves of fatigue; balancing carefully, he yanked the slicker back over his head to hold in as much body heat as possible. Then he pried the staff out of the muddy bottom and slid the end of it down his leg to probe the opening where his boot was wedged. His fingers had told him that the rocks were both large and jagged, and any shift in the wrong direction would not only keep him prisoner, but crush his ankle in the bargain. He was already losing sensation in his toes.

Weaving in the rushing water, crudely balanced and panting from exertion, he tried to gather strength. The flashlight in his belt shone upward into a space of sky and onto the undersides of overhanging trees, creating an eerie dome. Theatre-in-the-round, he thought hazily and turned its beam briefly toward the debris dam; paralyzed, he saw a chunk of earth tear away and a torrent of water gush through the gap. He was already waist deep in muck and water, and one way or another it was going to end pretty quickly. He forced himself into action. Rest was a luxury he could no longer afford.

"Get out of this or die trying," he panted heavily. "Don't roll over." He collected his resolve, talked to himself, held on to courage as best he could. "The damned thing moved once, it can move again." Closing his eyes, he thrust his head under the water one last time and clawed at the rocks to establish which was smaller. The need to breathe forced him to the surface and he came out of the water gasping. Out of time, he repositioned the slender staff as a fulcrum and chose the rock on his left.

The beam of the flashlight at his belt went underwater; water was rushing under his armpits, and he didn't need to look at the dam to know it was coming apart. He tested the tension on Joh's staff, knowing his chances were getting slimmer by the instant. Counting to ten, forcing as much air into his lungs as possible, he prepared himself to lunge against the wooden stick and prayed it would work. Half an inch would give him enough room to slip his boot out of the trap.

He shouted her name as prayer, expelled his breath, and drove his full weight onto the staff with all his might. The stone gave slightly before the brittle wood snapped and he plunged backward under the water, going down hard, grazing his back on the imprisoning rock. This time it took enormous effort to regain his footing and forever to thrash to the surface; choking and coughing up dirty water, he managed to clear his nose and mouth. Without the staff's support, he was all but helpless.

He began to comprehend the futility of his struggle. An hour had not passed, and Joh would not find him in time. That was a certainty. With the realization came an bizarre calm. When the mud and limbs and rocks of the dam gave way, he would drown. Even if the water didn't cover him, he couldn't fight the current forever. It had all happened before. He'd cheated death as a child, in a rainstorm, a sudden chocolate river. He knew what would happen now. Eventually he would lose his strength, then his balance, and go under.

The most surprising thing was his acceptance; as his tranquility progressed he understood at last the significance of the dream that had plagued him since childhood. Now that he knew why, the revelation brought an even greater sense of peace. *Everyone dies. Some people choose the when and where of it, and leave people they love behind.*

By refusing chemotherapy, Natalie had chosen; his mother had chosen when he was six years old by pushing him to safety before she'd been swept away to drown. He'd always thought she'd given up, but he knew now that she hadn't; she'd held on from sheer maternal will, past being tired, past her strength, in order to save his life. The minute the car slid off the canted bridge, it had filled with brown, turgid water, pouring in through the open windows; but they'd gotten out and were in the water for a long time before the men came. She'd sang to him, held him close as the current pulled them slowly downstream, and kept them on the side of the car nearest the riverbank.

A human rope of men had been within inches, seconds, of grabbing her. Even then she'd had a choice. Could have reached out, saved herself, but she'd chosen him instead. Unfastened his fingers from her shoulders and pushed him away, screaming, shoved him into a stranger's arms before disappearing forever. The moment she'd known he was safe, her strength had failed. He'd seen her relief, watched her eyes close as the car rolled over and she disappeared.

He, however, was not being given a choice. He was simply in the wrong place at the wrong time, and death was here to collect. In the larger scheme of life, it made no difference. One human more or less in the universe. His eyes would close, too.

Poor Andy, he thought placidly. His brother, who'd never had any luck in this family; raised with photographs of their mother without ever knowing her, Andy would be the one to have to tell their father that his oldest son had drowned, too. Break the news to their grandmother. In San Jose, with Frazier. And Charlayne . . .

I'll be the next one to discover what's out there. The next to know if there really is somewhere to see my mother again. And Natalie . . . Find out if she's still pregnant, or if "life" goes on and she had the baby. Andy's not going to forgive me for this one. . . .

Charlayne was dozing in the dry hollow of an ancient tree when Mala suddenly trumpeted, shattering her eardrums and scaring her half to death; she bolted upright in alarm and snapped on Jimi's flashlight. "What on earth—"

Jimi caught her arm and motioned for silence. Mala turned restlessly to face away from the river and trumpeted again, a piercing blast of sound.

"She hears Khalli," Jimi said, grinning widely in the beam of light.

Charlayne heard nothing, but her heart was leaping with relief. They were found! God love an elephant! Mala went down on her knees and Charlayne scrambled on board her saddle while Jimi walked up her face; within minutes of leaving the hollowed tree behind, they came upon a second stream with muddied water running over its banks.

"*Joh?*" Jimi shouted. "*Hallo?*"

From upstream Charlayne heard a male voice shout her name. She sat upright on the saddle. "That's not Joh, that's Jordan!"

They both screamed his name, but there was no answering shout. Jordan would not be here without an elephant, she thought happily, which meant that Joh or someone was with him. They'd be out of this nightmare soon.

Mala followed the bank upstream, splashing through water at every step, and they called out as they went. Rounding a small bend, Charlayne gaped in horror. Caught in the beam of the flashlight, Jordan was chest-deep in water, and behind him a dam of debris was sagging into slow collapse, pouring mud and water into the stream.

Jimi urged Mala into the river and they did a slow swim to Jordan's side. Charlayne held out Jimi's staff, and Jordan grabbed onto it while Jimi slowly maneuvered Mala's massive body around him to become a living dam. The elephant jammed her hindquarters against the remaining obstruction and effectively held a third of it in place as the rest collapsed; limbs and rocks and mud-slick water rushed into a widening breach at her side and were channeled past them to crash downstream.

Charlayne saw the flood surge of water reach Jordan's chin, lift his body, causing him to groan in obvious pain, but miraculously not cover his head. After a moment he released the stick and raised his arm over Mala's trunk; with great effort he planted a kiss on her hairy nose. "You're beautiful," he croaked.

"We'll get you out," Jimi said to him. "Can you hold on?"

"My ankle's caught. You'll break it off," he rasped tiredly, and steadied himself against Mala's jaw. "Rock slipped. Couldn't get it . . . Twisted."

Charlayne played the light on the pile of debris. The flow of water had lessened and it seemed reasonably safe to reposition the elephant. "What if I hold him up and Mala moves the rock?" she asked Jimi.

"We can try."

She quickly removed her boots and tied them to the saddle by their laces, then shed her sodden jacket. When Jimi had secured the flashlight onto the saddle, she hooked her arm into Mala's lead rope and slid into the water next to Jordan; his arm was stiff with cold and she had to help him let go of the elephant's trunk and push his fist under the rope. He was unable to hold on and immediately slipped under the water.

She hauled him spitting and choking to the surface and this time scissored her legs around his body and crossed her ankles; grabbing him firmly under one arm and around his neck, she locked her hands together behind his head. "Got him," she yelled. "Hurry!"

"Take a breath," Jimi warned. In front of her the elephant's eyes disappeared into the water as Mala lowered her massive head, taking Charlayne and Jordan with her; the world became a dirty, choking, swirling sea. When Charlayne was certain she couldn't stand another instant, they were raised up again, both coughing up water. She shook her hair out of her face and knew from the look of despair in Jordan's eyes that he was still trapped.

"She can't push from here," called Jimi, "and if we let go of him, he'll drown. We have to wait until the water is lower. We can tie him to the saddle as a last resort."

Jordan shook his head, trying to fight the lethargy of exhaustion; the coldness had crept into his center. It was his nightmare. The part where she was still alive. He could see her occasionally in the light that kept flashing over and under the water. Submerged to her chin in chocolate water, with leaves and twigs in her hair, she was holding him in a death grip, and he knew from the dream what would happen next. He would try to hold onto her and she would push him away, disappear from his life.

Strength flowed into his body and he clung to her, determined not to let go. Not this time. This time she would live. This time he would save her. He could hear her voice, sounding through his chest as she spoke to someone. Him. She was talking to him.

"Jordan!"

Suddenly it was Charlayne and he tried to focus. How had she gotten here? She was bloody gorgeous. Her breasts were pillowing his chin. He could feel their warmth and softness through her shirt, and one of her nipples, hardened, cold, rubbed gently against his cheek. Rust and rose . . . If he had another half ounce of strength, he thought dreamily, he just might be able to move the three or so inches to her lips and actually kiss her. But the half ounce was missing.

"You're wonderful," he rasped groggily. "I love you."

"I love you, too," she responded, her words a soothing whisper.

"No, I really mean I love you." *The way I love Natalie* . . . "Natalie," he echoed defiantly.

She pulled back her head to smile at him with a leaf stuck to her chin. "I really love you, too."

She wasn't taking him seriously, and it was important that he prove it to her. "You're terrific. Andy wants . . . go for it."

"I'm glad that's the way he feels," she said slowly. "We're going to get you out of here."

Somehow he was excruciatingly tired and conversation wasn't going in the proper direction.

"Can you stand on your own?" It was Jimi's voice from somewhere above him.

"I . . . try." His own voice belonged to someone else and

WISH LIST 263

the pain in his ankle roared to a new level. There was no strength in his knees.

"Can you hold your breath at all?"

He tried, but nearly lost consciousness. The pain was all. And Charlayne; warm around his middle, soft against his face.

"He's too tired, Jimi."

He began hallucinating. Above her face, in the canopy of trees, his theater, came a play of light and the voice of God.

"Hallo!"

"Over here!" Jimi's voice rang out again. "Quickly!"

And Charlayne's. "Hurry!"

Sweetheart, you can't tell God to hurry. Somewhere in the firmament there was a rapid exchange in Nepali, and suddenly another elephant was coming toward him in the water, and Joh's frowning face.

"Hey, you're late," Jordan said brilliantly, and tried to laugh. He took a mouthful of water instead and began to choke.

Charlayne held his face out of the waves generated by the elephants while Joh maneuvered Khalli closer. It took all her strength to keep him from drowning while Khalli, working on her knees with her head underwater in tandem with Mala on the other side, bullied one of the rocks aside, and Jordan was suddenly freed. He began to drift away from her in the current.

Joh grabbed him and together they held on. The elephants continued their partnership, with Khalli backing carefully out of the ravine with Jordan's body supported by her trunk, and Mala following with Charlayne clinging to her lead rope until they reached the bank.

He was too weakened to stand until he'd coughed up half a quart of water, and after that Khalli boosted him onto Mala's back and they returned to the hollowed tree; the three of them, and Khalli, were able to position Jordan into the dry space inside. While Jimi constructed a rough lean-to of small limbs propped against the entrance, Joh built a fire from rotted wood torn from the tree's interior. Charlayne worked Jordan's feet free from his boots. His injured ankle was swollen and bruised, but there were no bones through the skin and it didn't appear broken to her layman's eye.

As he began to get warm, Jordan drifted in and out of exhausted sleep while she took off her own boots, then used Joh's all-purpose knife to cut off his jeans at the knees and slide both bottoms onto his foot as a makeshift ankle support. Crudely cutting the shirt off the front of his body, she ripped the softer fabric into strips to tie the denim in place. Then she huddled next to him under his slicker until warmth began to return to the both of them.

Joh was standing next to the patient Khalli and talking with Jimi. A few moments later the elephant raised the old man onto her back and the two drifted away into the night.

"Where's he going?" she asked Jimi tiredly.

"He goes to look for Mitch," Jimi explained. "They found the Jeep but Joh didn't see him anywhere along the river."

She shivered with apprehension, and hoped for his sake that Mitch had taken refuge in the forest after all. Then she spooned her body against Jordan's warm stomach to join him in sleep.

24

Last chance . . .

She opened her eyes to a thin shaft of sunlight and looked past the lean-to into a ceiling of green leaves and pale golden sky. Sometime during the night the rain had stopped, and she was lying on her side in Jordan Kosterin's arms.

In a hollow tree.

Not quite her fantasy, but close enough. She stretched stiff muscles and smiled at her situation, enjoying life immensely; her motion caused him to clasp her to his stomach. "No," he mumbled and pulled her hips closer.

She willingly relaxed into his embrace, then edged onto her back so she could see him, savor the warmth and strength and mud-stubbly cheek of him. "I think it's morning," she grumbled halfheartedly, uninterested in disturbing her tranquility, but the events of last evening swamped her memory in a rush. They were lucky to be alive. By all accounts he should have drowned, and if she hadn't stayed with Jimi and Mala, she could very well have lost her life as well.

Fastened in his arms, Charlayne looked around and came to the conclusion that they were alone. Jimi and Mala were gone, or at least out of sight, but the little fire in front of the opening had fresh wood on it and was burning merrily on a ring of stones. Someone must be nearby. Her and Jordan's boots were impaled on stakes, side by side with tongues hanging out, drying by the fire.

She eased a couple of inches away from Jordan's body to begin a personal assessment. Her hair was reasonably dry, but plastered to her skull in what was bound to be an unattractive mess. Teeth: abominable; and there was sand under her tongue. She wrinkled her face in distaste and spat it out. Her jacket had disappeared somewhere in the water last night, and her shirt and jeans were still damp and clammy, but warm against her skin. No doubt the river had swept away the bag with her change of clothing along with her tent, her camera, and everything else she'd brought, and she'd have to wear what she had on until she managed to get back to park headquarters.

"Nurse Jones," Jordan mumbled next to her. "What are you doing?"

She grinned at his sleepy banter. "I'm spittin' grit."

He burst into a gruff chuckle, and she raised herself on one elbow. "Come back here," he demanded.

"No, I'm revolting." She sat up. "Besides, I want to see how your ankle's doing."

He protruded a hairy leg from under the slicker and looked at his bandaged ankle and the new shorter version of his denims in surprise. "Hey, these were my favorite jeans."

She laughed out loud at his scrambled priority. "Well, now they're cutoffs." In their cramped quarters she scooted awkwardly a few inches toward his feet and managed to pull his ankle into her lap and unwrap the cloth. The swelling had gone down, but his skin was raw in places and a sickly purple in color. "Can you put weight on it, do you think?"

He pressed his toes gingerly against the interior of the tree and grimaced. "Not more than two hundred pounds. Come here," he repeated, and waited impatiently until she retied the fabric and returned to her position next to him, then covered her with half the slicker. "This is going to make some kind of book."

"I hope I can make it as exciting in prose as it was in real life," she said with conviction. "Lord knows I can't make it as wet. By the way, I discovered the antidote for motion sickness," she told him snappily. "Terror."

"That'll do it every time." With a burst of strength, he pulled her closer and kissed her throat fervently, moving his face up to whisper roughly in her ear. "I'd have drowned without you. Don't ever go into the jungle without me."

Her temperature soared off the scale in the wake of his emotion and she felt herself blush. "I promise."

He blinked at her in the bleak sunlight, still serious. "I have to talk to you about Andrew."

She slid far enough away to give him a sober look. "I'm sorry, Jordan, but I have no interest in your brother. It's nothing personal, he's a nice guy, but . . ." She shrugged as he gazed at her, no longer blinking, and she braced herself for his response.

"That's good because I have no intention of sharing

you." He grinned and reached out to cup her chin with his palm. "We've already talked about it and he knows where I stand." He came up on one elbow to kiss her lightly. "I meant what I said last night. I do love you."

Her emotions surged at his words and the look that had come into his eyes.

"I have a thousand things I want to say," he continued, music to her ears. "I need to explain what's been going on with me, if I can. It's all pretty strange, but what it really comes down to is I'm in love with you. I don't know how it's going to square with my feelings for my wife, but unless you have an objection . . ."

She kissed him. She couldn't help it. Her heart was full to bursting, and he was so serious and so handsome that, grungy, mud-stained, beard stubble and all, she laid her body across his naked chest, pushed him to the ground and kissed him as if her life depended on it. And in a way, it did. He'd come looking for her last night, nearly died in the process, and, God forbid, if he had, she'd never have heard any of the wonderful things he'd just said to her, never have the incredible feeling that was jumping around in her chest—and never have survived if she'd lost him to the river.

He kissed her in return and surprised her once again with the intensity of his feelings. Gradually, outside, she became aware of the gentle, blowing snorts of elephants and the squishy sound of human footsteps on wet leaves. At the scrape and clank of metal against rocks, the hiss of water on hot coals, and the smell of ground coffee, she reluctantly disengaged herself from his arms. "I think the neighbors are back."

He kissed her quickly, then held her close. "To be continued," he whispered harshly, and she nodded into his chest. Absolutely.

"We're up, we're awake," she sang out to Joh or Jimi or whoever was out there. "We're alive and kicking."

"Kicking or kissing?" Joh ventured dryly.

Jordan laughed when she blushed again. "We were doing that, too," he called amiably. "And, Joh, your timing sucks."

The old man laughed and was spooning coffee into a pan of heating water when they crawled past the lean-to to join him on a small tarpaulin next to the fire. Jimi was squatting nearby, sharpening the forked ends of half a dozen sticks. Charlayne spotted a blanket and draped the thick wool across Jordan's shoulders before covering herself with his slicker; he dragged his weight on hands and hips to protect his injured ankle, then pulled her down next to him onto the tarp. "Except for last night," he amended emotionally. "Your timing couldn't have been better. You guys saved my life, probably hers, too. I don't know how to thank you."

Jimi smiled and Joh shrugged philosophically. "A life for a life, perhaps." The old man glanced back and forth between the two of them. "It was not your time . . . or perhaps there are plans for you. Who knows?"

Jordan clasped Charlayne to his side and spoke for the both of them. "Whatever it is, we're in your debt and we won't forget."

"Mrs. Jamieson sent a few things," Joh continued, his face beaming with pleasure from their show of gratitude. He handed Charlayne a small cotton pouch that contained a toothbrush, antiseptic, a plastic razor, soap, and a towel.

She showed the contents to Jordan with a gay smile. "Marthae's an absolute angel," she declared.

Charlayne made use of the alcohol on Jordan's ankle as Jimi began piercing thick slices of bread with the forked sticks; staked into the ground surrounding the fire, they became toasting devices. Soon came the heady perfume of warm, yeasty toast—ambrosia topped with spoonfuls of grape jelly. It was ravenously devoured as fast as the bread turned the least bit brown, and washed down with cups of ink-black, wonderfully hot coffee.

Life! Life was sweet! Jordan saw the world anew in bursts of color overlaid with the most minute of details. Rain-washed air was alive with mellow fragrances: centuries of humus beneath their feet, crisp earthy moisture, and the fresh smell of creation. Across from him, smudged and tousled and tearing into her breakfast with gusto, Charlayne was radiant, more beautiful than he could have imagined even twenty-four hours ago. She was flushed and rosy in his sight; he drank in the look of her as she came to his side, and wondered about the nearest place he could lay her down. Probably the bunkhouse, he mused. His room. Hers. Whatever she wanted.

It was as if life itself had begun again, overnight, and in his desire for her, Jordan recognized all the earmarks of a brand new wish list. Then he remembered Mitch and briefly turned his attention to Joh. "Did you find Baltine?" His former rage at the man was wan and meaningless in the light of this new day. Next to him, Charlayne paused in her search through the cotton bag, awaiting Joh's response.

"The Jeep is gone this morning," Joh reported. "It was on the bluff last night, so he must have found shelter in the forest."

Jordan nodded, relieved; he saw Charlayne's tension ease as well, and she looked at him saucily, holding up the toothbrush.

"Go ahead," he offered.

She shook her head. "Nope, fair is fair. Does anyone have a coin?"

Joh and Jimi shook their heads, seeing no logic or purpose to her question, but Jordan laughed merrily and searched his "cutoffs," coming up empty-handed. "Nothing but dirt." He picked up a small flat stone and marked an X on one side with a piece of char from the fire. "X is tails," he said. "Call it."

She studied the stone. "Heads." He flipped it into the air, and she gave him a cheeky grin when it came down with the clean side showing. "Me first." Satisfied, she walked a short distance away, turned her back, and proceeded to scrub her teeth with vigor, using her coffee as liquid toothpaste.

"Nurse Jones, save some of that for me," he called. Joh and Jimi, amused at their antics, shared the remainder of the coffee before Jordan poured off the dregs into his cup; inspired at her ingenuity, he dunked the bar of soap into the liquid, then rubbed it onto his beard, producing a reasonably warm, if aromatic, lather of sorts, and, to the delighted astonishment of the Nepali men, began to shave.

Jimi disappeared toward the river with Joh's knife, returning a few minutes later with a length of sapling. He peeled away the bark with the cumbersome implement, then pared down the remaining wood until the shape of a staff emerged. Jordan watched the man's skill, fascinated.

When Charlayne returned to the campfire and handed him her cup, he took his turn with the toothbrush, then gave her an impudent smile. "We'll have to notify Starbucks. They may want to take a look at the possibilities."

"Do you both feel well enough to travel?" Joh asked quietly.

They nodded at him in unison and his eyes twinkled, the old spy. Then, with the help of Jimi's freshly hewn staff, Jordan cautiously got to his feet to test his ankle. As he feared, it would accept little weight without a great deal of pain, and he balanced on one foot with the help of his new "cane."

Charlayne and Jimi poured river water onto the campfire, scattered the stones, and wrapped utensils and the remaining supplies inside the tarpaulin. Mala knelt at Jordan's side. Joh tied the bundle onto the back of the saddle and helped Jordan pull himself onto her back; it took a great deal of effort, and he was conscious that even with food energy, his strength had not fully recovered. Still twinkling, Joh indicated that Charlayne should ride with Jordan. "Mala has rested the night and Khalli has been working," he explained.

Jordan slid backward on the saddle until he felt the tarpaulin, in order to make room for Charlayne to climb up in front of him; as soon as she had, he immediately opened his blanket to enfold her firmly inside. She settled into his arms and fit neatly against his chest. The rejuvenating, life-giving heat he'd slept with seeped once again into his stomach, and it seemed that every blade of grass, every bird song, every flower and rock—everything he smelled and heard and saw—was brand new, fresh, and wonderful.

Khalli moved out with Joh and Jimi on her back, and Mala followed. They crossed the lowered river, the water still muddy with runoff from the storm, and headed cross-country; Mala paced herself a steady twenty feet in Khalli's wake. Charlayne's concern that the animal was unguided prompted Joh's assurance that the elephant would follow without need of command; appeased, she fussed with the blanket and slicker, and Jordan helped her create a mini-tepee to surround the two of them, preventing chill air from finding its way inside.

This time there was nothing neutral about riding close

behind her; his body was too alive and too highly aware of their contact—ten times greater than the night in the car. He gripped the edges of the blanket and maintained fists under her breasts as he held her body next to his chest. She adjusted her hips to fit snugly between his thighs, and the damp fabric of her jeans set up an unbearably delicious friction against his crotch, hard against her and getting harder by the moment.

Concerned at his growing indiscretion, he eased himself away in order to preserve a semblance of decorum and spread his legs in an effort to slide backward, but there was nowhere to go, and she immediately shifted her hips to fill in the gap; her deliberate pressure brought him fully rigid, instantly, permanently, and he quickly lost contact with propriety.

A viscous, sexual heat expanded to fill up his veins, molding his body; tension took over his being, radiated from his sex, tight against her. Ahead of them Joh and Jimi were deep in conversation in Nepali as they entered a light woods with a dense undergrowth of saplings still wet from the storm. Thin sunlight filtered through to the watery green around them and shimmered in the brisk air. Bombarded by stimulation, Jordan was glad for the light in the sea of leaves; glad for the rough wool blanket tenting their shoulders, shielding their bodies; glad to feel the soft globes of her breasts as they rode the tops of his wrists and shifted subtly with her movements. Their weight and warmth alone would have kept him hard as a rock.

He wanted to feel the rust of her nipples, pinch and knead them to an erection as taut and heated as his own, make them rub against her shirt, create the same thrust of fire in her loins that he was enduring. He slid his thumbs over the cups of her bra and onto the swell of immeasurably soft, ivory cleavage. When she made no objection, he freed one hand to explore damp, silken breasts, butter slick and smooth as melting cream, and got harder, if that was possible, risking his own control in the process.

"I want more," he whispered. "Hold the blanket." When she complied without a word, he quickly worked his fingers under her shirtfront, unfastened the snap to her bra, and spilled the satin undersides of her breasts into his palms, thumbs and forefingers greedily seeking rose aureoles; he took enormous delight in slowly, deliciously, teasing her nipples to stiff points and eliciting sighs of pleasure. The feel of her breasts, her body warm and tight against his chest, her legs resting along the tops of his thighs, drove his need to the singular thought of laying her down, of moving on top of her, having her, owning her, while the ache in his testicles built to a crescendo.

Still, he continued to make himself crazy with want. In truth, there was no contest; he'd choose the masculine price of confinement for hours rather than give up the feelings that were racing through his body. His chin came to rest at her ear level and he kissed her lobe, caught her flesh gently in his teeth and felt her shivered reaction.

"I want to make love to you," he whispered urgently. "I want to make you as crazy as you're making me."

Reveling in his confession, Charlayne laughed and worked her hips against him in a calculated, sweet revenge, making him pay for all the moments she'd wanted him, for the hours and days she'd been convinced he was impossible, compensating him in kind for the trilling ecstasies his fingers were sending through her breasts to fill her body at this very moment. From the instant he'd gone hard, she'd been unable to help herself. It hadn't been difficult to keep in tight contact with him, boldly rubbing her seat against his swollen penis, sturdily thick behind her, as she did her best to increase his pleasure.

His hands were supporting her breasts, thumbs and forefingers impishly, expertly, plying her captured nipples, sending sensation tumbling toward her center, exciting her brain, overriding any objection as to time or place, or anything else for that matter. All she wanted was to make love with him as soon and as often as possible. She moved forward to scissor her thighs a bit to tease him, gauged her success by his quick intake of breath, then eased back to enjoy the feel of his spasms. He could do whatever he wished, as long as he didn't stop streaking those lovely tremors through her—

"Be careful." His hoarse voice, wonderfully taut as he caught his breath once again, interrupted her reverie. She heard the warning and ignored it. Relentlessly exerting pressure, she repeated her subtle movements against him, demanding with her body that he either stop or share the pleasure he was creating.

The little witch was at it again, he realized, purposefully driving him crazy. "It's going to be my turn, you know. As soon as I get you in the bunkhouse," Jordan assured her recklessly, helplessly, and groaned. Her rocking body was willfully squeezing his erection with slow, tantalizing undulations; the small, relentless bursts of pressure were bringing him to the point of no return. "Two can play at this," he warned.

When she continued, he relinquished a breast in order to slide his hand past her waist and quickly worked his fingers to the base of her jeans. He cupped his hand and, by exerting a firm hold, prevented further motion, which kept her from driving him over the edge. Barely. Heat built under his fingers and he felt her ragged breathing. She struggled to move, but he held her fast.

"Last chance," he murmured, and when she purposefully sat back against him, he exerted pressure of his own. Soon, with an all but silent moan, she turned her head to seek his lips and poured the light and energy of her climax from her mouth into his. The joyous game was over and he'd won. He held her in his arms, kissing her neck and shoulders, loving her, enjoying the knowledge that he'd pleasured her. Against her bottom, his erection slowly subsided into an ache of immeasurable proportion as he paid the cost that only sex with this woman would relieve.

For the rest of their journey he counted the seconds until he could properly lay her down and satisfy his body as well. To his heart's content, as soon as she'd let him.

25

I was deciding whether or not to pretend . . .

    Charlayne rinsed shampoo from her hair, reveling in the tepid water running down her skin, cleansing and sensual across her breasts, still sensitive from Jordan's attentions. A sexual ripple tingled upward through her body, an aftershock of sorts; his intimate treatment hadn't been the first she'd received at the hands of a man, but it was unquestionably the most delicate. And enjoyable.

Jordan's hands. She flushed at the memory, astonished by her recent behavior with him. It had been wanton and completely out of control, the first time in her life she'd had total disregard for the outside world.

Right this minute he was waiting his turn in the camp's

shower, and soon they would make love, properly, in a bed and naked for each other; she felt a double rush of excitement at the thought of him, at the excitingly private things they'd share, and she knew from the ache in her body that she was ready. There was no question that she had a hunger to feel his embrace, know him fully and feel the hard shaft of his body slide inside her own, praying she wouldn't disappoint him.

Jordan limped the length of the compound, leaning on his cane and swearing at his inability to walk with any degree of comfort. Somehow he'd figure out how to work around his bum leg and make her his. Exceeding the pain in his ankle was the dull throbbing of his testicles, and all he could think about was how soon he could lay down with her. And how soon she'd be out of that damned shower so he could get clean enough to do it!

Halfway back to his room he saw her emerge and wave to him; he angled toward her, cursing his injury for slowing him down. Kissing her, he issued a fevered ultimatum. "My room in ten minutes." Then, as delicately as possible, "Um, what are your views on birth control?"

She looked at him distractedly and blushed. "I didn't pack anything, I didn't expect—"

"We'll manage." He kissed her again, loving her for her honesty.

Minutes later he was stripped and in the damp stall where she'd stood naked. He grabbed the bar of soap, slick from her use, and got a soft erection as he used it to lather himself. He leaned on his cane to scrub his hair and skin, anticipating the heat of her, of laying claim past the cream and rust and rose he now knew intimately, to the smooth, round, and wet of her. He doused himself with a chill water rinse then shaved again in front of a mirror, insurance against damaging fragile skin.

As he toweled down, his ankle began to protest in earnest; he wrapped himself in damp terry cloth—clothing being a waste of time since he planned to be naked with her in five minutes anyway. When he finally hobbled up the bunkhouse steps, the door to her room was ajar, but she was not inside.

Disappointed, irritated, he looked around the grounds for her, in no mood to hang around in the brisk air, and definitely not in the mood to twiddle his thumbs. When she did not appear, he limped into his room, closed the door, and tried to decide whether or not to get dressed after all. Maybe she was having second thoughts?

Frustration ate at him. Enough was enough. They'd arrived in camp over two hours ago; he'd been tight as a bloody drum when he let go of her body, eager to get her alone, only to endure an endless interview with Professor Jamieson, who'd had a late breakfast waiting. Then nearly an hour of cooling his heels while the cook heated water; the professor had been anxious for their safety and, totally unaware that he was throwing a monkey wrench into Jordan's sex life, had gone to a great deal of trouble to arrange a hot shower—his answer to speeding recovery from their near miss with disaster, as well as his manner of showing appreciation that they'd come through it safely.

While they'd waited for pails of water to simmer, Jamieson insisted they eat scrambled eggs and more toast, while he elicited the details of Jordan's rescue and confirmed that earlier that morning, when Mitch had shown up in the Jeep, he'd personally dismissed him from doing further research at the park. As far as he knew, Mr. Baltine had returned to Tiger Tops. In view of her innocent participation in the fiasco, however, Jamieson had granted Charlayne permission to stay on, so it hadn't been a total waste of time.

Jordan punched his pillow in frustration. Where the hell was she? It was practically eleven o'clock, and to make matters worse, they were expected for lunch in little over an hour. Not that he'd last that long. Christ, he couldn't remember a time he'd been so ready. At this rate he'd go off halfway through kissing her hello. He disposed of the mosquito netting and settled onto the bunk to rest his sore ankle on the mattress. Somewhere in this mess was sanity and control; he simply had to find it again.

It was an eternity before he heard her footsteps along the porch. She paused at his door, then continued on into her room and he heard the rustling of paper, the whisper of clothing. Finally, she opened his door and stood in the doorway wearing a thin orange shift, her body framed in weak midday sunlight.

"Where the hell have you been?" he demanded as reasonably as he could master. "I was afraid you'd changed your mind."

She laughed and tossed a paper sack to him as she closed the door. "I was bribing the cook."

The aroma of fried chicken began to seep from the bag. He set it aside, more interested in watching her cross the room in his direction. Blood began to pulse a new, high, pressing need in his body.

"And . . ."

She sat on the opposite bunk to remove her sandals. Beautiful toes with coral polish emerged. He wanted to kiss them. Lick between them.

". . . I've advised Professor Jamieson that you are entirely too exhausted to come to lunch and will probably need the entire afternoon to recuperate from your ordeal."

"And evening," he added firmly, adoring her foresight. As she moved in the dim light, he saw that her breasts were unconstrained under the flimsy cotton, and he made plans to kiss them, too. Suck the rust of her to a full, rigid erection, hard and tight as his own. As soon as he could reach her he was going to show his appreciation in more ways than she could imagine.

"And evening," she echoed, and stepped self-consciously out of her shift, totally nude in his sight.

He caught his breath, desperate to have her in his arms, under his body.

"It seems that I, too, am exhausted, and I have secured 'No Visitors' signs to both our doors."

Blood increased its insistent swelling. "Come here, Chara." He held out a handful of Roget's condoms. "I have plans to use every one of these."

Charlayne accepted the condoms, but her interest was fastened on the towel wound loosely around his waist with a conspicuous lump in its front, large and enticing. She sat at his side and lightly trailed her fingernail along the mounded terry cloth, watching his face. "I think we've met."

"You're about to meet again," he said heavily. "Unless I die of a heart attack. Which is possible if you do that again."

She tore the seal from one of the condoms, then deliberately slid her hand inside the terry cloth and traced her index finger up and down the length of his erection before opening the towel to reveal his rigid penis, making him wait while she enjoyed his torment. Ever so slowly smoothing the condom into place, she enjoyed lightly pressuring her fingers over the sensitive head and every inch of his sturdy shaft.

As soon as it was in place, he grasped her in a frenzy,

pulled her forward until he could kiss her, and rolled her onto his naked body. Cupping her buttocks in his hands, he ground himself into her abdomen as they kissed.

"It's been too long," he said raggedly. "Don't make me wait. Not this time."

She gave in to his need. "Tell me what you want."

"On top," he pleaded.

Not her favorite position, and little better than frustrating in past experience. But she quickly placed her knees on either side of his body as he took care to fit himself inside. "Oh, God," he breathed. "You're incredible. I can't believe this."

She began lowering herself by inches until there was close contact between their bodies. Gaining confidence from his gasps of pleasure, she tilted her pelvis forward, seeking to please him. He grabbed her shoulders. "Stop. Oh, Chara, stop. Don't move or it's all over."

She complied, determined to do as he wished. After a moment she felt his fingers slide down her breasts to the tips of her nipples; he carefully pulled her forward, then raised his head and began to kiss first one then the other. "Don't move," he pleaded as he switched from side to side. "Oh, God, it's so good I can't stand it."

It was tempting to defy his request and send him over; at the same time, she wanted to keep him hard and full between her legs, to continue the slow build of pressure in her own body, so she held herself still, acceding to his demand. Moments passed as he fought for control. Finally, he gave up and asked her to raise herself very, very slowly. When she was high enough, he quickly positioned his thumb intimately against her body, then pressed her hips in a signal to lower herself upon him once more.

He worked himself in a stabbing rhythm as she came

down, and it was a streak of fire melting into an icy glissando in one long, smooth, liquid motion; she moaned from the bliss of it, and he crushed his mouth against her breast, quelling his shout as he drove himself inside her body as far as he could manage, and again, until he was spent.

Little by little his body relaxed beneath her, with an occasional spurt of pleasure. Thick with her own sensation, she eased her aching breasts forward onto his chest and extended her legs prone against him, locking him inside her body; they lay content for several minutes. "I've wanted to get in bed with you since the first time I saw you," she confessed, her lips brushing his throat. "You were the most beautiful man I'd ever seen." She saw his embarrassed grin in the dim light.

"No one's ever called me beautiful."

"Well, it's true," she insisted.

His chest heaved slightly with his snort of disbelief. "You kissed my brother," he said indignantly. "Took him to your room for half the night."

She laughed. "Well, it took me a little while to decide. . . ."

"Decide what?" he demanded darkly.

"Whether or not to pretend he was you," she teased.

He reared his head back to look at her with narrowed, questioning eyes. "I didn't know women did that."

She shrugged, secure in his arms, but tight with the need for more of him. "You have no idea how many dreams I've had about you. I couldn't believe it when I saw you here."

"Andy's doing." As he explained his brother's machinations, Jordan moved onto his side to make room for her on the bed and settled an arm under her head.

She was wide-eyed when he finished. "You're kidding."

Then she cocked her head and punched him in the ribs in mock annoyance. "You mean your brother's not madly in love with me? It was an act?"

"To tell the truth, I'm not really sure," he said contentedly. A heady feeling curled up from his toes. She was his. He'd had her. He'd have her again. As soon as he could manage it. Reaching over to tease her breasts, he kept her ready, watched her face as she arched against him; her breasts were swollen globes, giant peaches with stiff rust stems and sensitive to every nuance of pressure. He wished he could be hard for her again. "I couldn't stop thinking about you," he confessed. "Being unfaithful to my wife's memory was making me crazy, and then when it looked like you and Andy had—"

She shook her head emphatically.

"I know. But it made me nuts at the time." He slid lower on the bed, smoothed her soft tummy with his hand, lightly toying with the glossy hair that bordered her sex. "I'm walking around with all this guilt because I was thinking, 'My brother's in love with her,' but I couldn't stay away from you."

He slid lower and kissed the mound, his blood heating with anticipation. "Still can't." She'd been generous, understanding of his need, careful to make his enjoyment supreme. He was about to return the favor. "Now it's your turn."

Comprehension dawned gradually in her face, further exciting him with the knowledge that she hadn't intended to admit she wasn't satisfied; a gratifying arousal quickly worked its way to the base of his spine. Some men, he knew, found giving oral pleasure to their partners one of the most exciting forms of sex; many, however, did not. In his mind, lovemaking in this way was something he supremely enjoyed, second only to getting to his own orgasm. He separated her knees and parted her feminine cleft, slick and proud under his fingers.

Attuned to her submission and determined to carry her as far into euphoria as he could manage, he eased back the tiny hood, and she caught her breath in a long, delicious sigh as he exposed the distended nub of her sex and blew it gently cold before encircling it with the tip of his tongue. Paying careful attention, and guided by her moans and ragged breaths, he probed her most sensitive sites, learning how to provoke the most pleasure, and how long to stroke and how much pressure to bring against her. Enjoying her bliss, he drove his own excitement at the thought of possessing her again.

He knew she was close; he also knew that the longer he held her in readiness, the deeper and more satisfying her orgasm would be. Having waited hours before reaching his own explosive climax moments ago, he could attest to the truth of it.

Diverting her with licks and kisses to her thighs, he came back occasionally to massage the small peak with his tongue, draw that small bit of her flesh into his mouth in a soul kiss to the base before making her wait a few moments more. She was moaning continuously now in mindless, wordless pleas, and he knew from the pressure of his own erection that it was going to be soon. He prolonged his teasing until finally he wanted her too badly, then guided her into heaving, rigid spasms by holding her hard against his mouth. He lost himself in the jerking contractions of her, and refused to let her cease; alternately, he brought friction and pressure, finally slicking the shivering surface gently until she came again.

Soon he had her skimming, and shared in her ecstasy by controlling her orgasms, one after another, sometimes giving her only seconds between, occasionally letting her drift into a moment of relaxation before taking her up again and sending her crashing into yet another series of paroxysms. She was gasping for breath, deliriously sensitized, and literally quivering under the touch of his lips. Finally, she began to plead. "No more. Please, no more."

He let her rest, watching with satisfaction as muscle contractions rippled through her body. She was his. He'd given her pleasure, in the extreme; it was as much his as hers, and he was proud. He eased his leg aside to allow room for his erection, sheathed and hard and more than ready for her as soon as she'd let him enter. It would be a few minutes before she'd be able to receive him again; at the moment, her sex was too sensitive to continue, but it was temporary. He knew the wait would not be long, and for her the next session of lovemaking would be even better. He caressed her breasts as he waited, content to suckle her nipples and feed the ache in his groin, anticipating release.

Thus went the afternoon.

And evening.

26

They're talking about us . . .

Charlayne woke from deep, healing sleep to discover that she was indeed still lying next to Jordan Kosterin. He'd been an erotic force in every dream she'd had since they'd met, and, incredibly, her fantasies could not compare with reality. He'd shown the way to vast reservoirs of feelings she could not have imagined. In the process, he'd become an obsession. Her body was bruised from taking his weight, tender from joining with him, sore from the nips and licks and teethings that had been exploring her for hours. But she wanted more. She wanted the sweetness of kissing him, of probing his secrets with her mouth, to feel his tongue, his gentle fingers sliding into no-longer-secret places, his erections that seemed ever larger, more insistent, and designed to fit her body alone.

Nothing in her experience had prepared her for the series of orgasms he had caused in her; high-pitched, shattering convulsions had gone racing, one after the other, obliterating her thinking as they produced torrents of light at the base of her thighs. Each time making way for even greater sensation as he entered her body, again and again. Driven to the end of herself, she'd lost track of time, place, sense of tomorrow, yesterday. There was only Jordan. Making love to her. Having made love to her. About to make love to her again.

Oral sex was something she'd abhorred with her husbands as obligatory and demeaning, but with Jordan she couldn't get enough of him. At her insistence, he'd shown her how to add to his pleasure in the way she'd received her own; she'd taken delight in learning his most sensitive areas, and was soon rapidly, and regularly, bringing him to a state of readiness that even he found amazing.

He'd sneaked naked next door at one point to retrieve bottles of water, and she'd followed him to the door, unwilling to let him out of her sight. They'd fed each other cold fried chicken and, still ravenous, continued making love.

She'd learned his limits, to gauge how long she could tempt, then make him wait; she'd refused breathless appeals to cease her motion in order to compel his orgasm at her will, and had become intimately acquainted with the heretofore unexplored world of condoms in the process. Every time a new one was necessary, she delighted in readying him with her mouth, her lips, her fingers, and her own brand of taking charge, teasing and tantalizing him before letting him take possession.

She'd introduced him to Sailor Green, who appeared

during their mutual rest after one particularly obliterating session of lovemaking; he'd bobbed his head in apparent approval before scuttling through a crack in the wall, and they laughed about his opinion for an hour.

It was now long past dawn. Hungry, she was unwilling to remove her body from the man at her side. He stirred against her, fumbled for her breasts and gently claimed her ravaged nipples. "I've never had a night like that in my life," he mumbled against her hair. "I think you're a witch."

She sighed and snuggled against him, more alive than she'd felt in years. "Think anyone knows what we're doing?"

"If they do, they're jealous."

"I wish we had room service. Wouldn't have to get dressed, wouldn't have to walk all the way to the kitchen . . ."

He looked around. "Are we out of water?"

She nodded. "We're also out of these." She held up an empty foil packet.

He laughed. "I know where we can get more of those."

She grinned at him happily. More was an absolutely fabulous idea.

"And room service," he teased. "And hot water. Your wish has become my command, Nurse Jones. Leave it to me."

She watched him dress, reveling in the tall and lean of him. "God, you are a good-looking man," she praised from the warmth of their bed.

He tossed an empty foil at her. "Cut that out unless you want to tempt fate."

She pretended to think it over, then shook her head as he approached. "No thanks. Right now what I need is food."

"*Energy* food. I've been running on adrenaline for the past two hours. Not that you're not worth it."

She giggled as he went through an elaborate ritual of discretion: knocking on the door to her empty room, he pretended a conversation, then retrieved her travel bag so she could get dressed as well. They left the bunkhouse, and the cook fixed them a late breakfast, chattering in Nepali to his helper as he scrambled eggs and made a fresh pot of coffee. Whenever Charlayne caught them staring, they'd turn away to break into the chortles of conspirators. "They're talking about us," she whispered, unsure if she was embarrassed or proud.

Jordan was unruffled. "If we were them, we'd be talking about us, too. My guess is the whole camp either knows or suspects by now."

The professor came in for coffee and joined them. "You two seem to be recovering nicely," he said, pleased. Either naive or the soul of discretion, his observation was confirmed by Jordan's assurance that his ankle was improving hourly and that despite his injury, he'd managed quite a bit of rest. Fresh snickers erupted from the kitchen.

Charlayne flushed, but Jordan gave her an angelic smile, shocking her once again with his incredible good looks. He addressed the professor in an offhand manner, man-to-man. "She'd like to go over to Tiger Tops for a couple of days, see if we can get a few tiger photos."

"Fine, fine," granted the professor. "Joh's giving Khalli and Mala a three-day rest, and I must say, they've earned it." He rose from the small table. "Well, I'm off. Time to replenish supplies again. Seems that's all we do when we're not gathering data. We have a few things to repair as well."

Jordan opened his billfold. "If it's not too much trouble, I'd like to treat the elephants to a couple bags of sugar. Our way of saying thank you. Sorry I don't have rupees."

He handed Jamieson twenty American dollars. "Plus twice that for Joh and Jimi." He glanced into the kitchen. "And a bag for the staff, if you'd be so kind." Sugar was a rare luxury, consistently in short supply due to its cost. "Is this enough?"

"Ample." The professor was appreciative. "I'll certainly see to it. Their families will be thrilled."

"Well, it's little enough, considering." Jordan's smile faltered. "How's Sunita doing?"

The professor sobered and shook his head.

Charlayne was alarmed at their change in mood. "What happened? Has she been hurt?"

"She lost her parents." Jordan took her hand as she caught her breath in shock.

"She seems pretty resilient," the professor said fondly. "She has her brother and sister to look after, which seems to be helping."

Jordan added another fifty dollars. "Whatever they need."

"Thank you," Jamieson responded. "It's much appreciated."

"What's going to happen to them?" Charlayne chastised herself for being oblivious. She'd never been happier in her life, and children were suffering.

"They'll live with us as long as we're here. We'll try to have them placed with local families. Unfortunately, there are already several orphans in the village. But this will help people take them in." He pocketed the money and bid them good day.

Charlayne felt hollow. "We have to do something," she said fervently. "Find someone to take care of them."

Jordan nodded agreement. "I thought maybe we could talk to Anup. A couple thousand a year is an enormous amount of money here. I can manage that easily, and it will give these kids a better life than they'd have had otherwise." His jaw tightened. "Of course, no amount of money replaces a parent."

"I can dedicate a portion of book royalties." She sighed, relieved that they had a solution, but equally troubled that a solution was necessary. "Life doesn't play favorites," she said unhappily. "I keep forgetting that. And it can all be taken away in a heartbeat."

He took her hand again. "It can be restored in a heartbeat, too. Don't forget that. I'm living proof."

She was able to smile. "I won't."

At noon they walked to Anup's Campgrounds. His grandchild, a boy, as Joseph had predicted, had arrived at last, and Anup's obvious pride in the newborn reminded Charlayne of her father. She and Jordan proposed their plan to aid Saura's orphaned children. When they finished, Anup agreed to act as guardian for Sunita and her brother and sister; he was also willing to administer a fund for the others on an as-needed basis. Then he drove them to Tiger Tops.

They secured a room with a huge, king-size bed in it—plus a new supply of Roget's black market birth control items—and after a lengthy bout of slick joining in a steamy, hot shower, during which Jordan introduced her to the joys of being soaped and rinsed with attentive loving care, they slept naked and exhausted for the next few hours.

Jordan was still sleeping when Charlayne decided to place a call to Andy. "Thanks again for my photographer," she said to him joyfully, "who is currently sound asleep."

Andy laughed self-consciously. "It's the least I could do for acting like such a jerk." Then he added seriously, "After Natalie, he just didn't come back, and we were losing him. When I saw his reaction at the Taj Mahal, I knew it had to be you."

She was suddenly tearful. "You're a very caring person, Andy. I hope you find someone in your life as special as you deserve." She pulled herself together. "I called to see how you're feeling."

"Well, they still won't let me fly, but I'm able to drive again. How's Jordan doing?"

"He's a little beat up, actually, but due for a medal." She laughed. "As soon as I get back to Los Angeles, I have plans to teach your brother to swim." She described Joh and Jordan's search for her and the incident in the river.

Andy's voice became intense. "My brother went into floodwater looking for you?"

She could hear his astonishment. "He told me about nearly drowning," she said soberly. "Being caught in the river must have been torture for him."

It was a few seconds before Andy commented circumspectly, "God, he must really love you."

They chatted a few minutes longer before a sleepy Jordan rolled over and took the phone from her hand. "Hey, little brother, I just want to tell you that you were nuts to let me have Nurse Jones," he said rudely. "And, now that I'm awake, you have to go away." To her shock and astonishment, he deliberately banged the instrument on the side table. "Hello? Did you hear me? Are you still here?"

With Andy's laughter issuing very clearly from the receiver, she was mystified at Jordan's behavior. "What are you *doing*?"

"It's a family thing." He whacked the phone again. "If you're still there, don't call back for two days." He hung up the phone and pulled her into his arms.

Thereafter, room service supplied sustenance, bottled water, and ice; Jordan supplied everything else. They engaged in sex. Truly, madly, deeply, no-holds-barred sex, interspersed with bouts of tranquil rest. Jordan's injury no longer required careful physical planning, and once again Charlayne became aware that orgasms weren't a sometime thing. With Jordan Kosterin, they were on time, every time, and there was nothing whatsoever remaining on her wish list in that department.

That night they slept the genuine sleep of the emotionally, physically, and sexually depleted. The next morning, they roused themselves early enough to claim seats on a howdah and went out with a group of tourists at six A.M. to look for tigers. Their wish to view the marvelously striped gold and black cats in the wild was fulfilled, and Jordan was able to photograph two young males, brothers according to their guide, at their toilette. As the young tigers licked each other's faces with obvious affection, Charlayne madly scribbled notes and began plans for a Twin Tiger series, "Pete and Re-Pete."

She and Jordan retired to their room, reveled once again in the joys of room service and, since his ankle was complaining about the level of their recent activity, a much needed rest. Two hours into sleep the phone rang, an unexpected, ominous sound that jarred them both awake.

"It better be a wrong number," Jordan mumbled darkly, reaching across her body to pick up the receiver. "Who's calling?" he demanded. After a moment he handed her the receiver. "It's the operator."

She came awake immediately and took the phone. "Yes?"

"Sorry to disturb you, Miss Pearce. We sent a driver to Chitwan and he's just returned to advise us that you're our guest. An Egan Hawke is trying to reach you from the United States."

Charlayne's heart pounded a terrible rhythm in her ears. "Is there a message?"

"'Please call as soon as possible,' and a number."

It was her uncle's home in Texas. She asked the operator to place the call, aware that it was after two in the morning in Dallas. "It must be my father," she explained to Jordan. "It can't be good."

He nodded and began to dress.

It seemed to take forever for the connection to go through, and she was thrilled when her father answered the phone. "Daddy?"

"Hello, sweetheart. I guess you know we've been trying to get in touch with you. I hope it isn't too early there, or late. I can never remember which way the time difference goes."

She could hear avoidance in his voice. *Oh, God, Mother?* "It's tomorrow afternoon here. What's wrong? Is it—"

His voice broke as he gave her the news. "Sophie's gone. Early this morning." He sobbed into the phone. "Her heart."

Charlayne's relief that it was neither parent was short-lived, flooded over with pain at the loss of dear, dithery Aunt Sophie. Her eyes filled with tears at his obvious distress, combined with her own growing sense of grief. She and Jordan had been discussing death at Chitwan about the time . . . A cold chill passed through her body.

"Sondra flew down with us," her father said haltingly, "but . . . it seems your mother's not handling things very well, and I'm afraid . . . I don't suppose you could—"

"I'm on my way," she said quickly. If her father was this distraught, her mother must be frantic. And her poor uncle . . . "How's Uncle Egan? Is he all right?"

"He's not good. It was a terrible shock, of course. No warning. He found her . . . Blames himself."

"That's probably normal. It'll take a while for me to get

back. I'll call as soon as I know when I'm arriving. Where's Mother? I'd better speak to her before I hang up."

"She's sleeping. I'll tell her you called."

Which meant she'd taken a tranquilizer. Indeed things were not good if her take-charge mother was sedated. Not good at all. "How's Sondra?"

"She's been helping your mother and Egan make arrangements, but she's not terribly strong, you know. Not like you. Of course, your mother's worried about her pregnancy.... How soon do you think you can be home?"

"I'm not sure. It took me almost two days to get here, but I'll fly straight through. Think in terms of twenty-five or thirty hours. I'll hang up now and start working on it. Give everyone my love . . . I love you, too." She put down the phone and fumbled through her purse until she located Mr. Pujji's card, conscious that her hands were trembling. "I have to go home," she said dully, trying to make it real.

She was grateful when Jordan took the card from her fingers.

"I'll work on this," he said. "Get dressed."

While she showered, Jordan reserved seating on the resort's afternoon flight to Kathmandu and determined its arrival time, then called Pujji's number. He gave him her Texas destination and asked about connections through New Delhi. "What city in Texas?" he called to Charlayne.

"Dallas."

"Dallas," he repeated into the phone and waited in silence. "Right . . . He says its best to get to New Delhi tonight, otherwise it's a ten-hour delay."

She nodded and he gave Pujji the go-ahead, then hung up the phone. "You'll connect either through New York or Washington, he doesn't know yet. Call him when you arrive in Kathmandu and he'll tell you which flights.

There's nothing from Delhi direct to Dallas." He looked at her closely. She was practically in shock, dressing methodically, vaguely aware of her surroundings. "All this is pretty hasty planning. Are you sure it's a good idea? Maybe you should take a few minutes to think about it." He had a partial solution. "I'll go with you to Kathmandu."

"No, it's not necessary," she insisted. "Really, I'll be OK as soon as I'm on the plane."

Going with her now would cost him a day's delay. He'd left his passport and cameras at Chitwan, and there'd be no time to get them before she left; he'd have to come back for them, then fly to Kathmandu again, which didn't solve the visa problem. Jordan helped her pack, wanting desperately to go with her, to take care of her. Without proper documents, he could only slow her down. "The plane leaves in twenty minutes. We have to go now to catch it. You have your passport? Plane ticket? Visa?"

She focused long enough to nod yes each time.

He made her check to be sure. "Money for taxis and food?"

She nodded again.

"Are you sure you don't want me to go with you?"

"I'm positive. I'm perfectly capable of flying alone. I got myself here, didn't I?"

He couldn't very well argue that one. "OK, let's not miss the flight. I'll tell Jamieson what's happened. Is there anything else I can do?"

"If you could have him send the rest of my things?"

"I'll do better than that. I'll bring them."

"Just get me on the plane."

She was tearful but under control as they ran toward the airstrip. Standing with the other passengers, wrapped in his jacket, he held her close to his side, furious that he hadn't pursued getting a visa, frantic to go with her and help her though this. Another part of him knew she'd be all right. She was tougher than she looked, and she'd have the duration of the commuter flight to pull herself together, to think and plan, and be ready to function by the time she arrived in Kathmandu.

"If you miss a flight, call me," he instructed as the passengers began to board. "If you can't reach me, call Andy and he'll track me down, and if you need anything—"

"I'll whistle," she bantered tearfully. "Call me in Texas. You have the number."

He patted the paper in his pocket, then kissed her, long and deep, possessive, unwilling to say goodbye. The pilot started the engines and he was forced to let go of her. "Go safe home." She boarded to passenger applause and he smiled sheepishly, fighting emotion. She was disappearing from his side into whirlwind and everything was upset and unsettled, everything the neatness freak in him abhorred. Death is never convenient, he reminded himself. Not when you love someone.

He watched until the plane was out of sight, an ache in his chest the size of New Jersey, then realized he'd best get cracking on his own arrangements. He returned to the hotel, placed a call to the American embassy in Kathmandu, and felt a rush at the lingering sandalwood fragrance in the room; several transfers and explanations later, he had convinced an executive and his superior to bend a few rules. Under the circumstances, they were willing to issue an exit visa and have it waiting for him as soon as he arrived. The next call was to Andy, bringing him up to speed and making arrangements to let him know later what his travel plans would be.

Finally, he called Mr. Pujji and asked him to arrange flights to Los Angeles; he learned that Charlayne had been confirmed to New Delhi at eight o'clock. According to Pujji, barring delays or cancellations, she would arrive in Texas about ten o'clock the following evening, Nepali time.

Within the hour Jordan was on his way to Chitwan, with Roget speeding his convertible along the gravel road; there were no more flights out of the resort tonight, and as soon as he'd gathered their things, the fastest way to Kathmandu would be to drive, which meant they'd be spending most of the night on the road.

She'd be in New Delhi by the time he arrived, and he missed her terribly already. The next couple of days were going to be hell.

27

. . . the old girl did a pretty good job . . .

When Jordan explained Charlayne's emergency and his visa problem to the professor, Jamieson expressed his sympathy and suggested that as soon as he finished his duties, he'd be willing to use the park's station wagon to drive Jordan to Kathmandu. "I have to file a report of our damage with the king's agent, and it will be a good opportunity to pick up a window glass for my office." He smiled with husbandly discretion. "Mrs. Jamieson needs a few things that can't be obtained locally, as well." Since it was an estimated eight to ten hour drive at night, and the vehicle actually had a semblance of shock absorbers, Jordan was glad to accept. He gave Roget an additional twenty dollars for his trouble and bade the source of his black market bargains a genuinely fond farewell.

The remains of Charlayne's tent and the contents of her water-soaked duffel were spread about the wooden floor of her room to dry. Apparently they'd been recently located along the river and returned to her by one of Joh's men. Her camera was past salvaging, but a flashlight was still operational, and he used it to sort through the remaining items. Most were hopeless, and he made arbitrary decisions on her behalf to eliminate muddy items such as socks, underwear, nondescript T-shirts, a pair of Reeboks. Anything he felt she might want was packed into a separate compartment in his bag.

Next, he took care to pack his film, carefully labeled and sealed in dust-proof plastic bags; there were thirteen exposed rolls in all, and he couldn't wait to get to a darkroom. Then began the difficult task of uprooting himself from the group of people with whom he'd shared a rebirth of sorts, and a great deal of his life, in a very short period of time.

At six o'clock he searched the sky; the compound grounds were visible under a bright quarter moon in a clear, starlit night. Charlayne's plane would be landing in Kathmandu about now. He interrupted his packing to hang around Jamieson's office, hoping she'd have an opportunity to contact him. He gave it up as improbable when the professor explained that hotels equipped with short-wave for public use were all in Kathmandu proper. To leave the airport for a hurried round-trip via taxi might put her flight to New Delhi at risk.

Determined to keep himself busy, Jordan studied the heavy night air and thought about what she'd want him to do. He wandered to the capture pit to check on the rhino juvenile; at his unfamiliar smell, the youngster heaved itself to its feet and resumed a fearful bleating for its absent parent, pacing its confinement in a ceaseless search for escape.

It hit him again that Charlayne was gone and it would be days before he would see her again. "Life plays no favorites," he advised the restive animal quietly. "I know it doesn't make a damn's worth of difference, but I know exactly how you feel."

He used Charlayne's flashlight to illuminate his watch, and felt closer to her with it in his hand. Nearly seven. She'd be checking in for her flight to New Delhi about now. He pictured her swinging through the airport in her long denim skirt and his jacket, pleased that he'd been able to contribute a bit of comfort at least. She hated being cold. It would be a long time before he could keep her warm again. He tried not to dwell on the thought and concentrated on how good it was going to feel running his hands along her body. Taking her to bed. Making love with her until he was exhausted. Then kissing her past exhaustion and doing it again.

At the elephant area, he watched Madhav construct the nightly treats for the elephants: a mixture of rice, salt, and sugar bound up in a banana-leaf bundle to the size of a small cantaloupe, and made sure Khalli and Mala were pampered by personally feeding them an extra one each.

He watched Joseph back the station wagon next to the bunkhouse, its red taillights dimly visible across the compound; apparently the professor was ready to go. Emotional goodbyes to Joh and Jimi caught in his throat; impossible to leave the men and beasts who'd literally saved his life, equally impossible to stay. He shook hands and patted trunks all around and walked swiftly away.

At the bunkhouse, he transferred his bag of film and his luggage to the car, then used Charlayne's flashlight to make one more pass through his room to make sure he wasn't overlooking anything. He made a wistful addition to his new wish list—that he could someday relive the day and night with Charlayne that had taken place in this room. *God, how long before I'll see her? Make love like that again?* He quickly stepped next door, and Sailor Green bobbed at him from the safety of a rafter. Remembering the saucy lizard's intrusion upon their intimacy, Jordan smiled. "Voyeur . . ." he accused.

He turned to find Sunita in the doorway. "Hello, sweetheart." Her sad face broke his heart. "How's your little sister? And your brother?"

"They're OK." She looked past him to solemnly inspect the empty room. "Did Charlayne go away?"

"She had to go home," he hedged, unwilling to upset her further.

"She didn't say goodbye," the little girl said miserably.

"Well, she asked me to do that for her. She was sorry that she wouldn't see you." He took Sunita's hand, at a loss as to how to console a child who was losing people she cared about at an alarming rate. He decided to be honest. "Someone died in her family, too."

She looked up at him, hollow-eyed, but with an eight-year-old's insightful understanding of a fellow sufferer. "Was it her mother?"

"No, but someone she loved very much." He heard the rhino calf in the distance, calling plaintively for its parent. "Sometimes it happens when you're young, but it happens to older people, too." He walked with her onto the porch. "My mother died when I was your age, and it feels awful. Hurts worse than anything I know." He searched for healing words, knowing there weren't any. "Someday you'll feel a little better, I promise. And you won't forget your parents. I promise that, too. I remember my mother very clearly."

She nodded, silent, eyes on his face, and he had a thought. He pointed out the small green lizard on the bunkhouse rafter. "That's Sailor Green," he said. "Charlayne asked if you'd make sure he didn't get hungry. You think you can do that?"

Sunita nodded, her attention diverted.

He jammed the light into his hip pocket in order to pick her up. So thin, so frail in his arms, he squeezed her tightly, wishing he could make her pain go away; then he put her down and gravely handed over the balance of his Nepali rupees. "I almost forgot. Charlayne sent this." She would have, if she'd had a moment, he justified.

"It's for cookies for you and Sailor Green to share. She said to keep in mind that he doesn't eat very much, and not to give him too many, OK?"

The child smiled at last, instantly seeing through his ruse about who should get the lion's share of cookies. They went down the bunkhouse steps together and he hallooed Joh and Jimi a final goodbye. Joseph was halfway up the compound, and Jordan started forward to say goodbye to the new father and wish him well, then paused to hoist Sunita in his arms once again. This time she giggled when he buried his face against her neck to give her a kiss goodbye. "I gotta go, kid. You take care of yourself."

At the other end of the compound the elephants began to screech and trumpet, and he became aware of hoarse shouting. When he looked up, Joseph was waving frantically, pointing behind him; he whirled to his worst nightmare. Worse than the water, worse than the drowning. Out of the gray darkness a gigantic creature was pounding toward him, head down in its charge. He had nowhere to go.

His first thought was the child in his arms. Sunita. He spun on his heel, felt his ankle give as he used every ounce of strength he could summon to hurl her away from him and through the air to Joseph. In the next instant the impact knocked him senseless and he felt his own body lift in some kind of slow-motion, bizarre fragment of reality. He had the dazed sense that the world was upside down and that trees were falling.

He hit the ground hard with nothing to breathe. Unable to work his legs. Still in the rhino's grip, he made an effort to curl himself into a ball, trying to protect his head and throat. Arms refused to lift. The animal had its head in his lap, its jaws and teeth locked onto his body, ribs . . . grinding, shaking, whirling him like a rag . . . things were breaking in his chest, tearing inside his body. . . .

The last thing he saw was a maddened, white-rimmed eye.

He woke to a world of pain. Surging and ramming in a fury through his head and heart and body. More pain than was possible. Screaming, red-hot needles nauseated his stomach; dull knives sliced through the stem of his brain. His hearing was drowned in the roar of an engine, loud and incessant. Dark, lightless motion, hurting his body and jabbing more pain, bursts of it, building to an agony. . . He was blind. In a vehicle. He tried to speak. "Wha . . . "

"Damn, he's wakin' up."

The male voice was only vaguely familiar.

"Hell, I thought we'd have another 'our at least."

Baltine? What the hell is the Batman doing here . . . the naked son of a bitch! He struggled to move, and torture shot through his body in all directions.

"Jordan, Mitch and I are driving you to a hospital."

That's Jamieson, but where the hell did Mitch come from? Reeling and disoriented, he tried again. "What's . . . "

"Anup notified your brother. His company's flying him out at first light and he'll meet you in Kathmandu Hospital." Jamieson's voice was strained.

"They patched you up at Tiger Tops, gave you some morphine and all the antibiotics they had on hand. They couldn't get a plane up there till daylight, and that woulda been twelve hours, so we're drivin' you." This time it was Mitch's voice. "I'as on my way home anyway, and it's a two-man drive."

Yeah, right. Whatever, you rotten asshole. You damned near got her killed. The pain was winning and it was hard to breathe. "Where's Char?"

"She's gone home. . . ." Mitch's voice kept coming from somewhere he couldn't find. "I think he's losin' it."

"At this rate, medication's not going to last," Jamieson muttered.

"Figure I owed you this, Kosterin. I ain't gonna kid you, you're not in great shape and we got another four hours of hard drivin', so don't waste your breath. . . ."

Jordan moaned against the hurt, a giant wall against his chest.

"We better stop and give him the rest of that morphine. He's gotta be in a whole bunch of pain."

"Right."

Motion came to a halt and Jordan tried to grapple the agony monster under control, but he couldn't move, let alone sit up. Inside his head the rhino came at him again and he remembered throwing the little girl. *Oh, Christ, did it get her, too?* "S'nita?" he managed.

"She's fine," Jamieson's voice assured him through the darkness. "Joseph got her into the car. Joh and Jimi turned the elephants loose, but the old girl did a pretty good job on you before they could drive her off."

The car exploded with the opening of a door, shredding his nerves, searing him with hot pokers; nauseous to the point of despair, he began to sink out of sight.

"Dear God, he's losing a lot of blood. . . ." Jamieson's

voice was closer, but the rest was lost in the red haze that was the hurt, and he went away from it.

On her way to New Delhi at last, uneasy in her skin and uncertain if she'd have enough time to make her connection to Frankfurt, Charlayne looked out the Air Nepali window into the black of night after an unsuccessful try at sleeping. Half of her was missing: half her energy, half her ability to function, half her willingness to think and plan and be. Within seconds of boarding the plane at Tiger Tops, she'd hated being away from him. Distance had not improved the feeling. She tried to hold on to his words. "Go safe home." He'd be in Los Angeles by the time she returned home from poor Aunt Sophie's funeral.

Thoughts of her dear aunt brought fresh tears to her eyes. Sophie and Egan Hawke had been together forty-five years. He'd loved her blindly, had retired from the military so she could spend the rest of her life in her beloved Texas. Charlayne shivered. Her mind flew back to the night of the storm, when Jordan had been within inches of death; a chill forced its way through her heart. Somehow the powers had taken Sophie but allowed her to keep Jordan. She vowed to sleep next to his body, never leave his side, make love to him a thousand times.

Eventually exhaustion forced her into a light sleep, but edgy, thin-steel threads of ice ran nagging through her dreams. Unable to call his face into being, she woke afraid.

28

Not in a hundred years . . .

    The sight of Mr. Pujji at her arrival gate in New Delhi helped lift her spirits; he hurriedly chaperoned her through the evening airport throng of harried tourists, displaced families, and crying children, finessed her through customs and immigration, and told her that he'd spoken to Jordan. "He called from Tiger Tops soon after I spoke with you. I believe he plans to drive to Kathmandu this evening and should have a visa early tomorrow, at which time I can complete his travel arrangements."

Grateful for the information, she thanked him profusely, and through his intervention with airport procedures, was able to make her connection to Frankfurt with moments to spare. The last passenger to board, she buckled herself

– 308 –

into her seat with the feeling that she'd stepped into someone else's life. It seemed a lifetime ago that she'd been making love with Jordan, falling into exhausted sleep in his arms. For the past five hours she'd been rushing: packing, boarding planes, running through airports, trying to catch her breath long enough to grieve for poor Aunt Sophie, and think ahead to her next step.

In Frankfurt, despite the early hour, she used her two-hour layover time to call Andy's office, hoping to get a message to Jordan. When there was no answer, she called Texas and spoke briefly with her father to see how things were going and let him know her next stop was New York. Her mother had rallied somewhat, insisted on adding her sleepy comments to the call, and elicited Charlayne's promise to phone as soon as she'd arrived at JFK.

Frustrated that she couldn't reach Jordan, Charlayne contented herself with the fact that he was on his way to Kathmandu, and placed her concentration on getting from Air India's terminal to Delta's in the vaguely familiar German airport. She checked in at the gate, and after one last try at reaching Andy, boarded through the proper doorway; this time during her flight, she ate the microwaved meals in a determined effort to maintain her strength, and calculated the hours of Jordan's drive. When eight hours had elapsed from the time of her Delhi departure, and she was certain he'd arrived in Kathmandu, she was able to sleep and dreamt her way back into his bed.

When she landed at JFK, Charlayne confirmed her flight to Dallas, notified her family of her arrival time, and called India again. This time she was able to ascertain that indeed Andy had gone to see his brother "yesterday," whatever day that was. The person in his office had limited English and could not provide the name of his hotel, a phone number, or further information as to where he could be reached—or when he would return. Aware that Andy had flown Jordan into the country without a proper visa, she thought he might have gone to assist in his departure process. Whatever, if Andy was in Kathmandu, it meant that Jordan was in Kathmandu, too, and that was progress. She left her uncle's phone number and word that she'd be in Dallas that evening, and asked that Andy call as soon as he received her message.

Encouraged, she boarded her flight for the final leg of her journey. Even if Jordan's visa problem caused delay, he'd be home soon, and she held on to that. As the hours passed and the plane drew closer to Dallas, uneasiness rode in her stomach like a stone and she was unable to eat or sleep. She missed him more than she thought possible; without Jordan's presence for the space of one day, everything seemed ten times more difficult, a hundred times more lonely. Poor Uncle Egan; without Aunt Sophie, he'd be lost. So permanent. So total. So unfair.

She stepped out of the jetway at the Dallas airport, bone-tired, and into her father's waiting arms—desperately through with flying and desperately glad to see him. In the bizarre world of airplane travel, she'd flown nearly twenty-four hours against the clock and time had slowed to a crawl. Two days blended to become one. It was too mind-boggling to deal with. However, her mother's absence shocked her. She couldn't remember the last time her father had been alone.

"How's everyone?"

"Holding up. Your mother doesn't want to leave your uncle just now. He's not himself."

She nodded. "Sondra?"

"She's fine. Ryan keeps her busy." He helped with her carry-on. "The funeral's tomorrow." He wiped away tears.

"Always took for granted it'd be me. Never even considered Sophie."

Soon after she had greeted her mother and sister, and cried with dear Uncle Egan, Charlayne crawled into a bed, blind with fatigue, to sleep the sleep of homecoming.

The following morning she awoke jet-lagged, hollow and despondent, and inside the vacuum there was an unnameable feeling that wouldn't go away. Things were terribly wrong for everyone just now, and the combination was bound to affect her, she reasoned.

Finding her way groggily into her uncle's kitchen, where she discovered little Ryan at breakfast, she kissed him hello and poured herself a cup of coffee before facing the small boy across the table. Death must be terribly frightening to children, who had no way of understanding the why of it, and she was reminded of Sunita. As soon as she spoke with Andy, she'd ask him to contact Anup and see how the little girl was faring. Sipping her coffee, she savored the taste of home while Ryan toyed with his Cheerios, his usually sunny manner subdued by the aura of grown-up sadness that sat in the house like a pall.

"So, I missed you," she said lightly, in an attempt to lift his spirits. "You got awfully tall while I was gone. Are you sure you're still my nephew? He was a much shorter kid."

Ryan grinned at the game. "Daddy went to Mexico," he announced with six-year-old importance. "He and Mommy had a big fight."

Sondra rounded the corner and entered the kitchen. "Ryan, I told you Daddy had business in Mexico that he couldn't avoid." She added a spoonful of sugar to her cup of coffee. "And it was an argument, not a fight."

Charlayne was too exhausted to put up barriers, and sighed with relief when her sister seemed as muted as her child. It was a welcome respite from their war.

"I'm glad you came home," Sondra said after a moment.

Charlayne looked at her, unsure that she'd heard correctly. No anger, no hostility, just a simple statement with no hidden agenda? She responded in kind. "I'm glad you're here, too."

"I'm worried about Mother," Sondra admitted carefully. "I thought Dad would be the one to crumble. . . ." She seemed to shrink into herself. "I brought an extra dress and a pair of black shoes, if you still wear sevens."

Charlayne was genuinely appreciative of her thoughtfulness. "Thanks. I'm sure they'll be fine."

Sondra looked as if she had more to say, but she glanced at her son and kept silent.

Charlayne dropped her gaze to Sondra's slender abdomen with concern. "Are things OK? Dad seemed to think there might be—"

"Things are fine." Sondra tapped the table with nearly translucent fingers, nails chewed to the quick; the tapping, a nervous habit, was intermittent. "Things are fine." She drank her coffee and fussed with Ryan's napkin.

Obviously things weren't fine, and Charlayne had learned it was always best to be prepared for Mark's entrances. "Is he coming in for the funeral?"

Sondra's face went to stone. "No. He hates funerals. You know how weird he is about certain things."

Charlayne laughed lightly, astonished to discover that she was no longer defensive about her past relationship with her sister's husband. "Yes, now that you mention it, I do."

"Are we going to a funeral?" Ryan asked his mother timidly.

"Yes, dear, we are." Sondra was suddenly near tears. "What time is the car?"

Charlayne searched through her foggy memory and remembered that her mother had ordered limousines so no one would have to drive. "They're picking us up at one o'clock."

The rest of the morning passed in a blur. Sondra's shoes were fine but the borrowed black dress was disastrously small across the bust line, which led to the controlled chaos of a rushed trip to Neiman Marcus with her mother. Fielding phone calls from her aunt and uncle's friends, accepting their expressions of condolence, and verifying the when and where of services kept the phone busy, and every time it rang Charlayne prayed it was Jordan. If he or Andy were trying to reach her, it would be all but impossible to get through.

Frustrating calls to Narmada produced an endlessly ringing telephone in Andy's office, nothing more, and she swore that as soon as Jordan arrived, she'd insist he ship his brother an answering machine. In the limousine and on her way to church, she swallowed her disappointment by reminding herself that Jordan would be here when he got here, and no amount of wishing and wanting could hurry the process. She comforted herself with the possibility that he was already on a plane, and was able to concentrate on dedicating the balance of the day to dear Aunt Sophie and her memory.

The eulogy was dominated by concern for her parents and Uncle Egan, whose steely military bearing carried him through dry-eyed and erect, followed by a graveside service that left everyone tearful and emotionally wrung out. When they returned home, it was dead of night in India, and there were no messages. Sondra was insisting on returning to San Francisco on an evening flight, and before Charlayne could pause to rest, she was obliged to accompany her father as he drove Sondra and Ryan to the airport.

The trip sealed her exhaustion. She fell asleep during the drive back to her uncle's home, and barely remembered finding her way to her room.

Charlayne rolled over to look at the clock, dismayed to see that it was two in the afternoon. Groggy for a moment, she verified with sunlight that it was indeed afternoon, and sagged with annoyance. It was the middle of the night again in India. Another day lost. "Damn time zones anyway!" she grumped unreasonably.

She found her clothing laundered and folded on her dresser, her notebooks stacked neatly to one side. A mother was a mother as long as she lived. In and out of the shower, she quickly dressed, grabbed her shoes, and threw Jordan's jacket over her shoulders. Maybe they hadn't been willing to wake her. Her barefoot approach caught her parents in candid conversation about Sondra, which ceased at her entrance. She couldn't help asking, "Did anyone call?"

"No. Why aren't you sleeping?" her mother demanded, testy and flustered by her sudden appearance.

"Good afternoon to you, too, Mother. Thanks for the laundry." She gave her a kiss on the cheek.

"I didn't have a choice," Lucille sniffed. "Your things were filthy. I take it they don't manufacture soap in Nepal."

Charlayne laughed and added a spontaneous hug. Lucille Delamere would never change, and that was OK, too. "Actually, I don't know. I'll have to go back and do some research on it," she teased, and kissed her father on the top of his head in passing as she headed for the coffeepot. "So, fess up. What's all this about Sondra?"

There was an awkward pause.

"Mark not being here for the funeral?" she guessed into

the silence. "You may as well tell me. I'm family, too, you know."

Her mother pursed her lips. "I think there may be trouble in your sister's marriage," she admitted.

"Wouldn't surprise me, he's a jerk." Charlayne paused, startled; she was actually conversing about Mark without edits to spare her parents' feelings. Clearly a new day had dawned somewhere in the past two weeks.

"I've always thought so, too," her father concurred, and she stared at him, astonished. Her father had never voiced a negative opinion about Mark in her hearing.

She cornered them with her eyes. "What's going on?"

"Your sister's pregnant and he's gallivanting in Mexico, that's what's going on," her mother snapped. "Important business deal, indeed. You tell me a situation where a family emergency doesn't take precedence over the sale of a painting, and I'll show you something fishy." She cast her eyes toward the floor.

Whoa! Major revelation here. Her mother suspicious as well? Charlayne was aghast. What on earth had changed during her absence? How had fair-haired Mark Hunter fallen off the pedestal, second grandson notwithstanding?

"You may as well know. He's asked your father for another loan," Lucille said bitingly. She whopped a damp linen towel against the counter in irritation. "He actually had the effrontery to suggest that Henreid not mention it to me. He was worried that I wouldn't 'respect him.'" She plopped herself onto the kitchen chair opposite her husband. "Asking my husband of thirty-eight years to keep a secret from me? 'Respect him,' indeed. Well, I can assure you that the answer will be no."

Her mother's mouth was pinched in her distress, and Charlayne was uncomfortable. "I shouldn't have asked. This really isn't any of my business."

"Well, actually, it is." Her father pushed his coffee aside with a heartfelt sigh. "Your mother and I have been thinking over things where your sister is concerned for some time. I know this isn't the best time to discuss it, but we wondered if you'd act as trustee for a fund we've created for Sondra's children. It's set up with Mark and Sondra in that capacity at the moment, but in view of the way things are going . . ."

Her mother was more specific. "The way Mark's mismanaging their finances. Not to mention their marriage." Lucille sighed as well. "We've discussed it with Sondra and she's agreed. Of course, it's up to you. Considering your history with Mark, if you don't feel it's something you'd be comfortable with, we can—"

Charlayne stopped her, disbelieving. "Wait a minute, Sondra's agreed . . . to me?" The world was coming to an end, and she was the last to know about it.

"Yes. We discussed it with her as soon as she told us about the new baby. Then when Sophie . . ." Her mother's eyes filled with tears and she struggled to keep her composure. "I happen to know that Ryan is named in Sophie's will and she's directed a rather substantial sum of money to be transferred into the children's trust rather than set up a separate fund. Your uncle feels very strongly that Mark should not be named as trustee." She glanced at her husband. "We agree."

Charlayne sat down heavily. "Why not Sondra alone?"

"She doesn't want the responsibility," said her mother.

"And she'll give it over to me?" Charlayne's confusion was growing. "Why?"

Henreid spoke up. "What she said was, she wasn't sure she'd be able to say no to her children's father every time he wanted to invade the trust."

A harsh self-judgment on Sondra's part, Charlayne

realized, but accurate. Unfortunately, she knew how persuasive Mark Hunter could be when he set his mind to something. Sipping her coffee, she rolled over the immense responsibility they were proposing to confer upon her. Power to thwart Mark. The ability to protect her nephew and nephew-to-be from their profligate father. With yes and no decision power over Sondra as well? See that her children had a good start in life, the college of their choice, whatever they needed? Could she hold neutral ground and act fairly toward a man she despised? Maybe. With Jordan's help, absolutely. "Yes . . ." she answered slowly. "That's fine with me."

Her parents were visibly relieved, and she saw that they'd been a great deal more concerned than she'd realized. "Good." Her father noded approvingly. "The revision's already drawn. We'll sign the papers as soon as we get home."

Uncle Egan came into the kitchen and her mother immediately moved into her sisterly "Lucille" mode, pampering and patting him, fussing to get his coffee just the way he liked it—treatment he would ordinarily have rejected out of hand. This time he submitted without so much as token protest, and Charlayne's heart went out to him. Her father harrumphed and cleared his throat to cover his own emotion, and the four of them sat in silence, mired in their loss of Sophie.

Somewhere in the house the telephone rang, and Lucille sprang to answer it. Charlayne crossed her fingers and made a silent wish that it was Jordan at last, and joyfully readied herself for a summons to the phone. When her mother called out that it was the pastor, Charlayne's attention returned to the table. Her father and uncle were watching her carefully, and she blushed.

"Ahhh," her uncle ventured with a hint of his former self. "And who did we think that might be? Mr. Jacket?"

Crimson to her ears, she gulped a huge mouthful of coffee and waited until her mother returned to the kitchen. "I've met someone." The admission prickled its way through her body, adding to her already rosy skin. "He's a lawyer—"

"A lawyer . . . that's nice." Her mother's interest was satisfactorily piqued and she reached out to pat a sleeve of the obviously masculine jacket. "Good, stable occupation, comes home nights."

"And a photographer . . ." she added quickly, to slow her mother down.

Her father's eyes began to twinkle. "On a week-to-week basis, wasn't it?"

"Oh, God, I hope not!" she erupted, unable to play it cool. Not even wanting to. She felt like opening a window and shouting it to the world. "He's wonderful, and he couldn't come with me because he lost his exit visa and, well, he lives in Los Angeles and . . ." She told them everything she knew about Jordan Kosterin, omitting the dangerous night of terror in the thunderstorm, which could wait until he was present and helped calm negative reactions; nor did she recount the subsequent bedroom activity, which wasn't exactly material for parental ears, but she had the feeling from amused glances that flew around the table that her family was doing just fine reading between the lines.

Her mother surprised her by coming around the table to administer a huge hug. "Well, you're certainly due for someone terrific," she said tartly.

"I'll drink to that." Her father lifted his cup and they drank the toast. "We'll look forward to meeting your young man."

Her mother spent the balance of the day making arrangements for Uncle Egan to accompany them to San

Francisco. "Why don't you come as well? Just for the weekend. We haven't seen you for ages, and I'm sure there are things about your trip you'll want to share with us."

"Let me think about it," she stalled and held out while her mother arranged with the phone company to have her uncle's calls forwarded to their number in San Francisco.

"I'm worried about your father's health," her mother wheedled, "and you can see how horribly upset Egan's become. They both need diversion and you need rest. I won't accept no this time," she stated decisively. "You can go to Los Angeles when your young lawyer arrives. It's only an hour flight."

When there were no messages on her home machine, to her mother's delight Charlayne threw in the towel and took over the chore of arranging their flight home. There was space at eight o'clock that evening, and she pitched in to help her mother pack Uncle Egan for the trip. Two hours before departure, she called for a taxi, and while they were waiting for it to arrive, she tried Andy's office again.

This time, finally, a well-spoken man answered the phone and she was able to explain that she'd been trying to reach Andrew. "Have you heard from him? Does he know I've been calling?"

"When he left, he was most specific, Miss Pearce. He said he would not be checking in with us, and that we were not to expect him for several days. I wish I could give you more information, but that's all I can tell you at the moment."

"Would his superior know?"

There was a beat. "I am his supervisor."

"I'm sorry." If anyone in India could get in touch with Andy, this should be the man. "Well, when he calls—"

"I've given strict instructions that he's to receive your messages, miss, and where to reach you in Texas."

It was a good thing she'd called after all. "I'm leaving for San Francisco." She gave him the number. It was all she could do. "Thank you."

The instant she hung up the phone, it rang. She grabbed the receiver. "Hello!"

"I have a collect call for anyone, from Mexico. Will you accept?"

"Oh, God . . ." She was in no mood for Mark "I Hate Funerals" Hunter. If the line was busy when Jordan tried to call, she'd kill him.

"Will you accept?" the operator repeated with the charm of an AT&T wrestler.

Charlayne forced temptation aside with enormous effort. "Yes . . ."

"Hey! Charlie!"

Her temper snapped and she gave him the benefit of a small tantrum. "If you want to talk to me, Mark, it's Charlayne. Not Char. Not Charlie. Not sugar cookie, honey baby, tootsie, or 'Hey, you' . . . Got it?"

"Wow, sweetie, sounds like you could use a good lay. Things must have been tough in the jungle. Let me talk to my wife."

She came that close to hanging up, but gave him a good, long pregnant pause instead.

"Charlayne?" Mark's voice became strained. "I want to talk to Sondra."

"She's not here."

What was amazing was the change in his demeanor. "Where the hell is she?"

"San Francisco. She left last night."

"Shit!" This time there was silence from his end.

"Oh, I agree entirely," Charlayne said sweetly, the

put-down opportunity too tailor-made to resist. The rescuing beep of a taxi horn sounded from her uncle's driveway, and she welcomed the legitimate excuse to get off the line. "Our taxi's here. I have to go."

"Wait, don't hang up, Charlayne. Please."

Please? And a second use of her given name? A new world groveling record for the dear boy. She gave him a break he didn't deserve. "What is it?"

"Well, I'm real embarrassed to ask you this, but I need some money. You think you could—"

"Mark, I'm on my way to the airport with my parents. The meter's running and we don't have a lot of room to make the flight. In addition to which, I probably have something like twenty dollars American, and a couple of rupees." *Which not even you can use, you toad.*

"Give me a credit card number."

"Not in a hundred years. Call your wife, I have to go."

"Charlie . . . you were always a bitch." The phone line went dead.

Preoccupied, she joined her parents.

"Was that him?" asked her mother.

"No, it was a wrong number," she answered, the beginnings of concern creeping in around the edges. *Where the hell was Jordan?*

29

. . . is grass green?

      He was in bed with her. And it was hot. Sweat from his body was running in golden rivers onto white sheets. He was helplessly lost—wrapped in her arms was the one place he could go that didn't hurt. As long as he stayed with her, there was peace.

"Jordy." The voice was white, and Jordan ignored the voice to stay with her.

"I know you're there, goddammit."

Andy. He reluctantly left her side to rise through the agony-heat to the surface, peeked out briefly into white-hot sun, and decided to go under again, into the chocolate-brown haze that had become his life; at the last moment he recognized his brother's face. Andy looked like a three-week drunk on bad booze.

"Christ, I thought you'd never come around, you asshole.... *Nurse!*"

His brother disappeared.

It hurt to think, so he didn't. But it was nice to see Andy again, so he decided to stick around for a few seconds to wait for him to come back. Find out what was on his brother's mind.

"You've been here for two days. It's a hospital."

Hospital? Oh, yeah... You had an accident... Damn. Must be why you look so bad.... He couldn't move his head, so he wandered his eye instead, trying to find Andy again. Shards of pain sheared through his skull, and he shut them out by closing his eyelid.

"He was awake. He opened his eye just seconds ago. Can you get Dr. Pillai in here?"

Even with his eye closed, everything was white. And the white definitely wasn't preferable to the brown. *Christ, it's hot.* Sweat was running into his eye, made him want to blink. Since it hurt to blink, he kept it closed. And drifted.

Andy's voice was close to his ear again. "Don't you leave, you son of a bitch. You listen to me."

It was too much trouble to answer. So he didn't. Something grabbed his hand, and he moaned when pain shot through his arm.

"Can you hear me?"

Fingers squeezed his hand, hurting him again; annoyed, he squeezed back. And that hurt, too. He moaned again.

"Oh, God, thank you!" The fingers pressured again. "You can hear me, I know you can. Squeeze my hand if you understand me."

He thought about it and decided not to. It would hurt like hell if he tried to exert pressure. Pain had shrieked up his arm the first time. It was not possible.

"Once for yes, two for no. Talk to me!"

OK, little brother, but just this once. He squeezed again and bought the pain. It got hotter and he was panting for breath. More pain. Jesus!

A blurble of voices followed.

"He's conscious, Doctor."

"This is a very good sign. Did he speak to you?"

"No, but watch."

Sounds of activity swam vaguely into Jordan's hearing. Icy cold eased onto his forehead and he opened his eye in surprise; his brother's face swam in and out of view. As usual, he was on a roll. "That's better. You're pretty whacked out, so stay with me on this. This is Dr. Pillai, he's a surgeon from New Delhi. He and I want to move you to a hospital there. You need surgery and they can't do it here. You got three kinds of infection out of control, and Pillai tells me you could die if we move you before they get you stabilized. You think he's right, yes or no?"

Die? Things must really be serious. Jordan tried to pin down the dying part. Not as long as he could stay with Charlayne. He really didn't care about anything else. He rested a few moments, then squeezed Andy's fingers.

"Good, I agree and that settles it." Andy's voice drifted a few feet away. "We're moving him. My dad's coming in on a private plane, and we need to get him ready to go as soon as he arrives."

More fragments of conversation invaded the white space; something about "won't be responsible" and "don't give a damn, he'll die in the air, maybe, but he's not gonna die here."

Activity in the room ceased. He'd slipped into the red zone and was well on his way to the brown by the time he heard his brother speak again. "Now, by all that's holy, let me ask the right questions."

His brother's fingers, thin cold sticks, slipped into his hand once again.

"Do you remember what happened?"

It came swimming out of the red, huge and black and ugly, to trample him one more time. He tried to speak, but breathing was a serious nightmare of hurt. He squeezed Andy's fingers instead.

"Are you in pain?"

Jesus, Andy, is grass green? He could barely stand to move his fingers.

His brother's voice broke. "They can up it a little, but if they give you much more, you'll buy the farm. You're a goddamn doorstop as it is."

Christ, don't make me laugh!

"Dad's got a corporate jet from one of his clients. Probably be here in an hour. I know you can't stay awake that long, but try to wake up again, OK? I'm going to leave now, take care of getting you more medication and see if I can get through to him on a phone." There was a pause. "Oh, Jesus, what about Charlayne? You're a mess, and she's been trying to—"

Alarmed, Jordan squeezed twice and the pain level shot off the scale. He didn't care. *No! Absolutely not! We're fine. Don't mess with anything.*

"Hey, relax! It's OK."

It occurred to him that his brother's voice was scared. *Damn . . . things must be pretty serious.* He released Andy's fingers.

"I'm not your brother for nothing," Andy reassured him. "I know you don't want her to see this, but she'll kill me if you die and I didn't let her know. I'll make you a deal. You don't kick off, and I swear I won't call her until you give the word."

He was tired. And it was still too hot, the agony too raw. It was all he could do to pressure his brother's fingers one last time, then he went away. Andy didn't need to call her; he knew where to find Charlayne.

30

. . . chalk on a blackboard . . .

She settled into her seat on the plane, suspicion pounding at her heart. Something was wrong. There was a sad, eerie feeling in the back of her neck that had nothing to do with the loss of Aunt Sophie. She'd been in Texas two days and there'd been no word from Jordan. No messages at Uncle Egan's; nothing on her answering machine at home—she'd checked again from the Dallas airport and practically worn out the replay code during the past forty-eight hours.

Why hadn't she heard from him?

And what could be so important that Andy would suddenly leave his job? Andy, who'd scrupulously checked with his office every time they'd been together.

As soon as she crossed her parents' doorstep, she decided if there was no message waiting from Jordan she'd start tracking him down. She'd call information in Los Angeles and find his father's law office. How many attorneys named Kosterin could there be? It was too late to reach anyone tonight without declaring it an emergency, and tomorrow was Sunday. Maybe someone would be there anyway, preparing a case or something. Certainly he'd have a service. One way or another, she was going to get some answers or know the reason why.

That determined, she debated whether to discuss Mark's call with her family, and elected to keep it a "wrong number." There was no harm done, and his asking for money would only upset them further. The best thing was to be patient and let time do its work for everyone concerned. Herself included.

He'd call. Soon. If he didn't, she'd call him. Somehow. But the creepy feeling hung around her shoulders like a shroud.

They landed on time, and met their driver, who helped them with luggage. The trip from the airport was endless, and she selfishly wished a hundred times that she'd been able to say no to her family and simply go home to her own life; the vehicle's slow crawl up the hills scratched at her nerves like cheap chalk on a blackboard.

Maybe he hadn't gone to Kathmandu after all. She searched her memory. Andy's office had said Kathmandu—no, they'd said he'd "gone to see his brother." She'd assumed Kathmandu. She checked her watch. If she called right away, they could still radio a message to Chitwan, find out if Professor Jamieson had information about Jordan. Maybe Pujji! Pujji would know, and she could call him yet tonight, too.

Absorbed in her thoughts she followed Uncle Egan up

the steps to her parents' home and found a distraught, nightgowned Alice embracing her mother in the foyer.

"Thank God you're home," the housekeeper cried tearfully. "I was about to go out of my mind. I think she's losing the baby, she won't let me—"

Her mother blanched. "I knew it. This has all been too much. Where is she?"

"In her room. I tried to talk her into going to the hospital, but she insisted on waiting for you. . . ."

Sondra appeared at the head of the stairway, defiantly twisting the ties to her robe; she came down a few steps to address them. "I am not going to a hospital."

Lucille, agitated, began to argue. "Of course you are, I won't hear otherwise. It's out of the question."

"Mother, I'm fine." Sondra was adamant. "It's just a little seepage. It's happened before and there's nothing to worry about. What I need is rest, and now that you're home, I'm going to lie down again. I'm sorry if I upset you, Alice, but I do know what I'm doing."

Undeterred, Lucille Delamere started up the stairs.

"Mother, I swear there's nothing wrong. Just let me get off my feet! What would *help* is if you and Dad could get Ryan back to sleep! He's been having nightmares and is giving me fits!"

Her mother, assigned a task, was somewhat mollified, but continued upward. "I'll talk to him, but your pregnancy is far too tenuous to—"

Sondra's face worked with emotion and she deliberately turned her back. "Mother, *please!* He's not up here, he's in the living room!"

Lucille was halted at last by this unexpected rebuff; head high, she retreated from the stairway, nodded a wounded acquiescence to Charlayne, then walked stiffly down the hall toward the living room.

Sondra paused at the head of the stairs to look back at Charlayne. "You think I could I see you for a few minutes?"

"Sure. Of course," Charlayne called up, uncertainly. "Give me a couple of seconds and I'll be right there." When her worried father and Uncle Egan had followed her mother into the living room, and she'd hugged and kissed her tearful, cranky nephew good night, Charlayne ascertained from Alice that there were no messages waiting.

"I'm sorry, hon. There hasn't been a word," Alice said distractedly. "I've been here all evening with your sister."

Discouraged, Charlayne took a deep breath and started upstairs, trying to divine what on earth Sondra would want to discuss that couldn't wait until morning. And how soon she could free herself to get to a phone and start to work on the dilemma in her own life. At the doorway to her former bedroom she saw that it had been transformed. The bed was naked. The handmade amethyst coverlet from her grandmother had been replaced by dull blue woolen blankets and masculine striped sheets, currently in a wad on the floor; prints and paintings that had hung on the walls for years had been replaced with photos of Sondra and Mark and Ryan; the glass in three of the frames had been smashed.

She stared at the mute evidence of her sister's tantrum, worried for her baby, and a frightening thought crossed her mind. This was pretty strenuous activity for someone with a difficult pregnancy. Surely Sondra wouldn't deliberately try to miscarry.

Suddenly apprehensive, she stepped inside. Sondra came in from the bathroom sipping from a glass of orange juice; a half-full carafe was sitting on the bureau, and Charlayne had the strong suspicion that there was more in Sondra's glass than juice. She spoke from concern, trying not to start an argument, but unwilling to look the other way. "Should you be doing that?"

For an answer, Sondra kicked the bedding out of her path, mauling it with her foot until it was under the bed. She was her old sarcastic self. "Believe me, sister dear, it's absolutely safe."

"OK, if you say so. It's your baby's health, which I'm sure you know, but I'm not going to argue with you. I'm not going to put up with 'sister dear,' either," she warned.

Sondra surprised her by backing down a peg. "Good. I don't want to fight anymore. I'm sick of fighting."

There was a stiff silence as Sondra began to pace about the room, a frozen look of contemplation on her face between sips of her drink. Charlayne was tired, and impatient to leave. She had problems in her own life, and daylight was rapidly slipping away in India. "Mark called from Mexico before we left Dallas," she said to break the impasse.

Sondra snorted derisively. "Let me guess. Money?"

She nodded. "We were leaving for the airport, so I told him to call you."

"Good." Sondra broke at last, came apart all at once, and hysterical sobs issued from her thin body as she collapsed on the bed.

Charlayne went to her side, unsure what kind of response to give, but torn apart by the sound of her sister's grief. She took the glass from Sondra's hand and pulled her into her arms. "Hey, it's going to be all right," she soothed. "Every married couple fights. This can't be good for the baby."

"I'm not pregnant!" Sondra burst out disjointedly. "I'm having my period. Alice caught me washing out underwear."

Charlayne was stunned at her confession, unable to react for a few moments.

As she admitted her deception, Sondra began to calm down. "I'm glad I'm not, I mean I'd love to have a baby, but not with him. Not now. I was going to tell everyone I'd had another miscarriage, but it's too late. If I go to a hospital, they'll figure it out in five minutes."

"Oh, Sondra. Why'd you do this?" But Charlayne knew the answer even as she asked the question.

Sondra sagged, abject. "I thought I was trying to save my marriage, but it turns out there's nothing to save. Never was, I guess." She freed herself from Charlayne's arms to pick up her drink. "He's in Mexico with a woman named Viveca Sandhurst. I found out about her six months ago."

Charlayne wasn't particularly surprised; she'd had to field Mark's hands and innuendos every time they were alone together. Now that she thought about it, there was no reason to assume he'd limit his attentions where other women were concerned.

Sondra faced her, ashamed. "I guess what I did to you finally came back to haunt me. I'm sorry. I've never been able to say that until now, but I've been sorry a long time, believe me. I know what this is going to sound like, but he did seduce me."

She began to cry softly, and Charlayne realized that for once the tears were genuine. Mark seducing Sondra had never occurred to her, and she began to examine the idea as she listened to her sister's tearful explanation.

"I was always jealous of you, and he knew it, and I used to flirt with him, I admit that. But I swear it was his idea. You remember the night he took you to the airport? You had that meeting in New York?"

Charlayne nodded, a rush of nerves tickling their way up her spine. There'd only been one New York meeting, and it had taken place in July, four months before the breakup of her marriage. Sondra had been four months pregnant when she and Mark had gotten married....

"He called me from the airport and asked if he could stop by to talk, that it was important. He showed up with a bottle of sake, and I didn't throw him out. And I should have. And I'm sorry. He said you two were having problems and that you wouldn't sleep with him." She bit her lip, embarrassed. "Anyway, we got drunk and I got pregnant that night. I know it doesn't change anything now, but after a baby got involved, I had to make the best of it."

Uneasy, Charlayne got up to cross the room. "He told me you'd been having an affair for two years."

Sondra glanced up at her, clearly disturbed at the statement. "That's not true! It started in July and he kept coming back.... When I told him I was pregnant, he said we'd get married. He said things were over between you anyway." She blinked, getting angry. "Two years? That's not true. You have to believe me."

Charlayne tried to take it all in. A confession, an apology, the exposure of a lie, and contrition from her sister, all in one massive rush. She felt overwhelmed, unsure what to say. Rage at her ex-husband began to boil in her veins and she nodded, beginning to consider that Sondra might be telling the truth. What could she gain at this point by lying?

She decided to think about it later, knowing it would be a long time before she'd be able to accept anything from her sister at face value, if ever. Sondra was rambling on, the liquor loosening her speech.

"They met a year ago. They've been having an affair for a long time, and I thought she was some kind of art groupie. Turns out her husband died and she's rich... but I guess she doesn't want to marry him." She gave a grim chuckle. "At least that's what she said."

WISH LIST   331 -

Charlayne was surprised, and appalled. "How do you know all this?"

"Oh, I called her." Sondra got off the bed and began pacing again. "Told her we had something in common. A revolving door: I'm out, she's in—preceded by, my sister's out, I'm in. It's like a pattern. Previous marital history suspect. For all I know, he's had a dozen wives." She drained her glass.

Charlayne started. It was true. She knew very little about Mark's past. No parents, no brothers or sisters. That was about it. She was boggled and still dealing with her nonconfrontational sister calling the other woman.

"She knew about Ryan, but when I asked her if Mark had mentioned I was pregnant, she got real upset."

"Holy cow, what'd she say to that?"

"She thanked me." Sondra poured more orange juice into her glass, then retrieved a bottle of Bombay gin from the bathroom and opened it to splash in a good deal of alcohol. "And guess what? He started coming home nights. I didn't say anything, and he never said anything, so . . . I assumed she didn't tell him. And I thought it was over. Then this trip to Mexico suddenly comes up. Right after Christmas. He said it was business."

She tipped her drink toward Charlayne. "It's always business with Mark. I told him I didn't believe him, that I thought he was having an affair. I didn't say with who, 'cause I didn't want to get into how I already knew and all that other stuff."

Charlayne got a plastic glass from the bathroom and poured a drink of her own. This was entirely too good to miss.

"He said my hormones were running my brain, that being pregnant was the reason I was a 'jealous nutcase'— except, guess what, I wasn't pregnant. Anyway, he said he was going whether I liked it or not, and if I didn't believe in him, to call and check." She sighed pensively. "Then Aunt Sophie died."

"And he didn't call off his trip."

"No, the bastard." Sondra studied her glass, bleary-eyed. "So I did."

Charlayne sat on the bare mattress, mesmerized with this new side of her sister. Clearly, more than one person in this household had changed in the past few weeks. "Did what?"

"Called the hotel, asked for his room." Sondra gave her a tortured grin. "I had Alice ask for her so he wouldn't recognize my voice. Men are so stupid. He didn't even ask who was calling, he just handed her the phone. When I said it was me, she told him to wait downstairs."

Charlayne laughed with appreciation. "Told him?"

"Apparently he's a good little lapdog. I wonder if he's better in bed with her than he was with me."

Charlayne choked on her drink, snorting gin and orange juice up her nose.

Sondra giggled at her and handed over a box of tissues from the bureau. "Bad with you, too, huh? We'll have to compare notes sometime." She resumed her tale. "Then I told her about him not coming back for Aunt Sophie's funeral, and said as far as I was concerned she could keep him, I didn't want him back."

"What did she say?"

Sondra laughed. "She said, 'Honey, tell you what. I'm going to do better than that. I don't want him either. I'm gonna give him a little gift and a big hotel bill.'"

Charlayne's jaw dropped.

"Yeah, and I said that suited me just fine. Then she said something about women sticking together, and suggested that I get a good lawyer."

Charlayne broke into laughter, still having a hard time believing her ears. "When was all this?" she managed finally.

Sondra looked at her, clearly no longer sober. "When I got home. He called all day today, but I just let the answering machine pick up until this afternoon, probably right after he talked to you. Alice answered the phone before I could stop her. He had this story about how he's been robbed and how soon could I wire him some money?" She gave an elaborate shrug. "So, I told him, sure, honey. Just 'wait downstairs.'"

Charlayne held her breath. "You didn't."

"I sure did. As far as I know, he's still 'waiting downstairs.' Wire him some money." Sondra raised the age-old single finger salute. "Too bad I can't wire this."

Charlayne laughed until she nearly fell off the bed, and clinked her glass with Sondra's in sisterly celebration before emptying it.

Sondra eyed her empty glass and proceeded to pour in orange juice for another drink. "Oh, wait. There's more. You won't believe it."

"I already don't believe it."

Sondra handed her the bottle of gin, then opened the top drawer of her bureau to take out a large manila envelope. *GIFT* was scrawled in block print across the front. She showed it to Charlayne. "This little jewel was delivered a couple of hours ago. It seems the very rich, very annoyed Miss Viveca had him investigated." She tossed the envelope into Charlayne's lap. "Read it, I don't mind."

Charlayne put down her drink long enough to empty the contents into her lap. The top document was a copy of a private investigator's report addressed to Viveca Sandhurst, with several attached pages outlining a date book over the past three months: times, names, and upscale addresses of two women appeared with regularity. There were half a dozen black-and-white photographs of Mark and a woman in a swimming pool. Naked. In severely compromising positions.

"Yipes." She tapped her finger on the word *GIFT*. "You think she gave this to him, too?"

"That's my guess."

Charlayne ran her finger down the list of women's names. Viveca Sandhurst was not included.

"You'll notice they're both single, lots of money. It seems our soon-to-be mutual ex-husband has been shopping around for a better marital situation. My guess is . . . it's been getting more difficult to stay on the Delamere payroll for providing a grandson and heir. Mother says he asked Dad for money the day we moved in."

Charlayne was past stunned. Aghast. Astonished. Proud of her sister for the first time in years, but worried that she might not stick to her guns. "What are you going to do?"

"Already done. Followed Viveca's advice and called a very expensive lawyer. I have an appointment Monday morning, ten A.M."

Charlayne searched for a word to properly express her feelings, and found it. "Bravo!"

Sondra's eyes filled with tears. "Now all I have to do is tell Mother and Daddy I'm not pregnant. They're already mad at me."

Charlayne took her hand. "Sondra, trust me. I don't think they're going to be upset."

Sondra sat her drink aside. "Think I've had enough." In the next instant she reverted to scared little girl. "Promise you'll stay with me? Promise you won't leave until it's all over."

Charlayne nodded happily. "I promise." Another item on her wish list had been accomplished. An important one. Trust would take time, but she and her sister were friends again; a tenuous friendship, to be sure, but the joy of it was worth its weight in gold. She glanced at the bureau clock; it was already Sunday evening for the people she needed to speak with. She'd call Pujji and Jamieson tomorrow to find out if Jordan Kosterin was still on the other side of the planet. Right now she had to get her sister into bed.

"And you'll go to the lawyer with me? I don't think I can do it by myself."

Sondra Delamere Hunter, who'd confronted the other woman, who was about to hang her cheating, conniving husband out to dry, had crumbled, but Charlayne knew her sister would be fine. She just needed to climb a few mountains.

"I'll be there. You'll handle it just like you did Mark, but I'll be there, I promise." She walked Sondra down the hall to her former room, no longer destined to be a nursery, and helped her into bed.

As welcome as it might be, four A.M. was too late to spring this on their parents.

31

What was missing . . .

The next morning Charlayne was proud of her mother. Lucille Delamere came through like a champ. There was momentary regret that there would not be an additional grandchild to pamper, perhaps, but the news that Sondra was filing for divorce was greeted with no opposition whatever, no remonstrances about keeping her family together "for Ryan," not even a hint that perhaps Sondra was being hasty. Thankfully, there'd been no need to introduce the damning evidence contained in the "gift"; if anything, acceptance of Sondra's decision had bolstered the family's unity, and everyone's thoughts turned to how best to protect Ryan from the situation.

However, all day Sunday, Charlayne couldn't help but

notice that her family exhibited unusual cheer in her presence. Aside from the fact that there was no postdecision quarterbacking of Sondra's actions, or declarations that Mark should have his side of the story on record before judgments were made—and while it wasn't exactly celebratory—the atmosphere in the Delamere home was pointedly lighter. Brunch was a jovial affair marked by the presence of several of her favorite foods, courtesy of Alice, but discussion seemed to be limited to weather conditions and whether or not the Delameres should try to upgrade their opera seating. What was missing was any mention of her trip, and the fact that "Mr. Jacket" hadn't phoned.

After consultations with her mother and sister, Charlayne and Uncle Egan took Ryan for an outing, to give Sondra an opportunity to pack Mark's clothing into moving cartons. There were four boxes in the foyer when they returned, all marked *GIFT*. But no smiling face telling her someone had been trying to reach her.

That afternoon, she failed at taking a nap, couldn't interest herself in a favorite author's new release, was unsuccessful in taking her mind off the silent phone. Something was wrong, she could feel it in her soul. With one eye watching the time, she forced herself to indulge in a facial, conditioned her hair, treated herself to a manicure and a pedicure in her room with Eric Clapton's guitar solos wailing from the stereo, and pushed herself through waiting and wondering until six o'clock.

Then she began to work the telephone with a vengeance. Andy's office manager insisted that they still had no knowledge of his whereabouts, but said he would be happy to take another message. Not logical. Something was definitely out of whack. She discovered a few minutes later that Pujji had taken a short leave from his business to attend a wedding in Bombay. His office staff was helpful and cooperative, but found nothing except "pending" travel arrangements for Jordan Kosterin. They were still waiting to hear from him.

Apprehension mounting, she called the Kathmandu Guest House; the radio operator agreed to contact Professor Jamieson at Chitwan. She held on the line nearly an hour only to learn that the professor, his wife, and staff were in transit to the zoo in Bangkok; they were accompanying the rhino calf to its new home and could not be reached until their arrival two days from now. Since she couldn't be patched through to Chitwan, she managed to inquire how long ago Jordan Kosterin had departed. She heard the radio operator translate to Madhav, who was there to care for the elephants; according to his translated reply, Madhav was insisting that the professor had personally driven Jordan to Kathmandu several days ago. She gave up at last and thanked them for their trouble.

Having reached a dead end for the moment, and unable to shake off her concern, she took Jordan's jacket from the hall closet and wore it through dinner. Evening brought no respite. Fog closed in from the bay as she sat through a repeat of *60 Minutes*, drank two glasses of white wine with Alice's famous sole Veronique, and watched *Aladdin* with Ryan until she could recite all the genie's lyrics. Sufficiently unwound, she couldn't wait to escape to her room and sleep, the one sure place to be with Jordan until she could wake tomorrow and contact his father's office.

Charlayne's in Texas at a funeral.
Jordan opened his eye.
There's a number . . . I have to call her.
Incredibly, there was less pain. Shrieking torment had

been replaced with a languid, floating sense that his body belonged to someone else. His ribs, however, were caught in a vise. His eye traveled the length of a tube that emerged from his wrist and attached to a bottle suspended upside down next to his bed. A saline drip. Then reality invaded by inches. He was in a hospital. He'd been mauled and mangled by the mother of all rhinos.

He struggled and failed to sit up as vague conversations about surgery entered his thinking. Gradually, he became aware that his head was swathed in bandages; most of his upper torso was also wrapped in white, and sprouting tubes as well, plus one of his legs. It must be over. He twisted a smile. Apparently, he'd lived. It hurt when he tried to swallow.

In front of him, his brother was asleep on a chair, and he was astonished to see his father stretched out on a nearby cot. He tried to speak to them, but the inside of his mouth had the consistency of rubber cement. Throat cotton-dry and sore, he was able to cough, but it came out a croak. His brother came awake, and his father rolled over, both staring at him.

"Hey," he managed. "Dad."

His father, the strongest man he knew, broke into tears, his haggard face speaking volumes. Jordan felt terrible at upsetting him. Andy hobbled to his side using a crutch and pressed the call button; his father took a seat at his elbow. "How do you feel?"

"Gainin' on 'm," he mumbled, and was relieved to see his father try to smile. "Somebody . . . want 'ell me . . . s'goin' on?"

His dad took a death grip on his hand; an Indian nurse with a red dot on her forehead came in to take his temperature. While she checked his blood pressure and poked efficiently at his IV, his brother gave him a sip of water and told him about the surgery. "They took out a rib that was ready to puncture one of your lungs, gave you megadoses of fungicides for everything from hoof and mouth to malaria. You're probably sterile, but what the hell, I hear you weren't usin' it anyway."

He tried to grin. "Heard wrong."

His father took over. "We don't know about your eye yet. It's possible you'll lose the sight in it." He fought more tears. "As Andy says, they think the infections are under control, you were in surgery six hours."

"Yeah, you got a road map of Utah on your stomach. Not only that, they shaved most of your hair. I'm the handsome one in the family now, so you know how ugly you are."

Andy had tears in his eyes also, and Jordan looked around. There were no mirrors in the room. "How bad am I?"

"You're pretty chewed up," his brother said, doing his best to make it fly. "Between the damage from the rhino and the holes the surgeons cut in you, you're this year's candidate for Frankenstein."

Dr. Pallai came in and, after being reintroduced and listening to his explanation of the multiple source of infections—open wounds from rhino bites, lack of proper initial cleansing and treatment, too long before sufficient antibiotics were available, loss of blood—and the whys and wherefores of surgical incisions to repair broken bones and skin damage, Jordan immediately thought of Charlayne. "Do I have anything contagious?"

"Not so far as we know. That would be unusual in a case of this kind."

Jordan relaxed, only to encounter a new concern. He wanted to see what Charlayne would see, and asked for a mirror. The doctor tried to talk him out of it. "You're still swollen from surgery and your body's overloaded with fending off infection. Wait a few days."

Before ceding the issue, the doctor insisted that dressings on his wounds be opened, examined, and changed; Jordan cringed at the great red-raw gashes that were slashed across his body. How had he survived? Eventually, a small hand mirror was located. Jordan looked at himself and gasped, horrified at his ballooned face, discolored skin, purple and yellow stains surrounding the bloodshot eye that was visible. Unable to recognize himself, he was rocked to his core. He no longer looked human. He'd never thought of himself as vain, but to lose his face, his identity, was the most frightening thing of all.

"You were in good physical shape or you would never have survived this," the surgeon stated pragmatically. "I have seen men die from less damage than you have sustained. In the context of living and dying, you are lucky. I know you will not think so at first, but all this will heal. Plastic surgery can work wonders these days, and two years from now most of the scars will be minimal."

"Two years!" Jordan was overwhelmed and sought something to counteract his fear—reassurance that it was really him, and he was here, and in control. "How soon before I look normal?"

"That depends, of course. Usually a week will—"

"Can I travel?" He didn't have a week. He had to get home. Make sure she was all right.

The surgeon sighed. "Barring complications, and only under the conditions I have described to your father, or I will not be responsible. You must be accompanied by a nurse, of course, and only to another hospital. The infections are only under control, not eradicated. You could still experience renal failure, half a dozen other equally difficult possibilities. If you are determined go right away, I must insist on a hospital in New York."

Blind in one eye! Two years of plastic surgery! All this

as punishment for not paying attention for one split second! His mind screamed for restitution. Restoration to the man he'd been! What woman could be expected to look past this kind of ugliness?

When their father left to talk privately with the doctor, Andy pulled a small glass bottle from his pocket. It was sealed with a wooden cork and half full of water; he held it close enough that Jordan could see a pale wash of sediment swirling in the bottom.

"What's this?"

"It's from Baba. Been putting it on you since Kathmandu. Figured it couldn't hurt." Andy blinked back tears. "They made me boil it first."

Jordan was struck by the old man's gesture and his brother's faith. Since he was still here, maybe Mata Narmada had extended her protection past India's boundaries. Thanks didn't seem enough, but it was all he had. "I give praise to the river. Will you tell him that?"

"I will." Andy regarded him for a moment, fighting emotion.

"What about Charlayne?"

Jordan lay back on the bed, exhausted, his mind grinding with indecision. Christ, he wanted to see her. But not like this! "I don't know. I can't face her yet. I need to get used to things first." He looked in the mirror, unable to believe that any part of the grisly image was his face. "You can call her when I'm home and some of this is gone."

"Jordy, she's not gonna care."

"I don't want her to see me like this! Ever. It doesn't go away. When Natalie died . . . her death face was all I could see for months. It doesn't go away," he repeated, upset at the thought. "I hope to God it's better by the time I get home."

"What do I do in the meantime? She's already called

my office half a dozen times. My boss has been telling her he can't find me, but she's sure as hell going to track one of us down. If she contacts the park, Jamieson will tell her, if he hasn't already."

"I don't know!" Jordan was rattled. Everything was moving too fast, too many quick decisions were being called for. "OK, you're right. I'm sorry. Call her, and if she doesn't know, say I'm stuck in Kathmandu. Tell her I was arrested, can't make phone calls, I don't care what you make up—but whatever you do, keep her away from me until I know which way it's going to go." Christ, *kidney* failure? What the hell else could happen?

"Dad's arranged a private room at New York Hospital as soon they'll let you travel."

"We're leaving tomorrow."

"OK by me, but I don't think—"

"Tomorrow!"

"Then can I call her from New York?"

"You get me to New York tomorrow, you can call her. Not until." He studied his brother's face with his working eye. "I don't want her meeting me there. I want your word."

"Oh, come on, Jordan, what do you think I'm going to do, run and get her?"

"Your word. You won't tell her until I say so."

"I won't tell her until you say so," Andy parroted, not meeting his eyes.

Jordan pursued him doggedly. "No more manipulations. Not this time. Word of honor," he demanded.

Andy got stubborn on him. "I said I wouldn't call her. Take it or leave it."

"It's good enough. You're my brother, and I trust you."

Andy sagged into the chair. "Damn your ass."

32

..a teaspoon of salt . . .

Charlayne sat on a navy raw silk sofa to use the extension phone at the far end of Ira Rust's elegant office. When Sondra said she'd called an expensive attorney, she'd been dead serious. The sofa alone would dent an average annual household income, and the parquet flooring was some of the most elaborate woodworking Charlayne had seen anywhere.

While Sondra examined and signed the documents that would bring a divorce action against Mark Hunter, Charlayne dialed her home phone number. Two beeps. Two messages! Heart thumping, she pressed her playback code and listened to a reminder from her dentist's office that it was time for a checkup. There was also a hesitant call from Judy Baltine: "Hi, I heard about the accident from Mitch. Hope everything's OK. Give me a call when you get a chance. 'Bye."

Charlayne experienced a stab of irritation. Mitch was responsible for Jordan's near-drowning, and she had very few good words to say where Judy's brother was concerned. A return call could wait until she was back in Los Angeles. Then came the telltale beeps that signaled no additional messages. She depressed the disconnect button.

Nothing this morning. Nothing yesterday. It was now the middle of tomorrow night on the opposite side of the planet. After four days, there were no more excuses. Maybe it was as simple as he'd lost her uncle's phone number and didn't know how to reach her, or as complicated as he'd changed his mind for some unknown reason—or something with a perfectly rational explanation had happened. Like a case of amnesia, or beamed aboard a UFO.

For a while, in the middle of last night, she'd even considered that the whole thing had been some sort of elaborate male hoax and now that they'd slept together . . . She dismissed the idea as ridiculous paranoia because, Mark Hunter notwithstanding, she wasn't *that* bad a judge of character. Jordan had been protective, caring, concerned for her. He'd nearly gone to battle with Mitch over his lack of caution where she was concerned. There had to be another explanation.

She hung up and placed a second call, following the numbers written on a piece of her mother's stationery, and waited for the law offices of William P. Kosterin, Esq. to respond. If Jordan's father didn't know anything, she'd call Bangkok and talk to Jamieson—start tracking him down from the other end. Anything was better than not knowing what had happened. If she had to, she'd fly to

Kathmandu. The law office answered and immediately put her on hold.

Charlayne waited, short on patience, and watched Rust's secretary come into the room to stand by her boss as the lawyer's confident voice traveled the length of his office. "With the evidence from the investigator and the record of loans from your family, if you two can agree on custody and visitation rights, I'd say you can pretty much assume a divorce as soon as we get you on the calendar."

His secretary took up the executed copies and disappeared out a side door. "We have a messenger standing by to run this downtown, and it will be filed by the time you've finished lunch," he assured her.

"He can be served today?" Sondra stood to leave.

"Anytime after it's filed. Is it known when he's getting back from Mexico?"

"I have no idea, but I'll stop back after lunch. I'm not going home until I have something to serve him with."

"You can't serve him," the attorney warned. "It has to be a third party."

"You don't know him. He'll be back today. All he has to do is call one of those women." Sondra gestured in Charlayne's direction. "Is it OK if she gives it to him?"

The lawyer nodded. "That would constitute valid service, yes."

Charlayne, still waiting at the phone, nodded agreement and held up her thumb. She'd like nothing better than to serve Mark Hunter with a divorce petition. A receptionist's voice answered, "Kosterin, Culp, Saunders and Recob, thank you for holding," and Charlayne's attention reverted to her call.

"Mr. Kosterin, please."

"Which Mr. Kosterin?"

She took a shot. "Jordan."

"I'm sorry, he's on leave from the firm. Can I connect you with someone else?"

Well, he hadn't come home. Or if he had, he wasn't in his office. "I meant William, sorry."

She was required to give her name before being transferred to an executive assistant to the senior law partner.

"Mr. Kosterin's not in, Miss Pearce. I'm Miss Zeigler, how can I help you?"

Divorce from Roberts two years ago had prepared Charlayne for Miss Zeigler's type: name, rank, and serial number attitude, vacuum sweeper mentality—everything in, nothing out but air. "Will he be in today?" she responded, serving notice that she knew the drill and wouldn't be intimidated easily.

Miss Zeigler gave it back to her. "I don't expect him, however, I anticipate that he will call. Have you been referred by one of Mr. Kosterin's clients?"

Drawing on larger ammunition, Charlayne cut to the chase. "I know his son, Andrew. We met in India a few weeks ago."

There was a slight thaw from Miss Z. "I see. So this is regarding Andrew?" There was an expectant pause.

"It's sort of a personal matter. When's his father going to be in the office?"

Iced-Z was back. "Personal for William Kosterin or Andrew?"

"Andrew. I've been trying to reach him in India, and his office doesn't have a location right now. I was wondering if Mr. Kosterin might know where he's staying in Nepal."

"I see."

The ice had retracted into something-below-zero, and Charlayne realized she probably sounded like a teenager who'd missed her period. Unquestionably, she'd have to be more forthcoming. "Actually, I'm looking for Andy's brother, Jordan. He's had some difficulty over there, as I'm sure you know, however, I'm an author and he was taking some photographs for an upcoming series of my books. Unfortunately, my publisher wants the shots sooner than I'd anticipated. . . ." She was running out of improvisation.

"I see. And what was your name again?"

"Charlayne Pearce." She was thanked politely and put on hold.

Sondra caught her eye with a wave of her hand. "I'd like to get away after Mark is served. Is it all right if Ryan and I stay at your place for a while?"

"Sure." Anything to keep her nephew out of the line of fire. "Whenever you want."

Miss Zeigler came back on. "Well, as it happens, Miss Pearce, my son is very well acquainted with your work. *Charlie Cougar . . . ?*"

"*Goes to See*, yes. That's mine."

She must have passed the test because the voice was instant charm. "Well, it's an excellent book and nice to know that Jordan's done some work for you. His father's out of the city, and while I had you on hold, I tried to verify their flight schedule. Unfortunately, it's still somewhat up in the air, however, I can tell you they're planning to return to Los Angeles sometime within the next three days. Would you care to leave a number where you can be reached?"

In terms of plane flights, three days could very well mean distance. And "they" was plural! Maybe there'd been some kind of legal tangle in Nepal that had compelled William Kosterin to join his sons. Charlayne forced her voice to remain level. "Is Andy traveling with them?"

"I'm sorry, I don't have that information. Did you want to leave word for him as well?"

By offering to take messages, Miss Zeigler apparently

expected to have someone to give them to. A strong indication that either Andy or Jordan was traveling with their father. Maybe both. "This is where I can be reached in San Francisco if you hear from them in the meantime."

Charlayne gave Miss Zeigler her parents' number, thanked her, and hung up the telephone with elation spinning through her chest. Within three days someone could give her answers! Someone would be in Los Angeles! If it wasn't Jordan, she'd get in to see William Kosterin if she had to climb over Miss Zeigler's body!

Her excitement carried her through the remainder of Sondra's consultation with Rust, after which they took a trolley to Ghirardelli Square to rendezvous for a late lunch with her parents, Ryan, and Uncle Egan. Lunch stretched into nearly two hours, but Charlayne was serenely unconcerned. There was no hurry now. He was on his way, she was sure of it. She'd be in Los Angeles within three days as well, and after that it was only a matter of time until she had some answers.

While Ryan and Uncle Egan scouted the pier for seagulls worthy of leftovers, she and Sondra alerted their parents to Sondra's plan to take Ryan to Los Angeles. Afterward, her father insisted on driving them past the attorney's office to pick up a copy of the divorce complaint. At four o'clock they were on their way to Baywatch Street.

Jordan turned from the mirror to look out the window at New York's skyline, the familiar buildings backlit with trace remnants of what had been a magnificent sunset. A need to see Charlayne weighed heavily on his mind. One thing for sure, she'd never call him good-looking again. And he sure as hell couldn't meet her family with half his face in bandages. He'd never survive the questioning looks, the shocked expressions. The suspicions about his health.

From what the doctors were telling him, he wasn't entirely out of the woods by any means. An infection in his damaged lung had been classified in the exotic variety, and was hanging on with unexpected tenacity. His open wounds could have been exposed to animal blood and there was some question as to whether he was contagious after all. The hospital was taking no chances. Everyone, including his father and brother, was supposed to wear face masks in his presence, but Andy usually pulled it away as soon as he stepped inside the room, with the logic that if he was going to be exposed, it would have happened by now.

Definitely not the way he wanted to see her again.

He ran his hand through the itchy stubble of his beard and up the side of his head where his hair had been, feeling like an autopsy case. When there were head injuries in a murder, the victim's head was shaved by the coroner for a more complete examination. He'd seen pictures a hundred times in the course of his career, and the resemblance was too resonant. Definitely not the way to meet her family.

He'd just gotten off the phone with his grandmother after assuring her several times that he was indeed in New York and that everything was fine. Except it wasn't, unless you were preparing for a lengthy Halloween with Freddy Kruger. The dear woman had beaten around the bush for a few minutes, in the manner of her generation, then hesitantly admitted that she and Frazier had been getting on famously, and did he think it would it be all right if she kept him a bit longer? He'd turned over the cat's ownership on the spot. Natalie would approve, he was certain, and another element of his marriage was laid to rest. As soon as he got to his apartment, he planned to wipe the dust off the bottle of champagne that had been waiting six years, drink a final toast to his marriage to Natalie, and pour the rest down the drain.

Andy hobbled through the door, pulling away his mask as usual. Finally! His brother and his father had been meeting with doctors and filling out paperwork for hours. "Can we place the goddamned call?" Jordan asked suspiciously. "Or did you already talk to her?" His breathing wheezed into a cough, which sent static through his stitches, annoying him further.

Andy grinned at him. "Well, you're grumpy. They say that's a good sign."

"That's not a denial," he accused. "If you want to keep my blood pressure over Denver, you'll keep it up. When I get off this bed, I'll break your leg all over again." He wheezed again, knowing it was an empty threat and that he was talking too much. Andy would be back in India by the time he could walk without help, let alone do damage.

"Keep your shirt on. I lost her folks' number and couldn't remember her father's name. I had to call my office."

"Delamere. Delamere! Let's do this before Dad gets back," he said irritably, "or another nurse comes in, or a doctor wants more blood, or some other damned thing." He'd been poked and prodded, temperatured and blood-pressured and X-rayed and unwrapped and examined and rewrapped ever since he'd arrived, had given fluid samples until he was ready to scream. The only thing on his mind was hearing her voice.

If he heard her voice, he'd be able to relax. Since his agreement with Andy that they'd call her from New York, it was the carrot he'd held out for himself through every obstacle. His mental wish list, patterned on Natalie's. Cross off "Getting to New York" and you can call her. Cross off "Living with pain" and "Positive test results" and you can dial the number.

He'd been out most of the flight from New Delhi, except for about ten minutes when they landed to refuel somewhere in Europe, but it had been the sleep of drugs. It was knowing he was home that would make natural sleep possible; that, and assurance that the person he loved was safe and well. Touching her. Having her body under him as soon as he could get on his knees.

"You want to call her at home, or at her parents?"

"Her parents." His anticipation mounted.

Andy dialed the number on an extension. Jordan picked up the receiver on his bedside phone and held it to his ear so he could hear the ring. She could be on the phone any second, and his throat tightened with need.

"And you don't want to talk to her," Andy baited.

"No! I've told you a . . ." He threatened to disconnect the call, more nervous than he'd been on his first date. "You got it straight? You know what you're going to say if she answers?"

Andy nodded emphatically. "Shut up so I can hear."

A recording kicked in after the third ring, and Jordan tried to contain his disappointment. "Delamere residence . . ." It was a man's voice, probably her father. ". . . leave a message at the sound of the beep."

Andy began speaking on cue. "This is Andrew Kosterin. We're calling Charlayne Pearce. I know you've been trying to reach me about Jordan, and as I'm sure you've figured out by now, something pretty serious has come up, which I feel you should know about. . . ."

Jordan cleared his throat in warning and shook his head.

WISH LIST   355 -

Andy ignored him. "He doesn't want me to tell you, but in view of your relationship I think you have a right—"

"Hello?"

Andy paused at the sound of the voice. It wasn't her father.

"Hello, who's this?" the man repeated.

Andy looked at Jordan and shrugged. "Andy Kosterin. I have this number to reach Charlayne Pearce. I'm calling for my brother because she's been trying to reach us for several days."

"Really? Well, I'll take a message, she's not here."

"That would be terrific, thanks. When do you expect her?"

"I have no idea."

"All right. Would you tell her Jordan cares about her very much and"—ignoring Jordan's furious signals—"hopes everything went well in Texas. He'll be in Los Angeles in the next couple of days and really wants to see her."

"He'll be wasting his time," said the voice.

Stunned into silence, Andy swung to face him; Jordan felt his own face lose color under his sense of shock and entered into the conversation. "What do you mean?"

"Who's this?"

"My name's Jordan."

"Hell, Jordan, she didn't come back from Texas. She and her ex-husband sort of got together at the funeral. Medical guy. They went to Mexico. Anything she told you, you have to take with a teaspoon of salt. I learned to do that a long time ago."

33

Don't screw me up on this one . . .

  Charlayne stepped gingerly in the door and left it open for Uncle Egan, still at the curb with her family; she'd come ahead to intercept Mark in case he was aware of their arrival, and was glad to see him on the foyer phone. He turned, met her eyes, and gave her a big grin.

"... went to Mexico. Anything she told you, you have to take with a teaspoon of salt," he continued. "I learned to do that a long time ago ... Hold on a second, I want to write this down." He put his hand over the phone, still grinning. "Hi, Charlie. I'll be through here in just a minute."

"Take your time." Grated at his insulting attitude, she matched him stare for stare; he picked up a pen to begin writing on a message pad, smiling at her all the while. Sondra had been right—he'd managed to get home in record time. Charlayne wondered which woman in the investigator's report had sent money she'd never see again.

Mark was still writing. "Uh-huh . . . I'll tell her as soon as someone hears from her, but she swore to me they were reconciled. Big, hot romance last I heard. Somewhere on his yacht, right now . . . I'm Mark . . . No, that's not true. Never happened. That's quite all right, Jordan. Any time."

Caught off guard, Charlayne was a beat late in starting for the phone.

"Will do . . . Goodbye."

Before she could reach him, Mark put down the receiver, a flint-hard gleam in his eyes. "Looks like *you* got burned on this round, honey. Maybe you'll think twice next time I ask a favor. I would if I were you."

Charlayne was beside herself with rage and humiliation. "You creep bastard!"

Mark ripped off the page, too happy to read her its message. "'Jordan' says he knows you've been trying to reach him. Says he's been thinking it over and it's not going to work. Sorry." Smug, he held it out with an ugly smile, then looked past her in surprise.

Uncle Egan was standing in the doorway. He nodded a stiff acknowledgment to Mark, who recovered smoothly. "Hell, I'm on your side, Charlie . . . Just getting even for you. Hello, sir."

Her uncle did not respond.

She grabbed the message. Mark couldn't have known about him, so it had to have been Jordan on the phone. She couldn't stop her eyes from scanning what was written. Essentially word for word as Mark had said, and there was no phone number. She felt as if she'd taken a giant fist in the heart. Numb, she turned to Uncle Egan. "Are they gone?"

At his nod, and shaking with anger, she opened her purse and reached inside. "Mark, I have something for you, too." The envelope shook as she handed it to him. She gave him a venomous gaze, hating him and everything he stood for. "It's a divorce petition. You're history in this family. Personally, I hope you eat dirt."

He made a move for the stairs. "Where's my wife?"

"Mark!"

Her brother-in-law froze mid-step at Egan Hawke's rigid command. "Sondra saw your car outside. She and Ryan have gone to a hotel for the night. Right now I think it's best that you take your things and leave."

Mark opened the envelope and confirmed its contents. "You can't do this."

"It's done. You're done." Charlayne pointed to the boxes of his clothing. "You can take these now, or I'll personally drop them off at the Salvation Army as soon as you go."

Mark was noticeably jolted when he read the word "Gift" on the packing boxes. Slowly his bravado collapsed into a need to salvage his belongings; he picked up the nearest box and started out the door. Her uncle stepped aside to let the younger man pass unhindered. When all four boxes were stacked on the curb next to his car and Mark was unlocking the trunk, Charlayne closed the door and turned the lock. Then she dissolved into defeat, her strength deserting her at last. "Surely he wouldn't leave a message like that.... He'd talk to me. He wouldn't just..."

Her uncle picked up the phone and spoke to an operator. "We received a call a few minutes ago which was accidentally disconnected. We're pretty certain it came in from overseas, possibly India, maybe Nepal. Is there any way to trace the call?" After a short pause, he thanked the operator and turned to face her. "Sorry. Can't be done," he said consolingly.

"Mark lied to him," she sobbed. "Said I'd—"

"I heard it all. . . ." He started to replace the receiver. "Wait a minute."

Looking up at his tone, she saw the blinking message light. Her sobs disappeared and she stabbed at the playback button, reciting a litany. "Oh, please, oh, please, please, please . . ."

A pall descended as they listened to the partial message: "This is Andrew Kosterin. We're calling Charlayne Pearce. I know you've been trying to reach me about Jordan, and as I'm sure you've figured out by now, something pretty serious has come up, which I feel you should know about . . . He doesn't want me to tell you, but in view of your relationship I think you have a right— Hello?"

At Mark's voice, the recording ceased.

Her tears resumed as Charlayne played it again, then a third time, her reaction more and more dismal. Andy's voice was strained. It was obvious he hadn't wanted to make the call, but felt obligated to tell her a truth of some kind. Every time she listened, the only thing she could think of was Mark's version of their conversation. For once in his life was the lying bastard telling the truth?

She cried without stop until her parents returned with Sondra and Ryan an hour later, then hid in the kitchen until her sister had put her sleeping son to bed, to make sure she didn't wake him. Finally, Alice's hot chocolate brought her around and she was able to halt her grief long enough to sign the verification of service with a trembling hand, and give the document to Sondra to provide to the attorney.

If it was true, why on earth wouldn't Jordan tell her in person? Why have Andy call?

Unable to fit into her skin, she tried to think things through. To wait forever to hear from him only to get a message that he was dumping her; and worst of all, not to know for sure. Not to hear it directly, to have nowhere to call, no one to tell her it was a lie. For the first time, she began to doubt her judgment of Jordan.

Suddenly dead as wood, she decided to go home. She'd been away much too long. Had had too much contact with Mark, too much pain and disappointment in too short a time. Losing Aunt Sophie, losing Jordan, maybe losing her sanity . . . She couldn't even think about the status of her writing career. The books she'd planned. She wanted to sleep in her own bed, wake up with her head on her own pillow, enjoy solitude for a few hours. Make her own coffee, walk to her kitchen for a drink of water in the dead of night without turning on a light. She wanted to be home.

Her family was understanding, but in view of her obvious distress, reluctant to accept her decision. Well past additional concessions, she was determined, and with Sondra's support, plus Uncle Egan's, she was able to convince her parents to allow her to leave. When her father insisted on driving her to the airport, she said tearful goodbyes to everyone and promised to be at LAX when Sondra and Ryan arrived the following day. But right now, she was going home.

In New York, Jordan watched Andy put down the phone and sagged against the pillow, his legal mind stacking things in order. Something was too wrong with this picture. Mark, the brother-in-law, had been entirely too glib, too eager to trash Charlayne to strangers. Something about the guy's voice was wrong, too. Not only was he a bad actor, but he'd been enjoying himself.

Andy approached the bed, confused and shaken. "Jordan, I don't know what to say. Am I crazy, or . . . You don't think the guy was telling the truth?"

Jordan shook his head. "Not a chance."

Andy sat heavily. "Well, if it's his idea of a joke, it sucks. Let me call back. I'll talk to someone else."

"He'll be expecting that. If someone else was there, he wouldn't be saying any of that crap."

"Why'd you ask if he'd been married to her?"

"Because her first husband was a lying asshole, and I figured that was him."

"So now what?" Andy stretched tiredly.

Belatedly, Jordan realized that his brother had to be on the brink of exhaustion. They'd shared the same marathon from Kathmandu to New Delhi to New York, but Andy had been awake, keeping track of details, coordinating flights and money and doctors and hospitals, making decisions and taking care of him. "When's the last time you got some sleep?"

"As soon as I leave here. Dad and I have a suite at the Dorset." Andy glanced at his watch, shoulders drooping with fatigue. "He'll be here in about ten minutes. You think everything's OK out there?"

"No, but there's nothing I can do about it from here." Jordan was unable to control his own yawn. "He's obviously not a mental giant, probably thinks I'll go away."

"So what now?"

"Now, I think you better leave a message for her in Los Angeles. Tell her you'll be there in a couple of days and you need to talk to her."

Andy reached for the telephone.

Jordan studied himself in the mirror. "Don't even think

about leaving this number, or she'll fly here. Tell her you're en route, or something. You're about to get on a plane. That'll be true because we're going to leave as soon as I can talk Dad into cranking up the engines. You can sleep all the way to Los Angeles." His thumb hovered over the disconnect button. "You've had your fun. Don't screw me up on this one."

"OK." Andy grinned in defeat, and began to punch the number. "What if she's there?"

"I'll talk to her."

His brother raised his eyebrows. "Oooh, now you'll talk to her."

"You heard me. Keep dialing."

34

... definitely out of sync ...

Her flight landed a little after seven-thirty that evening, the early dark of a January evening in L.A. matching her mood as she secured a taxi and gave him her address. OK, assuming it was real and he didn't want to see her again ... what about the photographs? Why hadn't there been any mention of them? And what about her things? He was supposed to be bringing everything she'd left in Nepal. And why wouldn't he talk to her directly? Why have Andy call?

Something was definitely out of sync with the person she'd made love with, with the person who'd put her on a plane and bade her "Safe home."

Well, she was "safe home," where the hell was he? Her

brain was about to explode! She resolutely shut out further deliberation by concentrating on the sights and sounds of homecoming.

Little by little, familiar city sights perked her up during the commute to her apartment. The peculiar Southern California mélange of surf and desert, concrete and palm trees, the eclectic mix of bungalows, condos, and high-rise office buildings with neon names glowing in the dark. The L.A. Marathon painting on the freeway's retaining wall greeted her just after the La Cienega on-ramp tunnel sporting mismatched patches of paint over recurring graffiti—at least the gangs had stopped spraying over the running figures and were using the spaces between. Some concessions were better than none.

Through the oily windshield of the taxi, streetlamps had the soft focus of light through fog, and red taillights ahead of them on the freeway fractured into starbursts.

Home.

She'd left her apartment before Christmas; it was now more than a week into January. Things had changed totally. Jordan Kosterin had turned her life upside down, then disappeared.

She dropped her bags inside her front door, happy not to have to think about unpacking, unwilling to even consider turning on the TV or the stereo; to permit sound of any kind was to scrape against already raw nerves. There was an accumulation of mail on the dining room table, courtesy of her neighbor, who had a key, and she was relieved to find that her plants had survived her absence. Peace began to soak through her body, the relaxation of entering a familiar, safe place.

She pushed the mail aside. Anything urgent would just have to wait until tomorrow. Also on the table was a note referring her to a fresh carton of milk in the refrigerator and the loaf of French bread she'd requested. In the kitchen, she took out the milk carton and drank from it thirstily—a guilty luxury she seldom indulged, and one that her mother would find appalling, but there were some joys of living alone, and this was one of them. She located a can of frozen mushroom and barley soup she particularly liked and put it on to simmer, intending to take a long soak in a hot bath, enjoy a light dinner, and turn off the world for the rest of the night.

With the bathwater running, she used her bedroom phone to call San Francisco and spoke briefly with her mother to let her family know she was home and safe. During her bath, it registered that her answering machine light had been blinking three times, not two. Eliminating her dentist and Judy Baltine, there was a new message since she'd last checked. That it was Jordan was too much to hope. Unable to bear the suspense, she got out of the tub and walked naked to the room that served as her office, stood dripping on the carpet to punch the playback button.

"Charlayne, it's Andy. I'm about to get on a plane, so I can't leave a number, but I have something very important to discuss with you about Jordan. As soon as I get to Los Angeles, I'll give you a call. Probably in a couple of days. He wants me to tell you—"

An abrupt disconnect.

She sank slowly onto the carpet. There was no way of knowing if he'd called before or after his conversation with Mark. Who knew what other damning statements Mark might have made about her before she stepped in the door? Too wary at this point to allow herself to count on anything positive, she played the message again, willing herself to hear something new. Some nuance that could give her a clue. The only thing that was similar to the recording in San Francisco was the tenor of Andy's voice. He sounded desperately tired.

Had the chain of calls gone in the opposite direction? she wondered. Had he tried to reach her at this number first, then called San Francisco? What did it matter? If the object was to end her relationship with Jordan, nothing mattered.

There was no solution. She gave up and traipsed back to her bath, but her enjoyment was destroyed. Eventually she was able to eat a bite of dinner and fall into bed, but sleep was slow in coming.

The following morning, she waded through her mail, found a wedding announcement from Maxwell and Shelley Cox-Caulfield, and set it aside, then sorted correspondence into high, low, and follow-up priority levels, and relegated the balance to the recycling bin.

Then she tackled her luggage, determined to eliminate evidence of the trip and get her life back on an even keel as quickly as possible. She found Jordan's jacket, which she'd forgotten, neatly folded in tissue—her mother's inimitable style. The sight of it loosed the questions and started their nagging dance through her head, giving her no respite throughout the day.

She called William Kosterin's office, learned he was still out of the city, and obtained the firm's street address. No longer certain that she wanted to confront the senior Mr. Kosterin after all, she found herself tucking it into her wallet and taking the fall-back position of waiting to see if Andy would call, as promised. In spite of filling her apartment with music, the silence inside her head was deafening, and she began to look forward to the visit from her sister and nephew, if for no other reason than that the

WISH LIST 367 –

chaos generated by their presence was bound to keep her doubts and unanswerable questions at bay.

Sondra and Ryan arrived that evening. On the drive from the airport, Sondra gave her a riddle. "What calls on the phone, threatens, screams, cries, pleads, begs, says it's sorry, and swears on a stack of Bibles that everything is just a mistake . . . and nothing works?"

Charlayne was unable to guess and Ryan gave up as well.

"I don't know either, but it's *still* not going to work," said his mother.

Ryan lost interest. "That's a dumb riddle, Mummy."

"You're right. I'll see if I can think of a better one."

Relieved at Sondra's resolve, Charlayne filled in for her sister. "What's black and white and read all over?"

Wednesday morning. Sondra began her round of questioning about Jordan, and Charlayne realized that obviously her sister had found out about him from the family. In view of their new status as friends, and her own involvement with Sondra's divorce, she did her best to be honest in her responses.

"I don't understand what's happened," she admitted. "I was ready to make a serious commitment. I thought he was, too." As she talked, she realized how short her time together with Jordan had actually been and was disheartened. "For some reason, he won't talk to me, but Andy's supposed to call by tomorrow," she finished.

Ryan was pulling at his mother, demanding she make good on her promise to take him to the park.

"It's down two blocks," Charlayne directed. "Can't miss it. Take a key in case I go out." It was her sister's first visit to her apartment, so she walked them to the corner to make sure Sondra had her bearings. When she came back inside, the phone was ringing and the machine was playing her instruction to leave a message. She grabbed the receiver. "Hello!"

She banged the wall with her fist in irritation. "Hello, Judy."

35

If she'd done this to him...

"*Thanks, I'll call you soon.*" Pale with emotion, Charlayne slammed down the phone. "OK, that's it. I've had enough." She hastily scribbled a note for Sondra: *Am going out. Have no idea when I'll be back. Will call later. Char.*

Eyes filling with tears, she grabbed her purse and her car keys and headed for the door.

Jordan answered the phone by his bed, expecting Andy's voice. "Well?"

"I tried calling her apartment. Her sister says she's gone out, doesn't know when she plans to return. Nasty lady, that one. Nearly bit my head off when she found out who I was."

"You still at Dad's office?"

"Yeah, I thought I'd drop off the film at her place, then come by the hospital."

"I'd rather hold on to it until I can talk to her. The doctors have verified that I'm not infectious. Some kind of bug from ingesting river water, for Christ's sake, but they have it under control."

"Well, that's a bit of good news. I'll see you in about half an hour."

"As soon as you get here, I'm going to call until I reach her." Jordan ran his hand through the quarter inch of dark hair covering his skull. "I still look pretty frightening, and I think it would be a good idea to have you here to help her through the initial shock. . . ."

"No problem. See you in a bit."

While he waited, Jordan debated how best to prepare her, trying to find a way that would upset her the least. He didn't want to do it over the phone unless it was absolutely necessary. Send Andy to get her? Frustrated that he couldn't at least walk in to see her on his own, having Andy pick her up was probably the best he could do. Any way it happened, she was going to be furious by the time she reached the hospital. He couldn't blame her. If she'd done this to him, he'd be chewing the scenery.

To fill the time, he called his office and asked his secretary to make out checks on his personal bank account. "One to Joh for a thousand dollars, another thousand for Jimi, and five thousand to Anup, as trustee, and send them by messenger for my signature. They're to go in care of Professor MacArthur Jamieson at Chitwan National Park, and prepare a letter that authorizes him to add their last names. I'll sign that, too. Oh, and add one for Baby Joseph for five hundred dollars."

Forty-five long minutes later his brother clomped through the door, no longer using a crutch, but hampered by his new cast. He'd been lucky. For a while there had been some question of rebreaking and resetting the bone.

Andy seemed antsy. "Did you call her?"

"Not yet. Maybe you should go to her apartment after all. Call me when she arrives. That way you could drive her here and have her somewhat prepared by the time she sees me."

"I'm ahead of you. I stopped to get her on my way over, but she wasn't there. Let me tell you, that sister of hers is some good-looking woman. She's a major piece of work, but if she's single, I plan to get to know her a whole lot better. Hope to hell she likes desert countri—"

The door behind them opened. A furious Charlayne flew into the room like a dervish. "How dare you!"

Jordan was frozen in shock at the unexpected sight of her, Andy equally stunned, as she threw down her purse and confronted them in outrage. "You are the two most heartless people I've ever met!"

She gave Andrew a stinging slap on the cheek. "Both of you! You're lower than dirt!" Then, glaring at Jordan, she sized up his bandaged body. "Where can I hit you?" she demanded. "You better tell me before I pick someplace that really hurts."

Andy moved away from the bed, trying to get out of her line of fire. She whacked him on the shoulder as he sidled past. "That's for not telling me!" She followed him to punch him again, harder. "How *dare* you not leave a message at least! Not let me know? You *toad!*"

She returned to Jordan's side as a concerned nurse came running into the room. "What's going on here?"

"I'm about to kill these two," Charlayne muttered darkly. "Don't try and stop me. They have it coming."

Andy grinned and stepped forward to intercede with the nurse. "It's fine. Really. She's perfectly within her rights. They're in love."

"Well, she'll have to keep it down," the nurse insisted, "or I'll ask her to leave the floor."

"Just take me with you," he said, and hustled her out the door.

"I'll keep it down, all right." Charlayne stood, rigid with fury at Jordan's bedside. "You didn't answer my question."

Jordan looked up at her, no longer nonplussed, just bloody glad to see her and loving the hint of sandalwood that had invaded the room with her. "About the only places that aren't damaged are my butt and my mouth," he answered, unable not to smile. God she was *gorgeous* when she was mad. "You can kick my butt as soon as I can get out of this bed, but I'd rather you didn't hi—"

Charlayne kissed him. After a moment she slapped him hard enough to hurt on the hand that was creeping up the inside of her thigh, then kissed him again.

From the corner of her eye she saw movement as the nurse peeked in, then disappeared. She closed her eyes and kissed him some more. It was quite a while until she'd had enough and settled back onto the side of his bed. "I thought I was going to die before I got in here," she said angrily.

"I was looking for you, I swear it," he whispered huskily. "Ask Andy. He'll tell you." He looked at her, totally baffled. "How'd you find me?"

She debated whether or not to tell him. Vengeance was roaming in her head like a tiger looking for lunch. "Your brother," she admitted finally.

He frowned, and she saw his disappointment. "He gave me his word he wouldn't call you."

She debated whether to rescue Andy's hide or let him fry awhile longer, but decided that revenge wasn't half as much fun as kissing Jordan. Besides, she was dying to reveal her detective work. She ran her fingers through his buzz-cut. "This is rather nice, actually. Tickles." She lowered her fingers to trace the shell of his ear, and looked with concern at the bandage covering his eye. "That looks pretty serious."

"It's better than I'd hoped. Looks like I'll keep about sixty percent of my sight." He ran his hand along her forearm, took hold of her fingers, kissed the tips one by one, watching her face. "I can't believe how good you look. I've been going out of my mind thinking about you—"

She kissed him again, slowly this time. Deliberately caressing his tongue with her own to tease him, make him want her. Make him prove it.

Long moments later he broke the kiss. "Maybe we better take a break here," he said, his rapid breathing telling her what she wanted to know. "I can't believe Andy told you. He swore he was going to let me call."

She ignored his attempt to change the subject and kissed him again. When she was sure she'd made her point and he was going down for the count, she relented long enough to murmur an explanation between kisses. "After I found out you were hurt, I went to your father's office. I was going to make someone tell me which hospital you were in, but I saw Andy leaving the parking lot when I got to the building, so I followed him."

She kissed his ear and deliberately pushed her tongue inside, just a little, which she knew from experience made him crazy. "When he stopped at my apartment, I almost went inside after him, but I knew Sondra didn't know where to find me, so I gave him a test. If he stayed longer than ten minutes, he was going to wait until I got home to tell me; if he left sooner, I'd have to follow him." She slid her fingers under the hospital gown to see if Jordan was wearing underwear. He wasn't. "He stayed seven and a half minutes. Oh, my. Not sure I can keep it down, after all."

"Oh, God. You're going to do this to me, aren't you?"

"Uh-huh." She gave him an evil grin. "Nurse Jones has plans to get even." Putting her fingers in motion, she licked her lips with satisfaction at the look of utter helplessness coming into his face. "How dare you decide when I can see you," she lectured. "What gives you the right not to see me? Because you look like a bus wreck? And where are my pictures?"

Jordan lay back with a smile, fully prepared to enjoy her punishment, mentally creating a brand new list of wishes, getting her into bed at the top of page one. Getting even immediately under that. "In protective custody," he said happily. "If you promise to keep that up, I'll be happy to give them to you in about six months."

Escape to Romance
and
WIN A YEAR OF ROMANCE!

Ten lucky winners will receive a free year of romance—*more than 30 free books*. Every book HarperMonogram publishes in 1997 will be delivered directly to your doorstep if you are one of the ten winners drawn at random.

RULES: To enter, send your name, address, and daytime telephone number to the ESCAPE TO ROMANCE CONTEST, HarperPaperbacks, 10 East 53rd Street, New York, NY 10022. No purchase necessary. This contest is open to U.S. residents 18 years or older, except employees (and their families) of HarperPaperbacks/HarperCollins and their agencies, affiliates, and subsidiaries. Entries must be received by October 31, 1996. HarperPaperbacks is not responsible for late, lost, incomplete, or misdirected mail. Winners will be selected in a random drawing on or about November 15, 1996 and notified by mail. All entries become the property of HarperPaperbacks and will not be returned or acknowledged. Entry constitutes permission to use winner's name, home town, and likeness for promotional purposes on behalf of HarperPaperbacks. Winners must sign Affidavit of Eligiblity, Assignment, and Release within 10 days of notification. Approximate retail value of each prize $250.

All federal, state, and local laws and regulations apply. Void where prohibited. Applicable taxes are the sole responsiblity of the winners. Prizes are not exchangeable or transferable. No substitutions of prizes except at the discretion of HarperPaperbacks. For a list of winners send a self-addressed, stamped envelope to the address above after January 1, 1997.

Harper Monogram

Let HarperMonogram Sweep You Away

MIRANDA by Susan Wiggs
Over One Million Copies of Her Books in Print
In Regency London, Miranda Stonecypher is stricken with amnesia and doesn't believe that handsome Ian MacVane is her betrothed—especially after another suitor appears. Miranda's search for the truth leads to passion beyond her wildest dreams.

WISH LIST by Jeane Renick
RITA Award-Winning Author
Only $3.99

While on assignment in Nepal, writer Charlayne Pearce meets elusive and irresistibly sensual Jordan Kosterin. Jordan's bold gaze is an invitation to pleasure, but memories of his dead wife threaten their newfound love.

SILVER SPRINGS by Carolyn Lampman
Only $3.99

Independent Angel Brady feels she is capable of anything—even passing as her soon-to-be-married twin sister so that Alexis can run off with her lover. Unfortunately, the fiancé turns out to be the one man in the Wyoming Territory who can send Angel's pulse racing.

CALLIE'S HONOR by Kathleen Webb
Only $3.99

Callie Lambert is unprepared for the handsome stranger who shows up at her Oregon ranch determined to upset her well-ordered life. But her wariness is no match for Rafe Millar's determination to discover her secrets, and win her heart.

And in case you missed last month's selections...

JACKSON RULE by Dinah McCall
Award-Winning Author of *Dreamcatcher*
After being released from prison Jackson Rule finds a job working for a preacher's daughter. Jackson may be a free man, but Rebecca Hill's sweet charity soon has him begging for mercy.

MISBEGOTTEN by Tamara Leigh

Only $3.99

No one can stop baseborn knight Liam Fawke from gaining his rightful inheritance—not even the beautiful Lady Joslyn. Yet Liam's strong resolve is no match for the temptress whose spirit and passion cannot be denied.

COURTNEY'S COWBOY by Susan Macias
Time Travel Romance

Only $3.99

Married couple Courtney and Matt have little time for each other until they are transported back to 1873 Wyoming. Under the wide western sky they discover how to fall truly in love for the first time.

SOULS AFLAME by Patricia Hagan
New York Times Bestselling Author
with Over Ten Million Copies of Her Books in Print

Only $3.99

Julie Marshal's duty to save her family's Georgia plantation gives way to desire in the arms of Derek Arnhardt. With a passion to match her own, the ship's captain will settle for nothing less than possessing Julie, body and soul.

Harper Monogram

MAIL TO: **HarperCollins Publishers**
P.O. Box 588 Dunmore, PA 18512-0588

Yes, please send me the books I have checked:

- ❏ *Miranda* by Susan Wiggs 108549-X . . . .$5.99 U.S./ $7.99 Can.
- ❏ *Wish List* by Jeane Renick 108281-3 . . . .$3.99 U.S./ $4.99 Can.
- ❏ *Silver Springs* by Carolyn Lampman 108432-8 . . . .$3.99 U.S./ $4.99 Can.
- ❏ *Callie's Honor* by Kathleen Webb 108457-3 . . . .$3.99 U.S./ $4.99 Can.
- ❏ *Jackson Rule* by Dinah McCall 108391-7 . . . .$5.99 U.S./ $7.99 Can.
- ❏ *Misbegotten* by Tamara Leigh 108447-6 . . . .$3.99 U.S./ $4.99 Can.
- ❏ *Courtney's Cowboy* by Susan Macias 108405-0 . . . .$3.99 U.S./ $4.99 Can.
- ❏ *Souls Aflame* by Patricia Hagan 108219-8 . . . .$3.99 U.S./ $4.99 Can.

SUBTOTAL . . . .$_____
POSTAGE & HANDLING . . . .$_____
SALES TAX (Add applicable sales tax) . . . .$_____
TOTAL . . . .$_____

Name _____
Address _____
City _____ State _____ Zip _____

Order 4 or more titles and postage & handling is **FREE!** For orders of less than 4 books, please include $2.00 postage & handling. Allow up to 6 weeks for delivery. Remit in U.S. funds. Do not send cash.
Valid in U.S. & Canada. Prices subject to change.   M034

Visa & MasterCard holders—call 1-800-331-3761

The Best in the Romance Business Explain How It's Done

A Must for Romance Readers and Writers

edited by
Jayne Ann Krentz

Nineteen bestselling romance novelists reveal their secrets in this collection of essays, explaining the popularity of the romance novel, why they write in this genre, how the romance novel has been misunderstood by critics, and more. Contributors include Laura Kinsale, Elizabeth Lowell, Jayne Ann Krentz, Susan Elizabeth Phillips, Mary Jo Putney, and many others.

Harper Monogram

MAIL TO: **HarperCollins Publishers**
P.O. Box 588 Dunmore, PA 18512-0588

Yes, please send me the book(s) I have checked:

❑ Dangerous Men and Adventurous Women 108463-8 . . . . $5.99 U.S./ $7.99 Can.

SUBTOTAL . . . . $_____
POSTAGE & HANDLING . . . . $_____
SALES TAX (Add applicable sales tax) . . . . $_____
TOTAL . . . . $_____

Name _____
Address _____
City _____ State _____ Zip _____

Order 4 or more titles and postage & handling is **FREE!** For orders of less than 4 books, please include $2.00 postage & handling. Allow up to 6 weeks for delivery. Remit in U.S. funds. Do not send cash. Valid in U.S. & Canada. Prices subject to change. M03311

Visa & MasterCard holders—call 1-800-331-3761